WESTERN

Rugged men looking for love...

United By The Twins
Jill Kemerer

The Cowboy's Secret Past
Tina Radcliffe

T0362984

MILLS & BOON

UNITED BY THE TWINS
© 2024 by Ripple Effect Press, LLC
Philippine Copyright 2024
Australian Copyright 2024
New Zealand Copyright 2024

First Published 2024
First Australian Paperback Edition 2024
ISBN 978 1 038 90273 3

THE COWBOY'S SECRET PAST
© 2024 by Tina M. Radcliffe
Philippine Copyright 2024
Australian Copyright 2024
New Zealand Copyright 2024

First Published 2024
First Australian Paperback Edition 2024
ISBN 978 1 038 90273 3

MIX
Paper | Supporting
responsible forestry
FSC® C001695

Published by
Harlequin Mills & Boon
An imprint of Harlequin Enterprises (Australia) Pty Limited
(ABN 47 001 180 918), a subsidiary of HarperCollins
Publishers Australia Pty Limited
(ABN 36 009 913 517)
Level 19, 201 Elizabeth Street
SYDNEY NSW 2000 AUSTRALIA

Cover art used by arrangement with Harlequin Books S.A.. All rights reserved.

Printed and bound in Australia by McPherson's Printing Group

United By The Twins

Jill Kemerer

MILLS & BOON

Jill Kemerer writes novels with love, humour and faith. Besides spoiling her minidachshund and keeping up with her busy kids, Jill reads stacks of books, lives for her morning coffee and gushes over fluffy animals. She resides in Ohio with her husband and two children. Jill loves connecting with readers, so please visit her website, jillkemerer.com, or contact her at PO Box 2802, Whitehouse, OH 43571.

Commit thy way unto the Lord;
trust also in him; and he shall bring it to pass.
—*Psalm* 37:5

DEDICATION

To my Black Friday crew—
Eva, Ceci, Cali, Sarah, Olivia and Brandon.
You bring so much joy to my life. Thank you
for waiting with me in the BBW line for however
long it takes. I cherish our annual shenanigans!

CHAPTER ONE

AFTER FIFTEEN YEARS, his mother's dream of expanding her bakery was about to come true. The stately brick building on the corner was finally available.

Marc Young inhaled the cold air, common for early April in Jewel River, Wyoming, and shoved his hands into his coat pockets as the door to Annie's Bakery clanged behind him. His mother, Anne Young, had opened the small shop when he was sixteen, not long after his dad had left them. If it hadn't been for her hard work and sacrifice, Marc wouldn't know where he and his sister, Brooke, would be today. He certainly wouldn't be the proud owner of the now-thriving ranch they'd almost lost.

His mom's patience was about to pay off. Over the years, she'd described her vision for the bakery countless times, always insisting the corner building was the only one that would do. Two months ago, Gus Prater had retired, leaving the former jewelry store empty.

It wouldn't be sitting empty much longer.

He turned toward his truck as a movement across the street caught his eye. A woman dug through a large purse on her raised knee near the corner building's entrance. The brick exterior boasted two huge picture windows to display Mom's donuts, cookies and freshly baked breads, and the ornate door had a transom window to let in light.

Marc couldn't place the woman. Her stylish outfit stuck out in their small town. Maybe she was the leasing agent Gus had mentioned when Marc had paid him a visit a few weeks ago about purchasing the building.

He'd been surprised to learn Gus didn't own the place. The man had kindly given him the contact information of the property manager, but she hadn't known much beyond the fact MDW Management held the deed. Marc's research showed that the late Dewey Winston had started the company, but no one seemed to know who'd taken it over after his wife's death last year. It was strange not knowing who made the decisions for the company.

Maybe this woman would have the answers

he was looking for—mainly, how could his mother buy or lease the place? The last thing he wanted was for someone else to swoop in and steal it out from under her.

Marc looked both ways, then loped across Center Street, the main drag of downtown Jewel River. After a hop onto the sidewalk, he slowed his pace.

"Excuse me," he said as he approached the woman, still digging in that pit of a purse.

She straightened quickly, tossing a glance over her shoulder. Her face arrested him. Big light brown eyes—so light they were almost gold—widened under sculpted eyebrows. Her straight nose was sprinkled with pale freckles, and her lips were a raspberry tint he couldn't decide was natural or the result of gloss. Brown hair rippled down her back, and she was wearing a tailored dark gray wool winter coat with a cream-colored scarf carefully wound and tucked inside the neck. Slim-fitting black pants and tall boots completed the look.

Not from around here and dressed up? The leasing agent. She had to be.

"Hi there. I'm Marc. Marc Young." He circled to stand in front of her, forcing a welcoming smile as he nodded to her purse, still resting on her lifted knee. "Can I help you with that?"

She blew an errant lock of hair away from her face. "My purse? No, thanks. I've got it."

Her voice was melodic, smooth. As pretty as her delicate features.

"Are you here about the building?" he asked. He stretched his neck to peek inside the window closest to him, but without the lights on, there wasn't much to see.

"How did you know?" She lifted out a set of keys and hauled the purse straps onto her shoulder before giving him her full attention.

"Gus Prater mentioned you'd be coming by."

"Gus Prater?" She edged toward the door, gripping the keys. Was he making her uncomfortable? Didn't want her under the impression he was coming on too strong. He stepped back to give her more space. That should set her at ease. She hitched her chin. "The name isn't ringing a bell."

"Gus. The man who owned the jewelry shop for twenty years. This building."

"Oh, right." She stared at him and didn't move. Seemed to be waiting for him to continue on his way so she could unlock the door. Wasn't happening. This woman had no idea how important this building was to his mother. And why would she? They'd never met.

"My mom's been waiting years to open her bakery here." His palms were getting sweaty. What was his problem? He wasn't the nervous type. "So whether you're putting it up for sale or for lease, I want to be first in line. In fact, we could work out the terms now. Or anytime, really."

The woman gave her head a slight shake as her cheeks grew flushed. "I'm not putting it up for lease or selling it."

He rocked back on his heels. Then why was she there?

"You're not?" He tried to figure out what was going on but came up short. "You're the leasing agent, right?"

"No," she said quickly. "I'm Reagan Mayer. I own this building."

She *owned* the building? How was that possible? She seemed too young. He scrambled to regroup.

"Nice to meet you, Reagan," he said so quickly he might as well not have said it at all. "When you're ready to sell—or rent it out— give me or my mother a call. I can write down the contact information for you or text you my number if that's easier."

She tightened her hold on the purse and inched backward. "I don't think you understand."

"What?"

"I'm not selling or leasing this place. I'm starting my own business here."

Starting her own business? The words didn't compute. Had she recently purchased it? How had she gotten the jump on him?

Why hadn't he known it was for sale?

"But you can't." He puffed out his chest as he firmed his stance.

"Why not?" Her head tilted in genuine curiosity.

"Because it's my mom's," he sputtered, kicking himself for being unable to form a cohesive argument.

"The deed's in my name."

"The deed is owned by MDW Management." He clenched his teeth, his molars grinding together. What was he missing? He felt blindsided and helpless and...upset. Really upset.

"I'm the sole owner of MDW Management."

"You?" He drew his eyebrows together. This woman—Reagan—couldn't be more than twenty-five years old. Twenty-six, tops. He gave her another glance. Okay, maybe twenty-seven. "How old are you?"

"Twenty-eight. Not that it's any of your business. How old are *you*?" Her offended tone alerted him he was crossing lines he shouldn't be crossing. *Get yourself under control. You've mastered the art of it over the years.*

"Thirty-two."

"What did you say you did again?" She narrowed her eyes.

"I own Young Ranch, about twenty minutes east of town. I'm also a member of Jewel River's planning and zoning commission. My mother, Anne Young, owns Annie's Bakery, across the street." He pivoted to point to the narrow building wedged between an insurance company and a dental office. Just seeing her tiny storefront gnawed at his heart.

His mom deserved this building. She'd risen before dawn for years and years to run the bakery, and she'd always clung to her dreams of expanding it right here, in the corner brick building.

This pretty outsider wasn't going to take it from her.

"What will it take to convince you to sell?"

He crossed his arms over his chest. As soon as the words were out of his mouth, he knew they were the wrong ones to say.

"I'm not selling." Her lips drew into an offended line, and he expected to see sparks of fire in her eyes, but all he saw was resignation and a hint of vulnerability. "Now, if you'll excuse me."

He wanted to stand there and argue and convince her. But what would be the point?

He wouldn't let Mom's dreams be snuffed out. Not after all they'd been through. Not after all they were still going through. He'd find a way to get the building for her. He wasn't letting this get snatched away from her, too.

IF ONLY SHE wasn't such an unorganized mess, she would have easily found the key, unlocked the building and slipped inside before that unfortunate confrontation with Marc Young, the man she'd instantly dubbed Hot Cowboy.

Reagan Mayer waited until Marc was across the street before turning to unlock the door. She fumbled with the key, then unlocked it with a click, pushed open the gorgeous wooden door and went inside. She dead-bolted it behind her just in case anyone got ideas about coming in. And by anyone, she meant Hot Cowboy.

Her heart was still pounding over the encounter.

She'd taken one look at him and her mouth had gone as dry as the bread she'd popped into the toaster and forgotten about earlier. The man was tall—she guessed around six feet three inches—muscular and dressed like a typical rancher in jeans, cowboy boots, a Carhartt jacket and a simple Stetson on his head. His hooded brown eyes, straight nose, thin eyebrows and chiseled jaw all added up to gorgeous.

But then he'd gone and opened his mouth. She could handle a simple misunderstanding—clearly, he felt entitled to this building due to his mother—but his dismissive attitude? No. She couldn't handle that. And asking her age as if she were a twelve-year-old with no clue what she was doing? So condescending.

If only she'd had a snappy comeback. Her sister, Erica, would have had one; she always did. After getting divorced two years ago, Erica had moved to Jewel River to live with their great-aunt Martha on Winston Ranch. Then Martha had died, and Erica had inherited the ranch, while Reagan had inherited MDW Management, founded by her great-uncle Dewey. Her brothers had inherited Martha's investments. The company's assets comprised three commercial buildings, including this one, a hefty bank account and a small house four blocks away that had been sitting empty for more than a year.

With the help of her large family, Reagan had moved into the house on Saturday. Hard to believe she'd slept in it two nights already. It needed some TLC, but the two-bedroom home within walking distance to this beautiful building was perfect for her.

Let's see what I've got to work with. She inhaled deeply—it smelled dusty, old, with a hint of mildew—then flipped the light switches on. A sense of wonder filled her heart.

This was it.

Her chocolate shop would no longer be an idea she was chasing—it would be reality. Her reality.

Reagan brought her fists just under her chin, savoring the burst of delight rushing through her. She needed this. Needed a new creative venture. Needed to see if she could make it on her own away from her loving, and overbearing, family.

After spending her entire adult life working alongside her mother as they'd built a hugely successful online candle business—Mayer Canyon Candles—Reagan was ready to do things her way. And who knew? Maybe Jewel River would cough up the perfect guy for her in the process.

She wanted to get married and have her own family. But only with a man who accepted her and didn't try to change her mind when she decided to act on intuition rather than logic. Her parents affectionately called her a dreamer, and she supposed she was. An optimist, too.

The downside was that she'd spent her entire life avoiding conflict and ended up doing things everyone else's way. Not anymore.

Reagan set her purse on the counter and slowly ambled around the store, trailing her fingers along the dusty glass cases where the jewelry had been displayed. Then she studied the walls filled with shelves as she made her way to the back, where two offices, a bathroom, a break room and a storage space were located. A hallway led to the rear parking lot.

She returned to the main showroom and started picturing all of the chocolates she'd learned to make in Denver over the past six months as she'd apprenticed under a gourmet chocolatier.

Creating things—coming up with unique combinations—came naturally to her. It hadn't been much of an adjustment to switch from the precision required to make candles to the precision required to make chocolates. And now she could make her own special candies. Yes, a new creative challenge was exactly what she needed.

But first she had to get the business set up, along with all the paperwork, phone calls, permits and everything else necessary to remodel this building. It gave her a headache just thinking about it.

Maybe she *should* have asked Erica to join her today. Her sister was analytical and determined. She'd been the business end of Mayer Canyon Candles for several years. Plus, she used to run one of her ex-husband's dealerships and was in the process of creating an event center—the Winston—on her ranch. Erica was good at getting things done.

However, the whole point of Reagan coming to Jewel River was to make her own decisions. Find her own path. No more falling in with everyone else's ideas of what she should do and how she should do it.

Reagan rooted around in her purse until she found a notebook and pen. Then she leaned against one of the glass cases and began to sketch the space, leaving out the current displays and adding ones she'd need. As ideas came, she flipped to the next sheet to write them down inside random circles. She'd figure out how the ideas connected later.

Tapping the pen against her chin, she wondered how much of this she could keep. The maroon carpet was worn and faded. It had to go. A nice hardwood or vinyl-plank floor would work well in here.

She could picture the pretty navy boxes she'd picked out for the chocolates stacked on the shelves. Her sister-in-law Holly—a marketing genius—had been emailing her designs for logos. Reagan had narrowed it down to three, all with her company name: R. Mayer Chocolates.

Hugging herself tightly, she did a twirl. Then she stood still for a while to soak in the place.

She'd discussed her plan with her mom and two sisters-in-law. The three of them were now the heart of Mayer Canyon Candles. They'd all agreed Reagan's chocolates would be the perfect companion product to feature with the candles. They were adding a tab for R. Mayer Chocolates on the company's website to link directly to Reagan's online store once she was ready to open and had her website set up. This would allow her to sell the chocolates exclusively online until she had a feel for how much interest there was in them. Later, she'd bring on employees and open this store to the public.

A knock on one of the windows made her jump. *Please don't let it be Hot Cowboy.*

At the sight of Erica's face, Reagan let out a happy squeal and ran over to the door. She unlocked it and let her sister and Erica's three-year-old son, Rowan, inside.

"We thought we'd pop over and see how Auntie Reagan's doing, right, Rowan?" Erica waited for Rowan to hug her before coming in for her own embrace. "So, this is it, huh?"

Reagan nodded, her stomach starting to clench with nerves. This was where her outspoken sister would tell her exactly where everything should go and how she should do things. And if Reagan contradicted her, Erica would give her a skeptical look, the one she'd inherited from their mother. Then Reagan would second-guess herself and eventually do it Erica's way because *maybe* she was right. In her heart, though, she knew her way made more sense. Maybe not to anyone else, but it did to her.

"I love it! Look at these windows." Erica's eyes sparkled as she gravitated to one of the picture windows.

Reagan joined her. "It's going to be fun changing the displays seasonally."

"This place has so much character." Erica looked around in awe. Rowan was busy sprinting from one wall to the other in the open space behind them. "It's big. Way bigger than it appeared when the jewelry store was still in here."

Reagan slowly circled to take in the space. Now that Erica mentioned it, it *was* big.

Could it be too big?

Nah. Once she had the counters and sinks installed along the back wall, along with all the chocolate-making equipment and the racks, the space would feel just right.

"Slow down before you trip and fall," Erica called over her shoulder to Rowan.

"But I'm fast, Mama!" He continued running at top speed. "See?"

"I know you're fast. You'll probably run sprints in high school, but not in here." Erica turned back to her and rolled her eyes. "I can't wait for the weather to break. Keeping him cooped up indoors all day is wearing on my nerves and Gemma's. She never complains, though, unlike me."

"How is Gemma?" Erica's middle-aged housekeeper/babysitter was a sweet woman. Very private, Gemma rarely left Winston Ranch.

"Great. Johnny Abbot finally got up the nerve to come out and visit her last weekend. I've never seen her so flustered. I told her they could have tea in my house if she didn't want him in her cabin, but shockingly, she declined. I know she was nervous because she made three kinds of cookies, apple bread *and* a sour cream coffee cake."

"Who is Johnny again?" She couldn't remember if Erica had already mentioned him. Her sister had shared so many stories about the various residents of Jewel River, and especially the members of the Jewel River Legacy Club, that Reagan had a hard time keeping them straight.

"The nicest man, Reag. He's sixty-five—older than Gemma, but not by much—and he's kind of shy but not as shy as she is. They went to school together back in the day, and I think he's got a crush on her."

"That is so sweet." Reagan loved the thought of someday reconnecting with an old classmate who had a crush on her. Except none of her old classmates had ever had crushes on her, and her dating life back home had been nonexistent. At least in Denver she'd gone on dates with three men. They hadn't been the right guys for her, and that was okay.

The right guy was out there. Mom insisted he was. Of course, she also insisted that Reagan should settle down with a nice cowboy, and that hadn't happened. Still…a girl could hope.

Erica rubbed her hands together. "So, what's the plan with this place? What are you going to do first?"

Tempted to press the heels of her hands into her temples, Reagan forced herself to keep a cheerful demeanor. The looming tasks were daunting, yes, but she would figure it all out. Maybe.

"I'm not sure. Now that I'm here, I'll start getting a plan together."

"You'll need permits. Henry Zane is the building inspector. Nice guy. Oh, and did you file the paperwork to register the name of the chocolate shop yet? Once you get that done, you can get your Employer Identification Number and your online banking system figured out."

"Stop." She thrust her arms out. "I have

plenty of time. I'm not going to rush. I haven't even unpacked my house, and this is the first time I've set foot in here."

"I'm not rushing." Erica flicked her fingernail against her thumb. "I'm simply excited for you. And I want to make sure every *i* is dotted and *t* is crossed."

"I know, and I appreciate your enthusiasm. But this isn't Mayer Canyon Candles. I'm older now. I'm capable of figuring it all out." At least, she hoped she was. One huge blessing from all of this was that she was financially secure. The buildings and bank account she'd inherited, along with her stake in the candle company, would pay her bills indefinitely. She could take her time learning how to get this business launched.

Erica gave her a look that screamed *if you say so* as she shrugged. "I'm glad you nixed the idea of using the other two buildings for your shop. They would not do at all."

She agreed with her sister there. One of the buildings was currently leased to a thriving convenience store, and the other, while empty, was more suitable for industrial work, not a retail shop.

"Well, if you can't get a hold of Henry—Angela's been keeping him busy—and you need help navigating the permits, call Marc Young. He's a member of the legacy club and on the planning commission. He can help you out."

Reagan was reasonably sure she grimaced at the sound of his name.

"What was that look for?" Erica asked.

"I met Marc. Right before I came inside."

"He's pretty cute, huh?" She waggled her eyebrows.

"Yeah." She left it at that.

"Uh-oh. What happened?"

"Nothing."

"Come on. I know you better than that."

She might as well give her the short version. Her sister would only pester her until she did anyhow.

"He seems to think his mom is opening a bakery here."

"Here? As in this building?" Erica cringed and peeked over at Rowan. He'd taken a toy car out of his pocket and was running it on the shelves as he made *vroom, vroom* sounds. "I didn't realize… I mean…it's well-known that Anne wants to expand her bakery. She's been waiting for the right space to open up. I didn't realize *this* was the space she had in mind."

"Do you think it's going to be a problem?" Reagan nibbled on her fingernail as visions of angry townsfolk boycotting her chocolates came to mind. She'd spent her entire life in a small town. She knew how they worked. Loyal to a fault, the residents would rally around Anne. Leaving Reagan—the newcomer—the loser.

"I hope not. She'll be disappointed, but she'll understand." Erica's gaze shifted toward the window. "But Marc? I don't know. He's like Jet. Protective of his mother and his sister, Brooke. And the past year has been awful for Brooke. Her husband died in an accident overseas—Ross was in the air force—and six months later she gave birth to identical twin daughters. That was back in January, so she has her hands full."

"Oh, no, that's terrible." Reagan's heart hurt for the poor woman. Losing her husband while pregnant? And having twin babies to raise on her own? "Does she live around here, too?"

"Yeah, Brooke moved back to Marc's ranch after Ross died. And once the twins arrived, Anne moved out there, too—temporarily—to help out with them. Anne has her own house here in town."

"It sounds like the entire family has their hands full." She bit the corner of her lower lip.

"I feel bad about his mom and sister, I really do, but this building is mine. I said goodbye to everything I know—besides you—to move here."

"Exactly." Erica put her arm around Reagan's shoulders. "And once this town tastes your chocolates, all will be forgotten and forgiven, although there's nothing to forgive. Why don't you come to the legacy club meeting tomorrow night? You can meet the members. They'll love you. Have I told you how happy I am you moved here?"

"Only a thousand times. I'm glad I'm here, too." She hugged Erica again. Her big sister always had her back. "Now, enough about me. How is the pole barn renovation coming along? Will the Winston be ready in time for the wedding?"

"Oh, it will be ready." Her eyes got the scary fire in them that meant she was on a mission. Erica and Dalton's upcoming wedding reception would be the grand opening of the Winston. "Dalton has to be tired of my never-ending to-do list. But the pole barn—you wouldn't even recognize it. It's been transformed. There are special rooms for the bridal party, a stage for a band or DJ, a state-of-the-art sound system... You name it. I've got it."

"I can't wait to come out and see it."

"I can't, either. That reminds me—your maid-of-honor dress is a slightly different style than we originally planned. I'll show you later. If you hate it, we'll go a different route."

"I'll love it." She would, too, no matter what it looked like. She wanted Erica to be happy with a man she deserved, and Dalton was that guy.

After catching up for several more minutes, the three of them went back outside. Reagan blew Rowan kisses as he waved to her on the way to Erica's truck, and then she ducked her chin into her scarf and strode down the sidewalk toward her house.

She hoped Marc Young and his mother didn't cause problems. The chocolate shop was all she'd dreamed of for months, and Reagan wasn't settling for anything less. She'd done things other people's way her entire life. No one—not even a hot cowboy—could make her compromise this time.

CHAPTER TWO

How COULD HE get Reagan to see things his way?

The following afternoon, after a long day of calving, Marc was finishing up paperwork in his ranch office. His pregnant cows were having calves left and right, so he had to be on top of everything. Rico Hart, the full-time cowboy he'd hired a decade ago, was taking the night shift. The additional ranch hand Marc had hoped to hire for calving season had fallen through, and instead of putting out the word to find someone else, he'd opted not to hire anyone. He and Rico had made it through last year on their own. They'd get through this year, too. Marc just hoped the next couple of weeks didn't bring any major storms.

His life was stormy enough.

Yesterday he'd made a lousy impression with Reagan, and when he'd called around this morning to find out more about her, he'd been mortified to find out she was Erica Black's sister. He and Erica volunteered together for the Jewel River Legacy Club, and he didn't want there to be any bad blood between them. Because of her efforts, the members were motivated to improve the town.

Out of habit, he checked his phone, then let out a sigh of relief. No messages.

For months, his phone had been filled with texts from his mom. Marc didn't hold it against her. He was worried about Brooke, too. His little sister was four years younger than him, and he'd slid into the role of father figure after their dad deserted them. If Marc could wipe away the devastating events of the past year for her, he would in a heartbeat. Since he couldn't, he'd done the next best thing—moved her back home so he and his mother could help with his infant nieces, Megan and Alice.

Even with their help, Brooke wasn't bouncing back to her optimistic self, and Marc had no idea how to fix it. She'd lost all the baby weight and then some, and she'd barely gained enough during the pregnancy as it was. Dark circles had taken up permanent residence under her eyes, understandable with the twins.

The few times Marc had tried to help her

with night feedings, she'd snapped at him. So he and his mother had formed a tag team during the day. As soon as Mom finished up at the bakery around noon—her part-timer closed shop at two—she rushed back to assist Brooke with the twins, and when Marc completed his ranch work by late afternoon, he helped with the babies while Mom made supper.

Again, he was struck by how much Brooke had been through—was still going through—and how much of a toll it had taken on his mother, too. It would be great to see Mom's face light up with the news she could finally expand her bakery. He hated letting her down.

Tracing his pen along the list on his legal pad, he reviewed his options. If he could just convince Reagan the building should go to his mom... But how? He didn't even know what she planned on doing with the place. A dozen potential stores came to mind, none of them good. A high-end clothing shop was the most likely option. Or maybe one of those smoothie bars so popular in cities these days. It could be a yoga studio or a tanning salon.

Yeah, you got all that in the two minutes you talked to her? Simply because she wore a dressy out-

fit? This is down-to-earth Erica's sister. The apple can't fall that far from the tree.

He thought back on how put-together Reagan had looked and how wary of him she'd been. There was something different about her, and he couldn't put his finger on it. She made him feel off-kilter.

Maybe Henry Zane knew something about the building that he didn't. He reached for his phone. After the usual pleasantries, Marc got down to business. "There's a new owner of the old jewelry store. Know anything about it?"

"It's the first I've heard. Are you sure?" Henry asked. "Deed hasn't changed hands."

"I'm sure. Met her myself. She owns the company that holds the deed."

"You don't say." Papers shuffling and someone calling Henry's name were in the background. "I haven't heard a peep. Who is she?"

"Erica Black's sister."

"Huh. I assumed you were talking about an older gal."

"Not old. Young." Twenty-eight wasn't that young, though. His sister was the same age, and she was already a widow with twins. Again, he couldn't shake the feeling of helplessness pouring over him. Why did Brooke's life have to be so hard?

"Maybe Anne will finally get you married off." The man let out a throaty chuckle, which then turned into a coughing fit.

Marc ground his teeth together. He was *not* getting married. Weren't his hands full enough just running the ranch and making sure his sister, his mom and the twins were okay? And, at the moment, they clearly weren't.

"I don't think so," Marc said.

"She's ugly?" He sounded genuinely surprised.

"I didn't say that."

"Christy Moulten will likely have her eyes on the gal for Cade or Ty. She won't rest until those boys are married."

"More power to her." He personally didn't like the idea of either Cade or Ty Moulten dating Reagan. And he didn't care to think about why. "There isn't anything that would stand in the way of her opening a business here, is there?"

"None that I can think of offhand. Of course, it depends on what she's putting in there. You know as well as I do if she's renovating the building, she'll need contractors lined up before she can get her permit. Then there's state licensing."

For once, Marc wished he lived in a bigger town with stricter rules about local businesses. Then he could deny her the permit for whatever she was opening.

He winced. Since when had he become so mean and petty? He would never abuse his position on the planning and zoning commission to prevent someone from opening a business.

He was better than that.

A few minutes later, they ended the call, and this time when Marc checked, there was a text from his mother.

Can you pick up diaper cream before your meeting tonight? Alice has a rash and we're all out.

Without giving it another thought, he texted back that he would.

Closing his eyes briefly, he cleared his thoughts. *God, these women mean more to me than anything on earth. Whatever they need, please help me provide it. And pave a way for Mom to have her building.*

It was getting late. He'd better change so he'd have enough time to stop at the grocery store before the legacy club meeting.

A few minutes later, he strode down the path from the ranch office, located in one of the barns, to the farmhouse. He might not know much about Reagan and her plans, but tonight would be the ideal time to find answers. He'd simply ask Erica.

After he'd cleaned up and dressed in fresh jeans and a button-down shirt, he descended the staircase to the living room, where his sister was buckling one of the twins into a bouncy seat.

"I hear we have a rash situation?" He kept his tone bright, teasing.

"Alice is as cheerful as ever, but it looks painful." Brooke gave him a wan smile. He'd take it. It was better than nothing.

"And how is Miss Megan?" He bent over the play mat where Megan lay on her back, grabbing her feet. She was wearing a yellow sleeper with ducks all over it. He tickled her tummy, and she gave him a slobbery grin. His sister always dressed Megan in yellow and purple outfits, while Alice wore pink and pale green outfits. It made it easier to tell the girls apart.

"Happy as always. Nothing bothers her." Brooke looked as frail as a corpse as she knelt beside Megan.

"Why don't I get you one of Mom's sugar

cookies and some chocolate milk?" He hated seeing her so pale and thin.

"And spoil my supper?" Her voice had an edge to it. "No, thanks. I'm fine."

Was she, though? She didn't look fine. She looked two steps away from the grave. He wasn't going to argue with her. It would only make her more defensive than she already was.

"Marc?" Mom called from the kitchen. "Can you come here a minute?"

He gave Brooke one last glance and made his way to the kitchen.

"What's up?" he asked, lifting the lid on the box of donuts she'd brought home. A cruller. *Yes.* He ate half in one bite.

She abandoned stirring the spaghetti sauce and turned to him as she wiped her hands on a towel. "The diaper cream."

"I know. You texted me." His mom assumed if she didn't remind him thirteen times, he'd forget.

"I took a picture of the tube for you."

"It's the same brand I bought two weeks ago, right?" He kept a lid on his temper. Mom was stressed out, too. This was her way of getting through it—by micromanaging everything.

"Yes, but I want to make sure it's the right one."

He stepped forward, putting his hands on her shoulders, and bent to kiss her forehead. "Don't worry, Ma. I'm taking care of it."

"Thank you." Her eyes gleamed with gratitude.

"You're welcome. Is there anything else I can pick up while I'm out?"

She craned her neck to peer through the archway that led to the living room. "She's too thin."

"I know."

"What if we buy that drink the nursing home uses?"

"I'll pick up some, but I doubt she'll touch it." Marc had been thinking along those lines, too. A nutritional drink might give her more energy.

"Grief is a terrible thing." Her eyes were downcast. Then she returned to the stovetop and began stirring the sauce again. "I'll talk to her about keeping up her strength for the babies. Maybe a guilt trip will get her to eat more."

Yeah, like the guilt trips Mom had given him over the years had worked. They'd tended to annoy him. Although, to be fair, some of them had done their job.

"I've got to go."

"Don't forget—"

"The cream. I know."

"I'll text you that picture…"

As Marc went to the mudroom to put on his boots and coat, the feeling of not being up to the task overwhelmed him. It was the same feeling he'd had the first couple of years after Dad had cut himself out of their lives—incompetent.

He just didn't know what to do about his sister.

Sure, he'd invited Mom and Brooke to move back in with him so they could all work together to take care of the twins. He was glad they were here. It was a privilege to make sure his loved ones had what they needed. But no matter what he and his mom did, they couldn't get Brooke to eat more, and no matter how hard he tried, he hadn't made a dent in healing Brooke's broken heart.

Reagan's face came to mind with her faint freckles and golden-brown eyes. Why did his thoughts keep returning to her? *Forget about her.* He was responsible for four women—his mother, Brooke, Megan and Alice. There was no room in his life for a fifth.

Now that she was here, Reagan was having second thoughts about attending the legacy club meeting. She wasn't the most outgoing person to begin with, and as soon as she'd entered the church's all-purpose room, she'd been swarmed. Apparently, the community center, where they normally held the meetings, was undergoing repairs and wouldn't be available until summer. Erica had promptly introduced her to a dozen people—Reagan had already forgotten most of their names—and the older ladies were peppering her with questions. They reminded her of her mother.

Christy Moulten, in particular, was overly interested in whether she had a boyfriend or not. Hopefully, the meeting would begin soon, and she could escape all this attention.

"Clem, this is my sister, Reagan Mayer." Erica appeared with a wiry, tough-looking rancher. At the sight of him, the ladies dispersed. "Reagan, this is Clem Buckley." His eyes were as hard as granite. A shiver tripped down Reagan's vertebrae. "He fills in for the building inspector occasionally. He can tell you what needs to be done."

Reagan *did* need help. She'd spent all day trying to determine the correct steps to start the business. The research she'd done online hadn't coughed up the information she needed.

In fact, she'd gotten so bewildered by the various government sites with their food licenses, registrations and various permits she wasn't even sure she needed that she'd stretched out on the couch with a cool washcloth on her forehead for a good half hour.

She was never going to be able to figure out everything on her own.

"Building? What building?" Clem's voice was as hard as his eyes. Erica excused herself to organize her notes for the meeting.

"The brick one on the corner—" Reagan said.

"Jewelry store. Got it." Did the man ever blink? "What kind of business are you putting in there, girly?"

"A chocolate shop." She licked her lips. Maybe she should remind him her name was Reagan, not girly. Or maybe she should not speak at all so he'd leave her alone. The man looked to be in his seventies, and boy, was he intimidating.

He let out a *humph* and made a sucking sound with his teeth. "Who's going to buy enough chocolates to keep you in business in this little town?"

The town *was* small. It was just one of the

reasons she'd decided to do the soft launch on-line before opening the store to the public.

"I'm selling them online at first."

"Then why do you need a big building?"

"I don't need a big building." She hated that her voice sounded so squeaky. "But I do need enough space for all the equipment to make them, as well as temperature-controlled display cases so I can select what I need for each box."

His skepticism was getting to her. Her breathing started growing shallow as all the reasons she never should have left the candle business came back in a rush.

"What about caramels?" He turned his head slightly and narrowed his eyes.

What about them? Did he have a problem with ooey-gooey deliciousness?

"I have my own recipe," she said. "I'm currently working on the perfect nut-and-caramel combo." She loved working with caramel. Making it from scratch required a lot of babysitting, and she'd learned the hard way not to stir it. But when it turned out right? Mmm… "Do you have something against caramels?"

"I do not." He straightened. "If there's a pecan or a peanut in there, I like 'em even better."

"You're really going to love my caramel collection, then." She went on to describe some of the chocolates she'd been mastering, and it was as if a weight was lifted from her shoulders. Discussing her craft always relaxed her. Clem asked more questions and his attitude softened. They were deep in a discussion about how much sea salt was too much sea salt when Erica asked everyone to find a seat.

Clem pointed to Reagan. "I'll talk to Henry Zane, the building inspector. He'll walk you through, nice and gentle-like, what you need to do to get the shop open." Then he patted her arm and—was that a smile?—retreated to the table.

Stunned, Reagan stood there a moment, then mentally shrugged before taking a seat next to Dalton Cambridge, Erica's fiancé. He leaned in and whispered, "We're in for a treat tonight. Angela Zane got her grandson to make a presentation for her Shakespeare-in-the-Park proposal."

"Jewel River has a theater club?"

"No, but that isn't stopping her."

"Is Angela related to Henry?"

"He's her husband."

Up front, Erica shushed them and they stopped

talking. After the Pledge of Allegiance and the Lord's Prayer, the meeting got underway.

Reagan looked around the tables set up in a U and noted the people present. Christy had a good-looking cowboy next to her—no doubt one of the sons she'd mentioned—and Marc sat two spots down from him. Her heart did a funny skipping thing she didn't like. He was even more handsome tonight, and she hadn't thought it possible.

She wanted to resent Hot Cowboy for being overbearing and kind of rude yesterday when they'd met. But did she resent him? Not really. Couldn't fault the man for looking out for his mother. Her brothers would have done the same.

"I may have found a veterinarian." Cade Moulten, the handsome man next to Christy, was speaking. "As a bonus, her father is considering opening a training center for service dogs in the old warehouse on Birch Boulevard."

"That would kill two birds with one stone," Marc said. "We want those empty buildings filled."

"Does this woman have the know-how to treat large animals?" Clem, back to grumpy mode, was leaning back in his chair with his arms crossed over his chest.

"Yes," Cade said. "Although she primarily works with pets."

"We don't need our horses and cattle dying if the doc doesn't know which end is which," Clem said.

Cade gave him a pointed stare. "I can assure you she knows which end is which."

"I guess we'll have to take your word for it."

"I guess you will."

The meeting progressed, and Marc stood and gave an update on the empty buildings. One of them was the industrial building Reagan owned. She'd have to figure out what to do with it at some point. Another thing to add to her list. He glanced Reagan's way when he finished, and she didn't know how to interpret the look. It wasn't accusatory. If anything, it was questioning.

Clem rose, mentioned the progress on having a new sign made to welcome people to Jewel River, then waved his hand as if flinging off a bug. "I can't believe we're bothering to discuss this, but Angela, here, thinks having a Shakespeare-in-the-Park doohickey is a good idea. With that in mind, it's time to suffer through yet another production by her grandson. You've all been warned."

The lights dimmed, and everyone turned their attention to the screen. A couple dressed in medieval clothing held hands as they walked across a prairie. Suddenly, a computer-animated explosion filled the screen as hard rock instrumental music blasted through the speaker. The maiden or princess—Reagan had no clue—ran toward a fence as a bull charged in the distance. A man's deep voice rumbled, "Shakespeare like you've never seen it before. Wyoming style. Run, Juliet, run. Or the bull will take you down." Another explosion and fireworks completed the clip.

As soon as it was over, everyone looked at each other as if they weren't sure what they'd just witnessed. Reagan didn't know, either, but she couldn't help it—she started applauding. And everyone else joined in. Someone even yelled, "Bravo!"

Erica turned on the lights and resumed her position as the chair of the meeting.

"Thank you, Angela, for that lively presentation," Erica said. "And please tell Joey, good job. That boy has a future in Hollywood for sure."

"I keep telling him that, hon." Angela, a full-figured woman in her early sixties, beamed. "Just think what having Shakespeare here could do for the tourism!"

"Tourism? Bah." Clem shook his head.

For several minutes, the club members debated the pros and cons of hosting the event. Then Erica took control of the meeting and addressed Angela. "Why don't you put out a survey to find out how much interest there is for locals to participate in the play? We'd need actors, sets, costumes—all of it."

"Will do, hon." Angela nodded brightly, licked her finger and pretended to mark the air with it.

Across the table, Clem looked absolutely disgusted with life. His chin was tucked and his arms were still crossed over his chest. Erica moved on to the next topic.

After the meeting wrapped up, everyone stood to leave. Some of the women came back over to Reagan, including Christy, who appeared to be dragging her son with her.

"Reagan, I want you to meet Cade, my oldest son. His younger brother, Ty, was supposed to be here, but he must have gotten busy."

"Nice to meet you." She smiled up at him, and he grinned, thrusting his hand out.

"Good to meet you, too. I hear you're opening a chocolate shop in the old jewelry store."

"Yes, I am." He seemed pleasant enough. She gave him a self-deprecating smile and shrugged. "Well, I will eventually. Once I figure it all out." She spotted Clem out of the corner of her eye. "Clem is talking to the building inspector for me. Hopefully, he'll be able to guide me through the process."

"Clem?" Christy's eyebrows soared to her hairline. "Voluntarily?"

"Yes."

"He must have a sweet tooth," Cade said, still grinning. "I know I do."

"Or he was charmed by your sweet personality, Reagan." Christy gave her arm a squeeze. "I'm looking forward to spending *a lot* more time with you."

"Um, thank you." She didn't know what else to say. While Cade definitely seemed like a catch, Reagan had more important things on her mind. Like Hot Cowboy. She glanced at Marc again, but he was on his way out the door with everyone else.

Soon she joined Erica and Dalton, and they headed outside into the cold night air.

"Have you decided to paint any of the

rooms?" Erica asked as they crossed the parking lot to their vehicles. "The house is so cute."

"I haven't made up my mind." She wanted to paint the living room, kitchen and her bedroom, but the right colors hadn't come to her. They would. They always did. She just had to give it time.

"When you know what you want, we'll come and help, right, Big D?" Erica elbowed Dalton's side.

"Of course. Just don't ask me to cut in the paint in the ceiling or corners. I'm all thumbs." He lifted his hands and wiggled his thumbs.

Reagan laughed. "I want to get things rolling with the shop first anyway."

They said their goodbyes, and Reagan noticed Marc a few parking spots down. She hitched her chin to acknowledge him. He gave her a weak wave and got into his truck.

Disappointment sank to her belly. If she wasn't robbing his mother of her dream, maybe Marc would have been someone she could have gotten to know better. Or maybe not. Men were somewhat of a mystery to her.

If there was one thing Reagan knew, she wasn't getting involved with someone who would try to talk her out of something important to her. She'd already been there and done that with her parents, her siblings…and even herself.

It was time to stand strong. Even if her plans didn't make sense to anyone else. Especially if they didn't make sense to anyone else.

God had made her the way she was for a reason, and she was finally embracing it. Who cared if Hot Cowboy approved or not? This was her life, not his.

CHAPTER THREE

HE PROBABLY SHOULD have asked what this meeting was about. Almost a week later, on Monday, Marc opened the door to the building inspector's office in city hall. Henry had called him earlier to let him know he would be twenty minutes late to an appointment on his schedule. Since Marc always worked at city hall on Monday mornings for the planning and zoning commission, he'd assured Henry he'd handle the appointment until the man could get back. Marc was well versed on the typical questions people asked about permits.

He left the door open and took off his coat before sitting behind the desk.

"Hey, Marc, how are those babies doing?" Donna Marquez, one of the officers on duty, asked.

"The twins are great. Getting big. They sure are cute."

"And Brooke?" Her sympathetic expression only added to the guilt he couldn't shake off.

"As well as can be expected." He didn't know what else to say. It had been nine months since Ross had died. Brooke had loved him very much, and Marc wasn't sure if it was her grief, caring for infant twins—or both—weighing her down.

"Anything I can do to help?" Donna asked.

"Pray. Keep praying for her." As much as he was tempted to ask Donna for advice on how to get Brooke to eat more, he didn't. He'd picked up a six-pack of the nutritional drinks his mom had requested. Brooke hadn't touched them.

"You got it." She gave him a wave and continued down the hall.

Marc studied the desktop for a sticky note or any information clueing him in on what this meeting would be about. Someone looking to build a home? Maybe a problem with a commercial property?

He'd find out soon enough. And then he'd drive directly back to the ranch. Several cows would be having calves any minute now, and he needed to get out there to check on them. It wouldn't be long. A day or two, tops. He hadn't lost a calf yet this season. He planned to keep it that way.

A soft knock on the door had him looking up. Reagan stood there, and as soon as she recognized him, she frowned.

"Oh, I'm sorry. I must have the wrong office." She stretched her neck back to check the plaque outside the door.

"Are you here for Henry?" Of all the meetings he'd been asked to fill in for, this was one he wished he hadn't agreed to.

He knew what this was about.

The building.

His mom's building. The one Reagan owned. The one she planned on keeping.

"Henry's running late. He asked me to fill in until he gets here." Marc gestured to the chair in front of the desk. "Have a seat."

He was proud of himself for sounding professional. He didn't want her to know how upset this situation was making him.

She slipped inside and closed the door. Then she unbuttoned her wool coat, revealing a lavender sweater, dark gray pants and dressy boots with a low heel. A delicate silver necklace with a cross hung at her collarbone.

"What can I help you with?" He folded his

hands and set them on top of the desk, trying to keep his composure. Her hair had been pulled back in a low ponytail with loose tendrils escaping around each ear. Her long eyelashes made her eyes appear even bigger than he remembered.

"Um, maybe I should just wait for Mr. Zane."

His thoughts exactly.

"If you'd feel more comfortable, I understand." He gave her a tight smile.

She lifted her chin, and there was a hint of wariness in the gesture. Was she suspicious of him? Now he did feel like a jerk. He'd made a lot of assumptions when he'd met her last week, and they probably hadn't been fair.

"I take it you're here to discuss a building permit." There, he'd gotten the words out and hadn't sounded mad or upset. She nodded, her cheeks growing pink. "Where are you at in the process?"

She clutched her hands together. If there had been anything between them, it would be strangled to death by now.

"I was hoping to find out what the process is." Her honesty impressed him, but the words were still annoying. If she didn't even know the basics about how the permits worked, was she qualified to run a business?

"We have an application to fill out. You can download it online, or you can take one home with you." He swiveled the chair to grab a packet from the cubby behind him. Then he swiveled back and handed it to her. "It's in here, along with a list of contractors who are licensed to do the work. Call one of them—or all of them—and have them give you an estimate. They'll draw up plans, and then you can fill out the application and pay the fee. Once they start the work, there will be inspections."

"Okay." She was staring at the packet as if it were written in hieroglyphs. "Do I register my company's name here or the county or…?"

"Um, I believe it's with the state." Her question confused him, though. "I thought you owned MDW Management."

"I do, but I inherited it after my great-aunt died. My great-uncle was the one who started the company. Dewey Winston."

Ah…now he understood how she'd come to own the company. She'd inherited it. A blaze of annoyance crushed his forehead like a bad tension headache.

Inherited the company. From a wealthy relative. Who had those?

Don't be a hypocrite. Brooke had inherited a life-changing sum of money after Ross died. Her husband had been raised by his much older uncle. The late uncle's fortune had passed to Ross, which had then passed to Brooke upon his death. Because of the inheritance, his sister didn't have to work. She could be independent.

But Marc would have provided for her no matter what.

His heartbeat began pounding like a drum in the marching band. He wanted to ask Reagan if she had any idea how to run a business or if she was just doing this on a whim.

Chocolates. That was what he'd heard. She was opening a chocolate store.

Her knuckles were white against her clenched hands. "I never appreciated how much work my sister did for the candle company."

"Candles?" he asked. "I was told it was going to be a chocolate shop."

"Oh, it is." Her eyes shimmered as they grew wide. "My mother and I started a candle company about ten years ago. Erica joined us to handle the business side of things. I came up with the new scents, and Mom and I made every candle by hand. I loved it." Her face brightened as she spoke. "But I needed a change creatively and…well… I just needed a change."

A change. The freedom to quit a company, to move to another town? He'd never had the luxury. Never wanted it, either. He had no intention of doing anything differently with his life.

Reagan pushed her chair back. "I'll call the contractors you mentioned." She stared at the packet in her hand. "I want you to know that I didn't move here to ruin your mother's dreams. When I realized the corner building was mine and that it was sitting empty, I felt like it was meant to be. I don't expect you to understand."

She had an honest, humble air about her, and her words drained some of the resentment he was clinging to. Before he could respond, his phone rang so loudly it made him jump.

His mom. She wouldn't be calling unless it was an emergency. The bottom dropped out of his stomach as he held up a finger to Reagan. "Give me one sec."

She nodded. He answered the phone.

"Marc, something's wrong with Brooke. She collapsed. I don't know if she fainted or what. I'm taking her to the clinic. Rico's here. He'll watch the babies until you can get back, but you've got to come home right away."

"I'm leaving now." He ended the call as his mind raced with fears. Brooke collapsed? He glanced at Reagan. "I have to go."

"Is something wrong? You look like you've had a shock."

"It's my sister. Mom's taking her to the clinic. I've got to get back for the twins. Rico is with them, but I don't know how good the cowboy is with babies." He realized he was babbling but was helpless to stop it.

Reagan stood, pointing to his coat hanging on the back of the chair. He looked back, then snatched it and put it on.

"The twins are babies, right?" she asked.

"Almost three months old." He wiped his chin with his hand as his brain seized. He had to get home. Where were his keys? He tapped the pockets of his jeans, then his coat. There they were.

"Is your dad going with your mom?"

"What?" The question blindsided him. Dad? What was she talking about? "I don't have a dad. He left years ago."

"I'm sorry. I didn't know." She opened the

door. "You should go to the clinic to be with your mom. I can take care of the twins."

"You?" He followed Reagan into the hallway.

"Yes. I've been taking care of babies for years. Your mom needs you. Your sister does, too."

Truer words had not been spoken. He'd just have to trust Reagan knew what she was doing. "Okay, do you want to follow me to the ranch?"

"Just text me the address. My phone will tell me where to go." She placed her hand on his arm. "I'll pray while I'm driving."

He clenched his jaw, nodded. Then they exchanged information, and he told her the basic directions to get to the ranch as they strode to the main door.

Reagan was right. His mom and sister needed him. But he needed them, too. Needed them so much, it hurt to think about losing either one of them.

REAGAN WANTED BABIES. Her own babies. And holding these darling three-month-old twins, one in each of her arms, had kicked the urge into high gear.

"They're two little honeybuns, aren't they?" Rico, the middle-aged cowboy on baby duty, had a deep voice with a slight drawl. His brown eyes sparkled as he hovered nearby. He wasn't tall, but he was fit, with black hair that was graying at his temples. He'd set her at ease the instant she'd walked into the two-story farmhouse.

"That they are." She looked up at him and smiled.

"The boss has been awfully worried about their mama." The way he was tapping his fingers against his thighs made her think he was worried about her, too.

"Oh? Has she been having health problems?"

"I'm not sure. With her man dying and all…" His forehead wrinkled. "They'd only been married two years, and he'd been gone most of the one on active duty. Got killed in a helicopter crash somewhere in one of those oil countries."

At the thought of these babies potentially losing both parents, Reagan's eyes grew watery. She bowed her head. *Lord, these girls already lost their daddy. Please don't let them lose their mommy, too. Take care of Brooke, and comfort Marc and her mother.*

"I didn't mean to upset you." Rico held out a box of tissues to her. But her arms were full with the twins, so he set it next to her and took one of the girls.

"Thank you." She shifted the child and pulled out a tissue, dabbing her eyes with it. "I'm sorry. I'm just…"

"No need for sorries. I understand. Gets me right choked up thinking about it, too. Brooke had been living down in Texas before her man died. The boss moved her back into her old room after the funeral. No way he was letting her raise these honeybuns on her own. And then Miss Anne moved back in after they were born."

Hearing the tale from Rico gave her a deeper understanding of how difficult life must have been for Marc, his sister and his mother this year.

"I know it's not easy on her. Miss Anne likes being able to walk to work. It's harder for her now. Leaves here when it's still dark to get to the bakery, and then she helps out with the babies all afternoon."

It sounded exhausting.

"You don't happen to know how to tell the girls apart, do you?" Reagan studied the baby in her arms. The Cupid's bow lips, big dark blue eyes, long eyelashes and chubby cheeks absolutely melted her. Her plump little body nestled into Reagan's arms, and once more she was struck by how much she wanted one of her own.

"You're holding Megan, and I've got Alice."

"How can you tell?" With her finger, she caressed the girl's forehead along her hairline. Such soft skin.

"Brooke's got a system. Miss Anne told me that Alice is always in pink or green clothes, and Meggie's in light purple or yellow."

"Smart," she said. "I can take her back now if you'd like."

"Oh, I can stay a bit longer. It's not often I get to hold a wee one." He cradled the baby, and Alice stared up at him as if he was the most fascinating person in the world. The man was all cowboy, yet he looked perfectly comfortable as he made baby talk and cooing noises to the child.

"I don't get to hold them as often as I'd like, either." She was blessed with nieces and nephews, but now that she no longer lived in Sunrise Bend, she didn't have daily access to them. "I grew up on a ranch with a big family."

"You missing them, huh?"

"Kind of. I mean, my sister—Erica Black, you

might know her—lives nearby. The twenty-minute drive from my house to her ranch is nothing. But the rest of them? Yeah, I'm not used to being on my own."

"Well, when you're feeling lonely, remember the Good Lord is always with you. My mama told me those words just about every day of my life. She still does. She's in the nursing home in town. It's small, but it gets the job done."

"I didn't realize there was a nursing home here. That's wonderful."

"It sure is. I couldn't take care of her anymore after she broke her hip. Now I can visit her every day and not worry about her falling."

Little Megan stretched her arms up and arched her back as her face scrunched and grew red. "Uh-oh. I think she's either getting hungry or going to need a change soon."

"Miss Anne left bottles in the fridge. She said they'd be hungry about this time. Why don't I warm 'em up?" He brought Alice to the infant seat on the floor and set her in it. She instantly began to whimper.

Reagan stood and settled Megan in the one next to Alice's. Then she knelt in front of them and talked to them as she made funny faces while Rico got the bottles ready. Neither baby was impressed with her attempts to entertain them. They both looked on the verge of tears.

Did they have pacifiers? She looked around, but all she could find were plush baby toys and a few receiving blankets.

"Here you go." Beaming, he brought two bottles over. "I checked 'em and everything."

"Thank you." What a nice man. She squirted a drop onto her wrist—not too warm, not too cold. "These are perfect."

She gave one to each baby and held the bottles as they greedily reached for them.

"I hate to leave you, but the boss will have a fit if one of our pregnant cows has a calf and I'm not out there monitoring the situation."

"I understand. Thank you for all your help."

"Let me give you my number if you need anything. I can be back lickety-split." He wrote down his cell number and left.

The babies had settled down after the initial gulps, and Reagan studied them as their eyelids began to droop. They truly were identical. She couldn't see anything different between them.

Brooke's situation reminded her of her late brother, Cody. Years ago, when he died in a car accident, his wife, Holly, had been pregnant with their child. No one in Reagan's family had even known Cody was married, let alone having a baby, though. And, weirder still, Holly was now married to Reagan's big brother, Jet.

Cody. Reagan sighed. He'd been the sibling closest to her in age. The baby of the family. A wild one. And being estranged from him the months before his death would hurt until the day she died.

She'd done the right thing coming here today so that Marc could go to the clinic to be with his mother. Hopefully, it wasn't anything serious. But if it was...

What her own parents would have done to be with Cody one more time before he died. What *she* would have given to see Cody one more time and tell him all the things she'd desperately wanted to say.

Someday she would. That was why she clung so tightly to her faith. She knew this world wasn't where it ended. In the meantime, she'd make the best of her time here, and feeding these babies was at the very top of her list.

MARC DRAGGED HIMSELF to the house later that evening. This morning felt like a lifetime ago.

Reagan's white crossover SUV was still parked next to Brooke's minivan. Would his sister ever drive it again? There were so many unanswered questions about her health.

He trudged up the steps to the side door and quietly let himself inside. In the mudroom, he took off his coat and boots and just stood there for a few moments.

Come on. You're used to this. Gird your shoulders. Get your game face on. You need to be strong. Reagan helped you out today. After she leaves…well, then you can fall apart.

That was the thing, though. He couldn't fall apart. Ever.

Too many people depended on him.

Falling apart would only result in him failing them. And he wasn't about to go down that road.

He straightened his shoulders and strode through the mudroom and kitchen. Continued to the archway into the living room and stopped in his tracks.

Reagan was rocking in the recliner with a baby in each arm. She was telling them a story—but no book was in sight. He leaned against the archway and listened as she went on about a girl with flowers for hair fighting a giant who was trying to cut down the tree she lived in. His lips twitched. Couldn't help it. Reagan was an original.

She looked up and their eyes met. Hers were so expressive. Surprise turned to welcome glimmering with sympathy.

"How is she?" she asked. The melodic tone of her voice soothed him.

He shoved away from the archway and padded to the couch, where he took a seat and let his head fall back against the cushion.

"Not good. She had a stroke."

"Oh, no!" Reagan kept her voice low as she glanced at the twins, almost asleep. "She's going to make it, though, right?"

Her concern surprised him. She'd never met his sister. Had no reason to care. Yet she did.

"It appears that way. Mom said the clinic thought it was a migraine at first, but they grew concerned when they examined her, so they rushed her to the hospital in an ambulance. Her left side is weak, but not paralyzed."

"A stroke." With her forehead furrowed, she shook her head. "But she's young, right? How old is she?"

"Twenty-eight." He swallowed as everything hit him at once. His little sister could have died today. She still wasn't in the clear. And what if she didn't get full range of movement back in her left side? How would she be able to take care of the twins?

He should have insisted she eat more. She hadn't been taking care of herself. Over the past weeks, she'd been vanishing before his eyes. He should have tried harder...

"Do they know what caused it?"

He inhaled sharply through his nose. "They're running tests. Her risk increased because of her history with migraines, and it was also elevated due to having the babies, although postpartum strokes are rare." He didn't even know what he was saying at this point. Just repeating things the doctors had said. He raked his fingers through his hair. "Never in a million years would I have thought my sister could have a stroke at her age."

"How is your mom holding up?"

"Good." It was true. His mom had been calm. Asked all the right questions. "She refused to leave her side. She's staying there tonight."

"My mom would have done the same. My dad, too." Her sympathetic expression was like the hug he needed, and all he wanted to do was to go over there and have her put her arms around him and tell him everything was going to be all right.

He must be losing it. Wanting a virtual stranger to comfort him? Unheard of. Uncalled for. He was the one who comforted, not the other way around.

"Do they have any idea how long she'll be in the hospital? By the way, what hospital did she go to?"

"She's at the medical center in Casper."

Reagan stared down at the babies, both now asleep on her lap. Her face was full of love for the girls, and gratitude filled him that the twins had been in good hands. One thing he hadn't had to worry about, anyway.

"I'll come over tomorrow morning to baby-sit," she said matter-of-factly.

He hadn't thought that far ahead. He didn't want to put her out or owe her anything. "No, that's okay. I've got it."

Her deadpan stare reminded him of his mother's. "You're in calving season. My brothers barely get more than three hours of sleep at a stretch when the cows are having their calves. You can't be everywhere at once. Let me take care of the twins. That way you can deal with the cows in the morning and then go to the hospital. Your mom will need the moral support."

"Reagan…" He liked the way her name sounded when he said it. "I can't ask you to do that."

"You didn't ask. I offered." Her tranquility eased the chaos inside him. "Look, it's going to be weeks before my shop opens. I have time on my hands, and I love babies. I especially love these babies. These cuties melt my heart."

Her shop. Right. His mom's dreams.

None of it seemed all that important right now.

What other options did he have, anyhow? The bakery would be short-staffed. Hopefully, Mom had called her employee, Deb, about getting someone to help her out tomorrow. All the pregnant cows he'd been keeping an eye on needed to be monitored. Rico had texted him that only one had given birth.

"You're overthinking it." Reagan's voice cut through his thoughts. "I'll be here at seven."

"Okay." He felt out of his league. "I'll show you where everything is and go over their schedule in the morning."

"Don't worry about this, Marc. I'm good

with babies. You worry about the other stuff. Leave these two sweethearts to me."

A sigh escaped his lips. Reagan was right. He had enough other stuff to think about. Not having to worry about the babies would be a huge relief. Not just for him but for his mom, too. And Brooke, when she gained full consciousness. She'd still been out of it when he'd left.

"I don't know when my sister will be discharged. I'll have to find someone to help me out with the twins until then."

"No, you won't." She smiled, shaking her head. "I'll babysit them while your sister is in the hospital."

Marc couldn't help admiring her. "Thank you. I don't know what to say but thank you."

"You don't have to say a thing. Now, let's get these babies to bed so you can get some rest."

He wouldn't argue with that. It had been the longest day of his life, and something told him the rest of the week would be just as rough. He was grateful for Reagan's help. And he would find a way to repay her when all this was over. He just had no idea how.

CHAPTER FOUR

REAGAN WAS USED to detours in her plans. She rarely fretted over schedules or deadlines. Even when the unexpected happened—like twin babies needing an emergency babysitter—she trusted God would give her the time and tools she needed to meet her goals. The few times she hadn't met them? It wasn't for lack of trying. So, this detour in her plans didn't bother her one bit. The only thing that bothered her was the fact it was for Marc.

At six forty-five the next morning, Reagan parked next to the minivan in his driveway and took a moment to mentally prepare herself. She'd brought her laptop, a notebook and the packet Marc had given her yesterday morning. Would she have a chance to research anything? Maybe. Maybe not. At least she had what she needed if she got any downtime.

Last night she'd called her mom and talked

for an hour about the twins and Brooke, how the candle shop was doing and all the latest from Sunrise Bend. Reagan missed her mom. They'd worked well as a team, and she'd learned everything about taking care of babies from her, too. So far, the twins seemed to be easygoing. She hoped it stayed that way.

She closed her eyes and said a quick prayer for Brooke. Then she took her large tote and purse in one hand, grabbed her travel mug of coffee with the other and stepped out onto the gravel. She shut the door behind her. The cold air was bracing against her face. The peach-and-periwinkle sky against the rising sun tempted her to take a picture, but her phone's camera would never do it justice.

As she walked toward the porch, she took in the ranch and couldn't help comparing it to the one she'd grown up on. Marc's was smaller in scale. No guest cabins, fewer outbuildings. In the distance, cattle roamed the pasture. The ranch might be smaller than her family's, but it was well-kept. Marc seemed like the type of man who cared about the details.

She reached the porch and knocked on the door. The door opened and Marc, bleary-eyed and unshaven, appeared. His button-down shirt was untucked, and he held one of the twins in the crook of his arm. The other twin was crying from somewhere inside. Probably the living room. "Oh, good. You're here. Come in."

He held the door open until she'd cleared the doorway, then shut it behind her and stalked to the living room. She followed. Yep, there was a baby in purple—Megan—kicking her legs and bunching her fists as she wailed from her bouncy seat.

Reagan set the travel mug on the end table and dropped her bags to the floor before unbuckling the child. Then she lifted her up to her shoulder, bouncing slightly as she made shushing sounds. "It's okay, Meggie. I know you miss your mama. It's okay."

"How did you know it was Megan?"

She turned to Marc. "Rico told me the secret about their colors. She wears yellow and purple. Alice wears green and pink."

The baby's cries were intense. Reagan figured it would take some time for her to calm down. However, a few moments of bouncing and cooing soothing words downgraded the wailing to whimpers. With a sigh, the child rested her cheek on Reagan's shoulder. Reagan rubbed her back, basking in her surrender.

"I don't know how you got her to stop crying." The bags under Marc's eyes and his general air of defeat brought a wave of sympathy over her.

"Are they hungry?" she asked.

"No. I fed them both before you arrived. And they had bottles at three."

She winced. It had to have been exhausting getting up with the babies after the day he'd had yesterday.

"Diaper change?" she asked.

"Fresh. Ten minutes ago."

"Maybe she's gassy." Reagan kissed the top of Megan's head and continued to caress her back. "Or she just misses her mama."

"I don't know." From the pinched expression on his face, she guessed the crying had given him a headache.

"Did you try a pacifier?"

"They never took to them. Spit them out from day one." Alice looked content as could be in her uncle's arms. He stared longingly at the couch, but he didn't sit.

"Ah. Does Brooke have a routine with them?"

"Yes. Rule number one—they do everything together. They eat at the same time. They nap at the same time. Brooke said she'd get zero hours of sleep if she didn't keep them on the exact same schedule. I don't really know what the schedule is beyond what I help with. Usually, I get ready, come down and change them out of their pajamas into clothes while Brooke grabs a shower. As soon as she's dressed, I head out."

Reagan tried to wrap her mind around the fact Hot Cowboy dressed two babies every morning. "Any word on how your sister's doing?"

"I talked to Mom earlier. She's the same."

That wasn't good. She'd hoped he'd have some indication his sister was recovering.

"Are you going over there today?"

"Yeah, as soon as I finish checking the pregnant cows and talking to Rico."

"Why don't you bring your mother a fresh change of clothes and some toiletries? I'm sure she'll appreciate it."

"I didn't even think of that." He brightened. "I will."

"I won't keep you. I've got this. You can take off."

"Are you sure?" He tried to tuck in his shirt one-handed.

"Of course."

"What if she starts crying again?" The way his eyes narrowed reminded her of her family's skepticism whenever they thought she was in over her head.

"We'll be okay." She shrugged. "I have a good feeling about it."

"A good feeling? About this? I'm glad someone does." He rubbed his chin. "Let me show you where we keep everything."

"I can figure it out. I found what I needed yesterday."

"It will only take a minute."

They proceeded to go upstairs. Reagan still held Megan and Marc carried Alice. He showed her where the twins slept in the bedroom next to their mother's. He pointed out diapers, lotions, clothes and blankets before returning to the hall and pointing to the right. "My mom's here. I'm down at the other end."

Reagan clutched the baby as she followed him down the staircase and into the kitchen, where he showed her the formula, bottles, bibs and everything else she might need. She'd found most of it yesterday, but it was still good to take the tour.

"Thanks." She craved her coffee. "If I need something, I'll text you."

"Okay." His jaw flexed twice. Then he brushed past her to return to the living room. She joined him as he crouched to buckle Alice into her bouncy seat. Then he tapped the tip of his finger on her little nose and told her to be good today before he straightened. Turning to Reagan, he kissed the top of Megan's head, and the scent of citrus and leather wafted to her. Whatever cologne or bodywash he used was as appealing to her as the affection he freely gave to the girls. Very appealing indeed.

"Thanks again." He gave Reagan a lingering look she didn't know what to make of and then strode out of the room. A few minutes later, the creak of the side door reached her, letting her know she was alone with the twins.

"Well, my darlings, it's just you and me now." Dare she attempt to set Megan back in the seat? Her gaze landed on the travel mug. Her coffee was calling her name. "Miss Meg, how do you feel about hanging out with your sister? I'll squish your seats together so close you two can hold hands if you want. Would you like that?"

Reagan bent to put Megan in the bouncy seat, and the baby's little lips began to wobble.

"It's okay, sweetie. I'm right here. I'll be here all day."

As the wobble grew more pronounced, she buckled the straps and began to hum. The babies seemed to like it, so she hummed louder while she retrieved her coffee, still hot, along with her tote bag and purse. Maybe the girls liked music.

She found her phone and swiped through a radio app until she found a nursery-rhyme songs playlist. Soon, both the girls were happily kicking their little legs and reaching for the toys dangling from the toy bars.

They were so precious. She couldn't help herself—she took pictures of them both. Maybe Marc could send them to his sister. It would help Brooke not to worry about the babies. She'd know they were in good hands.

Good hands? Reagan didn't consider herself a baby expert by any means, but she'd learned a thing or two over the years from her mother and from babysitting her nieces and nephews. The most important thing was not to panic. Babies got fussy; they cried; they gulped down their bottles one day and barely touched them the next. And teething was no fun. No fun at all.

"You two aren't ready to get your teeth yet,

are you?" She hoped they weren't. Megan blew a spit bubble. "I'll take that as a no."

As she drank her coffee, she decided to take advantage of this sliver of quiet time to get out her notebook. She looked over everything, but the big picture of what needed to be done still wasn't coming to her in a meaningful way. After digging around in her purse, she found a pen and drew a circle in the middle of a fresh sheet of paper. In it, she wrote Store Opening.

Then she created more circles and wrote tasks in them—Contractors, Estimates, Banking, Renovations, Licenses. As more tasks came to her, she gave them circles, too. Then she studied the paper and drew lines between any that related to each other.

Okay, it was starting to make sense. Sort of.

Alice let out a chirp, and Megan began pumping her legs. The twins were getting restless. Time to get them out of those seats. She set her notes aside and unstrapped one baby, picked her up, then unstrapped the other and awkwardly picked her up, too.

How did Brooke do this all the time? Not only was trying to carry two squirmy babies difficult, but it strained her muscles. Her arms and back were still sore from babysitting yesterday.

Maybe she needed to start lifting weights. *Yeah, right.* As if that was going to happen. She wasn't much of an exerciser. She let out a snort. That was an understatement.

Reagan took the twins to the couch and carefully sat down, then adjusted them on her lap. Alice yawned and snuggled deeper into her arms, while Megan curled her hand around Reagan's pinkie finger and stared up at her.

"You're not so sure about me, are you?" Reagan smiled at Megan. "*Who is this weird lady and what did she do with my mommy?* Well, pumpkin, I'm just filling in. Your mommy will be back soon."

She hoped it was true. It reminded her once again that life was short. She had no idea how much time on earth she had, and she needed to make the most of it. All she had to do was think of Cody to know it was true.

Once the girls fell asleep, she was going to take out her laptop and figure out what she needed to do to get her business name registered. Marc had said to take care of it with the state, right? Until then, she'd enjoy the babies.

"Why don't I tell you a little story? It's about a girl named Reagan, who wanted to open a chocolate shop. She learned all about how to make the chocolates from a kind man named Oliver, who owned a fancy store in faraway Denver. Every time she got a whiff of the rich scent of chocolate, she could picture the pretty candies lined up in their boxes. But Reagan had a problem. Before she could open her shop, she had to fight a scary beast called the Paperwork Monster. The Paperwork Monster was big and mean, and he told her if she didn't have all of her forms completed just right, she wouldn't be able to make the chocolates…"

Megan was wide-awake, drooling all over her tiny fist, which she'd somehow managed to fit in her mouth, and Alice was smacking her lips occasionally as she listened. These two darlings made all Reagan's problems seem like she could make them disappear with a poof.

Her problems were tiny compared to Marc's. Up in the night feeding the girls, doing the morning routine alone, riding out to check the cattle, driving to the hospital to be with his mother… He was destined to crash if Brooke stayed in the hospital for several days.

He seemed the type of guy who didn't ask for help often. But he needed it.

Reagan shifted on the couch to get more comfortable. The twins were growing sleepy, and she'd wait a bit to put them in their Pack 'n Plays, where Marc said they napped. Once they were asleep, she'd prepare more bottles and get some work done...if she had time.

Something told her she wouldn't be getting much research done today. Erica and her mother would insist she needed to stay focused. But the only focus she cared about at the moment was on the twins. Getting the rest of her life back to normal could wait.

LIFE WASN'T GOING to be returning to normal anytime soon.

It was after eight that evening when Marc arrived home from the hospital. He hung up his coat and washed his hands in the mudroom before dragging himself into the kitchen. Reagan was sitting at the table and typing away on a laptop. She looked up at him and smiled.

"How did it go?" she asked.

Closing his eyes momentarily, he traced the arcs of his eyebrows, trying to alleviate the pressure in his head. "Not good."

Reagan went to the oven and pulled out a covered casserole dish. "I kept it warm for you. I wasn't sure if you and your mom had eaten."

"You cooked?" He couldn't believe it. She'd

spent over twelve hours here babysitting the twins and had somehow found time to make supper? He'd underestimated her, and it only added another layer of guilt to his already full load.

"Yeah, it was tricky, but I did it in shifts. Chicken-and-stuffing casserole—it comes together quick. If you've already eaten, I understand."

"I didn't. We didn't." He removed a plate from a cupboard and dished out a large helping of the casserole. It smelled good. "Thank you. For this. For the girls. For…everything."

"You're welcome." She returned to the table, sat down and closed her laptop.

He took a seat across from her and dug in. It was delicious. Comfort food—exactly what he needed. He ate several bites before setting aside his fork. He needed to update Reagan on Brooke. But putting it into words? He dreaded it. Saying it out loud would make it all real. Too real.

He wished reality would go away. Wished Brooke was there. Wished Mom was, too.

"Why don't you finish your food before you tell me everything?" Her light brown eyes brimmed with sympathy, and her patience astounded him.

He wasn't all that patient. Brooke wasn't, either. Mom had the most patience of the three, but even she had a limited supply. Reagan seemed to have it in abundance.

"Okay." Agreeing with her was simple, a relief. If he wasn't so exhausted, he'd force himself to be strong and tell her everything now. To get it over with. But he didn't have to. She'd given him permission to eat his meal, and the simple gesture meant everything to him at the moment.

He almost made it through. Almost finished chewing the final bite. But all of his emotions hit him at once. He tried to swallow but couldn't. So, he spread his palms out on the table with his head bowed, willing himself not to choke, or worse, cry. Somehow, he forced down the final bite of food. Then he blinked and tightened his jaw.

"Do you want a glass of water?" She stood and tucked the laptop and her notebook into a large bag on the floor next to her chair.

"No, that's okay." That seemed to do it. A sense of calm chased away the intensity of his emotions.

"If it's too much to talk about, we don't have to—"

"No, I'm ready." He hoped he was, at least.

Watching him expectantly, Reagan returned to her seat.

He pushed the empty plate to the side and took a moment to get his thoughts straight. "We know more now. She had an ischemic stroke. Due to Mom's quick thinking and the clinic immediately sending Brooke to the hospital, the doctors were able to give her a special medicine to dissolve the blood clot that was preventing blood from getting to her brain. It's supposed to help her recover more fully than if she didn't have it."

"That's good news."

"Yes, it is." He just wished the rest of the news was good. "Unfortunately, she's really weak. She's in and out of it. Doesn't really know what's going on. Can't speak very well. We only understood a few words. Her left side has limited strength. She isn't paralyzed, but she'll need physical and occupational therapy."

"Will she recover?"

"Most likely." But what if she didn't? He wouldn't think about that now. "The doctors estimate she'll be in the hospital for a week."

"Then she'll come home?" Her hopeful expression hurt his heart. It matched the hope he'd been clinging to before the doctors had filled them in.

"Doubtful. Unless she shows outstanding progress over the next few days. They think she'll be transferred to a rehab facility." His throat was thick with emotion. He couldn't say another word if he tried.

"Can she eat and drink?"

He nodded, grinding his teeth together so hard, he was shocked none of them chipped.

Reagan got out of her chair and rounded the table to him. Then she wrapped her arms around his neck and leaned in to hug him.

"I'm so sorry, Marc."

Tears threatened. Reagan gently rubbed his upper back as she held him, and slowly, the out-of-control feelings passed, and he allowed himself to relax into her embrace.

He needed her gentle touch. Needed her comfort.

She pulled away, went to the cupboard next to the sink and grabbed a glass, then filled it with water and brought it back over to him. His fingers grazed hers as he took it from her. "Thanks."

He wished she'd hold him again, but she was

already sitting down. He took a long drink of the water.

"Can I pray for you and your family?" Reagan asked.

"Right now?" he sputtered. He went to church. Prayed before meals and when things were rough. But his family had never been demonstrative in the prayer department. Her shy nod helped push away his qualms. "Sure."

"Lord, You are all-powerful and know what Brooke needs. Please heal her from the effects of the stroke. Give the doctors and nurses and everyone taking care of her wisdom and skill as they treat her. Please comfort Marc and his mother as they adjust to this terrible turn of events. Help them trust You and rely on You as she recovers. In Jesus's name, amen."

"Amen." Her prayer touched him, but it also brought up uncomfortable feelings and questions he wasn't sure what to do with.

This terrible turn of events… Why had God allowed this to happen? Hadn't Brooke been through enough this year? And Reagan assumed Brooke would heal, but what if she didn't? What if she ended up unable to speak or to get dressed or to walk or to take care of Megan and Alice?

But the biggest question was the one he'd been flirting with for years and years. He'd never let himself sit with it long enough to get a satisfying answer.

Could he trust God?

Marc shifted his jaw and glanced up at Reagan. She seemed embarrassed.

"I don't normally go around praying for people like that," she said with her head hung low.

"I don't, either. But I appreciate it."

"The moment just seemed to call for it."

That it had. "I haven't had time to figure out a plan for the girls."

"Plan? No need." Her steady gaze implied everything was already worked out. "Until we know more, I'll keep coming over at seven, and I'll call my sister about getting some of the church ladies to take over in the afternoons. They'll be chomping at the bit to spend time with the twins. They'll probably bring food with them, too, so supper will be taken care of. You'll still have to get up with the girls at night, though. When do you think your mom will be coming back?"

Church ladies? Reagan here every morning? His house was going to be invaded. It was too much to take in. He gulped.

"Mom booked a room at a hotel near the hospital. Thankfully, she has her car, too. Her employee, Deb, asked her cousin to help out at the bakery in the mornings until she gets back. By the way, Mom appreciated the clothes and stuff I packed her. Thank you. I wouldn't have thought of that on my own."

"I'm glad. You were smart to pack more than one outfit." Reagan lifted her finger. "Oh, I forgot. I took pictures of the girls today. I'll text them to you to send to your mom. I'm sure Brooke will need some reassurance that the babies are doing all right."

Her fingers flew over the phone and, moments later, his chimed. He opened her text and instinctively smiled. The twins were clearly happy with Reagan.

"You don't have to do all this, you know." He leaned back, massaging one shoulder. "I can find someone else to help with the twins."

"Like I said, I want to. I have the time. It will be a while before I can open the shop."

The shop. He winced. He kept forgetting she owned the building of his mother's dreams. At this point, it was the least of his worries. The only thing he really cared about was getting Brooke back here. Healthy. Healed.

He didn't know how this stranger had popped into his life and solved so many problems at a critical time, but...well, that wasn't true. Reagan's prayer had shifted something inside him. He could clearly see God's hand in her being there.

Maybe he *could* trust God after all.

He couldn't get attached to her, though. He already struggled to be the man his sister, his nieces and his mother needed.

But he could still feel her gentle hands as they'd rubbed his back, and he wondered if he was wrong. Was there enough of him to go around to get close to Reagan, too?

No, there wasn't. A couple of days and he'd be himself again. He'd make sure of it.

"I FEEL TERRIBLE for them." Reagan stretched her arms over her head and savored the sensation of her tight muscles starting to loosen. She had her earbuds in as she talked to Erica on the phone. She'd gotten home from Marc's ranch an hour ago.

The day had been long. Fulfilling, but long. Those little babies had worn her out.

"They don't have any idea if Brooke will recover?" Erica asked. "You know, fully?"

"Not right now they don't. I hope over the next few days she'll get better and better so she can skip the rehab facility." Reagan swung her legs up on the couch, then leaned back against a throw pillow and wiggled her toes. Her fuzzy pink slipper socks felt soft against her skin.

"I hope so, too, but even if she did…well, I think she'll need help for a while."

"Yeah, I think you're right." Reagan reached for her mug of hot tea and took a sip. Perfect. Not too hot. Not too cold. Just right.

They discussed inviting the church ladies to help with the twins.

"I tell you what," Erica said. "I'll call Christy and explain the situation tomorrow. That way you can focus on the twins."

"Would you? That would help me out. As much as I love those babies, taking care of them for twelve hours is challenging."

Erica chuckled. "It's hard enough dealing with one. I have to admit, though, I miss those days. I'd love to have another baby."

"The wedding's coming up soon. You never know—maybe next year you and Dalton will end up having twins of your own."

"Don't say that! I said another baby. As in one. Not plural."

Reagan laughed.

"Enough about me," Erica said. "Where are you at with the shop?"

Her happy toes curled in dismay. Even the fuzziness of the socks felt rougher than they had a moment ago.

"Um…"

"Look, Reag, I applaud you for helping Marc and Brooke. They need it. But I don't want you to lose sight of why you're here. All of the forms and registrations and paperwork have to get done before you can even think about opening the store. And you need to get a contractor over there pronto."

"I know, I know." She sat up, accidentally spilling a few drops of tea on her pajama top. She tried to think of what to say as she dabbed at the spill. Her sister had never understood her thought process. She didn't really understand it herself.

"I have the links for the state," Erica continued. "I'll text them to you. It's not hard to register your company name."

Registering a company name wasn't hard for Erica. Reagan was well aware that her sister thrived on that sort of thing. So why was it so hard for her? It didn't matter. If Erica had the links, she'd take them.

"Thanks, Erica. I actually do need that information."

"No problem. If you need help figuring everything out, I'm here. In fact, maybe I should come over soon." It wasn't the words Erica said. It was her tone. Skeptical of her little sister.

"I'm handling it."

"Are you?"

"Why would you ask that?" Annoyance flared. "You know I was at city hall to talk to the building inspector yesterday morning. If I hadn't been there, I wouldn't have found out about Brooke. And I did some research and took notes today, too." Putting her thoughts in circles always seemed to unblock her. As for the research? Very little was achieved.

"Let me guess. You wrote things in circles."

Reagan wasn't even responding. Just because the rest of her family lived by lists didn't mean she operated the same way. Lists jammed up her mind and confused her.

"It helps me see the big picture." Why was she even justifying herself? She didn't need to explain anything. This was her business. Her life.

"Well, don't lose sight of all the little details that make up the big picture. There's a lot to do."

Like she didn't know that.

"Oh, and, Reagan, you might want to call McCaffrey Construction to come out and give you an estimate on remodeling the building. We used them for the Winston, and Ed did a great job."

She perked up at that info. Why hadn't she thought to ask Erica who she'd hired to tackle the event center's renovations? Sometimes her thoughts felt like fifty butterflies in a flower garden. All of them fluttering away in a different direction. "Thank you. I will call him. But, listen, I really am getting things done for the chocolate shop. You don't have to worry. I've got this."

But did she? Sketching out a bare-bones circle diagram and reading through Wyoming's Department of Agriculture website to figure out if she needed a state food license—she still had no idea—before Marc had walked through the door tonight could hardly qualify as making progress.

"Just don't get distracted, okay? I love you, and I want you to succeed."

"I'm not distracted. I'm babysitting. They need my help."

"And you're wonderful to give it to them. You have the biggest heart, Reag. But I don't want it to get you into trouble. This chocolate shop is your dream."

"It is, and I'm going to make it happen. Now, please, no more lectures."

"But I'm your big sister. It's my job to lecture."

"I'm twenty-eight. All grown up."

Erica sighed. "You got me. I don't mean to come on too strong. I just… I love you. I want you to be happy. I want you to be happy *here*, you know?"

"Yeah, I do know, and you don't have to worry about it. I'm going to love it here."

Reagan asked about Rowan, and they discussed the wedding for a while before ending the call. Then she went into the kitchen and heated up another cup of tea. Erica seemed to think she was distracted. Was she? Reagan gave the kitchen a once-over and concluded that, yes, she was distracted.

There was so much to do, and it all demanded her attention. Take this house. She'd unpacked most of her stuff last week. But she really needed to go shopping. Now that she was living on her own, there were things she lacked. New curtains for the living room, a set of pans—the one skillet and small saucepan she owned weren't going to cut it—accessories for the bathroom, decorative items...

Reagan fought her rising anxiety as she held her mug with the steam wreathing into the air. The house needed her. The building needed her. The twins needed her.

At least decorating the house could wait. Except for the color of the walls, the kitchen was perfect. U-shaped with a window above the sink, it had cabinets painted a creamy white, butcher-block countertops and taupe walls. The taupe had to go. She was thinking a nice periwinkle blue.

Marc's kitchen had a cozy country feel. His mom probably had decorated it. It was too feminine for a cowboy to have picked out. The cabinets were natural wood, but the walls were a pale sage green and all of the accessories had rose-colored accents in floral patterns. She loved how comfortable, how vintage and how pretty it was.

That was what she wanted in this house. For it to be comfortable and pretty.

Erica seemed to think she had to get everything done for the business and her house in the next twenty-four hours. But Reagan wanted to enjoy this time. She wanted to go at her own pace. Decorate her house, get the forms and licenses done one by one and take care of the twins until Brooke could come home.

Her phone chimed, and she saw the links Erica had promised. One less thing she had to figure out on her own.

She took her mug over to the couch and settled a throw across her lap. She couldn't help but think how fortunate she was to be able to sit on her own couch in her own house with her own cup of tea. Poor Brooke was stuck in a hospital far away from her babies.

And poor Marc. He had his hands full. Calving was hard enough on a rancher. Taking care of infant twins, too? Making the hour-and-a-half drive to Casper to visit his sister each day? None of it was easy.

That was why earlier she'd gone over to him, hugged him and rubbed the muscles straining in his back. He'd looked so tired and lost. She'd wanted to take away some of his burdens and let him know he wasn't alone.

She still couldn't believe she'd prayed for Marc out loud. So unlike her.

It seemed impossible that she could have comforted and prayed for the man she'd found so abrasive just over a week ago. But that was how life went. First impressions weren't always accurate. She hadn't known about his family troubles at the time.

And now that she did know?

She understood him a little better. Could see he was the protective type.

But that didn't mean she could grow close to him. She couldn't let his good looks and skills with the babies go to her head. The only man for her would put her first, not second-guess her decisions. She had no idea if Marc was capable of that. She'd just have to guard her heart. It was the safest thing to do.

CHAPTER FIVE

Looked like he'd found another one.

Thursday afternoon, Marc stopped the UTV far enough away to keep the cattle calm. A black calf was squirming on the ground in front of its mama, and they were already bonding as the mother licked it. A good sign. It was the second calf he'd found today. Grabbing his gear, he got out and approached the pair. The mother didn't like him near her newborn, but he quickly tagged the calf and made sure it could get to its feet. The little guy ran off to nurse.

Thank You, Lord, for another healthy calf. It made his job much easier when the cows and calves did what they instinctively knew to do.

He finished up and got back in the UTV to continue checking all of the places the cows liked to wander off to when having their babies.

Once he'd done a full sweep of the pastures, he drove back to the barn and parked.

Only then did Marc check his phone again. There were several texts from his mom. He ignored them for the moment. She'd been texting him all morning about the bakery and if he could make sure Deb had made the apple fritters and did he think sales would suffer if there were no pies this week? He'd responded that Deb knew what she was doing. More texts had landed. Mom asking him to bring more clothes and specifying exactly what items to bring, going so far as to tell him to take a picture of the shirts and jeans so she could make sure they were the right ones. He'd refused. It had gone on and on.

The new texts were more of the same. He replenished the calving supplies in the UTV before striding to his office. He kept reminding himself that his mom had been through a traumatic shock. This was her way of coping.

After logging the new calf's tag, he hiked down the path to the house and inhaled the crisp air. There was something about the in-between of winter and spring that spoke to him. Maybe it was simply the knowledge that warmer, brighter days were on their way.

He could use brighter days, that was for sure. At least the long drive to and from the hospital gave him time to clear his head. He didn't feel as frazzled when he could replay his list of ranch to-dos for the next day. As long as he didn't allow himself to think about Brooke's future or anything involving Reagan, he was fine.

Brooke's future was still uncertain, although she'd showed marked mental improvement yesterday. And Reagan? He was relying on her too much.

True to her word, she and Erica had created a volunteer list of babysitting teams to help watch the twins. Reagan would continue to drive to the ranch each morning and babysit until the volunteers arrived. He knew how tiring the twins were—he didn't want Reagan to get burned out. This schedule would free up her afternoons.

The first duo had been there last night when he'd gotten home from the hospital, and the next two weeks were covered. He hoped they wouldn't need help for two more weeks.

In the mudroom, he hung up his outerwear and continued through the kitchen to the living room. Reagan was kneeling on the quilted play mat with a bunny puppet in her hand, telling the babies a story. They were on their backs, staring up at her as if she were the most fascinating person on earth. He knew the feeling well.

"And then Betsy Bunny hopped over the fence," Reagan said in a silly voice as she made the puppet jump, "and landed right on a squishy frog."

Alice blew a raspberry in response, and Megan grasped her feet in the air.

Marc could have watched the three of them all day, but he really needed a shower. He stank. "How've they been today?"

"Great. As always." She grinned at the girls, scrunching her nose. "You two are the best babies in the world, aren't you?"

A longing bruised his heart. An unfamiliar longing. For this—a wife and child of his own. He hurried to the staircase, stumbling in the process. "I'll be back down in a few."

Reagan glanced over her shoulder, and her pretty eyes sparkled. "Have fun."

"I'll do my best." He gave her a cockeyed grin and took the stairs two at a time.

Twenty minutes later, he returned to the living room, feeling alive and clean in fresh jeans and a long-sleeved shirt. The babies were in carriers, drinking their bottles, and Alice looked asleep already. Megan was fighting to stay awake, but her eyelids kept drooping.

"Hey," he whispered, taking a seat on the couch.

"Hey," she whispered back with a smile. She took away Alice's bottle and placed a rolled-up receiving blanket under Megan's to prop it up. "She's almost out."

"I see that."

Reagan gracefully unfolded her legs to stand, then gave each foot a little kick before joining him on the other end of the couch. She looked tired. He didn't blame her.

"Any news on Brooke?" She kept her voice quiet as she gave him her full attention.

"Mom said she's much better cognitively." He glanced at Megan. She'd fallen asleep, too. What he wouldn't give to be able to stay right here for an hour or two. Rest his head against the couch and not think a single thought.

"That's good to hear. By the way, Marie Whitten and Leslie Grant are watching the twins later. Marie called to let me know they had supper for you. Baked ziti, salad, garlic bread and chocolate sheet cake."

His stomach growled just thinking about it.

"I appreciate all the trouble you and Erica

went through to line up babysitters. And Mom wanted me to thank you for all the pictures of the girls. Brooke keeps asking about them, and the pictures are helping her keep it together."

"We should take the babies to see her." Reagan tugged the sleeve of her dark purple sweater down her wrist.

Take the babies all the way to the hospital? Marc tried to think through the logistics of it. It would involve packing diaper bags, loading both car seats in his truck and driving a long distance with the girls. The whole thing gave him a headache. What if they cried? What would he do?

"She might be home in a few days." She wouldn't. Although the doctors had mentioned Brooke being discharged from the hospital in a few days if she showed enough improvement, they hadn't said a thing about her coming home. Everyone seemed to assume she'd be transferred to a rehab facility to continue physical therapy.

"You think so?" Reagan's nose scrunched. "I doubt she'll be home that soon. Even a week is an awfully long time for her to be away from the girls. I know you're busy, but what if I went with you on Saturday? The two of us should be able to handle getting the twins to her."

He massaged the back of his neck. Reagan was right, but he didn't want to deal with a long drive with three-month-old babies. Or with her. He owed her too much as it was. "I'll talk to my mom about it."

"Good."

"Ugh, where's my head at?" Rising, he jerked his thumb toward the staircase. "I forgot I needed to pack my mom some more clothes. I'll be right down."

Upstairs, he opened his mom's closet and found the items she'd requested. Once he'd folded them in a neat stack, a wave of exhaustion overcame him, and hoping it would subside, he perched on the edge of the bed.

He'd been doing so well, keeping his energy up, so why now was he sputtering on empty?

All he wanted to do was to curl up in his bed and take a twelve-hour nap. And when he woke up, he wanted Mom to be in the kitchen with a box of leftover donuts on the counter and Brooke taking care of the twins.

He wanted everything back to normal.

Knock, knock.

"Marc?" Reagan stood in the doorway.

"Yeah?" He got himself together and stood, grabbing the small pile of clothes in the process.

"Are you okay?"

"Yep."

"Have you been getting any sleep?"

"Sure. Why?" He didn't meet her eyes as he brushed past her to get to the hallway. He descended the staircase.

Reagan followed. "Why don't you rest for a little while?"

"Can't." He strode past the sleeping twins to the kitchen, where he rummaged through a cupboard to find an old grocery bag. Plucking one out, he shoved his mom's clothes into it.

"Thirty minutes. Just stretch out on your bed or the couch and close your eyes." She leaned her hip against the counter. "I'll set an alarm."

"Mom needs me. Brooke needs me. The girls need me. The cows need me. I don't have time for naps." His tone was too rough. Another thing to feel guilty about. Later. For now, he had to move. Just had to keep moving before he collapsed, before he fell apart.

Her hand on his arm halted him. He stared down at it. Short, groomed fingernails capped off long fingers. No polish. His gaze traveled up to her concerned face.

"The world won't end if you rest for half an hour. I promise."

He tossed the bag on the counter and braced

his hands against the edge, letting his head drop. Then he glanced sideways at her. "Why do you care?"

"Because you're right. Brooke and your mom and the ranch and the twins need you. You won't be able to help anyone if you don't take care of yourself."

"I am taking care of myself."

"Okay." She brought her hands to her chest and backed up a step. "I'll shut up."

"I've got to go." He grabbed the bag and gave her a lingering look. There was so much he wanted to say to her. To thank her for. He wanted to tell her he wasn't mad at her even though he was snarling. He wanted to tell her how much it touched him that she would give his well-being a second thought after spending hours taking care of the babies.

But the words wouldn't come and the clock was ticking.

"I'll see you tomorrow." He turned and left the room.

For the first time in a long time, he could admit to himself that his best wasn't good enough. Reagan deserved better than his bad mood. But it was all he had to give right now. And he doubted it was going to change any-time soon.

WHAT A LOUSY AFTERNOON. Frustrated, Reagan tossed her phone on her bed.

After Marc—clearly miffed at her suggestion that he get some rest—had blown her off, she'd gotten bottles ready and tidied the living room to prepare for Marie and Leslie. They'd arrived at three and assured her they'd be fine with the babies. Between them, they had seven kids—all grown—and thirteen grandchildren.

She'd given them a quick tour and explained the girls' schedule as best as she could before they'd interrupted with personal questions.

"Do you have a boyfriend?"

"A chocolate shop, you say?"

"And you're living in town?"

"Raised in Wyoming?"

"Early service or late?"

By the time Leslie insisted Reagan meet her youngest son, Phil, who "might be a touch old for you, but you'll love him," Reagan was ready to sprint out the door.

And she basically had.

When she'd arrived home, she'd forced herself to call McCaffrey Construction. A receptionist took down her information and assured her Ed McCaffrey would call her back when he got a chance. Then she'd called the next contractor on the list only to have the man act like he was doing her a huge favor for even talking to her. His dismissive attitude and rude questions had made her stammer, and that had bothered her more than his tone.

Forget about it. She snatched up her phone, strode to the living room and laced her athletic shoes. Some fresh air would do her good.

Five minutes later, she found herself in front of her building. She tilted her head back and studied the brick with its ornamental stonework. The contractor's words from the phone call mocked her. "A former jewelry shop? You *do* realize you're going to have to add plumbing and electrical. We'll have to frame new walls. Sheetrock them and paint everything. It's not going to be a quick or easy project."

She'd responded with "I know," and he'd acted like she hadn't spoken. "Those old buildings usually need all new wiring and HVAC. There could be foundation issues. It'll be expensive."

If only she had retorted with "I'm not stupid. I know it's going to cost a lot of money. Do you want to give me an estimate or not?" But she hadn't. She'd simply listened to him drone on and on until he'd finally told her he'd get out there in a couple of weeks.

A couple—did that mean two? Three? More?

She really didn't want to work with anyone so dismissive and rude to her. For all she cared, he could lose her number permanently.

The air was still cold, and she burrowed her hands deeper into her coat pockets. If she went inside the building now, she'd start finding things wrong with it. Then she'd second-guess herself. She already doubted herself enough at the moment—not about making chocolates for a living—about little things. Like choosing the right contractor. Figuring out the links Erica had sent her. And if it had been a mistake to stick her nose in Marc's private life.

She hated making mistakes. Hated conflict even more. And as much as she liked being around the cowboy, she also knew allowing herself to get emotionally close to him would be a big mistake. He was too stubborn—conflict would be inevitable with a guy like him. And she'd be right where she'd been her entire life—backing down and doing things his way, the same as she'd done for years. She couldn't live like that anymore.

After one more glance at the building, she

began to walk down the sidewalk toward the diner. With Marie and Leslie on duty at the ranch, she'd had no need to cook, and the thought of cooking for one tonight didn't excite her. Supper at Dixie B's it was.

Oof. Her body collided with someone. She stepped back and groaned. Of all the people to literally run into, Clem Buckley was the last person she'd choose.

"Watch where you're going, girly." He let out a huff, and those steely eyes pierced her all the way to her soul.

With a shaky inhalation, she attempted to get her nerves under control. "I'm sorry. I didn't see you there."

"I'm well aware of that." He narrowed his eyes as he studied her face. "You ain't sick, are you? You look poorly."

Poorly. Yes, that was exactly how she felt.

"I'm not sick. I just have a lot on my mind."

He pulled back his shoulders and skewered her with a look full of doubt. It made her feel twitchy, like every nerve ending was about to fritz. She should excuse herself and move on, but no, it appeared she was rooted to the concrete sidewalk.

"You aren't about to cry, are you?" he asked.

Yes. She hadn't even realized it until he'd mentioned it.

"No." Her voice was squeaky. She tried to toughen up, but all she could muster was a melancholy sigh.

"Come on." Clem adjusted his cowboy hat and cocked his head to the side. "I can see you need sustenance. You'll feel better after a meal at Dixie B's."

Unexpected gratitude flooded her, making her feel even more off balance than she already was.

"I was just heading there," she said, sniffing. Oddly enough, she didn't mind the thought of eating with Clem. It beat eating alone. "You don't have to come with me."

"I know I don't have to. But someone has to make sure you eat. You need to get some meat on your bones." He started striding toward the diner. She caught up to him and matched his pace. "Don't go making a fuss about it, either, girly. I don't do tears, and I don't do nonsense."

No tears. No nonsense. Got it.

Reagan remained silent the three blocks it took to get there, and when Clem opened the door for her, she gave him a genuine smile before entering the diner. Straight ahead, a row of booths against the wall was filled with hungry families. Tables of four lined the center of the room, and a counter with built-in stools was off to the left. Framed pictures of families and wildlife hung on the forest-green walls.

Clem guided her to the only empty booth near the back. Customers greeted him along the way, and he acknowledged everyone who did. He took the bench facing the front of the restaurant, and she slid into the bench opposite him. Laminated menus stuck out between the wall and the salt and pepper shakers. She took one and opened it.

The warm air carried conversations punctuated with laughter and the smell of chicken soup and French fries. She wasn't all that hungry. Whenever her mind was troubled, her appetite tended to disappear.

"Well, hey there, Clem. Who's this you got with you?" A smiling, curvy woman in her thirties stopped by their table. She was wearing a maroon T-shirt with the Dixie B's logo on it, jeans and an apron. Her dark brown hair was pulled back in a ponytail, revealing a dragonfly tattoo behind her ear.

"Molly, this is Reagan—" he turned his attention to Reagan "—what's your last name, again?"

"Mayer." She smiled at Molly. "Reagan Mayer."

"Oh, right," Molly said, pointing her pen to Reagan. "You're helping out with Brooke's babies, aren't you? We all feel so bad for Miss Anne and Brooke."

"Yes." Reagan shifted her gaze to the menu. It wasn't only Anne and Brooke suffering. "And for Marc."

Molly continued as if she hadn't said anything. "Deb's been asking around for help at the bakery, but we all can only do so much, you know? I spent a few hours there yesterday, but Tag didn't have preschool this morning, and I don't have a babysitter, so—"

"We're ready to order." Clem's firm tone stopped Molly in her tracks. Her sideways glare blasted disapproval.

"Right." Molly's cheer was gone, replaced by a wooden expression. "Go on, then."

"Ladies first." Clem nodded to Reagan.

"I'll have a bowl of your chicken noodle soup."

"Anything else?"

"No."

"What to drink?" Molly looked up from her notepad and pen.

"Do you have lemonade?"

"We sure do." Molly turned to Clem. "And you?"

"Bring her a BLT on grilled sourdough, too." He addressed Molly, then faced Reagan. "Unless you're vegetarian."

"I'm not a vegetarian. But I don't need—"

He'd already dismissed her. "Bring the BLT. I'll have the Reuben, fries and an iced tea. No lemon."

She gave them a curt nod. "Be back in a few with your drinks."

Reagan was about to tell him she wasn't that hungry, but he spoke up before she could. "What's troubling you, girly?"

Put like that… "It's nothing. I mean, it's not nothing… I don't know where to begin."

"Start somewhere."

It was on the tip of her tongue to mention Erica and how organized she was and how inferior Reagan felt compared to her in that department, but this was Clem. No tears, no nonsense Clem.

She picked up her napkin and began twisting it. "You see, chocolate? I understand. Running a business? I can do that, too. For the most part." She was confident in her abilities to make the chocolate, order supplies and package orders. The website designer she and her mother had used for their company had agreed to design hers when she was ready. And Mom had been the one to suggest linking R. Mayer Chocolates' online store with the Mayer Canyon Candles' website. "But getting the permits and renovations done? That, I don't understand."

"What do you need to do?" he asked.

"I don't know. Everything." Molly arrived with their drinks, and Reagan thanked her.

"You met with Henry?" He ripped the paper off his straw and dunked the straw into his iced tea.

"Tried to. He was running late, and I ended up meeting with Marc Young instead, but we were interrupted when his sister collapsed."

"Right, right." He nodded. "Where are you stuck?"

"I'm not sure." She already felt less anxious sitting here and talking to Clem, of all people. "My sister sent me links to register the business with the state, but I didn't understand everything. And I couldn't figure out the Department of Ag website at all. Do I need a food license or not? And how do I get one? Erica has mentioned banking and getting some sort of number, and I don't think I can even apply for one until I get the other stuff done. Today I called two contractors... That didn't go well."

"Sounds to me you bit off more than you can chew."

The lemonade soured on her tongue. Even Clem knew she wasn't capable of doing all this.

"But—" he pointed his finger to her "—it's fixable."

It was? "How?"

"My buddy Slim Nixon retired a few years ago. He's started several businesses and spent a decade on the board of the chamber of commerce. He knows how to do everything you mentioned. I can give him a call and, for a fee— he doesn't work for free, girly—I'm sure he'd help you get everything done."

It was as if the clouds had parted and the sunlight was shining right on her face.

She could hire someone to help her.

Her mouth curved upward. Why hadn't she thought of this?

"You really think he'd help me?"

"I can ask." One of his shoulders lifted. "I have a feeling he'll want to help you."

"Why? He doesn't know me."

"Fellas like me? We get bored. Need a challenge now and then."

Their food arrived, and Reagan couldn't believe the portion sizes. The bowl of soup could feed three people, and the BLT had to have a pound of bacon piled on it.

"Eat up." He picked up his Reuben and gestured to her with it before taking a big bite.

She dipped the spoon into her soup and glanced up at him. "Thanks, Clem. I needed this."

"I know." He wiped his mouth with a napkin. "The protein will fill you up."

"No, not the food—although it looks delicious—the help. Thank you."

"Bah." He waved her off. "It's nothing."

"It's not nothing. I appreciate it."

"Well, don't go blubbering about it. Eat your food."

No use in arguing about that. Her mood had completely shifted. She suddenly had an appetite. Clem had chased away the doom cloud hanging over her. He'd get in touch with Slim and, in the meantime, she'd relax.

Now she could babysit the twins tomorrow without tying herself into knots about making progress on her business during their naptime. And if Marc agreed to take the babies to see Brooke on Saturday, she wouldn't feel guilty about helping him with that, either.

She was doing this for the twins and Brooke, not for Marc. Yes, there was a connection there. But he wasn't the guy for her. She wanted someone who valued her opinion and listened to her. He might be attractive and protective, but she needed more than looks, needed more than a protective cowboy. She needed someone who understood her. Marc didn't, and she doubted he could.

CHAPTER SIX

MARC WAS STARTING the day off right—with a cup of coffee and an apology to Reagan. She should be here within ten minutes. He held Megan in one arm as he poured himself a cup and took it back to the living room, where Alice was fussing in her carrier. Megan had been on the verge of wailing before he'd picked her up. And look at her now...happy as could be.

"I know, I know, kiddo. Uncle Marc's back." He set the mug on a coaster and proceeded to strap Megan into her bouncy seat. Then he scooped up Alice and held her close. "See? Nothing to cry about. I've got you. I'll always be here for you."

She gurgled in reply and he kissed her forehead. Then he settled her in the bouncy seat next to her sister, sank into the couch and took his first sip of coffee. Pure bliss. He set down the mug and closed his eyes for a moment.

It had been a long night. The girls had woken up at three, as usual, and as soon as they'd had their bottles, he'd put them back to bed. As he'd dragged himself, bleary-eyed, to his own bedroom, a text had come through from Rico that he'd found a newborn calf with no mama around.

Normally, Marc would throw on a coat and drive out to the pasture where Rico had found the calf, but he couldn't. Couldn't just leave the twins in the house alone. Rico had taken the calf back to the barn and cared for it, but Marc hadn't been able to sleep as all the scenarios ran through his head. He'd finally dozed off about an hour before the twins were up for good. Fifteen minutes ago, Rico had updated him—he'd found the mother cow. He'd keep an eye on the pair until Marc was able to get out there.

If he wasn't so tired, he'd reach over and take another drink of the coffee. Maybe he just needed to sit here, eyes closed, for a few minutes. Get his bearings. Prepare for another long day...

"Marc?"

Something pushed against his shoulder.

"Marc?"

He opened one eye, then the other and stared into Reagan's golden-brown ones. "There you are."

Where was he supposed to be?

"Don't get mad." Reagan held Alice and backed up a few steps. Then she bent and un-buckled Megan. She managed to make picking up Megan while holding Alice look effortless. A baby in each arm and a smile on her face. His gut clenched. He'd never met anyone like Reagan.

"Why would I be mad?" The words sounded like they'd been tossed in gravel. He cleared his throat and glanced over at the mug sitting nearby. The coffee. He grabbed it and took a sip—ice-cold. How long had he been out?

"When I came in, you were resting, and I didn't want to wake you, so..." She gave him a small shrug.

He jerked to attention. The calf. Rico. The twins.

"I got here twenty minutes ago," she said in a singsong voice as she made faces to each of the girls. "And you looked so peaceful, I let you be. I know you need to get out to the cows, so I finally woke you up. Yes, I did, didn't I?"

Megan grabbed a lock of Reagan's hair and

promptly shoved it in her mouth. "You don't want that. Yucky." She laughed and glanced at Marc. "Could you take my hair out of her hand? I would, but..."

"Your hands are full." He stood and gently pried open Megan's fist to release the hair. Then he pushed the tendrils behind Reagan's ear. He tried not to think about how soft it felt or the feminine fragrance that lingered. He stepped away. "I'm sorry about yesterday."

"No worries."

"I mean it. I was short with you, and I feel bad about it."

"You're under a lot of stress."

"It doesn't excuse it."

"I know, but it really isn't a big deal."

He met her gaze, and he felt bad at the vulnerability lurking in there. She'd been so kind to him. He hated that he'd been rude.

"Did you talk to your mom about taking the twins to visit Brooke tomorrow?"

"I did." His mom had burst into tears right then and there. "I thought I had upset her because she started crying. But she was relieved. She misses the twins and thinks it will do Brooke a world of good to see them."

"And Brooke? Does she know?"

"Yes. When we told her about it, she said she was going to work extra hard with the therapist so she could try to hold them."

"Do you think she'll be able to?"

"One at a time. If we hand the baby to her. She's able to lift her arm and move her fingers, but the strength isn't there for much more than that."

"I'm sorry."

"I am, too." He caressed Alice's head. "The good news is that the doctors assure us that, with therapy, they think she'll make a full recovery. She's sharp—not slurring her words anymore—and the therapists are starting to see noticeable improvement in her left side. The doctors are running tests today to see if she could be released soon."

"To come home?"

"I'm not sure. I don't see how she could come home with her arm and leg still so weak. But maybe."

"What time do you want to go tomorrow?" Reagan shifted Alice to grip her better.

"If we left around nine, would that work? Then we could be back by early afternoon."

"Sure."

"I have to figure out the car seats. I don't know how to get them in the truck."

"Why not take her minivan?"

He smacked his forehead. "Why didn't I think of that?"

"Because you're thinking about a million other things." She bent to lay Megan on the play mat, set Alice next to her and reached over to the toy basket to grab toys for each of the girls.

"Yeah, I guess." He should head out and relieve Rico, but this time with Reagan was a reprieve from everything. "I never asked if you were able to talk with Henry or not."

"I wasn't. I need to reschedule our meeting." She gestured to the kitchen. "Mind if I grab a cup of coffee before you take off?"

"Not at all." He felt like a traitor for even mentioning Henry. Wasn't he supposed to be on his mom's side in all this? The building, the bakery—he couldn't muster up an ounce of energy about either at the moment. But Reagan… yeah, he could muster up energy for her. He wanted her to be happy. Just not at his mother's expense.

As soon as she was out of sight, anxiety rushed through him. He should have been out at the barn half an hour ago. There were cows to check. Chores to be done. Tonight he'd have to pack the girls' diaper bag for tomorrow, and he'd never done that before. Would he need to keep their bottles refrigerated? Bring a cooler? He almost hung his head. Taking the babies out of the house was new to him. And scary.

"Here, I figured you needed one, too." Reagan handed him a mug. Everything about her seemed to shine. She was open and easy, and he wished he could talk to her about the many things on his mind. How he worried about each pregnant cow and newborn calf. And how scared he was that his sister would be disabled for the rest of her life. Then there was his mom. He needed to explain to Reagan why her building was so important to his mother.

But it wouldn't be fair to burden Reagan with that, not when the building was important to her, too.

Unwanted memories crept up on him. Of his mother's haggard face the day she had come home and announced she'd leased a building in town to open a bakery. She'd tried to look cheerful, but he'd known how difficult that step had been for her. More than once, she'd joked that her bakery was the ugly duckling of Jewel River. Easily passed over. Too small to notice.

"Thanks." He accepted the mug and took a sip. *Come on, man, leave. Walk out the door. You have responsibilities.* "How are you settling into your house?"

She blinked rapidly and took a drink. "I have a lot of shopping to do. And painting."

"I'd offer to help paint…"

Her laugh brightened the room. "I think you have enough on your plate as it is."

"Yeah, I do."

"Dalton and Erica are going to help. I have no idea when. I haven't picked out colors or anything. By the way, I ran into Clem Buckley yesterday afternoon."

"Oh, yeah? Did he frighten any children?"

"No," she said, grinning. "He's been very helpful. He has a friend who might guide me through the process of filling out all my business paperwork."

He actually felt his face crumble. This conversation needed to be handled correctly without him being a jerk about it. He forced a smile on his face. "Any chance you'd want to check out the other empty buildings Jewel River has to offer?"

Her golden eyes darkened as the corners of her mouth pinched. "I don't think so. I've already got the right one."

They sat there staring at each other, sipping their coffees and pretending this obstacle wasn't a problem. But they both knew it was.

"Well, I'd better get out there." He stood.

"Yep. I'll see you later. Mary and Bill Steyn will be here later. They're bringing pizza."

"Great." Marc wanted to thaw the ice between them, but he didn't know how. "Thanks again. Text me if you need anything."

He was heading to the kitchen when he heard her soft voice say, "I won't."

I won't. His step almost faltered. He deserved it. All he'd done was take from her, and he couldn't even be supportive of her new venture.

It was better this way. Reagan's personality drew him to her. He wanted to get closer to her, but he couldn't. He didn't have room in his life—or his heart—for anything more. The women who needed him had all of him already.

"THIS AFTERNOON?" REAGAN frowned as she kept an eye on the twins, still napping in their carriers on the living room floor, while she talked to Ed McCaffrey. She hadn't expected him to call back so soon or want to meet her at the building today.

"Yes, I'm going to be out that way anyhow. We might as well do a walk-through, and you can fill me in on what you want done."

She hesitated.

"If this afternoon doesn't work for you," Ed said, "it will have to wait until the week after next. I'm booked out."

"I'll meet you there today. Can you give me an hour?"

"That works for me. I look forward to seeing you there." He ended the call.

Reagan frowned at the phone. This changed things. She scurried over to her tote bag and took out the folder with her notes. She'd been jotting down ideas as they came to her, and she wanted to make sure she didn't miss anything when she talked to Ed.

Before leaving Denver, she'd asked Oliver, the owner of the chocolate shop, what his must-haves were for a building, and he'd rattled off a number of things she wouldn't have thought of on her own. Where had she put the paper with his ideas? She flipped through the pages in the folder twice before she found it. After giving it a quick skim, she clicked a pen and jotted down a few more thoughts.

Earlier, she'd texted Erica to let her know Marc had agreed to take the babies to the hospital tomorrow. Should she text her again to ask her to join her at the building for the meeting with Ed? It would be good to have another set of ears and eyes there in case she missed anything. But what if Erica and Ed felt one way about something and she felt another? Would they team up against her? Make her doubt her choices?

It was a chance she was willing to take. She called Erica.

"Hey, Reag, what's up?"

"Ed McCaffrey is meeting me at the building in an hour. Any chance you'd want to join us there?" She held her breath as she waited for her answer.

"I can't. I'm dropping off Rowan to Jamie's early. Want me to see if Dalton can come out?"

"No, that's okay." She could handle this. Couldn't she?

"By the way, Dalton contacted Marc about going over there to check his cattle tomorrow. He figured if Marc was in Casper with you, he'd need the extra help."

"Really?" This was why she adored her sister. "That is so thoughtful of you guys."

"Marc would do the same if Dalton needed help."

She didn't doubt it. He seemed the type of cowboy who would step in at a moment's notice to help anyone…unless it was her.

It would have been nice to have the type of friendship where she could ask Marc to join her for the contractor meeting. He'd made it abundantly clear, though, he still wanted his mother to have her building. Therefore, he would be no help to her.

"Let me know if you change your mind about Dalton joining you."

"I'll be fine." After the call was over, Reagan was faced with a choice. Did she meet Ed alone? Or did she call someone else to join her? Clem would. She had no doubt. But that would bring up even more issues she wasn't prepared to deal with.

No, it was time to handle her business. She'd meet Ed alone and hope she didn't forget to mention anything important. She also hoped he wouldn't make her feel like a three-year-old attempting quantum physics.

Reagan checked on the twins again. Still

sleeping, the sweethearts. A knock on the front door alerted her that Mary and Bill had arrived.

After chatting with the quiet couple for a few minutes and explaining what the twins needed, Reagan drove to town and parked in front of her building. As she got out of her vehicle, a truck pulled in next to her. A man in his mid-sixties got out, adjusted his cowboy hat and stared up at the building. She joined him on the sidewalk.

"Hi, I'm Reagan Mayer." She held out her hand. He gave it a vigorous shake. The cheer in his eyes put her at ease. He reminded her of her father. Trustworthy and solid.

"Ed McCaffrey. Let's see what you've got here." He hitched his thumb to the entrance. He held an iPad and notepad under one arm. "This here's a beauty. You're Erica's sister, right?"

"Yes. I moved here a few weeks ago."

"Well, she has a good eye for detail. The Winston is coming along fine."

"She does. My sister is nothing if not thorough." Reagan unlocked the door, and he held it open for her to enter first. Inside, she flipped on the lights.

"I have to admit, it's been some time since

I've been in here. My wife left me long ago, so I didn't have a need for jewelry." The smile lines around his eyes emphasized his playful tone. "You're converting this into a chocolate shop, correct?"

"Correct." She set her tote and purse on the front counter and took out the folder with her notes. Her fingers trembled slightly. *Stop it. You don't have to be nervous.*

"How soon do you want it opened? Do you have a deadline in mind?"

"Um…not really. I figured it would depend on how long the renovations would take."

"Let's see what we've got." He nodded, booting up the iPad. Then he took out a tape measure from his pocket.

For the next thirty minutes, Reagan followed Ed around the entire interior and answered his questions to the best of her ability.

"It looks like the electrical wiring and ductwork was all replaced in the early nineties. That's what I'm guessing, at least. Probably when Dewey bought the place. I do recommend replacing the furnace and air-conditioning unit since they're well past their prime. If you want to hold off, though, I understand. That leaves reconfiguring the floor plan to add the work area, a small kitchen, a break room and re-modeling the bathroom and office. New floors throughout, fresh paint on the walls. We'll install the climate-controlled display cases, but you're in charge of ordering them. Now, how many tables do you plan on having up here?" Ed pointed to the entrance area.

"Tables?" What did he mean?

"You know, for people to sit."

"Oh, I'm not having a sitting area. No tables."

"Gotcha." He scratched his chin. "What are you going to do with the space, then?" He checked his notes. "I am correct that all of these displays are being taken out, right?"

"Yes, you're correct." Reagan bit her lower lip as it hit her how much empty space there would be up front.

"There's no crime in having some room to breathe." He smiled warmly. "And if you change your mind, you could easily fit several tables up there for customers."

She didn't know how to respond, so she remained silent.

"I'll work up an estimate for you next week."

"When would you be available to start the work?" She followed him to the front door, where he was staring up at the ceiling. Then he poked his finger along a piece of chipped paint on the door frame and made another note on his notepad.

"My crew will get started as soon as the building permit is issued. I'm sure you're eager to open your shop, so we'll work it in around our other projects." He pointed to the corner of the ceiling. "I'm adding a new alarm system to the quote. You want to be safe."

"About the building permit... What do I need to do to get one?" She clasped her hands, wringing them tightly. Her pulse was beating too fast. She dreaded having to deal with the permit.

"Leave that to me. I'll take care of all that for you. I work with Henry all the time."

"You will?" Could she hire him on the spot?

"I will. Okay, then, Reagan. I'll get this estimate to you next week. You have yourself a fine weekend, and welcome to Jewel River. I'm looking forward to trying some of those chocolates."

"Thank you for coming out here today. You've been a big help."

They said goodbye and Ed left. As Reagan gathered her things, hope chased away all her worries.

This was really going to happen. She had a great feeling about hiring McCaffrey Construction to tackle the renovation. Now, if she could get Slim to help her with the other paperwork, she'd be in shape to open the shop this summer. That meant...it was finally time to tackle the fun stuff.

She could start ordering all the equipment she needed to open the store.

After spinning in a pirouette, she grabbed her tote and purse, hiked them onto her shoulder and locked up the building. Meeting with Ed had been the breakthrough she'd needed.

The life she'd been dreaming about would be reality soon.

CHAPTER SEVEN

MARC FINALLY LOOSENED his grip on the mini-van's steering wheel midway through the drive to the hospital. He and Reagan had gotten a later start than expected. Alice had needed a complete outfit change after a major diaper blowout, and Reagan had taken one look at the bottles Marc had prepared and announced there weren't enough. She was right, of course, and she'd made additional bottles while he'd taken care of the diaper. Reagan had definitely gotten the better end of the deal on that one.

"Did you grow up in Jewel River?" Reagan asked as she adjusted the heat. They'd worked through a number of topics so far, including Dalton checking the calves for him and what to expect at the hospital.

"I did. Right on the ranch, too."

"Your mother has a house in town, right? I

mean, I know she's living with you now…but that's to help with the twins. Or is it permanent?"

"Temporary." He hoped so, at least. Not because he had anything against his mother, but he wanted her life to get back to normal. She loved her house in town, loved being so close to the bakery. If Brooke needed more care, what would that mean for the twins? For his mom?

"I know I'm being nosy, so don't feel like you have to answer, but why doesn't she live on the ranch? It's hers, right?"

"Not anymore."

"Is it yours?"

"Yeah. After my father left us, he filed for divorce and wanted his portion of the ranch assets. Mom ended up selling a lot of acreage to help pay his settlement. We couldn't afford a full-time cowboy anymore, and I took over running the ranch while she opened the bakery. Several years ago, we agreed it made sense for me to buy the ranch from her." What he didn't mention was how touch and go the finances were those first years. If it wasn't for the bakery, they might have lost the ranch altogether.

"How old were you when your father left?"

"Sixteen." He'd trained himself to feel detached, but moments like this made all his dormant emotions rise to the surface. Maybe it was the fact Reagan was the one asking. She wasn't just making idle chitchat. She actually cared.

"And you took over the ranch by yourself? You were young. Still in high school. I can't imagine how you managed it all."

"We still had a cowboy for a short time after my father left since the divorce took a while to finalize. I was able to graduate early from high school so I could concentrate on the cattle."

"Sounds like you had to grow up quick."

He shrugged, giving her a small smile. "Yeah, well, it worked out all right. Mom isn't interested in ranching, and I am. I took out a mortgage to buy the ranch from her, and she used the money to pay off the loans she'd taken out for the bakery. She hired a financial advisor to set up a retirement plan, and best of all, she was able to buy her house. She loves that house."

The past five years had been profitable for him, too. He'd paid down the mortgage and refinanced at a lower rate. His finances were in the best shape they'd ever been.

"My mom isn't into ranching, either, although she always lends a helping hand if needed." Reagan peeked at him through shy eyes. "Do you ever see your father?"

"No, I haven't seen or heard from him since the divorce." It hurt saying it out loud. Hurt thinking about it, too. Marc was older now, but knowing his father didn't want to be part of his life still stung.

"I'm sorry. That must be difficult. Painful."

"I survived."

"You more than survived. You've succeeded under very tough circumstances."

Her compliment seeped inside him, made him want to savor it. He'd done what he'd had to do. But it had been hard.

She turned to check on the babies. They'd stopped babbling ten minutes ago. "They're asleep."

"Good. They'll be fresh for Brooke." He checked the rearview and switched lanes. "So you grew up on a ranch, too, huh?"

"Yep. Mayer Canyon Ranch. I have two older brothers—Jet and Blaine—and they divided the ranch between them after my dad retired. My parents wanted everything to be fair, so Erica and I get a small percentage of the profits, and we each have a parcel of land on the property if we ever want to build a home.

My other brother, Cody, died in a car accident several years ago."

Her tone toward the end matched the one he'd used for his father—detached. "Were you close to Cody?"

She nodded, staring straight ahead. "Yes, I was." Each word was softer than the previous one.

"I'm sorry he died."

"I am, too."

The atmosphere had grown melancholy. He couldn't stand it. "Tell me how you came to own a candle business."

"My mom started making candles as a hobby when I was in high school, and I thought it looked fun. So we did it together, and before you know it, we were selling them. Dad told us we should convert one of the old pole barns into a workshop, and we did. Erica set up the business. She's great at that. And Mom and I made the candles. I loved coming up with new scents."

"You're really creative." It wasn't a question. It was a fact. He'd seen her telling stories to the twins. It didn't surprise him one bit that she would come up with new scents. Her chocolates would probably be delicious. As unique as she was, too.

"Thank you. I wouldn't mind having some of Erica's organizational skills, too, though. My way of doing things positively terrifies her."

"As long as it works for you, who cares?"

Her mouth opened then closed as she stared at him and frowned.

"What? Did I say something wrong? I wasn't trying to offend you."

"No, no." She turned her attention to the view out her window. "My family really doesn't get how I do things, and they have strong opinions about how I should do them. Well, everyone except my brother Blaine. He's pretty supportive."

He chuckled. "Let me guess. They don't do things the way you do?"

"Bingo." Her smile made her face even prettier than it already was. "I've been second-guessing myself for a long time."

"At some point, they'll recognize that you've figured life out."

"Maybe after I actually have figured life out…"

"Why do you say that?" Her self-effacement took him by surprise. "Are you having second thoughts about the chocolate shop?"

"You wish." She grinned.

He flashed her a surprised look, but at the mischief twinkling in her eyes, he relaxed.

"For the record," he said, "I have nothing against your shop beyond the location."

"I know." She settled back into her seat. "No, I'm confident about opening the store. I met with a contractor yesterday. It went much better than I'd expected. And I'm starting to get excited about ordering all the equipment I'll need. I really miss being able to experiment with the flavors. I had this idea for a cinnamon caramel that I just know people will love..."

As he listened to her talk about the chocolates and the decorating skills she'd learned using edible paint, his entire body relaxed. There was something soothing about hearing her obvious enthusiasm for making the candy.

All too soon, he was navigating the minivan through the city streets to the parking lot of the hospital. When he parked the van, he turned to Reagan. "Thank you. I couldn't have made this trip without you. In fact, I wouldn't have even considered it. I don't know what it's going to be like in there. My mom...she's usually the most welcoming person you could ever meet, but..." He didn't know how she'd react to Reagan, and he wanted his mom to like her.

Reagan placed her hand on his arm. "It's okay. She probably hasn't slept more than a few hours at a time all week, and you all still need answers about Brooke. Don't worry. I can handle this."

He was glad someone could handle it. Because he wasn't sure he could.

"Do you think we should feed them first?" she asked.

"Nah, let's get them into the double stroller. If they're hungry, Mom will help us feed them. She is probably having baby withdrawals after this week."

"Good point."

Marc got out and opened the back hatch to unfold the stroller. Reagan exited the minivan and slid open the side door. Marc rolled the stroller to her. "Here, let me."

He popped Megan's seat out of its base and locked it into where it fit in the stroller. Then he wheeled around to the other side and repeated the process with Alice's seat. The girls made noises like they were waking up.

"Are you ready for this?" He had a firm grip on the stroller. She hiked the straps of the diaper bag and her purse up on her shoulder and nodded. "Okay. Let's go."

They headed to the entrance, through the sliding glass doors and straight to the bank of elevators in the hall. Marc pressed the number for Brooke's floor and tried to ignore the acid in his stomach. Would seeing the twins be hard on Brooke since she couldn't be with them? Would the doctors have a plan for her release? Would his mom act weird with Reagan around?

Minutes later, they reached Brooke's door. With his nerves taut, he knocked. "We're coming in."

He pushed the door open and waited for Reagan to enter before propelling the stroller inside. Brooke, sitting up in the hospital bed, promptly burst into tears, and his mom jumped to her feet.

He wasn't sure what was happening. He glanced at Reagan, who smiled brightly as she set the diaper bag on the floor.

"The girls are here!" Mom didn't give him a second glance as she began to unbuckle Alice. She lifted the baby high in the air and kissed her cheeks again and again. Then she settled her against her chest and beamed at Marc. "Thank you, honey. These dears are a sight for sore eyes."

Reagan was unbuckling Megan, leaving

Marc surprised that neither baby had started to cry. Yet. They'd just woken up and were hungry.

Reagan brought Megan over to Brooke, who held out her arms, although the left arm wasn't as high as the right. His sister was clearly trying to pull herself together. As Reagan gently laid the baby in her arms, Marc hurried to Brooke's side in case she needed help.

"I'll get her bottle." Reagan turned away to pull out two bottles from the bag. "I'll see if I can warm these up." She left the room.

"Oh, I've missed you, Meggie." Brooke held her in the crook of her right arm. She slowly brought her left hand to Megan's forehead. Marc was surprised she was able to lift her hand so high. She truly was making progress. "It's been too long since I've held you. Mom, will you bring Alice over so I can see her?"

His mother stood and brought the baby to Brooke. A fresh batch of tears dripped down his sister's cheeks. Marc looked around the room and found a box of tissues. Grabbing one, he handed it to Brooke, and he was glad to see she was able to dab her face with it using her left hand.

"You're really getting your strength back."

He nodded to her hand. She reached out to him, and he took it. She squeezed it slightly.

"I am. I couldn't do that two days ago. The therapy is really helping."

"You should see her, Marc. All day long, she has occupational therapists and physical therapists coming to get her. She's working her tail off."

"It's exhausting." Brooke sounded tired, but her expression was full of love for Megan, settling deeper into her arms. "This morning we got some positive news."

"Yes," Mom interrupted with a worried glance to his sister. "Brooke is moving tomorrow."

"Moving?" Marc pictured bringing her back home. She seemed to still need a lot of care.

"There's a short-term rehab hospital nearby with a room for her. She'll be going there in the morning."

"That's great news." She'd improved enough to enter the next phase—good news indeed. "How long will you be there? And what kind of rehab are we talking?"

Brooke looked up from Megan to him. "Most people spend around three weeks there, but the doctor told me since I'm young and motivated, I could be home in a week or two."

His mom's smile was tender but concerned. "They told her to expect a minimum of three hours of work each day."

"Work? What kind of work?"

Brooke relaxed her head against the pillows. "Mostly physical therapy. I'm doing better walking. Haven't recovered full use of this hand, though."

"These should be warm." Reagan breezed back into the room and handed Brooke a bottle and his mom one. Mom sat in the chair again to feed Alice.

Two other chairs stood next to each other against the opposite wall, so he and Reagan sat in them. The only noises were the babies drinking their bottles and the beeps of the hospital.

"I should leave you alone. Give you some privacy." Reagan began to stand but Marc stopped her.

"I'm sorry—I forgot to introduce you. Mom, Brooke, this is Reagan Mayer. She just moved to Jewel River. Reagan, this is Brooke and my mother, Anne."

His mother's smile was full of gratitude. "Erica's sister. You've been so kind to us. I don't know where to begin. Thank you."

Brooke nodded, clearly choked up. "I was so worried when I realized I'd been in the hospital for a few days. Mom showed me all the pictures you sent, and it was such a relief. I can't thank you enough for all you've done."

"It's my pleasure. I love babies, and I have the time to help right now."

"Knowing they're in good hands has been the most precious gift." Brooke looked ready to cry again, so Marc went over and took Megan from her.

"I'll burp her and give her right back," he said.

"Actually, will you bring Alice to me? I need to cuddle her, too."

"You got it."

"I'll bring her over," his mom said, rising.

Reagan found a burp cloth in the diaper bag and handed it to him. The expression in her eyes made him feel like they were a team, and he appreciated it. He'd been feeling so lost and on his own ever since he'd gotten the call from his mom about Brooke collapsing. He shifted the baby to his shoulder and softly patted her back.

"Brooke's moving to a short-term rehab center tomorrow," Marc told Reagan. "Isn't that great?"

"That's fantastic." She beamed. "Do you need anything? Clothes? Supplies?"

His mom settled Alice in Brooke's arms. "I'll take care of all that, Reagan. I plan on coming home tomorrow night. Then I'll drive here during the day and spend my nights at home this week. We'll see where things stand after that." His mom's cell phone rang. "I've got to take this." She hurried out of the room.

"Marc, what's going to happen with the babies while I'm at the rehab facility?"

"I'll keep watching them," Reagan said. "Don't worry about the girls."

"Reagan's great with the babies." Marc nodded. "You just worry about getting healthy and coming home, okay?"

"It's so much, though, asking you to watch them." Brooke's forehead wrinkled. "I can pay you."

Reagan's laugh tinkled in the air. "I don't want money. Trust me when I say spending time with two of the cutest babies in the world is payment enough."

"They are really cute, aren't they?" Brooke smiled.

"The cutest." Marc kissed the top of Megan's head.

His mom came back into the room. An air of dejection trailed behind her.

"What's wrong?" Marc asked.

"Deb can't work at the bakery tomorrow. She had an emergency—don't worry, she's fine—and says she'll be okay to work on Monday. But I don't know what to do. I can't be there. I need to be here. There are a lot of moving parts involved with Brooke's transfer, and I don't want to miss any of it."

Marc's spirits dropped to the floor. Just when everything was improving, another thing had to go wrong. Why couldn't anything be easy for once?

"What about Jackie?" Marc asked.

Reagan kept quiet as she watched the exchange between him and his mother. For five minutes now, they'd been trying to work out a solution for the bakery. They both looked completely exhausted.

On the one hand, she was thrilled for Brooke to be moving from the hospital tomorrow. On the other hand, she could see the toll this week had taken on Anne. The woman clearly needed more sleep. Maybe even a week to sit on a couch, watch old movies, sip tea and do nothing else. It would help her tremendously.

"Jackie's out of town for the weekend." Anne seemed to be on the verge of tears, and Reagan got the impression this wasn't a woman who cried often—if ever.

"Who else knows how to make all of the pastries?" Marc's tone was patient. Reagan was impressed with how well he was handling his mother.

"No one." She pressed her lips together and sank into the chair, turning her head to stare at the wall. "Except you kids, and that won't work."

"Mom, you don't need to be here," Brooke said, but the insecurity in her eyes told Reagan otherwise. "I'll be okay."

A solution had begun to swirl in Reagan's head, but it wasn't her place to offer suggestions. Or was it? If it would help them, maybe she should speak up. Marc set Megan in his mother's arms, and Anne visibly relaxed as she held the baby.

"Marc, do you know how to make everything?" Reagan asked.

He nodded. "I do, but Rico's the only cowboy I've got at the moment. And then there's the twins. I can't leave them to head to the bakery at 4:00 a.m."

More puzzle pieces locked into place. Reagan held up her index finger. "What about this? I'll ask my sister to come out to the ranch to take care of the twins. If it's 4:00 a.m., they'll be sleeping. She'll probably bring Gemma— Gemma is her housekeeper and babysitter— with her. And you and I will go to the bakery and make all the goodies. Then you can go back to the ranch when you normally start your day, while I stay to run the bakery."

His mom opened her mouth to speak but must have thought better of it and didn't. Marc, too, seemed to be working his way through her plan.

"Do you think Erica would be okay with it?" he asked.

"She will. She's always willing to pitch in and help in times like this."

"Sounds like it's a trait that runs in your family," Anne said. "I don't know how you dropped into our lap at just the right time, but I sure am thanking the Good Lord in my prayers for you, Reagan."

"God knew you needed some help." She gave

Anne a smile. "He's sent me help when I needed it, too."

A new appreciation for her sparked in Marc's eyes, and Reagan had to look away. It was too much. The thought of him viewing her as anything beyond a temporary helper was scary. Because she wasn't doing this for him. But that look in his eyes? She'd sacrifice her time and more to see it again…and again.

How much was she willing to sacrifice for Marc Young? And was it any different from the compromises she'd made over the years, the ones she'd told herself she wasn't doing anymore?

She didn't know and didn't want to find out.

Reagan excused herself and left the room to call Erica. Her sister assured her she'd help with the twins and would ask Gemma to come with her. Gemma lived in a cabin on Erica's ranch. The woman loved children, so Reagan knew the girls would be in good hands. When she returned to the room, Brooke's eyelids were closing, and Marc's mom let out an aggressive yawn.

"The plan's on." She pocketed her phone and met Marc's gaze. "Erica will take care of the twins tomorrow."

"She knows how early she'll have to be there?" he asked.

"Yes, and she's asking Gemma to join her."

"What a relief." Anne barely got the words out before another yawn took over.

"Ma, why don't you go to your hotel room and get some rest? We need to head back to the ranch anyhow."

"I think I will." She slowly stood. "About tomorrow. I've changed the menu some. Focus on the donuts, cookies and pies. Put out a sign that we're out of everything else for the day."

"Got it," he said. "Don't worry about it another minute. I'll take care of everything."

Reagan gathered the bottles and packed everything into the diaper bag. Anne brought Megan over to Brooke to say goodbye, then buckled her into the car seat as Marc took Alice from Brooke.

"Thank you for bringing them to me today." Brooke cast a longing glance at the girls. "I'm going to work really hard this week so I can come home."

He kissed Brooke's cheek. "Don't burn yourself out. I know you'll work hard. And we'll take care of everything until you come back."

Brooke nodded, then motioned for Reagan

to come over. Reagan wasn't surprised when she took her hand. His sister was beautiful, even this tired. Her almost-black hair waved around her shoulders, and she had big, round dark blue eyes, full lips and pale skin.

"Thank you," Brooke said. "Thank you from the bottom of my heart for all you're doing for my babies. I will always be in your debt."

The words brought a burst of unexpected emotion, and Reagan swallowed to ease the tightness in her throat. She patted Brooke's hand. "Like I said, I'm happy to help. You don't owe me anything."

She glanced back at Marc. Alice and Megan were secure in the stroller, and they were getting fussy. He wiped his fingers across his eyebrow as his mom listed off bakery items. Reagan pressed her lips together to keep from chuckling—why it was funny, she couldn't say—and met Brooke's eyes, also twinkling.

"She'll text him at least a hundred times about what to bake and how to bake it," Brooke said. "You'll see."

Reagan squeezed Brooke's hand once more and joined Marc. They said their goodbyes and headed down the hall.

"Was that hard for you?" She stopped at the elevators.

"Yes and no." He pressed the button. "I'm glad Brooke's improving so much, but I'm worried about her and what will happen when she and Mom come home."

"You might need help with the twins for some time." The doors opened and they went inside. Reagan smiled down at the babies. They weren't fussing anymore. They seemed to be enjoying the ride.

"I know you can't do it." Marc's shoulders slumped. "You have your own life. I'm sure we'll be able to hire some part-time help during the day."

She faltered at his words. She didn't have her own life…yet. What would *her* life look like when they didn't need her help watching the babies anymore?

It will be fine. She'd be busy with the chocolate shop. R. Mayer Chocolates would be her new life. This was just a temporary arrangement. She wouldn't forget it.

CHAPTER EIGHT

HIS MOM WOULD be disappointed if he messed this up. Under the dark sky, Marc fumbled with the key as he unlocked the back door of the bakery. Reagan shivered in her coat next to him. After Erica and Gemma arrived at the ranch, he'd given them the rundown on what to expect with the twins, and then he'd hopped into his truck and mentally reviewed everything his mom had texted him yesterday about the various baked items.

He couldn't remember how to make a few of the things she'd mentioned. It was a good thing she kept a binder full of her recipes at the bakery.

The lock finally clicked, and he held the door open for Reagan. As she hurried inside, he caught the tail end of the delicate floral scent of her perfume.

He switched on the lights and pointed for

her to continue down the hall to the kitchen. After taking off his coat, he helped Reagan out of hers, then went to the office to hang them up. There wasn't time to catch his breath before returning to the kitchen. They had too much to do.

"Aprons are over there." He nodded at the stack in a bin under the freestanding stainless-steel workstation. Every time he was in here, the kitchen felt smaller. It could barely accommodate him and Reagan. How did his mom do this every day?

Reagan grabbed two aprons. She tossed him one, and it hit him in the chest. With her hand over her mouth, she giggled. He tried not to glare at her. It was too early for giggling, and he hadn't had even a drop of coffee yet. No one should be in a good mood this early.

"I'll put on a pot of coffee," he said.

"I'll poke around while you do."

It only took a minute to fill the carafe, scoop the grounds into the filter and get the coffee-maker started. Then he hustled next to where Reagan stood with her back to him as she reached up for something on the shelves along the wall.

Where was the recipe binder? He wasn't paying attention when she whirled around…right into his arms.

With his hands on her waist, he steadied her. "Whoa there. Where do you think you're going?"

Their bodies were close. He watched in fascination as her pupils dilated, then returned to normal. The sensation of being in her personal space made his pulse quicken. He let her go.

Today was about baking. Not Reagan.

It was impossible not to be aware of her, though—like he ever wasn't aware of her. He'd thought about her all day yesterday after they'd returned from Casper and again at night when he couldn't sleep. Her generosity, her amenable personality, her intelligence and kindness—all affected him. All tempted him.

She made him question if he *could* fit another woman into his life.

"This is great!" She rubbed her forearms. Her eyes twinkled as she took in the kitchen. "It's so cozy in here."

"Cozy is one way to put it," he said dryly. The binder. There. He opened it and set it on the counter. *Pretend she isn't here. Pretend she isn't two inches away. Pretend you can't smell her perfume.*

"What's that?" She stood all of two inches behind him and was looking over his shoulder.

How in the world was he going to pretend she wasn't there when she was practically touching him?

"Mom's recipes," he said gruffly.

"Oh, good. That will help. Or do you know how to make everything by heart?"

"Not even close." He found the page with the yeast donuts. "But Brooke and I have helped her out many times, so I'm confident we'll be able to make most of the things she sells."

"She mentioned pies. I'm not your girl for that. But cookies? Those I can handle."

He was glad she could handle cookies because, frankly, he couldn't handle being in this minuscule kitchen at all—not with her everywhere he turned. "Here's the list of what she makes on Sundays." He pulled out the laminated sheet.

Reagan took it from him as the coffeepot gurgled. He needed a cup desperately.

"Are these the quantities?" She pointed to the sheet.

"Yes. Do you want a cup?"

"Yes, please."

He poured coffee into two mugs and added

cream and sugar to hers before bringing them over. She smiled her thanks, and his heart did a backflip.

Gritting his teeth, he tried to focus. *I should be checking cows. But, no, I'm in this closet of a kitchen, standing next to the most fascinating woman I've ever met, and all I can think about is touching her hair, holding her hand and learning everything there is to know about her. I need to bake.*

"What do we do first?" she asked, holding the mug between her hands.

"I'll make up the yeast dough because it needs to go into the proof box. You can work on the cookies. Then I'll get the pies started. The cake donuts don't take long. Mom's pastries are too complicated for today, but if we have time, I'll tackle a batch of bars."

"Aye, aye, Captain." With two fingers, she saluted him. The gesture was so ridiculous, he couldn't prevent the corners of his mouth from curling into a smile.

"What's that? A smile?" She grinned. "You were getting a little uptight."

"Getting? That's generous of you. I've been uptight since the minute we met."

"You have your reasons." The shrug and

shimmer in her eyes made him forget why he was there.

Why was he there? *Dough. Right.* He found a mixing bowl.

"What cookies am I making first?" she asked.

He found the recipe and took it out of the binder for her. He gave her a quick overview of how to work the oven, pointed out the rack where the pans would go after baking to cool off the cookies, and then he gathered everything he needed for the donuts. They worked in silence for several minutes. Marc put the dough in the proof box to rise, started making the piecrusts and set the rounds in the fridge to chill.

Reagan popped three trays of chocolate-chip cookies into the oven and set the timer.

"Okay, Cap'n, what's next?" She glanced over her shoulder as she washed her hands at the sink.

"Sugar cookies. I'll get the recipe." He put the recipe she'd finished back in the binder and found the new one.

"You sure know your way around this place." Reagan wiped her hands off on a towel and joined him.

"Yeah, well, I had to learn." He filled the sink with soapy water and proceeded to wash the mixing bowls. "The year after my dad left, Mom and I—and Brooke, to a certain extent—worked night and day to keep our life from falling apart. If it wasn't for this bakery, we would have lost the ranch. Whenever Mom needed an extra hand or got sick, I was here to take her place."

"That's how my family is, too. We work together and pitch in when someone needs help." She dumped sugar and butter into one of the stand mixers and began creaming them together. "Yesterday, I could see how close the three of you are."

"They're my whole world." He glanced her way, and her thoughtful expression made him wonder. What did she think of him?

"It's obvious that you'd do anything for them."

"Yes." He didn't need to be reminded about why his mom was so important to him. This bakery symbolized her struggle. And a newer, bigger bakery was supposed to be her reward. But Reagan didn't know that, and he couldn't plead his case, not with all the help she'd lavished on him and the twins. And certainly not with her here helping in the bakery itself.

He cleared out the unwanted thoughts as he

prepared pie fillings. Then he wiped off the counter, sprinkled flour on the workspace and took the discs of piecrust dough out of the fridge. After rolling out the crusts, he carefully transferred them to disposable pie tins, added the filling, and quickly wove the lattice top crusts. He put the pies in one of the ovens and set a timer.

"Do you have a sweet tooth?" he asked. *Duh.* Of course she did. She was opening a chocolate store.

"Oh, yeah. I'm a candyholic. Is that a word?"

"If it isn't, it should be."

"I agree. What about you?" One of the timers beeped, and Reagan took out the cookies and slid them onto the cooling rack. Then she put the next batch into the oven and meandered back to the coffeepot for another cup. When she returned, he handed her the next recipe, and she gave him another salute.

"My sweet tooth gets worse every year. I can't resist Mom's crullers. Or anything she bakes, really. She usually brings home a box of leftovers, and I go to town on them." He brushed her shoulder as he moved behind her to check the cookies on the rack. They looked perfect, from what he could tell. It didn't surprise him. Reagan's talents seemed to apply to everything she touched. "You're good at this. Do you like baking?"

"I love baking." The mixer drowned out any hope of conversation for the next couple of minutes. Reagan turned it off and continued adding ingredients.

He should be starting the next item on the list, but another cup of coffee called his name. Plus, all these questions were bubbling up. Questions he'd normally ignore but, for whatever reason, here in this small space with Reagan, he couldn't.

"Have you ever been in love?" Why had he blurted *that* out? His cheeks burned, and he hustled to the coffeemaker, where a quarter of a pot remained.

"Um, no. How about you?" She sounded nervous. He could relate.

"No."

"Really?" She looked up from where she was shaping the sugar cookie dough into a log.

"Really."

"I find that surprising." She bent down to eye level with the log and squished one end slightly. Then she straightened and took it to the refrigerator.

"I find it surprising you haven't been," he said.

After shutting the fridge's door, she wiped her hands on her apron and leaned against the counter to face him. "I haven't met the right person."

His eyebrows arched as he took a sip. "And who would that be?" Why was he asking? Why was he pursuing this at all?

"Someone who respects me. Who recognizes I have my own way of doing things. Someone who supports my decisions."

"Is that all?" His mind raced around her words and, unfortunately, came up with results he didn't like. He respected Reagan. Who wouldn't? And he had no problem with her way of doing things. But he couldn't exactly support her decision to open the chocolate shop in the corner building.

"No, it's not all. I want someone who will put me first, the way my parents do with each other. Plus, my faith is very important to me, and I want kids."

"Yeah, I get that. Church is a big part of my life, too."

"Do you want kids?"

"If I were to ever get married, yes."

"The way you say it makes it sound like you don't plan on getting married."

"It's difficult for me to see marriage in my future."

"Why's that?"

"I've been the man of my family for fifteen years. After Brooke married Ross, I found my-self alone on the ranch, and the solitude suited me. But after Ross was killed and Mom and Brooke moved back...well, it was the wake-up call I needed."

"What do you mean?"

"I'll always be here for my family. No mat-ter what. And a wife might not understand my devotion to them. She might not support my decision to move everyone back to the ranch. But even if she did, I don't know if I could put anyone else first. My mom, my sister and the twins already have the top spot."

"I see," she said softly.

He doubted it. "I'd better get started on the cake-donut batter."

He could feel her gaze following him as he grabbed clean mixing bowls. Reagan wanted someone who would put her first. She deserved it. Part of him wished he could be that guy.

Marc scooped flour into one of the bowls.

His life was a raging mess at the moment. The one thing he didn't need was romance, and he wasn't going to go looking for it. He'd push away these inconvenient feelings. He had enough on his mind to last a century anyhow.

REAGAN WAS TIRED all the way to her bones. In five minutes, she could flip the Open sign to Closed and lock the bakery…if she didn't pass out from exhaustion first.

She took a spray bottle and clean cloth over to the three café tables and wiped them down. Then she cleaned the chairs and put away the supplies. The bakery was open from seven in the morning until two in the afternoon. Add the hours of baking earlier and it had been the longest ten hours of her life.

It wasn't that she hadn't enjoyed it. She had. Making all the baked goods with Marc this morning had been fun, informative—even flirty. Every day she learned something new about him. All the tidbits were adding up to give her a better picture of who he was. When he'd left before the bakery opened to relieve Rico from cattle duty, Reagan had immediately missed him.

Everyone who'd come in to the bakery had

been welcoming. She'd spent hour after hour filling bags and boxes with donuts and pies and everything else. The register hadn't been too complicated, and what she didn't know, the customers had been eager to explain. It had been really nice to get to know the residents of Jewel River better.

The only thing she was confused about had nothing to do with Marc or baking or customers. It had happened earlier, when she'd toured the bakery. It had been so sudden and unexpected that she still hadn't processed it.

When she'd walked through the space, she'd instantly pictured the interior of Annie's Bakery, from the front to the rear, completely reconfigured to be her chocolate shop.

As it was, the bakery was functional and cozy and smelled delicious. But somehow, in a flash, she'd mentally reconfigured the layout, redecorated it and replaced the current bakery display with her chocolate display cases. The front wall? Gone. It would be replaced with large windows and a glass door to let in light. Those three café tables? No room—and no need—for them.

The vision of her chocolate shop still blazed in her mind. And she didn't know what to do with it.

Reagan checked the time and decided to lock up a few minutes early. If even one more customer came in, she'd collapse in a heap on the floor and start whimpering. She was just that tired.

She was almost to the door when it opened. *No way. I'm telling them we're closed. I can't fake a smile right now. I can't. I just can't.*

But to her surprise, Erica and Gemma entered the store.

"Quick, flip over the sign!" Reagan pointed to the door. "Before anyone else comes in."

Erica's eyes grew round, but she backtracked and flipped the sign. "Want me to lock the door?"

"Yes." She resumed her spot behind the counter, took out two large donut boxes and began filling them with the few leftovers that hadn't sold. "You're taking these home with you."

"But Gemma already made me snickerdoodles."

"That's true. I did, dear." Gemma pulled out a chair and groaned.

"Are you okay, Gemma?" Reagan asked.

"Just a little tired. Johnny's coming over later. He might like the donuts."

"See?" Reagan beamed to Erica. "Johnny will like the donuts."

"Those babies are delightful," Gemma said. "But it's been ages since I've been up this early to care for infants."

"Me, too." Erica collapsed onto the chair opposite Gemma.

"Why are you here so early? Who's watching the twins?" Reagan finished filling the boxes. Then she wrinkled her nose at the register. "I have no idea what Anne does with the money."

"Is there a cash bag?" Erica asked.

Reagan rummaged through the drawer and cabinet below the register. She found a pouch of some sort and held it up. "Is this it?"

"Yes. Just put the cash and receipts in there. Do you need help cleaning the kitchen?"

"No, Marc and I took care of it before I opened the store this morning. I'll just give the floors a quick mop, and I'll be done. You still haven't told me who is watching the girls."

"Oh, right. Anne came home half an hour ago. She said the move went well, and that Brooke was already working on her mobility assignments when she left."

"That's good news. I'm glad she came home

early. This is the first time she's been home in almost a week."

"Maybe we should have stayed so Anne could take a nap." Gemma frowned, biting her lower lip.

"We tried," Erica said to Gemma. "She wouldn't hear of it."

"You're right, but still."

Reagan filled the mop bucket and almost broke her back trying to get it out of the deep sink in the utility closet. Using the mop handle, she steered the bucket on wheels to the front of the store and began to mop. "Thank you both for going over there so early and helping out with the babies. I really appreciate it."

"We were happy to, weren't we?" Erica said, smiling at Gemma.

"Yes, but maybe a little later in the morning next time."

All three of them laughed. Reagan's back and shoulders ached as she mopped her way to the rear of the store and into the kitchen. With Anne home in the afternoons, Reagan probably wouldn't have to coordinate babysitters for the twins anymore.

She dumped out the dirty water and put the supplies back in the utility closet. After washing her hands, she found her coat and purse and joined Erica and Gemma.

"I'm not sure what's going to happen next week with the twins." Reagan motioned for them to follow her to the back door. They emerged outside moments later. "Anne said she's going to be home in the afternoons, so I'm assuming Marc won't be driving to Casper anymore. If I watch the babies until Anne comes home, the two of them will probably be able to take care of Megan and Alice on their own."

Erica put her arm around Reagan's shoulders. "If you want to take off time to work on the business, we'll find babysitters to come out in the mornings."

The gesture and thought behind it were kind, but Reagan bristled anyway.

"That's okay. Ed's getting an estimate to me this coming week. I've got everything under control."

"But I know you want to paint your house and—"

"It doesn't need to get done right now."

"But—"

"It can wait."

Erica's gaze probed her for a long moment. Then she glanced around. "Where's your car?"

"Marc picked me up."

"Want a ride home?"

Normally, she'd decline. She loved fresh air, especially after being indoors most of the winter. But if she didn't get off her feet soon, she didn't know what would happen.

"I'd love a ride home."

Five minutes later, she waved goodbye to them and let herself into her house. She put on her softest joggers and favorite old sweatshirt with a big stain on the sleeve. Then she padded to the couch, stretched out her legs and closed her eyes.

Every muscle twitched. Every joint ached. And every thought ping-ponged between her vision of the chocolate shop being in the bakery and her interaction with Marc this morning.

He'd asked some personal questions. Given her personal answers. What he'd told her yesterday about his father leaving and then him taking over the ranch had become more nuanced today when he'd talked about his mom and the bakery. Anne's sacrifices had clearly touched him deeply. Reagan understood why he was invested in her success. She also understood why he'd moved his sister and the twins in with him. And she got his worries about finding a woman who not only grasped why he did the things he did for his family, but also approved of them.

But he didn't seem to think he was capable of putting a wife's needs up there with his mom's and sister's. And if he wasn't, there was no future for Reagan to be with him. She wasn't willing to settle for anything less than his top spot.

"I CAN'T MOVE." Marc lengthened the recliner as far as it would go. Megan was asleep in his arms. His mom was stretched out on the couch with her head on a pillow from her bedroom. Alice was sleeping on her chest. Earlier, he and his mom had warmed up a can of tomato soup and choked down a few grilled cheese sandwiches. It was all either of them had had the energy to make or to eat.

Had it only been this morning when he'd met Reagan at the bakery? Felt like a thousand years ago.

The television was turned to a cooking show that neither of them was watching. The noise from it relaxed him, though.

"Longest week of your life?" he asked, keeping his head against the headrest.

"By far. You?"

"Oh, yeah."

"I haven't even asked how the cattle are doing."

"They're good. Tagged another calf this morning."

"Glad to hear it."

The television was the only sound in the room for quite a while.

"What are we going to do until Brooke comes home? You know, about the twins and the bakery?" Marc asked. He didn't want to think about it, but they had to come up with a plan. Last week was a blur of Reagan arriving, him checking cattle, driving to the hospital, coming home to awkward conversations with the volunteers, then forcing himself to eat before crashing in bed. Reagan had already told him she'd be at the ranch tomorrow morning, but they couldn't sustain this for long. She'd already done so much for them.

"I can't think about it now," she said.

"Fair enough."

He wanted to close his eyes and sleep for days, but his practical side won out. He snapped the recliner back to normal and stood, regretting it as his knees and hips cried out, then carried Megan upstairs and gently placed her in her crib. He returned to the living room and took Alice from his mother, then went back upstairs and put her to bed, too.

After changing into sweatpants and a T-shirt, he brushed his teeth and reclaimed his spot on the recliner. Mom was conked out, her mouth ajar as she lightly snored. For the first time, it hit him that she looked old. Not senior-citizen old, just every inch of her fifty-nine years. It was no wonder after the week they'd had.

He drew the comforter over her, then took his spot on the recliner once more.

Marc had reached a breaking point today. It was all too much. He'd called Cade and Ty and Dalton about hiring another cowboy to get through calving. Ty had gotten back to him a few hours ago. One of his ranch hands had a brother who'd been helping them part-time and was looking for more work. Ty vouched for Trevor's experience and said he had good instincts with the cattle. Trevor would be at Marc's ranch tomorrow morning.

He should have hired someone earlier in the season. He'd foolishly told himself he and Rico would be fine dealing with calving on their own. But he'd been wrong. If Trevor worked out, he and Rico could get some much-needed rest.

And, no matter what way he sliced it, it was obvious his mother needed another part-time employee, too. Sure, she and Deb managed the bakery fine in normal times, but the second the twins had been born, everything had stopped being normal.

That led to the next issue. The twins. It was wishful thinking to imagine Brooke would be able to care for them on her own when she was released from the hospital. And he and Mom were spread too thin as it was. They needed to hire part-time help until Brooke recovered completely. But how would his sister feel about it?

Reagan had offered time and again to babysit until Brooke came home. Why couldn't he simply accept her help? She was great with the twins. Sure, he hated the feeling of being in her debt, but he didn't know how they would have survived without her help.

God, I haven't taken enough time to pray beyond asking You to heal my sister. But thank You for sending Reagan. We needed her. We still need her. I know we're taking advantage of her generosity, but I can barely deal with everything as it is. And know-

ing the twins are in her capable hands gives me the breathing room I need.

Their conversation while baking this morning came back to him. She was easy to talk to. He'd told her things he hadn't told anyone. He usually didn't discuss how hard it had been for his mom to get the bakery running or how overwhelmed he'd been when he'd single-handedly taken over the ranch. And he never talked about his romantic life. Maybe because he didn't have a romantic life. The last time he'd dated anyone had been three or four years ago. A teacher at the elementary school. Nice woman. Phoebe was now married with a baby on the way.

He had no regrets.

He would have only disappointed Phoebe, and she would have left him for someone who could meet her needs. So, he'd broken things off. But Reagan... She was unique. She not only understood how much his mom, sister and nieces meant to him, but she threw herself wholeheartedly into helping them, too.

What did he have to offer a woman like her? He didn't even know what she needed.

That's not true. She told you.

He closed his eyes, replaying her melodic

voice in the bakery this morning. She wanted someone who respected her.

Who wouldn't respect her? She was something special.

She'd also mentioned that she had her own way of doing things, and if he remembered correctly from previous conversations, her family didn't think her way was the right way. Hadn't she said she second-guessed herself a lot?

Then the clincher—she needed a man who would support her decisions and who would put her first.

Marc's heart sank. He lived with strong women. He supported their decisions, even when he didn't like them. But he didn't know if he could put a girlfriend or a wife first. When all this was said and done, he'd find a way to thank Reagan, and he'd resume his solitary life.

CHAPTER NINE

REAGAN'S PALMS GREW clammy as she kept an eye on the library entrance Thursday afternoon. *What if this is a mistake? What if he thinks I'm an idiot? What if he treats me like I'm incompetent?*

She'd found an empty table near the teen section. Her laptop, notebook, pen and phone were lined up in front of her. If Slim Nixon thought she was an idiot, she'd handle it. Somehow. *Yeah, like you handled it when Mom acted like you'd requested a unicorn for your birthday when you told her you were going to Denver?*

The only reason she hadn't caved to her mother's pressure to stay in Sunrise Bend was that she'd already lined up the chocolate job and put a deposit down on a short-term furnished rental. Reagan knew herself too well. One sign of doubt from her family and she'd fold like a cheap lounge chair.

If Slim gave her the impression he thought

she was in over her head, she'd just have to thank him and excuse herself. She'd drive straight to Erica's and beg her for help. Trying to figure out all these business forms was over her head by a mile, and she was tired of pretending otherwise.

A tall gentleman with a silver mustache and wearing a navy vest over a button-down shirt, jeans and cowboy boots walked through the doors. Rising slightly, she waved, and he acknowledged her with a nod.

"Reagan Mayer, I assume?" He leaned across the table and held out his hand. "It's good to meet you."

"Thanks for agreeing to come here. I'm... well..." She was getting flustered, and it had nothing to do with Slim. She just felt so out of her league.

"You don't have to say a word. I understand. It's a lot to figure out." He took a seat and opened a folder. "Clem mentioned a chocolate shop."

She nodded, unsure of what to say or what to do.

"Good, good. I like chocolates. Especially chocolate-covered strawberries. Do you make those?"

"I do." If Slim could help her wade through

all this, she'd make him a dozen chocolate-covered strawberries every week for the rest of his life.

"I'll be stopping in for them once your shop is open." His friendly tone set her at ease. "Now, why don't you tell me where you're at in the process?"

She swallowed, trying to tamp down her nerves. "Not very far."

"Have you picked out a name for your business?" He clicked open a pen.

"Yes. R. Mayer Chocolates."

"Good, good." He jotted it down. "And how do you want to structure the company?"

"Structure?" The word brought to mind steel beams and concrete, but she doubted that was what he'd meant.

"You can incorporate or create a limited liability company." He explained the different types of businesses and their pros and cons.

Right. Now she understood what he meant by structure. After going back and forth about the options, both agreed on which one would make the most sense for her.

"Okay," Slim said, "let's pull up the Wyoming Secretary of State website and do a search to make sure your company name isn't taken already. Then we can register it."

"Right now?"

"Sure. Why not?"

It was as if the dark clouds surrounding her to-do list had parted. What a blessing this man was. Slim wasn't just telling her what she needed to do—he was helping her do it.

Over the next hour, they were able to submit three forms to various agencies. He gave her instructions to work on the others at home. When they finished, he escorted her out the door to her car.

"Now, if you have any questions—I don't care how small they might seem—you give me a call." He shook her hand once more.

"Wait. How much do I owe you?" She should have asked before they'd gotten started, but whatever price he threw out, she'd happily pay him.

"I'll take a couple of those chocolate-covered strawberries after your shop opens."

"But I can't let you do all this work without paying you. I want to—"

"Nope. I'm retired. I like helping folks out. And you seem like an awful nice person to help."

She blinked as her emotions got the better

of her. What a kind, generous man. "The next time I see you, expect to take home a box of those chocolate-covered strawberries."

"I'm looking forward to it."

They parted, and Reagan got into her car and swiped her phone. She almost pressed Marc's number. But then she remembered that this conversation was off-limits with him. By his choice.

She sighed. It was too bad, really. They got along so well. Every morning when she arrived at the ranch, they had a cup of coffee together and discussed Brooke and the bakery and the calves. While he didn't seem to mind talking about making the chocolate—he hadn't showed any discomfort Tuesday when she'd mentioned all the equipment she'd ordered—he *did* mind any mention of the building. The few times she'd broached the subject, his jaw had tightened and the light in his eyes had gone out.

So she'd kept it to herself when Ed McCaffrey had called her yesterday to let her know he'd have the estimate ready this Friday. And she hadn't mentioned this meeting with Slim, either.

It seemed their relationship only worked on his terms. And that wasn't much of a relationship at all. If she couldn't share the things most important to her, then maybe she'd be better off not putting too much stock in their friendship.

After starting her vehicle, she drove down Center Street. She flicked a glance at the bakery. What was it about that particular space that appealed to her so? It was a hidden gem, for sure. Continuing on, she parked in front of her building. Without getting out of the car, she stared at the entrance, and all the anticipation she expected to feel was nowhere to be found.

What was her problem? Why wasn't it singing to her the way the bakery just had? Was she letting Marc's attitude about it get to her? Was she internalizing his disapproval and getting cold feet because of it? Trying to find a compromise so he'd let her into his world?

Pulling her shoulders back, she checked her rearview and backed out of the spot. Her chocolate shop would be in *this* building. The plans were moving forward. She'd made a lot of progress this week with the help of Ed and now Slim. It would be ridiculous to let Marc's bias affect her decisions.

This was her life, not his, and she was making the best of it. Starting with this building. If he didn't like it, too bad.

But as she approached the intersection to turn left, she couldn't help but wish he'd get on board. The building—her plans for it—was the only thing that seemed to be standing between them. And she'd spent enough time with him over the past couple of weeks to know she liked him. A lot. But if he couldn't respect her decisions...

She'd better put some ice on that attraction. She had too much to lose if she didn't.

"I DON'T KNOW about that." Marc set his mug on the counter Friday morning as he kept a firm grip on Alice. He was just starting to feel like himself again—a tired version of himself—and now Reagan was asking him to do this?

The week had gone better than he'd hoped. Brooke was making excellent progress, and the doctors were already talking about letting her come home later next week. Mom had been visiting her every other day and working at the bakery on the days she stayed in town. Trevor, the ranch hand Ty had recommended, was a hard worker who needed little supervision. Hiring the cowboy had allowed both Marc and Rico to catch up on lost sleep.

"Do you have something against taking pictures of the girls around the ranch?" Reagan held Megan in her left arm and calmly sipped her coffee. "It's a beautiful day, and I think Brooke would really appreciate seeing them in cute outfits outdoors."

"Why the ranch?"

She lifted one shoulder in a shrug. "I've taken pictures of them on their play mat and in their bouncy seats. Why not get them in the sunshine?" She set the mug down to snap her fingers. "What about taking their picture with one of the calves? You have a few in the corrals, don't you?"

"Ye-e-es." He grabbed his coffee again and took another drink. "Is it safe for the girls to be around livestock?"

"I don't know. I just thought it would be fun to have one in the picture."

"I suppose."

"When these two get older, they're going to love the calves. You can't stop my nieces and nephews from petting them. Clara and Maddie kiss them on the forehead. It's really cute."

"I don't want these two kissing any cows."

Her laughter loosened the tension spreading across his upper back. "I don't think we need to worry about them kissing cows just yet. I saw the most adorable little sundresses and head-bands in their closet. Would it be okay for me to dress them up?"

How would he know? His sister's plans for their clothes had gone out the door when she had the stroke.

"If it's not, I'll just find different outfits," she said. "But it sure would be cute to have them in those dresses."

"Go ahead," he said. "If Brooke or Mom say anything, I'll take the blame."

"Do you think they would?" Worry lines creased her forehead.

"No, not really." All week his mom had raved about Reagan every time her name was mentioned. And it was mentioned often. Too often. "Knowing those two, they'll probably love it."

"Good. And, listen, if you don't want the girls near a calf, that's fine. There are so many places on your ranch that will make a good photo op."

Photo op? It was news to him. While he loved his property, he was under no illusions. Anywhere you walked, you were going to smell manure. He kept the grounds tidy and the fences repaired, but it wasn't anyone's dream spot for selfies and photo shoots.

"I'm thinking I'll bring out that adorable quilt with the pastel colors I saw in the closet. And correct me if I'm wrong, but I did see kittens running around near the stables, didn't I?"

"You did. But I don't see how we can get barn kittens to cooperate with getting their picture taken."

"Point taken." Her face glowed with excitement. It made him want to say yes to everything she suggested. "No problem. We'll get plenty of other shots with the girls."

Her enthusiasm lifted his spirits. Reagan was right. This break in the weather was too good to pass up. The girls had never experienced being outside without being bundled up. And even then they'd simply been transferred from the house to the minivan. Fresh air and sunshine would do them both some good.

"What time do you want to take the girls out?" he asked.

"Let's do it after lunch. They'll be fresh from their nap. I know it means taking an hour out of your day, so if you have to check cattle or whatever, I understand. I just don't think I can get the pictures I want without your help."

He hiked Alice farther up his shoulder. "I can take an hour off. It's okay."

She nodded, a twinge of insecurity in her expression. He didn't like that she felt insecure about asking him for this. The twins were important to him.

"It'll be time well spent," he said. "Brooke is going to love it, and it will probably motivate her to work even harder so she can come home."

"I really hope the doctors clear her to move back soon." Reagan shifted Megan, kissing the top of her head in the process.

"Me, too." Disappointment settled in his gut. He figured Reagan was probably itching to get back to her own life. "Listen, we appreciate your sacrifice in coming out here every day. If you have stuff you need to do, just let me know. We can line up another babysitter or something. I know you have a lot to take care of."

"What? Oh, no, that's not why I said it. I want her to move home so she can be with her babies and start getting back to normal. I can't imagine how awful it would be to be separated from the twins for so long."

Of course. He should have known she would think of Brooke's feelings over her own inconvenience. This had nothing to do with her wanting her own life back. Why had he auto-matically gone there?

"Yeah, I want it for her, too." He drank the last of his coffee and set the mug in the sink. Then he lifted Alice up in the air near his face. "And you, little princess, be good for Reagan this morning. You and your sister are going to get a tour of the ranch after lunch. If you're good, you can see a calf. Maybe even some kittens." He kissed her nose and met Reagan's eyes. They sparkled with mirth and something else... Appreciation.

It was nice to feel appreciated.

"Where should I put her?" he asked.

"Let's try the play mat first. The girls can have some wiggle time down there."

"You got it." As he made his way to the living room, he wanted to ask her how her plans were coming along for the chocolate shop. The other day she'd told him about all the things she'd ordered—a machine to temper the chocolate, double boilers, food scales and all kinds of things he hadn't realized she would need—and he'd liked listening to her. Wanted to know more about her plans. But instead of asking the questions her list had brought up, a hard ball had formed in his chest and the words wouldn't come out.

Instead, he'd recalled all the times his mom had talked about moving the bakery to the corner building. She'd described exactly how she would display the baked goods in the windows for the holidays. And her eyes had sparkled as she'd estimated all the additional seating she'd have and how more people could hang out there in the mornings.

His mom had all these dreams, all these plans. And they all revolved around the place Reagan was using for her dreams, her plans.

Marc never thought he'd be in a dilemma about wanting to support his mom while at the same time rooting for the woman who stood in the way of his mother's dream coming true.

But this was Reagan. No ordinary woman. Didn't she deserve to have her dreams come true, too?

He carefully set Alice on the mat. A few seconds later, Reagan placed Megan next to her. When she straightened, he didn't step back, leaving them only inches apart. Attraction flared. He wanted to say something, do something, but the moment passed.

"I'll be back after lunch for the pictures." He

didn't bother waiting for her reply, just hurried out of the room with his face hotter than a broiler. *Come on, Marc, you're thirty-two. Grow up.*

This feeling had nothing to do with maturity, though. He was falling for Reagan Mayer, and it terrified him.

"IT'S PERFECT!" REAGAN couldn't believe Marc had come up with this. He'd found an oval galvanized tub and lined it with the quilt she'd mentioned earlier. The tub was nestled in the grass near a fence with hay bales stacked next to it. "Are you sure you weren't a photographer's assistant at some point?"

"I'm sure." He grinned, adjusting the quilt.

"And you didn't help design sets for the school plays?" She liked teasing him. The twitch of his lips and creases in the corners of his eyes told her he enjoyed it, too.

"Afraid not."

"Well, you got your talent somewhere."

"Probably my mom." He chuckled.

"Probably." Reagan knelt and laid Alice on the quilt in the tub, then held out her hands for Marc to pass Megan to her. He did, and she settled the girls next to each other. Then she straightened their little sundresses and head-bands and stood. They stared up at her with wide-eyed expressions.

"Okay, you stay close to them, and I'll take the pictures." She slid her phone from her pocket. Then she moved around to get the best angles. She took close-ups and pictures from above and from the side. When she was satisfied she'd gotten enough pictures, she faced Marc and held up her phone. "These turned out perfect."

"Let me see."

She handed it to him and watched as he swiped through them. "I still want to get a picture of them with a calf."

Chuckling, he picked up Megan, cradling her to one shoulder, then picked up Alice. He made carrying two babies look easy. And Reagan knew from experience it was tricky. She gathered the quilt, folded it and shoved it in the basket under the stroller. "Do you want the girls in here?"

"Nah, I'll carry them." He smiled at Megan, then Alice. "You like being out here, don't you? Just wait until summer. You're going to love it even more."

Reagan pushed the stroller as they headed toward the barns.

"I moved one of the calves to a pen earlier so you can get some pictures."

They continued past the barn to the corrals and a pen behind it. A little calf had curled up on the grass next to the fencing, and a gray kitten was sleeping against its side.

"Marc, would you look at that?" She pointed to the calf with the kitten. "How precious. I have to get a picture."

She entered the pen and quickly got a few shots of the sleeping calf with the kitten. Then she stepped back. "Hmm…any ideas on how to get a picture with the girls?"

"Why don't you crouch down there with them, and I'll take the picture?"

"I think Brooke would prefer to see you with them. You're their uncle."

"Yeah, but you're prettier."

He thought she was pretty? She liked the sound of that.

They argued back and forth about who should be in the photo, until finally Marc relented. Reagan helped him hold the girls so they would be cradled in each of his arms and facing the camera. Then he crouched on one knee next to the calf. Reagan started taking pictures. The kitten yawned, stretched her front legs and settled more deeply into sleep. The calf woke and looked up at Marc.

"Hey there, little guy," Marc said as the calf licked his arm. He shifted so the girls could see it. "You've got a couple of friends here today."

The calf extended his neck to sniff Megan. The babies couldn't take their eyes off him. Megan reached out and touched its soft forehead.

Reagan took picture after picture, knowing she was going to love each one more than the previous. After a few minutes, Marc winced.

"Would you take Alice for me? I'm in an awkward position, and I don't trust myself not to stumble getting up."

"No problem." She put away her phone and took the baby.

"What next?" He rose, holding Megan, and opened the gate for them. She gave the calf one more smile and exited the pen.

"It's so nice out. I don't want to go back inside yet. I think I'll spread out the quilt on the lawn for a bit."

"I'll join you." They strapped the girls into the stroller, and Marc pushed it in the direction of his backyard.

"Tell me about this place." She glanced around the outbuildings and took in the pastures.

"The ranch?"

"Yeah."

"My grandparents—my mother's folks—were newlyweds when they bought it. The farmhouse was already here and most of the outbuildings were, too. Mom grew up on the ranch. My grandfather died shortly after my parents married. Mom and Dad talked with my grandmother, and they agreed to take over the ranch for her. They moved into the farmhouse, and my grandmother moved to an apartment in town."

"That's sad about your grandfather, but I love that it worked out so your parents could take over." She pointed to a dry grassy area. "Is this okay?"

"Sure." He stopped the stroller, took the quilt out and spread it on the grass. They each took a baby and sat on the quilt. "Anyway, my grandmother passed away not long after I turned sixteen. It was hard. Brooke and I were really close to her. Being an only child, Mom inherited the ranch, along with all of my grandmother's assets. My parents argued about the inheritance. Then my father left us. A week after my grandmother's funeral."

As the impact of what he was saying hit her,

Reagan tried not to cringe. His father leaving them had been awful, but the circumstances made it even worse. Leaving so soon after his wife's mother died?

"I'm so sorry. I don't know what to say."

"There's nothing to say. From a young age, I worked alongside my father and our full-time cowboy on this land. And the second Mom inherited it, Dad walked away, knowing he'd get half of everything in the divorce. It was like this ranch meant nothing to him."

The unspoken words unraveled between them—Reagan could practically hear him say, *Like we meant nothing to him.*

"Didn't he like ranching?" she asked and immediately regretted it. She shouldn't be prying into such a sore subject.

"I thought he liked it. I mean, I never suspected he didn't." He stared off into the distance. "All of Grandma's money was used to pay off my dad. We had to sell acreage, too. And he took it. Took everything and left."

Reagan wanted to comfort him but, in this moment, she had no idea how. "Why? Why would he do that?"

"I don't know. I've asked myself that question too many times." He shifted to face her. The pain in his eyes broke her heart. "Why would he take everything that mattered to us? Why did he leave?"

Alice began to squirm and, as if on cue, Megan got fussy.

"They're ready for a nap. I should get them back inside." Reagan moved to a kneeling position before standing. She held Alice close and caressed her little cheek. Then she settled her back in the stroller. Marc buckled Megan in the stroller, too, and folded the quilt.

"I'll help you get them inside."

She pushed the stroller, steadying it as it hit a rut, with Marc next to her. As soon as they reached the side porch, Marc unbuckled the babies, both on the verge of crying, and carried them inside. "Just leave all that out here. I'll take care of it later."

Reagan went straight to the kitchen, washed her hands and went to the fridge to pull out the bottles she'd prepared earlier. She placed them in the bottle warmer.

"Should I change them out of these dresses?" Marc called from the living room.

"Yes, please." She filled a glass of water as the thump of his footsteps up the staircase echoed. Having him help right now was a relief. Her energy always flagged in the afternoon, and her upper back muscles and arms tended to ache from carrying the twins. From upstairs, the twins' cries reached her. Neither of them wanted to get their diapers and clothes changed, apparently.

Several minutes later, Marc descended the stairs with the babies—in onesies and stretchy pants—in his arms. Both girls continued to cry. Reagan rushed over, took Megan and gently bounced her on the way to the couch. The bottles were on the end table. She held one to Megan's mouth, but she was crying hard, and it took her a few tries before she'd take the bottle.

Marc had already given Alice hers and was sitting in the recliner. As soon as the crying halted, a sense of peace filled the air.

"Reagan?" he asked.

"Yeah?"

"Thanks for listening." His face was drawn. "I feel comfortable talking to you. Comfortable being with you."

The compliment spilled down to her toes, and she gave him a smile. "You're welcome."

"When life is back to normal, I hope…well… I hope we'll still be friends."

"I hope so, too." It was on the tip of her

tongue to say *Of course we'll still be friends— why wouldn't we be?* but she couldn't in good faith say it. Because when he no longer needed help with the twins, they'd have no reason to hang out. And when the work on her building started, Marc wouldn't want to spend time with her anyhow.

With that in mind, she decided to tell it to him straight. No more keeping her plans to herself to protect his feelings. "I'm expecting the estimate for renovating my building from Ed McCaffrey this afternoon."

"Oh." Was she imagining the regret in his tone? "He's a good contractor. He'll take care of you."

His response was more than she'd expected. Yet it was less than what she'd hoped for.

"I suppose this means you'll be ready to file for permits soon."

"I suppose it does."

When he didn't say anything, she tried to bury her disappointment. She'd always been one to take things to heart. Just like she'd also always been one to see the writing on the wall.

Marc had made it abundantly clear where his priorities were. And she'd never be one of them.

She doubted friendship would ever be enough

for her, and anything more was off the table from his point of view. If she kept reminding herself she couldn't have him, maybe she'd be able to convince herself she didn't want him.

Or was it already too late?

She didn't know and didn't want to find out.

CHAPTER TEN

The following Thursday, Marc helped Brooke out of the passenger seat of the mini-van. Her shining eyes filled with tears as she gave him a grateful smile. He hadn't seen her smile like that since before Ross died. A dart of hope pierced his heart.

"It feels like I haven't been here in years." She threw both of her arms around him and hugged him tightly. Her left arm put the same pressure on him as her right. She really had made a lot of progress.

She still had a limp, but it wasn't as notice-able as it had been when she'd first arrived at the rehab center. It was astounding how much she'd healed in less than two weeks.

Mom got out of the back seat and went straight to the trunk to grab Brooke's belongings. Haul-ing two large bags, she marched past them, then gestured with her head to the minivan. "There are a few more bags back there, Marc."

"Got it." He squeezed Brooke's hand and she squeezed it back. "Let me help Brooke inside first."

He tucked her arm in his, and they slowly made their way up the porch steps and into the mudroom.

"Are you doing okay?" he asked.

"Better than okay. I'm nervous about the stairs, but I think I could have managed the porch steps fine without your help." Brooke paused to get her bearings near the doorway to the kitchen. "Before we go in there, I just want to thank you. For everything. Moving me back here after Ross died. Helping with the twins before I had the stroke. Taking care of them after the stroke. I couldn't ask for a better brother. All of this must have been exhausting for you. On top of that, I know I haven't been easy to be around for a long time."

Marc gave her another hug. "I wanted to be here for you. You went through a lot after Ross died. We didn't expect you to be floating on happy clouds all the time."

"Thanks." She placed her hand on his arm and inhaled deeply. "I'm ready for my babies. I'm going in."

"You need my help?" He wasn't sure if he

should insist on walking her into the living room, where Reagan had the girls, or let her do it on her own.

She shook her head. "No. I've been working hard. I can handle this."

"I'll get those other bags."

A few minutes later, he entered the living room as his mother fussed with pillows for Brooke, who was sitting on the couch. Brooke held Alice and was raving about how much the girls had grown in her absence, while Reagan knelt on the play mat and dangled a stuffed elephant above Megan. He'd been prepared for awkward silence, but it wasn't the case. In three seconds flat, the women had found a conversational rhythm he'd never understand.

"I think we should set up a bed in the dining room for you, honey. That way you don't have to worry about the stairs." His mom gave a pillow one final pat, then straightened and frowned as she looked around for something.

"Too much work. I don't plan on using the stairs unless I'm going to bed or showering." Brooke's tone was pleasant as she made silly faces for Alice. "Everything I need for the day is down here. I want my routine back."

"We could move more of the girls' clothes

down here for you." Reagan shifted to sit cross-legged next to Megan. "That way, if they need a complete outfit change, you wouldn't have to worry."

He caught his mother's frown as she left the room.

"That's a good idea," Brooke said. "And more diapers, more wipes. They nap in their portable cribs."

Was Brooke being too optimistic? Maybe Mom was right that Brooke should move down here until she...what? He didn't know. Wasn't sure if the limp would go away or not. But one thing he did know? Trying to take care of two babies was going to be difficult with or without the stairs.

His mother rushed back with her arms full of bedding. She dropped a folded blanket and a comforter on the couch. "You can nap here until we figure out the sleeping situation."

His mom's I-know-what's-best tone alerted him to trouble. Marc slowly inched back toward the kitchen. He wanted no part of this upcoming conversation.

Brooke glanced at Mom. "My physical therapist told me I should push myself to do everything I did before the stroke, and when I get tired, to listen to my body and rest."

"I know." His mom pursed her lips, clearly keeping her frustration in check. "But you're not ready for stairs."

"Doctor Cleese told me I was." Brooke brought Alice up to her shoulder, sat back and addressed her mother. "I know I'm not all the way there yet, especially with my left leg. But I worked really hard—hours every day—to come here and have my life back. Can't we at least try it my way for a week?"

Marc was surprised at how calm Brooke sounded.

"And what exactly is your way?" Mom asked.

"If we hire someone to come in and help with the babies until you get home from the bakery, I won't worry about not being able to handle the girls. Plus, it will free up some time for me to continue with my exercises."

"I think we need to do that no matter what." His mom took a seat in one of the chairs. "But even with the help, you going up and down the stairs makes me nervous…"

As the back-and-forth continued, he made his way through the living room to crouch near Reagan.

"Hey," he said gently.

"Hey." Her eyes twinkled.

"Thanks for being here," he said so only she could hear. "This morning went smoothly. Knowing the twins were in good hands helped a lot."

"I love watching them." She kept her voice low as she glanced at Megan with eyes full of affection. The baby was mouthing a toy.

Brooke's voice grew louder. "If you or Marc help me, I can get up those stairs at night and down them again in the morning."

"What if you need something in the night?" Mom was starting to get snippy.

His sister huffed. "I'll wake one of you up."

"You promise? I know how you are. Never wanting anyone to help. Not wanting to be a burden. This is important, Brooke."

He exchanged a charged look with Reagan. Then he held out his hand. She took it, and he helped her to her feet. "Come on. Let's get out of here for a little while."

"Are you sure?"

"Where are you going?" his mother demanded.

"We're getting some fresh air." He took a few steps, then turned back. "Why don't you both just relax and enjoy this for the moment? We'll get everything sorted out later."

Mom closed her mouth, shaking her head, and Brooke mouthed *Thank you* to him.

He hitched his chin to her and led Reagan through the kitchen to the mudroom. After she put on her shoes, they went outside. The sun was shining and a light breeze blew.

"She seems to be doing well." Reagan strolled next to him on their way to the outbuildings.

"Yeah. It's more than physical, too. There's a new spark to her that was missing before the stroke."

"What do you mean?"

"I don't know. I feel like ever since Ross died, she's been barely holding on to get through life. Mom and I were worried about her. But today? It's like having my sister back—all of her."

They continued in easy silence until they reached the fence to the horse pasture. The horses were loving this warmer weather, too. Their tails flicked as they grazed.

With one arm resting on a fence post, he turned to Reagan. He didn't know if it was the relief of having Brooke home, the realization that the worst month of his life was almost over or his growing feelings for the quiet beauty by his side, but he couldn't keep his thoughts inside anymore.

"Reagan, I couldn't have gotten through this without you."

Wind tickled the tendrils of hair around her face as she turned to him. But she didn't speak. Now that he had her alone, the thoughts he'd been avoiding all came to a head.

"I don't want this—what we have—to end."

"What do we have, Marc?" She sounded curious, not sarcastic.

"I'm not sure. I just know I like being with you and want to spend more time with you."

"As friends?"

"Yes. And more." He shrugged, staring at the horses again. Had he really admitted that? Was he ready for more?

Would he ever be ready?

"I like being with you, too." She averted her eyes.

"But?"

"But I don't think we can get close enough for more."

The words surprised him. Why would she think that?

"Why not?"

She gave him a deadpan look. "There seem to be topics that are off-limits between us."

"That's not true."

"It is true." Her probing stare made him flinch. "I can't talk to you about my plans for the building."

He couldn't refute it but… "I liked hearing about all the supplies you ordered."

"I'll give you that," she said. "But whenever I mention the building, your face gets all pinched, and I can feel the strain between us."

Okay, it was true. He wasn't sure how he could overcome it, though.

"On Tuesday, Ed and I went over the plans and estimates for the building, and I hired him for the job. He's already filed for the building permit. I wanted to tell you all this yesterday, but I didn't feel like I could. So I kept it to myself."

He hadn't realized… Wasn't really prepared for the topsy-turvy sensation it brought to his gut. It bothered him knowing she didn't feel like it was safe to talk to him. "I'm trying to be supportive."

"I'm not asking you to be supportive. I know you're not trying to make me feel bad. But, Marc, I have plans and dreams, too. I don't think I can be transparent about them with you."

"What if I try harder?"

"That's just the thing." She sighed, shaking her head. "I don't want you to have to try harder. I just want…"

"What, Reagan?" He reached for her hand and caressed it with his thumb. "What do you want?"

"I want to be important enough to you that you don't have to try."

It had cost her a lot to admit it. He could tell by the way her lips pinched together and how she wouldn't meet his eyes.

"You are important to me. I just…"

"Don't." She shook her head. "I think I want too much."

At that, he dropped her hand. Shame ripped through him. Reagan expected nothing from him or his family, and she'd sacrificed her time for weeks to help them out.

"You don't want too much. You deserve to feel important."

She flashed him a surprised glance. "I don't want to just *feel* important. I want to *be* important. Why else would I give my heart to someone?"

And that was when it hit him. He trusted

her with everything, and she didn't trust him back. She *couldn't* trust him back. He'd made it impossible for her.

"You are important, Reagan. You're important to me." He shifted closer to her. "Can't you give me a chance?"

Her tongue darted out to moisten her upper lip. Was she scared of getting hurt? He knew the feeling well.

"I don't know. I want to, but I have a funny feeling about it."

"What do you mean?" He straightened his shoulders.

"I already explained."

She had, but it wasn't enough. He wanted to talk her out of her feelings. Wanted to convince her that the two of them could work.

But, at the end of the day, she was right. There was an invisible wall separating them, and until he made peace with the fact she was opening her shop in the building his mother wanted, he doubted the wall could come down.

FRIDAY AFTERNOON, REAGAN finished unpacking the tower of boxes she'd discovered on her front porch after returning from Marc's ranch. She'd helped Brooke with the twins again today until Anne had finished up at the bakery. She had to admit it was nice getting to know Marc's sister. They'd bonded over the babies, but they'd also opened up about their losses; Brooke's with Ross and Reagan's with Cody. For only knowing the woman a short time, Reagan felt remarkably close to her.

She was getting too involved with Marc's family. The babies were so dear to her, she actually didn't like thinking about not spending time with them regularly once Brooke no longer needed help. And then there was Marc...

Loyal, hardworking, self-sacrificing and so incredibly handsome.

If he'd just let her into his inner circle, he'd realize how good they could be together. But, for whatever reason, he wouldn't. It hurt knowing that he wouldn't be happy for her when she opened the store.

She hadn't heard yet if her building permit was approved, but she figured it probably took some time. The thought of moving forward with her plans kept bringing a strange mix of excitement along with hesitation, and she wasn't sure why.

Was it Marc? Was it normal nerves? She didn't know.

She cut the tape on the box from a gourmet chocolate supplier and opened it. Pouches of various chocolates had been packed inside, and she took them out one by one. Would it hurt to open each bag and breathe in their delectable scents? Not yet. Instead, she lined them on her countertop, took a photo and just stared in wonder.

This was happening. She *was* starting her company. She *was* creating her own chocolates.

Leaving her lovely bags of chocolate on the counter, she went to the box that held one of the tempering machines she'd purchased. All of the specialty chocolates she'd learned to make danced in front of her eyes. It had been almost a month since she'd made any treats, and she missed it.

The urge to experiment couldn't be ignored. But what to start with? The rich cherry ganache she'd been playing around with in Denver came to mind. It would taste like a chocolate-covered cherry, but it would be less messy, more refined. Marc was sure to love it, since he'd mentioned that chocolate-covered cherries were his favorite.

Oh, Marc.

Things had been distant between them since their heart-to-heart after Brooke came home.

Had she been wrong to tell him how she felt? Maybe she shouldn't have been quite so honest with him.

She wasn't any good at romance. Other women made it look so easy. They seemed to know how to flirt. They knew what to say and how to get guys to notice them.

Then there was her. Unable—or unwilling—to flirt. Never really knowing what to say. No clue how to get a guy to notice her and too blunt for anything to develop if one did.

Maybe the timing was off anyhow. Erica was right. Reagan had spent so much time and energy helping Marc with the twins, she'd begun to lose sight of what was important to her.

Blowing out a breath, she eyed all of the supplies now lining her kitchen counters. Then her attention wandered to the walls—the boring taupe walls. She'd been living here for a month and there wasn't a stamp of her identity or her style anywhere to be found.

It was time to change that.

She repacked all of the supplies in the boxes, then stacked them along the wall in the dining room adjacent to the kitchen. As much as she itched to play around with her new toys and start dipping chocolates, practical matters came first.

A trip to the hardware store to get paint swatches was in order. Reagan found her athletic shoes, pulled on a lightweight jacket, grabbed her purse and headed outside. Before she descended the porch steps, she paused to consider the covered porch. The boards were in good shape, but they needed to be stained or painted, and the faded light gray paint on the columns and rails was chipping.

Another thing to tackle soon.

She skipped down the steps onto the curved sidewalk that led to the driveway and turned back to take in the house. It was a Craftsman-style, one-story bungalow with dark gray siding. Tilting her head, she studied it. The exterior would be more appealing if she had the porch and columns painted white. With a little TLC, the house would pop. Plus, the porch needed some furniture and a wreath on the door to make it more inviting.

Reagan pivoted and made her way down the sidewalk toward Center Street. Her to-do list for the house was growing. Before today, it had all felt too overwhelming to think about. But now, for whatever reason, she was ready.

As soon as she finished selecting the paint swatches, she was going home, taking out the tempering machine and testing the chocolate she'd bought.

R. Mayer Chocolates, here we come!

IN AND OUT. He'd be back home before he knew it. That was what he'd told himself when his mom had handed him a list of things to buy for the twins. Marc had memorized the baby aisle of the grocery store at this point. It wasn't as if they were in desperate need of diapers. His mom was back to micromanaging everything, and he didn't mind. The sooner they were all back to normal, the better.

Marc tossed the bags into the back seat of his truck, shut the door and stood there with his face to the sky. The fresh air grounded him. With Trevor on duty at the ranch and his mom, sister and the twins doing okay, he realized he didn't want to return home right now. In fact, he wouldn't mind a break from the place.

He stepped up into the truck and fired the engine. How long had it been since he'd done anything for himself? If it didn't involve the ranch, the planning commission, the legacy club, his mother, his sister or the babies, he didn't take the time for it.

Maybe he needed to make time for his life.

There was only one thing he wanted to do on a fine Friday night like this.

Visit Reagan.

He backed the truck out of the spot and turned onto Center Street. He missed her. Hadn't spoken to her since their conversation yesterday. He'd already been out checking cattle when she'd arrived this morning, and she'd left before he was finished for the day.

Sure, he could have waited until she'd gotten there to talk to her, but he hadn't. He'd been mad at himself. Because she was right. He'd made the topic of her building off-limits. And he didn't see it changing anytime soon.

The thought of his mom's dream never being fulfilled hurt in a way he couldn't put into words. He wanted his mom to be happy. So much had been taken from her. Was it wrong of him to want her to have what she deserved? Just once in her life?

After Reagan's permit was approved, his mom's vision for her expanded bakery would be over. He'd have to get used to the thought.

Because Reagan showed no signs of changing her mind. He didn't have the heart to try to change it anymore, either.

He'd just have to get over it.

Soon, he was pulling into her driveway. As he got out, he took in the neighborhood. The street was lined with older bungalows. Her house held no personal touches, no welcoming decorations. He climbed the porch steps. Not even a welcome mat.

It hit him again how much time she'd spent helping him and his family when she could have been working on her own home, her own plans. Without overthinking it, he knocked. And looked over his shoulder as he waited. She might not be home. He knocked again.

The door opened, and Reagan's eyes grew round as she smiled. "What are you doing here?"

"I was in the neighborhood." His spirits lifted at the warm glow of the light behind her and the sound of relaxing music from inside.

"Come in." She held the door open, and he brushed past her, wanting to pause and take her hand in his. As he looked in her eyes, all he could think was how much he wouldn't mind kissing her.

He forced his feet forward, and she locked the door behind her. It smelled amazing in here, like walking smack-dab into a brownie.

"I'm in the middle of trying out some new equipment." She padded confidently to the kitchen and pointed to the stools at the U-shaped butcher-block counter. "Have a seat."

She stood on the other side of it and pulled on a pair of plastic gloves. Then she selected a small oval of what looked like cookie dough, balanced it on two upturned fingers, dipped it into a machine with melted chocolate, shook off the excess and flipped her fingers over to set it on a parchment-paper-lined tray. She did a little swirly thing with her finger on the top of it.

"What are you making?" After taking a seat, he let his elbows drop onto the counter and craned his neck to peek at the chocolate. What he wouldn't give to dip a finger into that chocolate and have a lick.

"Vanilla buttercreams." She was already midway through dipping another chocolate. "I wanted to see how the new chocolate-tempering machine works. Then I found myself whipping up a batch of buttercream centers, and by the time the chocolate was melted, the centers were chilled, and here I am."

"You do them all by hand?" he asked.

"For the most part. I pour the barks into molds, and I have a few specialty chocolates I use molds for as well."

"What happens after they're all dipped?" His mouth watered as more candies joined the others on the tray.

"They get chilled. I wish I had my temperature-controlled displays. My refrigerator is too cold. But these are just samples anyway. Go ahead and try one if you want."

He didn't need to be told twice. He reached over and popped one in his mouth. The chocolate hit him right away. Then the light texture of the cream and the rich vanilla flavor burst through right after.

It was the best chocolate he'd ever eaten.

"Wow." He eyed the rest of the tray. "That was delicious."

"Thank you." Her smile lit her eyes. "Have more. I don't want them to go to waste."

"What other kinds do you normally make?" he asked as he selected another one.

"The chocolatier who taught me had a set selection he kept on hand all the time. He added new items for the various holidays. I'm going to use a similar strategy, but I haven't settled on the exact chocolates I'll choose to be my regulars."

As she finished dipping the batch, she explained about the types of chocolates and caramels she liked to make. When she was done, she selected one of the chocolates and took a bite, then chewed with a thoughtful expression.

He wasn't sure what she was experiencing with her bite, but from the way one eye narrowed, he guessed it wasn't the taste-bud explosion he'd had.

"I was afraid of that. It needs more vanilla. I'll have to order vanilla beans and make my own extract."

"Really? I thought it was amazing."

It must have pleased her because she gave him a shy shrug. "I appreciate that." Then she began cleaning up. He offered to help, but she laughed and claimed there wasn't room for both of them. She had a point. They chatted about the twins as she tidied the counters and cleaned the equipment. When she was done, she wiped her hands dry on a kitchen towel.

"Have you eaten supper?" he asked.

"No." Her nose scrunched. "I haven't thought that far ahead."

"Do you want to order a pizza? Cowboy John's is the best." He tensed, waiting for her response.

"Sounds good to me."

"I'll order us one. What do you want on it?" He almost tripped as he got off the stool and searched through the contacts on his phone.

"Do they have a supreme? I like all the toppings."

"They do." He called in the order, then put his phone in his pocket and stood there awkwardly. "I like your house."

"I haven't done much with it." She began walking to the living room and waved for him to follow her. "It's more comfortable in here."

He passed into a cozy living room. A brick fireplace took up part of one wall. The dark gray sectional and matching chair and ottoman looked new. The end tables were bare except for lamps and a tissue box. A large television in the corner had him grinning. Big televisions meant good viewing when football season came back around.

"I still need to decorate." She sat on one end of the sectional and curled her legs under her body. "I finally got over to the hardware store earlier for paint swatches."

"Oh, yeah? What colors are you thinking?"

He sat at the other end and shifted to face her better.

"I'll show you." She scrambled to her feet and left the room. She was back within seconds. After resuming her spot on the couch, she handed him the swatches and scooted over to the cushion next to him, pointing to the squares in his hand. "I like this one, but I think it will end up too pastel in here. I should go with a darker shade."

"The darker shade would look good in here." He couldn't think straight with her this close to him.

"You think so? I could decorate with these accent colors." She shuffled through the swatches until she found the ones she was looking for.

"Accent colors, huh?" He didn't know much about those.

"Yeah, for pillows and throws and little items for the mantel." A dreamy expression crossed her face as she leaned in even closer to him and tucked her legs under once more. He could smell her perfume, along with a lingering chocolate aroma. Her hair was *this* close to his shoulder. It would be so simple to reach out and touch it. "It will feel more like home when I decorate it."

Even in its undecorated state, something about it felt like home to him now. He wasn't sure if it was the chocolate, the background music or Reagan herself, but he found himself relaxing more with every second that passed. The general sense of calm had been missing in his life for quite some time.

"Do you ever get nervous?" He inched his hand toward hers until their fingers touched. "Living by yourself in a new town?"

She didn't move her hand away. "A little. But not too much. I know if anything goes wrong, Erica and Dalton would be here in a snap."

"You can call me, too, you know." He wanted to be the one she called. Wanted to protect her, to help her, to fix anything she needed.

"I know."

Their eyes met and the urge to touch her was so strong, he no longer fought it. He tenderly touched her cheek, then pushed a lock of hair behind her ear.

"I want to kiss you, Reagan. Tell me I shouldn't." His voice was low; his gaze locked on her lips.

She shook her head, her eyes golden, and he didn't hesitate. He pressed his lips to hers. They were soft. So soft. Tender, like her personality. He needed this.

He needed her.

His hands cupped her face as he deepened the kiss. Sensations swirled. She tasted like chocolate, and her skin was smooth, satiny. His heart pounded. Impressions flashed.

Reagan was sunshine, determination, hope and joy.

How in just a few weeks' time had she become so necessary to him?

The doorbell rang, and he reluctantly let her go. He searched her eyes and was reassured by what he saw in them. She didn't hate him, that was for sure.

"Pizza's here." The corner of her mouth quirked up.

He stood and bent to kiss her one more time. "I'll take care of it."

He wanted to be the one who took care of anything she needed. He wanted to be the guy who took care of her.

As he approached the front door, questions swam to the surface. What if he couldn't? What if he didn't have enough to give? What if he tried and ended up neglecting his mother, sister and the twins in the process?

Marc opened the front door. He'd worry about all that another time. This was the first Friday night he'd enjoyed himself in ages. He planned to make the most of it and get the big answers later.

CHAPTER ELEVEN

How was it possible she still hadn't gotten any word on her building permit?

Over a week later, on Monday morning, Reagan checked her phone, but there weren't any missed calls or texts from Ed or Henry. There was a text from her mom. A picture of her nieces in matching sundresses and cowboy boots. She was definitely having that one printed and framed. But even their adorableness couldn't distract her from this antsy sensation.

It had been ten days—but who was counting?—since Marc had stopped by so unexpectedly. The pizza had been delicious. The company? Phenomenal. And the kiss? Had been everything she'd dreamed Hot Cowboy's kiss would be and more. She hadn't stopped thinking about it...or him.

She let out a happy sigh and returned to the task at hand—making chocolates for Clem and

Slim. She dipped a monster of a strawberry into the chocolate. Today was the first day she hadn't gone out to Marc's ranch to help with the babies. One of Brooke's friends had offered to help with the twins all week. As much as Reagan enjoyed taking care of the girls, it had been nice to sleep in and sip coffee in her pj's on the couch for as long as she'd wanted this morning.

Would Marc call her later? He'd been making an extra effort with her since their kiss. Each morning when she arrived at the ranch, he lingered over his coffee to chat. And when his mother arrived in the afternoon, he would meet Reagan outside as she headed to her car. They'd talk for a while. On Wednesday afternoon, they'd even toured the ranch on horseback. Reagan had always loved riding—as long as it was slow. She'd never been the galloping or rodeo-competing type. Then, Thursday, on a whim, she'd invited Marc over for supper.

It had been so nice, so easy. She'd made tacos, and they'd talked about all kinds of things. Childhood memories. Favorite foods. Movies they liked. And they'd gone deeper, too. About how hard life had been for him after his dad had left them. And she'd shared how much pain she'd felt when Cody cut off all communication from the family in the months before he died. Over the years, she'd made peace with it, but every now and then she still wondered if she could have done more.

Marc made her feel safe. He listened without giving advice—unheard of in the family she'd grown up in—and he made her feel interesting, pretty, even talented. All the things her family had assured her she was, but until she'd met Marc, she hadn't quite believed.

The only problem? He still couldn't bring himself to discuss her building. Instead, they tiptoed around the subject. At some point, it would come to a head, and they'd either continue exploring their relationship or it would end in a spectacular explosion.

She hated explosions. Wasn't a fan of conflict, in general.

Reagan dipped and swirled the strawberry, then set it on the parchment-lined tray with the others. Slim was going to love these. They'd met for an hour earlier this week to tie up loose ends. He'd simplified everything, and she appreciated his patience with her. Even Erica was impressed with all the progress she'd made with Slim's help.

As she dipped another strawberry, her mind

went back to the corner building and all the changes she and Ed had discussed. She had no doubt it would be welcoming and lovely when it was all said and done. But she could still see the vision of her chocolate shop in the bakery. And that was the one she continued to dream about.

Reagan lifted the lid on the square metal container of pink-colored white chocolate in one of the melting machines. It looked ready. She drizzled it over the chocolate-covered strawberries, then repeated the process with the red-colored white chocolate.

Why did she keep thinking about the bakery? Was it simply a distraction? Or was it more?

She shook her head. Too late now. She'd signed the contract with McCaffrey Construction. It made no sense to be fantasizing about a much smaller building tucked into the heart of downtown. Easily missed. Easily passed by.

But she kept seeing the floating shelves she'd install on the wall to the left of the entrance, and the entire front wall replaced with glass, bringing in light and allowing anyone walking past to see inside.

She wiped her hands on her apron. Why was

she doing this to herself? Why was she fantasizing about the wrong building?

If she asked anyone—right here, right now— if it made more sense to open R. Mayer Chocolates in her building or in the space where Annie's Bakery currently resided, they would laugh out loud and tell her the corner building. No question.

And if Erica or her mother knew the thoughts she was having, they'd blame it on her growing attraction to Marc. They'd tell her she was falling in love. That she was only having these fantasies about the bakery because she knew it would make Marc happy.

Would they be right?

She didn't know. And she didn't want to examine it too closely.

She'd stick to her plan. It was too late to back out now even if she wanted to. And the truth was, she didn't know what she wanted. All she knew was that whatever was growing between her and Marc felt precious…and she didn't want it to end.

"Hey, Marc, you got a minute?"

"Sure. What's going on?" Marc paused as Henry Zane came out of his office at city hall

Monday. Marc had just finished catching up on work for the planning and zoning commission. He hadn't had much time to deal with it since Brooke's stroke.

Henry's cheeks were red and he seemed flustered as he approached. He waved the paperwork in his hand. "Could you do me a favor? See that this gets to Reagan Mayer. She's still helping out with the twins at your ranch, right?"

"Most days, yes."

"Great." The man's face relaxed in relief. "I'm running late, and Angie'll have my head if I even think about canceling our trip to the city this afternoon. The permit slipped my mind last week, and I don't want Reagan to have to wait another day. Ed's out of town, too, or I'd give it to him."

Marc's lungs compressed, and a funny feeling rose up from his feet to his head—a hard feeling. Like he was turning to stone as Henry spoke. He'd known this day was coming, but he'd been putting it off, trying to pretend it would be okay.

And all he could see was his mom's pale, pinched face on the day the divorce was final. She'd turned to Marc and said so softly he'd almost missed it, "He could have left me before your grandma died. He waited one week after the funeral to tell me he was leaving. It's like he was waiting to take my inheritance."

"You okay?" Henry gave him a questioning look.

"Yes. Fine." He thrust his hand out to take the papers from him. "I'll take care of it."

"Great. You tell her if she has any questions, I'll be in my office on Wednesday."

"Will do." Marc nodded goodbye and marched down the hall, through the front entrance and straight to his truck. Once inside, he tossed the permit onto the passenger seat and just sat there.

What was he going to tell his mother? It wasn't like she didn't know Reagan was opening a chocolate shop in the corner building. She did. Everyone in town knew about it. But he hadn't brought up the subject, and neither had she. They'd been focused on Brooke and Megan and Alice.

But they'd also been helpless to change the situation, and maybe that had held them back, too. Sometimes he felt like the only thing that had gotten his mom through those rough early years in her tiny bakery was her dream of expanding—and not any old spot would do. The goal had always been the corner building.

And now he had to go tell Reagan that *her* dream was about to come true at the expense of his mother's. As much as he cared about Reagan, as much as he craved her company, as much as he enjoyed being with her and respected her, he didn't think she wanted that building as badly as his mother did.

His breathing grew shallow as scenarios raced through his head. Would his mom blame him for not talking Reagan out of it? Would she hold a grudge against Reagan?

He'd grown so close to her, was falling harder for her every day. What if it caused tension in his family? If his mother and sister resented Reagan, how could he in fairness offer her anything more than friendship?

Pull yourself together. He started the truck and drove away.

He'd give Reagan the permit and talk to his mom later. She was mature. She'd handle it. But it would break her heart, and he'd already seen that heart broken before.

It took less than five minutes to get to Reagan's house. As he got out of his truck, he tried to come up with something to say that would be appropriate, but words failed him.

His footsteps slowed the closer he got, and by the time he'd made it up the porch steps and knocked on her door, there was a sour taste in his mouth and his body felt heavy.

The door opened and Reagan beamed at him. She was so beautiful, he could only stare. Her beauty shone from within, and he wanted so badly to be the man she needed right now. It would be the easiest thing in the world to hand her the permit and take her in his arms and congratulate her with a kiss. To take her out to supper to celebrate. Let her tell him everything she knew about chocolates for as long as her heart desired.

But he couldn't work his mouth into a smile. Couldn't muster a whisper of enthusiasm.

"What's wrong? Did something happen?" She frowned as she stepped onto the porch in front of him. "Is it Brooke? The babies?"

"Nothing's wrong." Shame washed over him as it registered that her first thoughts were for his family. "It's good news." His voice sounded strangled.

"It is?"

"Yes. Henry Zane asked me to drop this off to

you." He handed her the papers, not taking his gaze off her face. "Your permit. Congratulations."

She scanned the top paper quickly, and a smile flashed, then disappeared.

"Thank you for dropping it off."

"Sure thing." He backed up a step, letting his head drop. *Just leave. Go home. Don't make this worse.* "I'll leave you to celebrate."

Reagan didn't answer, and when he glanced at her, her expression brimmed with hurt.

"I'll just go." He started to turn.

"Wait."

He gave her his full attention.

"Why can't you let me have this?" she asked quietly. "It's my career. I do want to celebrate. I'd like to celebrate it with you, but I know better."

He swallowed and shifted his jaw. "You won. Let's leave it at that."

"Won?" Her nose scrunched in confusion. "This wasn't a competition. It's not a game with winners and losers."

"Tell that to my mom." He opened his hands. "Because she's lost an awful lot over the years."

"I'm not the one who took anything from her."

"You kind of did."

"Is that how you see it?" She raised herself to full height, which was still several inches shorter than he was. "Your mother never owned the corner building. It was never hers. And it is mine. I own it."

"You inherited it."

"Yeah, so?" Her face was growing splotchy and he hated that he was doing this. This conversation was all wrong, and yet he couldn't stop making it worse. "It's still mine."

"She deserves it."

A breeze rippled between them, and the light in her eyes went dark. She stepped back, crossing her arms over her chest. "And I don't. Got it."

Now he really did feel like the world's biggest jerk. "I didn't say that."

"Marc, you've said it in so many words since the day we met. I just chose to ignore it. But we both know it's there."

He ground his teeth together, unable to deny it.

"I'm never going to be as important to you as your mom and your sister. I won't even be as important to you as the twins. And I deserve better than that." At the pain in her voice, his heart clenched. Were those tears in her eyes? "I think you should leave."

"Reagan…" He reached out to touch her arm, but she jerked it away, shaking her head. "You're important to me. You are."

"Not enough. I'm…" She blinked away the tears. "I'm not okay with this. I thought we had something special, and my feelings for you are real. I don't give my heart to anyone lightly, and I'm not giving it to someone who can't be happy for me. So why don't you just get out of here? I'm done."

Before he could say another word, she'd stepped back inside the house. The loud slam of the door rattled him. He stalked down the porch steps to his truck. Roared out of her drive and onto the street.

He was furious. Not with Reagan. With himself.

Because every word she'd said was true. And he hated himself for it.

REAGAN LEANED HER back against the front door as tremors rippled through her body. *No regrets, no regrets.*

She was full of regrets.

And she'd do it all again in a heartbeat. She'd

offer to babysit the twins. She'd get to know Marc. She'd sit on her couch and discuss paint swatches and let him kiss her. Yes, she'd do it all.

Still, how could she have been so delusional? Here she'd thought Marc cared about her. She'd hoped he'd eventually move past the problem of the corner building.

But she'd been wrong. Oh, so wrong.

And now what was she going to do about Brooke and the twins? She wanted to help out, but the entire family would probably hate her by morning.

What did they want her to do? Hand over the deed to Anne with a "you had mental dibs on it, so it's yours"? Wasn't happening.

She pushed away from the door and grabbed her keys and purse. There was no way she was sitting here alone and crying for hours. This situation called for her best friend. Erica would know what to say. Erica would know what to do. Erica would feed her Gemma's coffee cake and let her cry to her heart's content.

Fifteen minutes later—yes, she'd exceeded the speed limit and didn't care—she pulled into Erica's ranch and ran up to her front door. Erica opened it immediately, took one look at her and dragged her inside.

"What's wrong? What happened?"

"I got my permit." The words were choppy.

"That's good news."

"Marc didn't think so." And then the tears came. Erica hugged her until the sobs subsided, then led her down the hall into the kitchen.

"Have a seat." She practically forced Reagan onto a stool at the huge island. "I'll brew the coffee."

Reagan dug in her purse for a tissue, and there was so much stuff in there, it made her cry even harder. "I can't even find a tissue. I'm such a mess. No wonder I'm still single."

"What?" Erica dismissed her with a wave. "That's not true. You are not a mess. And if you weren't at Marc's ranch all the time, I guarantee the single guys around here would be lining up to ask you on a date."

"No one has ever lined up to ask me for a date." Reagan was trying to pull herself together, but she hiccuped through the entire sentence. "Guys don't like me. And I thought Marc did, but I'm nothing to him, and I was stupid for thinking he might be the one."

"You're not stupid. You're smart and beautiful

and kind and creative." Erica finished starting
the pot of coffee and left the room momentarily.
She returned with a box of tissues that she set
in front of Reagan. "Here."

"His entire family is going to hate me." She
pulled three tissues out at warp speed and proceeded to wipe her eyes and blow her nose
with them.

"What? No. They love you. You've been such
a help to them."

"I'm not going to be able to help with the
twins, and Brooke and I were starting to become friends."

Her sister moved to the other side of the island and took mugs out of the cupboard. "Is
that what you're worried about? The twins?"

Was that what she was worried about? "No.
I can handle being cut out of their lives. It'll
hurt, though, and I really do want to get closer
to Brooke."

"But?" Erica unwrapped a plate filled with
blueberry muffins and lemon-drizzle pound
cake.

"But getting over Marc is going to be hard."
She'd kept her growing feelings for him to herself, and acknowledging them now was both
painful and a relief.

Erica inhaled quickly and pointed her finger at Reagan. "You fell in love with him."

Had she? She squirmed, averting her eyes to the counter.

"And that jerk had the nerve to make you feel bad about getting the permit for a building *you own*?" The last two words seemed to boom through the air. "To think I thought he'd be good for you. And what does he do? Put his mother first. Like your shop doesn't matter. Who does he think he is? He doesn't own the store." Erica continued muttering all the things Reagan, too, had been thinking. She poured cream into the mugs, followed by steaming hot coffee, then set one of them in front of Reagan. "Don't worry. It's decaf."

The mug had swirly words spelling I Can't Even.

I can't even. Exactly. And Reagan gave in to another round of tears.

"Here, have a piece of Gemma's lemon-drizzle cake. It's melt-in-your-mouth good." Erica shoved the plate her way, and Reagan selected a small slice. "If you want to know what I think, he should be on his knees thanking you for all you've done for his family. He should personally be offering to help you remodel the building.

He should be shouting to the hills how wonderful you are."

The lemon-drizzle slice fell out of her hand to the counter. Wouldn't that have been nice? To have him appreciate her? Be supportive of her? Offer to help her?

She'd fallen in love with the wrong guy.

Erica's right. I fell in love with him. How stupid could I be?

"Why don't you tell me everything?" Erica perched on a stool kitty-corner from Reagan and glued her attention to her. "Did you two kiss?"

Her cheeks were hotter than the scalding coffee she hadn't even attempted to sip.

"You did!" Erica reached over for a muffin. "Was this like an everyday thing? He'd come back from the ranch and see you with the twins, and he just couldn't help himself?"

"No! Nothing like that." The burst of indignation chased away the threat of tears. "It's just…we've gotten to know each other. We've been spending a lot of time together, and one night after Brooke came home, he stopped by. We ordered pizza and talked and…"

"He kissed you." Her eyes grew wide. The

mug was practically dangling between her hands. "Go on."

"Over the past week or two, Marc and I have had more time to connect."

"Any red flags?"

"Only my building. Everything else is just right."

"But that's a big wrong."

"It is. It's the biggest wrong. I can't look past it anymore. I tried. I just wouldn't mention the building. The funny thing is, he had no problem talking about the chocolate."

"You felt like you had to hide something important. Oh, Reag, I hate that for you."

"I do, too. I should have known better. I *knew* the topic bothered him. I knew how much he wanted his mother to have the building. I shouldn't have let myself get close to him."

Erica lifted one shoulder. "You're better than me. I always get too close."

"But you don't put up with any nonsense."

"Come on. You and I both know that isn't true. I put up with mountains of nonsense when I was married to Jamie. Dalton is different. He's no nonsense in the best possible way."

"I wish I could have what you guys have." It was hard for her to admit it. "I wish I was savvy like you and smarter and had just the right comeback when people are rude."

"Me? No. You're way better. You're kind to everyone. Your creativity astounds me. You have more talent than I could ever hope for."

"But I had to get help with every tiny business detail. And I knew Marc resented me because of the building, but I ignored it. How dumb."

Erica reached over and squeezed her hand. "We all get help with things we're not good at. That's normal. And I ignored a lot of things I shouldn't have with Jamie and even a few things with Dalton. We're human. It's okay."

"Thanks." Her shoulders slumped, and she took another sip of coffee. Nibbled on a bite of the lemon cake. It really was melt-in-your-mouth good.

"You know, Marc is kind of a mystery." Erica tapped her fingernail on the side of the mug. "From what I've been told, he'd never gotten serious with a woman around here. Doesn't really date much, either."

Reagan gave her a glum glance. "So?"

"So, you're the first woman who's gotten this far with him."

"Well, another woman will have to get him over the finish line. I'm done with him."

She was, too. She only had a few rules about dating. No cheating. Mutual respect. And she refused to be anything less than number one in his life.

Two out of three wasn't good enough. And she wasn't changing her mind. She and Marc were through. For good.

CHAPTER TWELVE

"Mom, we have to talk." Marc waited for his mother to get settled on the couch later that night. Brooke had gone to bed half an hour ago, and the twins had been asleep for a while. This conversation needed to be between the two of them with no interruptions. And it had been gnawing at him ever since he'd left Reagan's place.

"What's going on?" She unfolded a fuzzy throw blanket and spread it over her legs.

"Reagan's building permit was approved today." He leaned forward in the recliner so he'd have a full view of her face. She nodded, then closed her eyes as her shoulders began to shake in silent sobs.

He went to her side, sat next to her and put his arm around her shoulders. He'd known this would be hard.

"I'm sorry, Mom."

She turned to him, wrapping her arms around him. He held her while she cried. Then she took a shaky breath and pulled herself together.

"I guess it's really over," she said. "The dream is over."

He wanted to tell her it wasn't over, that he'd find a way...but he couldn't.

"I wish I could have changed her mind," he said. "I tried, but I didn't try hard enough."

"No, Marc—" she shook her head "—this isn't Reagan's fault. She has her dreams, too. It's just... I'd put so much stock into mine."

"You deserve to open your bakery there. You had every right to dream about it."

She gave him a shrug that broke his heart. "It's not the first time I've had to let go of a dream. It will be okay. I'll just keep the bakery where it is and—"

"It's too small. It's always been too small." He ran his hand over his hair. "And if Dad hadn't taken everything, you wouldn't have had to open it in the first place."

"I'll always be glad I opened the bakery. I'm proud of my work."

"I know." He sighed. "I didn't mean to imply..."

"It's okay. I know what you meant. And your father didn't take everything," she said quietly.

"How can you say that?" His voice rose. "He made you sell off so much land. He took Grandma's assets, and he had no right to them. No right at all."

"I had you and Brooke. I kept half of the assets."

"*Your* assets."

"Legally, both of ours." She shrugged. "I survived. We survived."

"Yeah, and it was hard. You shouldn't have had to go through all that. Months of barely any sleep, worrying if we would lose this place. Loans and hard work and trying to settle accounts until business picked up. Your dream of moving the bakery should have come true. I wanted to make it come true."

"God provided for us."

"He hasn't done a very good job lately." He regretted it as soon as he said it, but he could no longer deny his feelings.

7"Brooke lost the love of her life. Then she had a stroke. You both had to move back here. I know how much that cost you. It hasn't been easy driving all the way to town before sunrise. I just wanted you to have this. I wanted the building to be yours."

"Life isn't easy. And, yes, Brooke lost Ross.

She also had a stroke. But she has beautiful twin baby girls. She has a big brother who moved her back home and helps take care of her and the girls' needs. She's working hard to recover. You can see how well she gets around. We need to be thankful for that."

"I am thankful." Not thankful enough, obviously.

"She could have died. Have you considered that?"

"Of course I've considered it! I thought of nothing else the week she was in the hospital."

"Then stop looking at the negatives and focus on the positives. We have our Brooke back. That's all that really matters."

He clamped his mouth shut. While his mom was right about Brooke, other things mattered, too, and he couldn't pretend they didn't.

"I prayed for over fifteen years for that building, Marc, and it's time for me to accept that God has other plans for it. I'll move on. I will. Don't worry about me." She got to her feet and stood in front of him. "I'm glad Reagan is putting something special in the building. We need to be happy for her. Look at all she's done for us."

"Happy for her?" What was his mom thinking? "I'm not happy for her."

She gave him a sharp look. "What do you mean? I have eyes. I can see you two have been getting close."

"Not anymore."

"She's good for you. She's the first woman you've let in—even a sliver. I hope you aren't pushing her away because of the building."

"I can't get past it. I need time. I'm too upset to even think straight at the moment."

"I love you, Marc. I want you to be happy. I want to see you settled. Reagan is good for you. Why would you push her away?"

"All these years, all you've talked about is expanding your bakery. And I told her how important it was to you."

"You can't expect her to toss out her plans for me. That's ridiculous."

"It's not ridiculous. Your dream is important. You're important. You and Brooke and Megan and Alice. All of you. Your happiness is important to me." The words came out more rapidly than he'd intended.

His mom frowned, tilted her head and studied him. He wasn't sure what she saw, but it didn't seem to be good.

"Marc, you've put our family first for over fifteen years. Maybe I expected too much from you. Maybe I put too much pressure on you. But my happiness has never been your responsibility. Nor has Brooke's. And don't get me started on the twins. We're all responsible for our own happiness."

He wanted to refute her but, as the words sank in, he couldn't.

"What's really going on with you? What are you afraid of?"

That you'll see I failed you and you'll leave me. Just like Dad did. I should have done more. Should have been more. Then he wouldn't have left and taken so much of what mattered to us.

He sat in the chair, propped his elbows on his knees and let his forehead fall into his hands.

"Honey, I love you. I'll get over my disappointment about the bakery. All those times we discussed expanding it filled me with optimism. But I never intended to make you feel responsible for making it happen."

"I know you didn't. I put it on myself."

"You've put a lot on yourself over the years, haven't you?" The words came out softly. "Maybe too much. Maybe Brooke and the girls should move to town with me. It might be easier for all of us."

"No!" He couldn't believe his mom was threatening to move out. "This is exactly what I was afraid would happen."

"What are you talking about?"

"I couldn't get the building for you, and now you're threatening to cut me out of your life just like Dad did!" As soon as the words left his mouth, he froze, stunned at the realization he actually believed it.

All these years, he'd never allowed himself to face his worst fears. And here they were. Tumbling out of his mouth.

"I would never cut you out of my life. Never." Mom cupped his cheek with her hand, and the outpouring of love from her eyes brought his anxiety down a notch. "Nothing you do could ever make me not love you. You and Brooke are my life. It would be like cutting out my heart. You've never had to earn my love. It's yours. It's always been yours."

As the words seeped in, he felt a sense of peace that had been missing since he was sixteen.

"I only suggested Brooke moving because it's

a lot having us all here. You deserve to have your own life, too."

"You guys are my life, Ma."

She patted his arm. "I know. I'm blessed. But there's room in your life for one more. Don't shut Reagan out because of us."

He didn't respond. Couldn't respond.

He'd already shut Reagan out. He didn't see a way back in.

Even if he did, he wasn't sure he was ready. It was easy for Mom to talk about making room for one more, but he'd already burned his bridges with Reagan and, unlike his mom and sister, he doubted she'd be able to overlook his shortcomings.

He'd fallen in love with her. And he'd hurt her. Chosen his mom's happiness over hers.

He never should have gotten close to Reagan Mayer. He'd known all along it would end badly. And it had.

THE TWENTY-FOUR-HOUR RULE for hosting a pity party had come and gone, and Reagan was no closer to moving off her couch and changing out of her stretched-out, faded leggings than she'd been yesterday. She didn't care, either. So what if it was late Wednesday morning? She didn't have a job. Didn't have any place to be.

A fresh batch of sadness whipped up to fill her heart.

If she had her way, she'd be with Brooke and the twins right this minute. She'd be telling Megan stories and kissing Alice's little cheeks. She'd be breathlessly anticipating the moment when Marc would join her in the driveway so they could catch up the way he had before he'd given her the permit.

But, no. Brooke had the baby help covered this week, and who knew what would happen after that? Marc hadn't reached out. No texts, no calls, no apologies. So why did she keep checking her phone?

Earlier, she'd gotten four texts and one phone call. The texts, in order, had been from Erica, her mom, Erica again, and the final one had been a reminder for a dental cleaning back in Sunrise Bend she'd forgotten to cancel. The phone call had been from Ed McCaffrey to let her know he'd be back in town on Monday to go over the timeline of her project.

As if she even cared at this point.

She wasn't sure if Marc had permanently tainted the corner building for her or if her irrational vision for opening her store in his mom's bakery was the culprit. Either way, the thought of renovating brought her no joy.

Her cell phone rang, and she kicked off the throw blanket tangled around her legs. Tripped as she got to her feet and lunged for the phone.

"Hello?"

"Hey, Reagan, how are you?" Her brother Blaine was on the line. He rarely called. She didn't want to panic, but her mind went straight to his two-month-old baby, Ethan.

"Is something wrong? Is it Ethan?"

"Nothing's wrong. Ethan's getting bigger every day. Wish he'd sleep a little more. Maddie's obsessed with him. Thinks he's her real-life doll." His chuckle calmed her nerves. She traced her steps back to her spot on the couch and sat down. "I haven't talked to you in a while. Thought I'd see how everything's going."

For years, Blaine had been her rock. Even before he'd married Sienna, he'd always included Reagan in his plans. She missed him. Right now, she missed her entire family, especially her mom, whom she'd talked to several times yesterday about the Marc situation.

"It's going." She didn't trust herself to say more without falling apart.

"You don't sound very happy."

"I'm not."

A long pause had her closing her eyes. She didn't want Blaine to worry, and he was the type to worry about her. But she also didn't want to hide anything from him.

"Is it serious?" he asked.

"Until a few days ago, it was going great here. I've been helping out with the cutest little babies—identical twin girls—I'm sure Mom has told you about them. And everything is moving along for the chocolate shop."

"What's wrong, then?" His low voice soothed her nerves.

"Everything." She fought back her emotions. "Marc, the twins' uncle, and I grew close, but he's not the right guy for me—"

"What did he do?" There was an edge to his tone.

"Nothing. He and I had different ideas on how my building should be used."

"What business is it of his? If this guy is bothering you, say the word and I'll leave right now to have a talk with him. In fact, I'll bring Jet with me."

Like that would go over well. Her two over-protective brothers riding into town to confront Marc? Her oldest brother, Jet, once had a stare-down with a classmate in high school who'd nicknamed her Scarecrow, and the kid had been so intimidated he'd avoided her in the halls from that day forward.

"No. It's not like that. His mom has always dreamed of moving her bakery into my building."

"I hope you told him 'too bad.' That's *your* building."

She let out a miserable sigh. "I did."

"Good."

"But, Blaine…" She'd always been able to confide in him. Out of all her family, Blaine was the safest person to tell how she really felt. "I don't know. Lately, I don't feel right about the building."

"That does it. I'm coming down there and talking to this guy myself. He cannot push you around."

She could feel a tension headache coming on. "He's not pushing me around. This feeling has nothing to do with him."

"Then what is it?" And that was why she loved Blaine. He was willing to listen.

"It doesn't feel right." Those four words brought relief. Admitting it—out loud—was like finding the key that fit.

"What doesn't feel right about it?" Anyone else in her family would have assured her she just had cold feet and that once the renovations were finished, it would be perfect. Not Blaine.

"It's bigger than I need. I have a floor plan that would be the envy of anyone opening a retail shop, yet all I can think about is this other building. It's half the size and wedged between two businesses. Makes no sense, I know. But when I go in there, I can picture my shop down to the tiniest details, from the floating shelves to where the display cases would go."

"Is it empty?"

"No, and this is where things get weird."

"I'm used to weird with you."

She chuckled. "Fair enough. Marc's mom's bakery is in there."

"The one that wants to expand into your building?"

"Yes."

"You're not giving yourself a consolation prize to win this guy over, are you?"

Was she? "I don't think so. In fact, I know I'm not."

"How can you be sure?"

"Because I broke it off with Marc on Monday."

"Is this your way of getting him back?"

"That's not it, either. I thought he could be the one, but I'm obviously not very important to him, and I'm not okay with that."

"Where did you get all your brains from?"

"We all know I'm not the brains of the family, Blaine."

"You're smart, and you mean the world to me, Reagan. Whatever you do, don't settle for second best. You're worth so much more."

Grateful tears pressed, and she took a moment to get grounded. "Thanks, Blaine."

"You'll know what to do. Trust your instincts."

Trust her instincts. She smiled to herself. Yes, that was why she'd moved here.

"I will."

"And if you need me to come down there and have a talk with this Marc guy, say the word."

"I'm good."

"Should I call Dalton to confront him?"

"No!"

"Okay, okay. I love you."

"I love you, too. Thanks for calling."

Talking to Blaine clarified things. She was growing more convinced every day that the corner building wasn't right for her shop.

Why couldn't she have figured all this out three weeks ago? She'd signed a contract with Ed. The renovations would be starting soon. Even if she wanted Annie's Bakery, she had no idea if it was even possible for her to get it. Did Anne own the building? Lease it? What would be involved?

Dear Lord, I keep feeling like I'm hitting a roadblock when it comes to my plan. Will You help me figure out what to do?

One thing she knew. Marc *would* treat her differently if she decided to give up on the corner building. But it wouldn't matter. Because deep down she knew when push came to shove, she wasn't as important to him as he was to her. And that was a deal-breaker.

No matter where she opened her shop, she had no future with him.

CHAPTER THIRTEEN

"WHAT'S GOT YOU down, boss?" Rico asked Wednesday after lunch. "You're less fun to be around than a wasp in a closet."

"Nothing." Marc cranked the wrench harder to tighten the bolt. He'd just replaced a part in the old truck they used to haul water around the ranch. Did it need to be replaced today? No. But he was determined to keep his mind occupied.

"Yeah, right." A skeptical *psshh* escaped his lips. "The honeybuns okay?"

"They're fine."

"And their mama?"

"Also fine. She made it up half the staircase all by herself last night before she got tired and needed my help."

"Good. What about Miss Anne? She okay?"

"Yes. She's okay." Was she, though? He tightened the bolt with one more crank, then straightened and tossed the wrench back in the tool chest. His mom seemed to be back to her normal self after their conversation Monday night. But was she hiding her pain?

"Then it must be Twinkles."

"Twinkles?"

"Yeah, Reagan. Her eyes are always twinkling."

Reagan's eyes *were* always twinkling. She had an amazing attitude. He missed those eyes. Missed that attitude.

"I noticed her car hasn't been around."

"Yeah, well, Gracie's been coming over every morning to help Brooke with the twins."

Rico rolled the air compressor back to the corner. "Why don't you take a drive? Go see Twinkles."

"Nah. I've got to check the new calves."

"You checked them an hour ago."

"Then I'll make sure the—"

"Look, boss, I don't normally involve myself in other people's beeswax, but it's clear to me you need a shove."

No, he didn't.

"Move this back to the side of the shed, will you?" Marc tossed Rico the keys to the truck.

Rico caught them with one hand. "I will. After you hear me out."

He didn't want to listen to a single word anyone had to say. He just wanted to be left alone. Forever. Or at least until his heart stopped crinkling up like an old burger wrapper being thrown in the trash every time he thought about Reagan.

"That girl is good for you. You could have a nice life with her. Settle down. Have a couple honeybuns of your own."

"I know, okay? I know. I blew it." Was his throat lined with lighter fluid? One wrong word would ignite the whole thing.

"Last I heard, most couples fight."

"We didn't fight." He almost said they weren't a couple, but they had been. For a short time.

"Whatever you messed up can be fixed."

"Not this."

"I don't believe that."

"Believe it or don't. Doesn't matter to me. I was upset that she's opening her chocolate shop in Mom's building. And she knew it. I couldn't be supportive, so we're done."

Rico rubbed his chin and nodded thoughtfully. "I can see how that's a problem."

Marc's shoulders sagged. It was a problem.

"She thinks she's not important to me. And

I take the blame for that. I'm still struggling with it. I wanted Mom's dream to come true."

"Go on."

He kicked at a cardboard box on the ground and instantly regretted it. Was it filled with cement? "It's all she's talked about for years, but Reagan is opening her chocolate shop there."

Rico's sigh irritated him.

"Why don't you leave it to the women to work it out?"

"There's no working it out. Reagan got her building permit. Hired a contractor. It's happening."

"Let me ask you something else." He brushed his hands down the sides of his jeans. "If you convinced her to give the building to your mama, could you live with yourself?"

"Of course. Why?"

"Because you'd be taking away Twinkles' dream. I've known you for a long time, boss. I don't think you'd feel so good about yourself if you did that."

Marc hadn't thought about that aspect. He hadn't really considered Reagan's point of view about her shop. He thought of all the times her face had glowed as she'd explained about how she'd learned to make truffles or her excitement at finding just the right chocolate to order. He'd loved listening to her. Loved being with her.

He loved her.

But how could he claim to love her when he'd purposely ignored what was important to her?

Chocolates were her passion. The building? She was right. She owned it. And he'd pressured her to step aside for his mother's sake. No matter what angle he looked at, the only conclusion he could come to was that Reagan was better off without him.

"I've got to go." He turned to leave.

"Go to town," Rico called. "Talk to her."

He wasn't going to town or talking to her. He was saddling up and taking a long ride. It was time to figure out how he'd become the kind of guy he loathed. The one who'd take away the dream of the woman he loved for his own selfish reasons.

Like father, like son.

There was no coming back from this.

REAGAN WAS TOWELING off her hair when she heard a knock on her front door. It had been a few hours since her conversation with Blaine. During that time, she'd fixed herself a bowl of soup and asked herself what she wanted. The more she thought about it, the more she realized it didn't matter how far along with her plans she was—she needed to do what was right for her. And that meant talking to Marc's mother. Just the two of them. She'd call Anne tomorrow. Maybe by then she'd have a clue how to present her plan.

She tossed the towel into a hamper, then padded to the front door. Marc's mom stood on the doorstep.

"Anne." Reagan was taken aback. "Come in."

Was she here to try to convince her to let her have the building for her bakery? Reagan didn't like the thought of Anne, too, thinking her dream was more important than her own.

"Are you sure?" Her lips curved into a weak smile. "This isn't a bad time?"

"It's a good time. I have nothing going on." She held the door open wider for Marc's mom to come inside. She led the way to the living room.

"I like your house." Anne took in the room. "We're practically neighbors—well, we will be when I move back to town."

"Thank you. Have a seat." Reagan sat in one

of the chairs as Anne perched on the couch. "Why are you here?"

"Marc doesn't know I came." Anne smoothed her hand over the throw pillow next to her, then met Reagan's gaze. "But I had to stop by for a couple of reasons. First, to thank you. The twins have been in good hands while Brooke recovered. Your generosity and kindness allowed Marc and me to focus on Brooke. I can never thank you enough."

"You're welcome. I wanted to help. I love those babies. I… I miss them."

Anne looked thoughtful as she nodded. "We'd love to have you come back, but I know it's probably not what you want to do."

"I want to." She hadn't been expecting this. Her heart softened.

"Really? After Marc… Well, I don't know exactly what happened, but I can guess." She stared at the throw pillow again for a beat. "Marc takes his responsibilities very seriously. He had to grow up awfully quick. It's made me happy—hopeful—to see how he is with you. I like that you bring out his softer side. But it was wrong of him to expect you to not open your business in the corner building. It's yours,

Reagan. And Brooke and I will be the first in line on opening day. We want you to succeed."

Relief and gratitude chased away her anxiety. "I didn't expect to hear that."

"I wish I'd been able to get to know you better these weeks, because then you'd know I think the world of you. We can never repay you for all your help, but we will always appreciate it."

What a kind woman. "There's nothing to repay. I know how important it is for family to stick together when trouble hits. You and Marc and Brooke needed each other, and I was happy to be there for the babies. Plus, I had time on my hands. God worked it all out."

"He did." Anne nodded. "Look, my son means well when it comes to my bakery—I take the blame since I talked about nothing else for years—but he should never have expected you to change your plans. Like I said, he takes his responsibilities seriously, and in his mind, that includes Brooke and me. I'm trying to set him straight."

"Yeah, well…" It was the opening she needed. "I actually have something I want to discuss with you, and it has nothing to do with Marc."

"What's that?"

"This is going to sound out there, so you're just going to have to take my word for it that this is truly what I want."

"Okay."

"When Marc and I opened the bakery that Sunday your employee couldn't come in, I immediately pictured my chocolate shop there. The entire vision for it came to me. I'm talking every detail. From tearing down walls, reconfiguring the displays, replacing the floors, to changing the color of the paint. All of it."

"My bakery?" Anne's eyes grew round. "That tiny slice of square footage?"

"Yes."

"But Marc said your permit went through."

"It did." She opened her hands and shrugged. "I don't think it's right for me. It's too big. All I really need is enough space to make the chocolates. The actual front reception area can be small. I have no plans to add seating, and most of the kitchen will be converted to an open workspace."

Anne blinked. "What exactly are you saying?"

"What if we swapped?" Reagan's voice grew stronger as she spoke. This felt right. More than right. "I don't know if you own your building or lease it, but I'd like to open my chocolate shop there. And you can open your bakery in my building."

Tears formed in Anne's eyes as she shook her head in wonder. "I couldn't take it from you. It's *your* dream, Reagan. I can't help thinking Marc is behind this."

She really was a lovely woman. Reagan liked her more and more.

"No." She smiled widely. "He actually doesn't know about it. I couldn't discuss my plans with him, and I kept trying to ignore how much your bakery would fit my needs. Like I said, this doesn't change anything between me and your son. I'm sorry. He's just not the right man for me."

Anne's face fell, but she nodded. "I understand. And I don't blame you. I love him, and I would love nothing more than for the two of you to be together, but…he needs to get his priorities straight. He needs to value you."

Why did his own mother understand and he didn't?

"Do you own the bakery?" Reagan asked.

"I do. I leased it the first three years, and then I bought it."

"Good. We'll have to figure out how to handle the legal aspects. Get them appraised. If you buy my building and I buy yours, I want a clause that I would get the first option to buy it back if you ever decided to sell in the future. It's a special building."

"Deal." Anne's eyes shimmered with hope. Reagan could see why his mom's happiness was so important to him. She was an easy person to love.

"What do you say we make an appointment with a real-estate lawyer early next week? Get this plan set in motion? And I'll talk to Ed McCaffrey about the logistics of renovating both buildings."

"I would love that." Anne stood and they embraced. "Thank you. For making my dream come true. I still can't believe it. If there's anything you ever need, I want to be the first person you call."

They chatted all the way to the front door. And when Reagan waved goodbye to her, her heart was full.

She'd made the right choice for herself and her business.

She just wished things could have worked out with Marc, too.

CHAPTER FOURTEEN

MARC WAS NOTHING like his father. He drove
through town Wednesday afternoon with his
heart beating double-time. A large bouquet of
red roses was on the passenger seat.

The horseback ride around the ranch earlier
had given him clarity. He loved every inch of
his land, and he'd never let it go. Just like he
loved his mom and sister and nieces—nothing
could make him turn his back on them.

His father had turned his back on all of them,
taken what he wanted and vanished. But Marc
wasn't like that. And Mom was right, too. God's
faithfulness had kept them together—had kept
him together all these years. And that had led
him to the uncomfortable truth—he loved Reagan, and nothing could make him leave her.
Not even the guilt over his mistakes.

Marc slowed his truck for the stop sign up ahead.
Sure, he'd messed up. He'd probably nuked

any chance that Reagan would ever trust him again. But the fresh air and the stillness of the ride had reminded him he wasn't the sum of his mistakes. He'd prayed about it. Asked for forgiveness for not trusting God enough.

God *had* provided for them all these years. And God had graciously spared Brooke from death or permanent disability. He'd also sent Reagan to them precisely when they'd needed her the most.

When Marc needed her the most.

Why hadn't he seen it? Why hadn't he recognized how wrong it was to insist she put her dreams on the back burner for his mom's?

No matter how things played out, he had to apologize to Reagan. He needed her to know in no uncertain terms how much she meant to him. How much he regretted not supporting her plans.

In a few short minutes, he'd be at Reagan's door, and he could only pray she would let him in.

What if she didn't? He'd find a way to make her listen. Throw pebbles at her window. Sing outside her door. Anything. He'd do anything to get her to hear his apology.

He slowed to turn down her street. His

nerves grew tighter as the first block went by. He was almost to her house when he saw his mother get into her car, back out of Reagan's driveway and head east.

What was his mom doing there?

Marc hoped she hadn't gone to ask Reagan to reconsider her plans for the building. If she had? He'd tell Reagan not to do it. Mom could keep the bakery where it was and find another building to expand in at some point. Reagan had poured too much into this to cave to his and his mother's demands.

He pulled into the driveway and grabbed the flowers. Before getting out, he smoothed his hand down his hair, adjusted his button-down shirt and took a deep breath. *God, You've come through for me over and over again. I don't deserve Reagan's love, but I don't deserve Yours, either. If she slams the door in my face or decides I'm not worth her time, help me remember I'm Yours and that's all that truly matters.*

Reagan's love mattered, too, though, and he couldn't pretend he wouldn't be devastated if she rejected him.

With long strides, he reached her door. Knocked twice. And waited.

What if his mom *had* tried to make Reagan

change her mind? It didn't make sense, but why else would she be here? Dread pooled in his gut. He'd already given Reagan enough reasons to never talk to him again.

The door opened, and Reagan stood there looking like his every dream come true.

"What was my mom doing here? Did she try to talk you out of opening your chocolate shop? I didn't put her up to it. I wouldn't do that to you. I know you have no reason to believe me but—"

"Why don't you come inside?" The corner of her mouth curved up and her eyes twinkled. She didn't look mad. Didn't seem upset.

He followed her inside and shoved the flowers into her hand. *Real smooth.*

She held the blooms to her nose and closed her eyes as she inhaled their scent. "Let me get these into water."

"It can wait." He reached for her hand, but he wasn't quick enough. She'd already turned toward the kitchen.

"It will only take a sec."

"Reagan, what I have to say can't wait." He hurried after her—this time he did clasp her hand—and closed the distance between them.

Took the flowers from her and set them on the counter. "I was wrong."

She dragged her gaze from the flowers to give him her full attention. "I know you were wrong."

Nothing if not direct. That was his Reagan.

"I never should have expected you to sacrifice your dream for my mother's. It was wrong and selfish and you didn't deserve that." He paused to take a deep breath. He was in over his head, but all he could do at this point was continue. "Regardless of what my mom told you just now, she and I had a long talk on Monday, and she told me she'd be okay without your building. And she will. So don't let her sway you. God will take care of her."

"You really believe that?" The words came out as wispy as a cloud.

"Yes." He nodded.

She tilted her head, her eyes searching his.

"I think God sent you here at a pivotal moment in my life," Marc said, "and I was too overwhelmed to see it. I knew you were an answer to a prayer my mom, my sister and I didn't even have time to pray. The twins needed you. We all needed you. But I needed you the most. I need you now. And tomorrow. And every day."

"What are you saying?"

"I love you, Reagan. I don't expect you to believe me after how I treated you, but I do. I love your generous heart. Mine is so small compared to yours. You remember the day Brooke had the stroke? I came home to the ranch and it was late. You were in the living room telling the twins a story. Not reading them one. Telling them one you made up. After hours and hours of taking care of infant babies you'd just met. I knew you were special even then."

Reagan was silent. Her eyes weren't twinkling. They were glistening with tears. He'd better get the rest out before she showed him the door.

"I'm sorry, Reagan. I'm sorry for being such an idiot. My priorities have shifted. Believe it or not, Mom helped me get them in line."

"I believe it." The tiniest of smiles appeared on her lips.

"Before you came along, I refused to make room in my life or in my heart for a woman. I already had four relying on me, or so I thought. But you wiggled in there and, instead of being a burden, you were a blessing, a comfort. I could listen to you explain how to make all the chocolates for hours. I could watch you kissing Alice's and Megan's cheeks and singing them silly songs every day for the rest of my life. I could talk about anything your heart desires as we share a pizza on your couch—and I want to. I want to share it all with you, Reagan. You told me you would never be as important to me as my mom, my sister and the twins. But you were wrong. You already are more important—I was just too stubborn to see it."

Reagan's heart was bursting with love, but she had to be certain she could trust him. Had to verify he truly was capable of putting her first.

"If I told you your mom asked me to give her the store and I did, what would you say?" She held her breath, hoping for the right words but bracing herself for the wrong ones. What if he simply thanked her? Hugged her and told her she'd just made his mom the happiest woman alive? She'd have to politely ask him to leave. Because that wasn't putting her first.

"Did she?" His face looked stricken. Then the muscle in his cheek pulsed. "Don't worry. I'll talk to her. You are *not* giving her your store. You've worked too hard to get to this point. I know I was a jerk about you inheriting it. I acted like you didn't deserve it—I'm sorry for treating you that way. I'm ashamed for thinking it in the first place. You *do* deserve it, Reagan, and I want to help you with it. Whatever you need, I'll be there, whether it's help painting or making sure the work is getting done. You can count on me."

"Your mom didn't ask me for the store." Her insides lit up like a carnival ride. Marc really *did* love her. "You should know your mom better than that. She stopped by to thank me for all my help."

He ran his fingers through his hair and sighed. "You're right. I don't know what's wrong with me."

"It's okay." She put her hand on his arm. "You've been through a lot this month."

"You've gotten me through a lot this month." He moved closer. "I don't know what I'd do without you, Reagan. I don't want what we have to end."

"I don't, either." She averted her eyes. "I have something to tell you."

His face went blank. "What is it?"

"Ever since I helped you that Sunday at the bakery, I've been having doubts about opening my shop in the corner building."

"But it's perfect for you. It has all that character and the big picture windows."

"It does have character, and I do love those windows." She nodded. "But it took all of two minutes in your mom's bakery for me to picture having my shop there."

"No." He shook his head. "You're just saying that to make me happy. I won't let you give up your dream."

Those words melted her even more than all his previous ones.

"Marc, listen to me. I could picture it—all of it—I could see every detail. And it feels right."

"Why didn't you say anything?"

"Because I was second-guessing myself."

"And I was pressuring you, which didn't help."

"It didn't."

"I'm sorry." He leaned down and touched his forehead to hers. "I'm really sorry."

She wrapped her arms around his back and hugged him. He held her tightly. After a few moments, she looked up at him.

"Your mom and I are swapping buildings. I don't know exactly how it will work, but we're setting up a meeting with a lawyer. We're both going to have our dreams come true, Marc, and

I'm not doing it for you. I'm doing it for me. It's important you know that."

He frowned a moment. Then his face cleared and he nodded. "Yes. I understand. You're strong. Made of steel and surrounded by whimsy. You broke the mold, Reagan Mayer."

Steel and whimsy? She laughed. Yeah, she'd take it. It might be the best compliment anyone ever gave her.

"I fell in love with you, too, Marc." It felt so good to say the words out loud. "Your greatest gift—your loyalty—is all I wanted. And I hope you know it is a blessing. The fact you'd sacrifice anything for your loved ones makes you oh so appealing to me. I love how much you care. About the cattle and the ranch. About this town. And most of all, about those sweet little babies and your mom and sister."

"Say it again." He smoothed her hair away from her face, looking deep into her eyes.

"I love you, Marc."

His lips were on hers—at first a whisper-like touch, then firmer, but tentative, as if asking if it was possible that she loved him. She kissed him back. Yes, she loved him.

She'd finally found the man she'd been longing for. The elusive man who got her. The one she could count on. A man who respected her. Her hot cowboy. Imagine that.

CHAPTER FIFTEEN

HE HAD A full day planned, and this was the first stop. Marc held Reagan's hand the next morning as they walked into his living room. Brooke was sitting on the couch with Megan, and Gracie was putting Alice in her bouncy seat.

"Good morning, Gracie. I'd like you to meet Reagan Mayer. Reagan, Gracie French."

"It's nice to meet you." Gracie glanced up with a smile. Gracie and Brooke had been friends forever. With long blond hair, a curvy figure and a smile for everyone, Gracie hadn't changed much since Marc had last seen her before she'd moved to Idaho.

"You, too."

Marc kept a firm grip on Reagan's hand and continued forward until they reached Brooke. "We have something to tell you. You were sleeping last night or I would have told you then."

"Ok-a-ay." Brooke's dark blue eyes couldn't have grown bigger.

"Reagan and I are dating. It's new, but it's serious. I love her." He turned to Reagan and grinned, wanting to kiss her again, but he'd already kissed her a minute ago as he'd helped her out of his truck in the driveway.

"That's the best news." Keeping a firm grip on Megan, Brooke struggled to her feet. He wanted to take the baby, but he also knew how important it was for her to continue everyday tasks on her own. Once standing, she hugged Reagan and let her take the baby before turning to hug him. "I'm thrilled for you both."

"Really?" he asked.

"Of course." She beamed and wiped away the moisture from her eyes. Then she turned to Reagan. "You couldn't do better than my big brother. I'm so happy you two are together."

"I am, too." Reagan caressed the back of Megan's head. "I missed you this week. Look at you—you got up so quickly with the baby this time."

"I know. Isn't it great?" Brooke said. "I still need help, though. Are you up for coming back next week? Just in the mornings?"

"Yes! I've missed the babies so much."

"I hope you know you are always welcome here." Brooke put her hands on Reagan's shoulders. "Always."

They shared a long look before Brooke stepped back. "I've been enjoying this week with Gracie."

"It's nice of you to help," Reagan said to Gracie. As the women chatted, Marc grew antsy.

"Listen, we've got to go." He kissed Brooke on the cheek.

"Already?"

"Yeah. We're stopping by Winston Ranch to see Erica, and then we have plans."

"A date." Reagan grinned.

"Well, don't let us keep you." Brooke took the baby from her.

Marc kissed Megan's cheek, then went over to Alice and tickled under her chin. Reagan, too, said goodbye to the babies. He reached for her hand and led her back outside.

Last night, they'd told his mom they were dating, and she'd actually burst into tears and hugged Reagan again and again, saying she'd made all of her dreams come true and that the Lord worked in mysterious ways.

In the driveway, he opened the passenger door to his truck and lifted Reagan by the waist to help her into the seat. Her laugh filled the air. "I could have gotten in by myself."

"Yeah, but I wanted to help. I can't get enough of you." He leaned in and kissed her, loving it when she wrapped her arms around his neck and kissed him back.

"Oh, my." She touched her lips.

She could say that again. He grinned, shut her door and loped around to the driver's side. Soon they were driving past his pastures and onto the main road.

"Tell me again about the peppermint thing you're working on." He glanced her way. She exuded contentment, and there were those twinkles in her eyes as she faced him.

"I found the richest dark chocolate to enhance the peppermint filling. It's going to be amazing when I get the proportions right. I'm using a mold for them, but I think I need to order a different shape…"

And just like that, he was in her world. A world of candy delights and possibilities.

A world he hadn't known he needed and couldn't imagine living without.

"I HAVE SO much to tell you." Reagan and Marc were sitting on stools at the island in Erica's kitchen. Reagan had already hugged Rowan when they'd walked in, and she'd gone to his room to check out his new toy tractor. Then Gemma had bundled him up to get to know his "horsey" with Dalton. Two small horses had arrived last week for Dalton to teach his son, Grady, and Rowan how to ride this summer.

"Obviously." Erica gave Marc a pointed glance that said she didn't quite trust him. "You two want coffee?"

"Yes," they said in unison.

She laughed. "Okay, then." She pulled out three mugs from the cupboard and filled them all. Then she set one in front of Reagan, one in front of Marc, and after she poured cream in her own, she slid the carton their way.

"We had a long talk yesterday." Reagan glanced at him and took his hand.

"I messed up." Marc stared at Erica. "I was wrong. I treated your sister badly, and I regret it. I apologized."

Erica narrowed her eyes, sipped her coffee and said, "Good."

"But before Marc came over, I made a decision. You might not understand it." It was important for Reagan to get this right. She didn't want her sister or the rest of her family to have any doubts where her intentions were concerned. "For a while now, I've been having a lot of second thoughts about using the corner building for my shop."

Erica frowned.

"But there is one spot in town…well, as soon as I saw it, I could picture my shop there. I know it's crazy. I know you're not going to understand. But I want to open R. Mayer Chocolates in Annie's Bakery. We're swapping buildings."

Reagan held her breath, bracing herself for the judgment sure to come.

Erica seemed to consider it, then lifted her chin. "You know, Reagan, I'm not surprised."

"You're not?" Her stomach clenched as she waited for her to say she was making a mistake.

"No." Erica placed her mug on the counter. "Tell me the truth, though. Are you doing this for you? Or for him?" She jerked her thumb to Marc. Reagan glanced his way, but he didn't seem offended.

"For me." As she thought about the new smaller shop, she couldn't stop a smile from spreading across her face. "I don't know why, but something just felt off about the corner building. And I talked to Blaine yesterday, and it just clicked. I guess I feel a bit like Goldilocks. My building was too big."

"And Annie's Bakery isn't too small?" Erica asked.

"No. It's just right."

Her sister hitched her chin to Marc. "What do you think about all this? You got what you wanted."

He squeezed Reagan's hand. The look he gave her was full of love.

"I did get what I want—your sister. I love her. Whatever makes her happy makes me happy."

Erica softened at that. "And if she changed her mind? Decided to open her shop in the corner building after all?"

"I'd help with anything she needed. I want *all* her dreams to come true."

That was why she loved him. Reagan let out a heartfelt sigh. "Thank you."

"Well said." Erica pointed to him. "Okay, Marc. Why don't you check out the new horse with Dalton while I talk to my sister?"

He glanced at Reagan and she nodded. She needed to make sure Erica truly understood where she was coming from. Marc rose from the stool and kissed her temple. "Is it all right if I take the coffee with me?"

"It's all yours."

A few minutes later, Reagan tried to mentally unravel the knots in her stomach as she prepared for a lecture from Erica.

"Do you trust him?" Erica asked. She looked more vulnerable than Reagan had ever seen.

"I do. He's sincere. I made the decision to swap buildings with his mom for my own sake, not for his."

Erica nodded, a thoughtful expression in her eyes. "Do you love him?"

"Yes."

"You know, I would have understood if you'd decided to let his mom have your building for his sake."

"You would have?" Reagan was surprised. Her sister always had such vocal opinions about her life.

"Yeah, I would have. But, man, I'm proud of you, Reag. That took guts. To know what you really wanted. When you told Anne to take the building, you weren't going to take Marc back, were you?"

"No, I wasn't." She shook her head as a sense of pride expanded in her chest. All her life she'd wanted her family to be proud of her. But most of all, she wanted to be proud of herself. And she was.

"Now I know you two are meant to be. He loves you. It's written all over his face, and I don't think you'll ever have to worry again about not being his top priority."

"I hope not."

Erica rounded the counter and pulled her into a hug. Reagan sank into her embrace.

"I'm glad I moved here," she said as they separated.

"I'm glad you did, too." She raised her mug. "To Great-Uncle Dewey and Great-Aunt Martha. If it wasn't for them, we wouldn't be here."

"We found our purpose—"

"And our partners—"

"Right here in Jewel River."

They clinked mugs.

"Now, let's go see what those guys are up to." Erica waggled her eyebrows and Reagan laughed. They linked arms as they headed out into the sunshine, giggling all the way to the paddock where Dalton had Rowan on his hip and Marc was petting the forehead of the new horse.

"We all good?" Marc asked Erica.

She grinned, let go of Reagan's arm and went over to give him a hug. "We're all good."

"Phew." He pretended to wipe his forehead. Then he reached for Reagan's hand. "And how are you? Ready for phase two of our day?"

She leaned into his side. "I'm ready."

"Then what are we waiting for?"

This. This was what she'd been waiting for. Her entire life. The man who got her, and the one she couldn't wait to spend her days with. "Let's go."

EPILOGUE

AFTER FIFTEEN YEARS of patiently waiting, his mother's dream of expanding her bakery was about to come true. Tomorrow was the grand opening.

All because of the beautiful woman by his side. Marc held out a chair for Reagan at the Jewel River Legacy Club meeting. It had been four months since they'd declared their love for each other, and he couldn't believe how much had happened in that time.

Once his mom and Reagan had hammered out the details of selling each other their buildings, Ed McCaffrey and his crew had undertaken the renovations of both locations. His mother had decided to temporarily close the bakery to give her more time with Brooke and the twins until the renovations were complete. Marc had never seen her happier.

Brooke had healed from the stroke with only a slight limp remaining. Marc wished he could take away her fear of having another stroke, but the doctors had warned her she was at a higher risk. All he could do was leave it in God's hands. Mom had moved back to town, and since it was a one-story house and easy to walk to everything, Brooke and the girls had moved in with her. They were all doing well.

Meanwhile, Reagan's vision for her chocolate shop had come true, from opening up the kitchen down to the floating shelves she'd pictured all those months ago. She'd spent these months honing her recipes and finalizing every aspect of the products, from the wrappers the chocolates sat in to the special packaging system she'd worked out. R. Mayer Chocolates would start taking online orders early next week.

"Did Alice start crawling yet?" Reagan leaned in with a whisper to Marc as Erica readied her notes at the head of the table.

"Not yet. She's on all fours, shifting back and forth. It's only a matter of time."

"I was sure she'd take off yesterday." She

shook her head. At least three days a week, Reagan went over to Mom's house to spend time with Brooke and the twins. "Megan won't be far behind."

"Thank you for coming, everyone." Erica's voice carried. "It's great to be back in the new—and improved—community center."

"It doesn't smell anymore." Christy Moulten looked around in wonder and turned to her son, sitting next to her. "Cade, I still think you should use the Winston for your wedding reception. Erica, yours was lovely. Truly impressive."

Reagan raised her eyebrows and glanced at Marc. "Is Cade dating anyone?"

"Not that I know of." He shrugged.

"Is there something you aren't telling me, Mom?" Cade asked dryly. "Don't tell me you ordered a bride through the internet for me."

"Smarty-pants." She made a *tsk tsk* sound and playfully slapped his arm. "If I could order both of you boys brides, I would."

"They don't want to get married," Clem said loudly in his exasperated tone. "Worry about yourself, woman."

"Me? I have just about had it with you, Clem."

Flames could have shot out from Christy's gaze and Marc wouldn't have been surprised.

Cade motioned for Erica to keep going.

Everyone stood to say the Pledge of Allegiance and the Lord's Prayer. Then Erica smiled at the people seated around the tables. "First, I want to thank Angela Zane and her grandson, Joey, for their exciting film. I have to admit, watching *Romeo & Juliet: Wyoming Style* on the makeshift screen in the park last month was a lot of fun."

"The whole town turned out for it." Angela's bright eyes glowed as she nodded. "When we could only get three actors on board, I thought Shakespeare-in-the-Park was done for. But my Joey knew better. He said, 'Nana, it doesn't have to be live. I'll film it, and those three can play all the parts.' We're so proud of him."

"I don't recall the book having Juliet fall from a hayloft into a pile of cow patties after Romeo tells her he loves her," Clem said. "Ditto for the bull charging at her."

"Wasn't that scene with the bull electrifying?" Angela seemed to not notice Clem's sarcasm.

Erica turned to Mary Corning. "Thank you

for setting up the crew for the kettle corn. It really added to the overall experience."

Mary smiled smugly. "I'm telling you we should install the equipment in the park for anyone to use. Who doesn't love kettle corn?"

"Yes, well, we've been over this before. Remember? The safety issues?" Erica gave her an apologetic smile. "Now, let's move on to the next order of business."

"Erica?" Cade stood. "I have an update."

"Go ahead."

"The veterinarian will be moving to town in the spring. She and her father have finally gotten their plans in order."

"Good job. Thank you for taking the lead on this. Anyone else?" Erica glanced around until her gaze landed on Marc. He nodded and stood.

"First, Reagan and I have an announcement. I proposed this weekend, and she agreed to be my wife."

A round of congratulations and applause filled the room. When it calmed down, Marc continued. "Tomorrow is the grand reopening of Annie's Bakery. I hope you all will go over to the new building and show your support. She sure is excited." Then he looked at Reagan and his heart filled with love. "And Reagan's chocolates will be for sale online beginning next week."

"When are you going to open the store for us to buy them?" Clem asked.

"Hopefully, soon. But feel free to stop in anytime, Clem. I'm making some new caramels for you."

"I'm taking you up on that, girly." He pointed to her and winked.

Johnny Abbot raised his hand.

"Yes, Johnny?"

"I just wanted to say how nice it is to see you all working together. Since I started coming to these meetings, you've gotten a new welcome sign for the town made up, added the nicest flowers along Center Street, gotten the whole town together for the Shakespeare film Angela's grandson made, and now we have two freshly renovated buildings downtown. This club has already made a lot of progress. I can't wait to see what you all will come up with next."

Marc took Reagan's hand under the table and squeezed it. "He's right, you know."

"I know." She smiled at him. "Jewel River is my favorite place to be."

"Wherever you are is my favorite place to be."

The Cowboy's Secret Past
Tina Radcliffe

MILLS & BOON

Tina Radcliffe has been dreaming and scribbling for years. Originally from Western New York, she left home for a tour of duty with the US Army Security Agency stationed in Augsburg, Germany, and ended up in Tulsa, Oklahoma. Her past careers include certified oncology RN, library cataloger and pharmacy clerk. She recently moved from Denver, Colorado, to the Phoenix, Arizona, area, where she writes heartwarming and fun inspirational romance.

Visit the Author Profile page at
millsandboon.com.au for more titles.

As far as the east is from the west, so far
hath he removed our transgressions from us.
—*Psalm* 103:12

DEDICATION

A big thank-you to Craig Wolf with Oklahoma's Child Support Services for patiently answering all my questions. As a writer himself, he had particular insight, and I am grateful. All errors are my own.

Thank you to my team, The Wranglers, who have supported me for the last five years. You'll find many of their names sprinkled throughout the entire Lazy M Ranch series. A shout-out to Natalya, who named the canine star of this book, Patch.

Finally, this book is dedicated to reader and reviewer Susan Snodgrass, who supported Christian fiction and touched lives daily with her promotion of the genre.

CHAPTER ONE

"I'm EIGHTY-TWO YEARS OLD. I don't need a babysitter."

Trevor Morgan's grandfather shifted position in the wheelchair, jaw set, blue eyes determined. Despite recovering from hip-replacement surgery, the Morgan patriarch had dressed like he would have on any other day on the Lazy M Ranch. Gus Morgan rejected the sweatpants that the hospital physical therapist suggested and instead wore a plaid Western shirt, Wranglers and boots. The Stetson that sat on his thick, wavy, caramel-colored hair belied his mature age.

"Gramps, it's not a babysitter," Trevor said. "She's a registered nurse." He had repeated the same information nearly half a dozen times, yet Gramps refused to change his stance.

"Same difference," Gus huffed. He inched

himself closer to the kitchen table and eyed the pastries cooling on the counter.

The drip and gurgle of the coffee maker was the only sound in the kitchen as Trevor took a calming breath. The aroma of fresh coffee mixed with the yeasty scent of cinnamon rolls called out to him. He would have liked nothing more than to answer by easing into a chair to enjoy a mugful of strong coffee and a pastry. But it was Monday morning, and the ranch came first. June in Oklahoma meant a list of chores piling up on the Morgan cattle ranch because the nurse scheduled for 9:00 a.m. was MIA.

"Gramps, this is not a debate," Trevor finally said. "The only reason your doctor didn't discharge you to the rehab facility in Elk City on Friday is because I gave my word that we'd have a home health team come to the ranch." He released a breath. "Besides, Bess is going on vacation to visit her grandbabies soon. We're going to need some assistance during the day."

Gus muttered under his breath and shook his head. "Define *soon*."

"Two weeks."

As if on cue, Bess Lowder, the family housekeeper and cook, walked into the kitchen with a basket full of towels to fold. She stopped, looked at Gus, and then at Trevor, her eyes round. "No nurse yet?"

"Nope." Gus glanced at his watch. "She was supposed to be here an hour ago."

Yeah, an hour ago, when his brothers Drew and Sam were here. They'd offered to postpone their vacation when it seemed clear that the nurse would be a no-show. Trevor refused to let that happen. The elder Morgan brothers and their families had planned a short trip to Branson, Missouri, months ago. A terrible plan, in his opinion. Though no one had asked him. Trevor's idea of a vacation was zero people, not a destination full of them.

His gaze moved to the refrigerator decorated with pictures of Drew and Sadie's children, along with the sonogram photo of Sam and Olivia's babies, due in December.

Seven years ago, a wedding picture of himself and Alyssa had been prominently displayed on that fridge. Bess had kindly removed it days after the funeral.

He pushed away the thought. Not going there. Not today.

"Did your brothers leave already?" Bess asked.

Trevor nodded. He'd practically shoved them out the door, assuring them that they could entrust not only the ranch, but also Gramps to him while they were gone. The ranch, he could manage. He'd been ranch manager for nearly two years now. But Gramps? Handling him was like trying to wrestle a greased pig.

And he hated being in the position of lecturing his grandfather. Gramps was the one who'd come to live with him and his siblings when their parents died twenty-two years ago. He was the rock they all depended on, who never once let down the four Morgan brothers.

So here he was, wearing a path on the kitchen floor, growing more and more annoyed and feeling guilty as the minutes ticked by and the nurse was nowhere to be found.

He paused when something caught his eye out the window. A small blue sedan kicked up the red Oklahoma dirt as it rounded the main drive and pulled up in front of the Morgan homestead.

A petite brunette in pink scrubs burst out of the vehicle. She carried what looked like a tackle box in one hand and slid a tote bag onto her shoulder. The woman said something to the passenger in the back seat of the car as she raced up the steps to the house.

Trevor tore out of the kitchen and down the

hall, yanking open the door before the woman could knock. The action caught her off guard, and she nearly toppled over. He grabbed her arm as she swayed.

"I'm—"

"I know who you are," he said. "You're late."

Her hazel eyes were wide with surprise as she adjusted the pink stethoscope around her neck. Standing straight, she pushed bangs from her face and tucked a strand that had come loose from her ponytail behind her ear. She met his gaze without hesitation, the warmth in her eyes moving to sub-zero temperatures, which was fine with him. He wasn't here to make friends.

"My apologies," she murmured.

Trevor did an about-face. "Follow me." While his boots clomped on the oak floor, her white shoes squeaked an irregular beat as she trailed him down the hall to the kitchen.

All eyes were on the nurse the moment she stepped into the room. Bess offered a welcoming smile. His grandfather perked up with interest.

"Mr. Morgan?" the nurse asked, addressing Trevor's grandfather.

"Call me Gus. There are five Mr. Morgans on this ranch. It can be mighty confusing."

"Gus, then. I'm Hope Burke, your case manager." She grinned, the smile lighting up her face.

"I apologize for my delay," Hope continued on a somber note. "Unfortunately, I wasn't able to call. It won't happen again."

"Aw, no problem," Gus said with a shake of his head. "Not like I had a hot date or anything."

Trevor nearly fell over. One smile and Hope Burke had his grandfather wrapped around her pink stethoscope.

"This is my grandson Trevor," Gramps began. "I've got three other grandsons. Two are on a short vacation, and the other is in Reno for a rodeo." He turned his head toward Bess. "And this beautiful woman is Mrs. Lowder. She runs the place."

"Bess. You call me Bess, dear." The housekeeper chuckled. "Don't listen to Gus. He only flatters me when he wants cinnamon rolls."

His grandfather laughed. "I plead the Fifth on that."

"It's a pleasure to meet all of you," Hope said,

her gaze moving between Gramps and Bess and avoiding Trevor.

Gus nodded toward the tackle box in Hope's hand. "Whatcha got in there? Are we going fishing?"

"Wouldn't that be nice?" Hope said with a wink. "Last summer, I caught a huge catfish over at Grand Lake. I'm ready to beat my record."

"Woo-ee." Gramps slapped the kitchen table with a hand. "A fellow angler. Glad to hear it. You be sure to sign up for the Homestead Pass Annual Fishing Derby. It's at the end of July. Cash prizes and lots of bragging rights."

"I will absolutely look into it." Hope patted the tackle box. "This is my supply kit. I'm on the road all day, so this is a convenient way to carry everything. My electronic notebook is in the tote bag."

"Looks like you're ready for anything," Gramps said.

She eyed Trevor dismissively and frowned. "Usually."

Points for the nurse. Trevor arched an eyebrow. She had spunk. He crossed his arms as the exchange continued, a bit intrigued by the woman.

"What's the plan?" Gramps asked.

"I'll be here twice a week. Each time I'll do a brief exam, including your vital signs and an examination of the incision. If your physician orders lab work, I'll handle that as well."

Gramps nodded.

"A home health aide will visit Monday through Friday mornings for about two hours. He'll help you with personal hygiene and assist with your home physical therapy."

"So I don't have to drive to Elk City for physical therapy?" His grandfather's expression was hopeful.

"You haven't been cleared to drive." Hope paused. "Someone will have to take you to PT three times a week." She smiled and once again looked at Gramps and Bess, ignoring Trevor. "Any questions?"

"Not so far," Gramps said. "How about you, Trev?"

"I'm good." Yeah, he was good until he could get Hope Burke alone and discuss the schedule. She was supposed to be here to help Gramps and make life easier for all of them. So far, that hadn't happened.

"All right, then, Mr. Morgan. Let's get you to your room, so I can do a quick exam."

Gus pointed to the left. "I'm staying in the guest room down the hall. Easier than the stairs."

"Perfect." Hope glanced around. "Where is your walker? DMEs are supposed to be delivered prior to discharge."

"DME?" Gramps asked.

"Durable medical equipment," Hope said.

"His DME is hiding in the closet." Trevor stared pointedly at his grandfather. "Gramps refuses to use the thing."

"Aw, well, I may have been a bit hasty last night," Gus mumbled.

Trevor nearly snorted aloud. A bit hasty? When Drew had suggested using the device, his grandfather had practically given a sermon on respecting your elders, complete with Bible verses to back him up.

"No problem," Hope said, her tone upbeat. "You've got a lot going on right now. I get that." She turned to Trevor. "Would you retrieve the walker, please?"

Sure, he could retrieve the thing. That didn't mean Gramps would actually use it.

When Trevor returned, Hope assessed the kitchen. "Your house is wheelchair-accessible.

I noticed the ramp on the far side of your porch and these wide doorways."

"Uh-huh. Trevor's daddy did that to accommodate my late wife when we visited," Gramps said. "We've got safety rails in the restroom as well."

"That's great." Hope looked at Gus. "Ready?"

"I guess so." Gramps eyed the walker, his face screwed up with distaste.

Trevor crossed his arms and leaned against the kitchen counter, trying not to appear amused. Though he surely was.

Hope locked the wheels of Gramps's wheelchair and met his gaze. Her voice was low and comforting, and with words of assurance, she talked him through standing, pivoting and gripping the walker while she held the aluminum device steady.

Once again, Trevor found himself surprised. She expected compliance and got just that. Not unlike when he worked with horses. A firm but gentle confidence got the job done. More points for the nurse.

"Nice work," Hope said, rewarding Gramps with a megawatt smile. She looked over her shoulder at Trevor. "The wheelchair can go away."

"You sure about that?" Gramps asked.

"I am. Walking is the best remedy for that hip."

"If you say so."

"I do. Now, if you lead the way to your room, I'll do an exam, then we'll fill out a bit of paperwork."

"Okey dokey," Gramps said. He began a slow shuffle down the hall, with Hope a step behind.

Trevor stared, stunned. If he hadn't seen it, he wouldn't have believed that the woman had managed to get his grandfather to do what he'd unequivocally refused to do last night.

"Now, that was amazing," Bess said. She turned to Trevor and grinned. "Don't you think?"

"What I think is that this is never going to work," Trevor grumbled. The nurse's smile and perky cuteness worked this time, but eventually, Gramps would catch on.

"Oh, don't be so negative." Bess swatted his arm. "I like her. She's a bit of sunshine. We can certainly use some around here."

"Are you calling me negative?" He looked at Bess.

"Well, if the wet blanket fits…" A smile hovered on her lips.

"I'm not negative. I'm forthright."

"Forthright, hmm?" Bess leaned closer. "You're getting to be a cranky old man, Trevor Morgan, and you're only thirty-five years old."

Trevor remained silent. To defend himself would only provide proof that he was cranky. He wasn't. Not at all. He was simply a straight talker.

"No wedding rings. Did you notice?" Bess continued. "It'll be fun to see the wranglers around here stepping over themselves to meet a cute young lady."

"I didn't notice."

"You didn't notice which? Her ring finger or that she's cute?" Bess teased.

He jerked back at her words. "Neither."

Bess's laughter rang out. She held up her wrist and glanced from the silver watch to him, her eyebrows arched. "My, my. Fibbing before noon. That's a new record."

Bess had been around for a long time, and it was rare, if ever, that he could pull one over on her. Yeah, Hope Burke was cute, and yeah, he'd noticed she didn't wear a ring. That didn't mean he was interested. Trevor scowled and headed for the coffeepot. "Mind if I have a cinnamon roll?"

"Not at all. Have two. Maybe they'll sweeten you up."

He sucked in a sharp breath. Though the Morgan household leaned toward being heavily male, all it would take was Bess's alignment with another female to throw the dynamics into chaos. He sensed chaos on the horizon. Yep, they were going to have some real weather at the Morgan homestead, and he planned to find cover and steer clear.

HOPE ADJUSTED THE tote bag on her shoulder. In one hand, she gripped the handle of her tackle box. In the other, she held a plastic container full of cinnamon rolls. Gus and Bess were certainly welcoming. For a little while, she almost forgot why she was in Homestead Pass instead of back home in Oklahoma City. She reminded herself to stay on task. Time was not on her side, and she couldn't risk being distracted from what she was here to do.

Unfortunately, her mission on the Lazy M Ranch involved the cranky cowboy she'd met this morning. She hadn't expected him to be quite so arresting. Trevor Morgan was tall and lean, with impossibly blue eyes and full lips that were wasted on his unsmiling mouth. There were shadows of sadness in the depth of his gaze, and more than once she found herself curious about his story.

It had only taken a few minutes to assess the Morgan household, and aside from the irritated cowboy, there weren't any red flags. As a home health nurse, she'd become adept at assessing family dynamics. Everything from mental-health issues to stress and undiagnosed physical problems. Part of her job also included evaluating a patient's home environment for potential hazards.

So far, the Morgans checked all the boxes, and she couldn't find a single outstanding issue besides what she was here to address—Gus Morgan's postoperative care.

An hour later, Hope completed the home visit without incident. The knot in her stomach eased a bit as she left the house. First visits were always stressful. Today, doubly so.

Hope scanned the ranch before her as she carefully moved down the front steps to the walkway lined with large terra-cotta pots of crimson geraniums. Overhead, a blue sky with wispy clouds framed the view. Green pastures stretched as far as she could see. To the right, there was a barn and a stable with a corral. The area buzzed with activity as men strode in and out of the buildings.

In the distance, the muted sound of a lawn mower filled the air. A warm, humid breeze brought with it the sweet scent of cut grass. The Lazy M Ranch was beautiful, and she couldn't deny a bit of envy at the wide-open spaces and large family that the Morgans most likely took for granted.

She'd spent her adult life in apartments in the city. Her patients had become her family, which was pathetic for a thirty-four-year-old woman to admit.

"Ms. Burke, I'd like to talk with you before you leave."

Hope halted at the sound of Trevor Morgan's voice. She'd nearly made it to the car and far away from the disapproving glare of Gus Morgan's grandson.

"Yes, Mr. Morgan." She turned and put a smile on her face as he approached.

He wasn't smiling. Perhaps he'd forgotten how. The man was formidable. She'd give him that. Well over six feet, he was wearing a navy T-shirt that only emphasized his muscular forearms. The family resemblance was evident, although Gus had been blessed with charm and humor, which his grandson had failed to inherit.

"Ma'am, I have a ranch to run." He tipped back his straw Stetson with a finger and then crossed his arms, assessing her.

Hope tried not to stare while at the same time doing her own evaluation, taking in the caramel-brown hair that peeked from the edges of his hat and curled a bit on his neck. She didn't know any men who wore a five-o'clock shadow so well at ten in the morning. Rugged. That was the thought that came to mind.

She searched Trevor Morgan's features for a resemblance to the boy sitting in her car, but found none.

"I will work to respect that," she answered. At her response, she once again felt his penetrating gaze upon her.

"You look awfully young," he said. "How long have you been a nurse?"

Stunned by the remark, Hope worked to hide her annoyance. "I've been a registered nurse for eleven years, Mr. Morgan."

"Are you always an hour late?" he asked, his jaw tightening.

Hope relaxed at that question. This man had much to learn about life and the medical profession. It was her job to gently explain things to patients and their families. Even if this particular family member was being a rude lout.

"Patient care doesn't always align with minutes and hours, Mr. Morgan," she finally said. "Sometimes the Lord has different plans."

"Pardon me?" He cocked his head and looked at her, clearly confused.

"My morning appointment. He went to be with the Lord. That was my delay." Hope released a sad sigh. There was rejoicing at a soul going home, yes, but part of her job included comforting the loved ones left behind. The morning had left her emotionally fragile.

"Oh, I..." His face paled, and the deep blue eyes flashed with pain.

Hope immediately regretted sharing the information. Had she misjudged the man? Perhaps he was all bark.

"Then I left my phone in my car, and the battery drained," she admitted. "I'm not making excuses. Those are the facts, though, I assure you, Mr. Morgan. It will not happen again."

The cowboy nodded. "Um, you can call me Trevor. As my grandfather said, there are a handful of Mr. Morgans around here. I've got three brothers. Drew is the oldest, then Sam, then my twin brother, Lucas."

"I see." Hope stood awkwardly, not knowing what to say to his transformation from cranky to civil.

She certainly did not want to actually say his God-given name aloud. It seemed far too personal. "I'll be going, and I apologize for causing you an inconvenience."

"Yeah. Sure. Thanks for helping Gramps. We all appreciate it." Trevor paused. "My grandfather means more to me than…" He swallowed and looked at the ground. "He's important."

"He'll get my best care." As all her patients did.

The answer seemed to satisfy him, and he turned toward the house.

With his departure, Hope slid into the driver's seat of the car, turned to the back seat and handed her nephew, Cole, the cinnamon rolls. "Here you go. Your reward for waiting for me."

"These are for me?" He closed his book and peeked into the blue plastic container.

"All yours. You can save me a bite." She smiled. "You okay?"

"Yes, I sat on the porch for a bit, like you said I could." Cole ducked his head. "I'm really sorry I used up the battery on your phone playing video games."

"It's my fault too. I should have brought the charger cord." Hope shrugged. "Everything worked out. The Lord has us in the palm of His hand."

"What does that mean?" Cole asked. The eleven-year-old hadn't spent a lot of time in church, but Hope planned to change that.

"It means that as long as we listen to His still, small voice, we'll stay on the path intended for us." She smiled. "Understand?"

"I guess." Cole inclined his head toward where Trevor stood watching them on the porch. "Who's that?" He narrowed his eyes, his gaze intent as he stared out the mud-spattered windshield at the cowboy.

"Trevor Morgan. His grandfather is my patient."

"Does he own all this?"

Hope glanced at the view out Cole's window, where Angus cattle grazed in yet another pasture.

"I think his family does. Lazy M Ranch. *M* is for *Morgan*."

She assessed her nephew as she backed out of the gravel drive and aimed the vehicle toward the exit. He was at that awkward boy-man stage. When he turned to her, soulful blue eyes searched hers. Hope would do anything to erase the deep sadness reflected in their depths. She'd been in his place when she was his age and had lost her mother. Only time and the Lord could heal his pain.

Her stepsister, Anna—Cole's mother—had fallen and gotten up more times than Hope could count, but despite her struggles, she'd loved her son unconditionally right up until her passing.

What about Trevor Morgan? Would he love Cole the same way when he found out the boy was his son? Hope blinked and swallowed back the tears that threatened. The ache in her chest seemed unbearable today, and she rubbed at the spot with her knuckles.

One step at a time.

Hope checked her rearview mirror as the tall cowboy faded into the distance.

The road into Homestead Pass was dotted with farmhouses and ranches—a pleasant drive into a very quaint town. Hope hadn't even known Homestead Pass existed until two weeks ago. She'd been going through the personal belongings that had been turned over to her after Anna's death. That was when she found a stack of newspaper clippings and Cole's birth certificate.

Cole Edward Burke. Her nephew's middle name came from Hope's father, who'd adopted Anna when he married Hope's mother. Though she'd given her son the family name, Anna listed Trevor Morgan as Cole's father. Her stepsister had never once mentioned Trevor, which was curious.

On the other hand, there wasn't anything about Anna that was not curious. She'd popped up at intervals in Hope's life. Usually, when she needed money, a place to land or a favor. That favor usually meant leaving Cole with Hope for *a little while.*

Hope had found online articles similar to the clippings Anna had collected. A write-up that highlighted rodeo events. Some even had photos. Although the clippings were from different newspapers, they had a common thread.

Trevor Morgan.

Bulldogger. She'd had to look that one up. He wrestled steer. And he was good at it.

One particular photo showed Trevor smiling broadly. That smile was a secret weapon. No wonder he didn't use it often.

She'd done a little digging and come up with Homestead Pass as Trevor's hometown. All she had to do was pull in a few favors with a friend at the home health company. She got herself transferred to the Elk City office for the summer. It was providence that Gus Morgan needed assistance, or maybe divine intervention.

"Where are we going?" Cole asked, interrupting Hope's thoughts.

"To the inn for now. It's a nice place. Don't you think?" The accommodation at Homestead Pass Inn offered an immaculate one-bedroom suite, and Mrs. McAfee, the innkeeper, had gone out of her way to make them comfortable.

Hope had given Cole the bedroom and slept on the rollaway. The inn also provided a complimentary continental breakfast. Her bank account would suffer, paying for this and the rent on her apartment. And it wasn't like she had a nest egg any longer. That was long gone when Hope paid off the credit-card debt Anna had rung up. Giving her stepsister the card had been a huge mistake, but what else could she do? Cole was the one who suffered when Anna was broke.

She looked at her nephew. Cole hadn't answered the question, and she knew he couldn't.

Because while the inn was far nicer than any place where he and his mother had lived, it wasn't home. Home was where Anna was, and that was no more.

"Will I ever go back to Tulsa?" Cole asked.

He deserved an answer, but she'd promised herself a month ago, when she'd picked him up from social services, that she wouldn't give him anything but the truth. And the truth depended on Trevor Morgan.

Cole turned to look at her, waiting patiently for a response.

"No. Not Tulsa." Never Tulsa. There was nothing in T town for either of them now that Anna was gone.

"Oklahoma City?" he persisted.

"That's where my apartment is, and for now, yes, that's home," Hope finally said. Eventually, they did have to return to OKC. But between now and then, she didn't know where the road would take them. One way or another, Hope had a list of decisions to make before she enrolled Cole in school at the end of summer. Where they would be at the end of summer remained the looming question.

Her nephew nodded slowly at her response, saying nothing more.

A profound sadness filled Hope at his response. Cole never argued or protested. Simply acquiesced. Eleven years old and far too accustomed to life happening to him without his permission. From now on, Hope would do everything in her power to change that.

CHAPTER TWO

On Thursday morning, Trevor stood at the corral with one boot on the rough-hewn fence as Slim Jim, the ranch horse whisperer, worked with a mare that had arrived on Saturday.

"You going to that barn-dance thing, boss?" Jim asked. The tall, lanky cowboy pushed back his hat as he stood at the fence, waiting for an answer.

"I don't see a good reason to." Trevor did his best to avoid social gatherings and the dreaded small talk that always ended in nosy questions about his personal life.

"It's a fundraiser for the Homestead Pass Clinic. Food catered by Moretti's and there's a country-music band. That's a good reason."

"I can send a check," Trever said. He made a mental note to make it a big check. Dr. Lakhno at the clinic had done an excellent job of getting Drew and his wife, Sadie, through their first year of parenting Mae, their adoptive daughter who had a heart condition.

"Couldn't hurt to get out and socialize," Jim continued as he ran a gentle hand over the horse's flank. "You've been in a holding pattern for seven years." Trevor leveled a gaze at his friend and the cowboy shrugged. "Just saying."

Not many people could get away with that kind of remark, but he'd known Jim a long time. The cowboy had attended Trevor's wedding.

At the sound of a vehicle approaching, Trevor turned and spotted Hope Burke's car coming up the drive.

If he hustled, he could stop and talk with her before she went into the house. Always good to check in with the caregiver. Especially since he might have been a little hard on the woman on Monday. This time he'd work on his knee-jerk responses and attempt to be more reflective before opening his mouth.

Trevor pulled off his gloves and shoved them in his back pocket as he started toward the drive. He did a double take when a furry streak raced past from behind, moving to the right, followed by Drew's dog, Cooper. Cooper, with his red coat and white patches, struggled to keep up with the energetic rescue pup the vet had dropped off yesterday. The rescue dog was part border collie, like Cooper, with the same pointed snout, except he wore patches of long, thick, espresso-colored fur, with a white face and belly. The pup had been in a fenced yard outside in the sunshine, but Cooper was a wily animal who'd no doubt unlatched the door and let his buddy out of jail.

"Cooper—here, boy. Cooper!" Trevor broke into a run, chasing the dogs so he could herd them toward the house.

Cooper's tongue lolled with abandoned joy at the game, his long legs working to keep up with his companion.

As Trevor got closer to the house, the back seat passenger door of Hope's vehicle opened, and a slight-framed boy of about ten or eleven got out and whistled to the dogs. Cooper shot straight for the kid, followed by the pup, and nearly knocked the boy to the ground. He recovered quickly and kneeled in the gravel, seemingly enjoying the attention of both animals.

"Hey, thanks. I appreciate the assistance," Trevor said when he caught up with the dogs.

The boy shoved shaggy brown hair away

from his face and offered a faint smile as he rubbed Cooper behind his ears. "What're their names?"

"Cooper is the red one. We haven't named his friend with the chocolate patches. He's new to the ranch."

"Patch is a good name," the boy said.

"Yeah, it is," Trevor said. He nodded slowly. "Let's call him that." Though the boy's face remained expressionless, Trevor didn't miss the twinkle in the kid's blue eyes.

"You're pretty good with animals. You have a dog?"

The boy shook his head, a shadow passing over his eyes. "No. My mom… No."

Trevor noticed a book lying in the gravel next to the car and retrieved the paperback, examining the cover. "*Space Knights*. Love this series. Isn't this the one where the spaceship lands on Mars and finds a colony of broken robots?"

Cole nodded. "Uh-huh." He paused. "You've read this?"

Trevor crossed his arms and smiled. "I own the entire series. From book one and the discovery of the parallel galaxy, all the way to…" He chuckled. "I better not let any spoilers slip."

The boy's mouth formed a silent O of surprise.

Few people realized that Trevor was a bookworm and he took pains not to share that nugget. It worked out fine that he was often underestimated. *Cowboy jock* was the term given to him and his twin, Lucas, in high school. He'd surprised a few people, including Lucas, by graduating second in his class and scoring a full scholarship to Oklahoma State University.

"You're a big reader, huh?" Trevor asked. "Most kids your age are into video games."

"Last time I played video games," the boy mumbled, "I accidentally used up all the power on my aunt's phone."

"Ms. Burke is your aunt?" Well, this was new information. Her nephew had drained her phone battery on Monday, and she hadn't thrown the kid under the bus. He might need to rethink his initial evaluation of the woman.

The kid nodded and accepted the book from Trevor.

"I'm Trevor. What's your name?"

"Cole Burke."

"Nice to meet you, Cole." Trevor paused. "Do you wait in the car while she sees her patients?"

"Yeah, nothing else to do in the summer."

Trevor's jaw dropped at Cole's response.

"Are you serious? There's nothing *but* stuff to do around here in the summer. Horseback riding for one. And swimming, and tubing in the creek. Then there's the Blueberry Festival and the Fourth of July parade, followed by a big fishing derby later in July. Lots to do."

"Yeah, but I don't live here."

"Where do you live?"

"I'm from Tulsa but...my mom died, so I'm staying with my aunt."

"I see," Trevor murmured. Though he sure didn't. Where was the kid's father? Sounded like a complicated story. Poor fella had lost his mother and was now stuck with his aunt for the summer when he ought to be out enjoying his youth.

Trevor recalled the summer his folks died. He'd been only a few years older than Cole. Lousiest summer on record. Yeah, he could absolutely relate to this kid.

"Would you like to look around the ranch?" The invitation jumped out of Trevor's mouth before he could think about the wisdom of the offer. Might not be a good idea to get tangled up in Hope Burke's business.

When Cole's head jerked up, and excitement lit up his eyes, Trevor knew it was too late to take back the offer. And maybe he really didn't want to.

Cole searched Trevor's face. "Really?"

"Sure. Ever been on a ranch?"

The boy shook his head. "Nope. But my mom used to ride horses in the rodeo before she had me."

"How about that." Trevor paused, his eyes on the house. "Wait right here. I'll run inside and ask your aunt if it's okay to show you around."

Trevor took the stairs two at a time. For some reason, the idea of showing this quiet, bookish city kid the ranch had a growing appeal. He'd mentored kids at the pastor's request in the past and always found the time fulfilling and enlightening for himself and his guest.

Maybe because the ranch meant so much to him. The Lazy M had provided a healing balm at the lowest points of his life. When he was hurting or confused, he'd ride far as he could and talk to the Lord. His Alcoholics Anonymous sponsor had told him numerous times how blessed he was to have a supportive family and all this space on the ranch to work out his thoughts.

He was right. Twelve years clean, and a day

never went by that he didn't thank the good Lord for every blessing.

Trevor found Hope Burke and his grandfather seated at the kitchen table.

Gramps looked up. "Hey there, Trevor, what's up?"

"Just checking in," Trevor said. "And I had a question."

"Because your brothers calling twice a day might not be enough checking in?" Gramps asked with a chuckle.

"We love you, Gramps." Trevor's gaze skimmed the papers on the table. "What's going on?"

"Hope is doing a *postoperative cognitive evaluation*." Gus looked at the brunette seated across from him, her back to Trevor. "Did I get that right?"

"Yes," Hope replied. She didn't turn to face him as she sorted the papers. "Your grandfather mentioned he had a few memory issues. I'm doing a quick evaluation, and then I'll report to his physician."

Heart pounding, Trevor gripped the kitchen counter. Memory issues? This was his grandfather. His rock. "Should we call a specialist?"

"There's nothing to be concerned about right now. It's not unusual for anesthesia from surgery to impair cognitive ability post-op. That's why it's so important for your grandfather to be mobile and exercise. I'll recommend some techniques to keep him sharp. You know, like word games and puzzles." She paused and looked at his grandfather. "He's very compliant. By far my best patient."

"You hear that?" A grin split Gus's face. "Her best patient."

"I don't doubt that." His grandfather appreciated the attention he was getting, and rightly so. He'd spent the last twenty-some years taking care of everyone else.

"What did you say you need, Trev?" Gramps asked.

Rattled by the conversation, Trevor nearly forgot why he was there. "I, um…" He paused. "I came in to ask Ms. Burke if she'd mind if I gave Cole a tour of the ranch."

Hope swiveled in her chair to look at him, her eyebrows knit with concern.

"Cole?" Gramps frowned. "Who's Cole?"

"My nephew," Hope said. "He reads in the car while I visit patients."

"That's got to be mighty boring," Gramps said.

"It's a temporary situation. I hope to have him in a summer program soon."

"Is that a yes?" Trevor asked. "I've got a

thirty-or forty-minute window before I'm due at a meeting with one of my vendors."

Hope's lips thinned and she frowned. "Oh, I don't know. Cole is…vulnerable. He's had a rough time."

"Trevor sure can relate to that. Maybe that's why he's so good with kids," Gramps said. "Tell her about your project."

"I, um…" Trevor hesitated. He didn't like to talk about himself, though he had to admit his grandfather's assessment was spot on. Yeah, he liked kids. They didn't ask awkward questions about his wife or his past, or pry into his business.

"You earned bragging rights, son," Gramps said. "Trevor here started a kids event on the ranch last August. Right before school began," his grandfather continued. "Brought in kids from the city. The Homestead Pass Community Church sponsored the program." He smiled. "Doing it again, this summer. Right, Trev?"

"Yes, sir."

"Really?" Hope cocked her head and assessed him. "You like kids?"

Don't look so surprised. Trevor worked to keep his mouth shut, for Cole's sake, and simply nodded.

"I suppose it will be okay." She paused. "You

aren't going to put him on a horse or anything, right?"

"No, ma'am. As I said, I have about forty minutes," he returned, frowning. What did the woman have against horses?

"Well, then, sure." Hope reached for her cell phone. "I should give you my number."

"Ms. Burke. He'll be fine." Trevor felt her gaze follow him long after he left the room.

"Did she say yes?" Cole asked when Trevor met him outside. The boy stood next to the pickup, eager-faced, in faded blue jeans a size too large and a once-white T-shirt with some sort of comic-book character on the front. He was stroking the velvet fur of the pup, newly named Patch.

"She sure did." Trevor smiled. "Come on. We'll put the dogs up and then get the ute."

"Ute?"

"A utility vehicle." Trevor pivoted on his boot heel and started toward the barn. He whistled for Cooper, who followed, with Patch bringing up the rear.

"How old are you?" Trevor asked Cole.

"Almost twelve." The kid scrambled along, his short legs moving like scissors as he worked to keep up the pace.

Trevor frowned and looked down at the boy at his side. "How almost is almost?"

The boy's face pinkened. The pinker he got, the more the sprinkling of freckles across his nose stood out. "In six months."

"Yep, that's almost twelve." Trevor swallowed a smile and tried to remember the best part of ranch life when he was Cole's age. Definitely the horses. "What do you want to see first?"

"Horses."

"Horses it is," Trevor said.

Once Cooper and Patch were put in the outdoor pen, with the latch firmly in place, Trevor cocked his head to the right. "The stables are right next to the barn."

The big doors were open, the fans moving the June air through the long building as they stepped inside.

"It smells kinda bad." Cole put his hand over his nose and mouth.

"Does it?" Trevor had long gotten over the many intense aromas on the ranch. All part of a day's work as ranch manager.

"What is it?" Cole asked.

"The smell? Manure." Trevor grinned. "You get used to it eventually."

His face pale and moist, Cole shook his head, contradicting Trevor's assertion.

Concern had Trevor putting a hand on Cole's elbow and leading him back outside. "On the other hand, maybe we should start you out slow. Let's go visit the corral, and you can see the horses in the fresh air."

Cole bent over and coughed once they were in the sunshine.

"There now. Take a deep breath."

"It really does smell bad," Cole said. He wiped his face with the tail of his T-shirt and darted a look at Trevor, his expression sheepish.

"You never had a pet?"

Cole shook his head.

"Cleaning up after an animal can be smelly," Trevor reassured him. "You get used to it." He nodded toward the wood fence. "You can sit up there and watch Slim Jim."

"You named the horse Slim Jim?" The boy's eyes widened.

"Not the horse. The cowboy. He's a horse trainer. We recently started boarding and training horses on the ranch." Both Trevor and Cole were silent as the lean cowboy in the corral slowly approached the chestnut mare with a striped blanket over his shoulder.

"What's he doing with that blanket?" Cole asked. The boy stepped onto a fence rung, his untied sneaker laces trailing in the dirt.

"He's letting the horse sniff the saddle blanket. Now, watch."

Cole stared with interest as Jim gently touched the blanket to the horse's neck and then his withers, finally settling it on its back.

"Why's he doing that?" Cole asked.

"You have to take it slow. Jim is allowing the animal to become accustomed to the weight on his back. Eventually, he'll put a saddle on the horse, and when the animal is ready, he'll sit on him and let the horse get used to the idea."

The boy nodded, his attention never leaving the corral. For minutes, they were silent as Jim continued training.

"I'd like to ride a horse someday," Cole said. "I'm kinda scared of them now, but I could maybe start like Jim. Just sit on one." He looked at Trevor, his guileless blue eyes questioning.

Quirky kid. Almost twelve years old. If Alyssa was alive, they might have had a kid or two by now. The thought didn't hurt quite as much as it used to.

Trevor smiled at the earnest expression on Cole's face. Something about this particular kid tugged at Trevor, and he couldn't say no to the unspoken plea.

"If you're here for the summer, we can work up to that," Trevor said.

Delight flickered in the boy's eyes, and then he frowned as though tamping down any premature expectations. "What does 'work up to that' mean?"

Trevor pointed a thumb toward the stables. "It means you have to get used to the stink because preparation to ride starts in there."

"Oh." Cole chewed his lip, thinking hard. "I can do that."

"You think so?"

"Yes, sir."

This kid had grit, and once again Trevor found himself longing to champion the boy. "Great." He offered a high five.

Cole looked at him for a moment before his palm shot up and met Trevor's.

"It's a deal then. All we have to do is get your aunt's permission." Trevor glanced around and then lowered his voice. "Leave that part to me."

Hope Burke wasn't going to be happy. She'd made it clear that she thought he wasn't qualified to keep an eye on her nephew. Trevor grinned. Was it bad that he looked forward to proving her wrong?

"AND THEN HE took me to see the cows. I mean cattle. There's a difference between cows and cattle, you know." Cole looked up at Hope as they strolled down Main Street. His brow was furrowed, his expression intent. "All cows are cattle, but not all cattle are cows."

"Yes. You said that." Hope's lips twitched at his serious tone. "I guess you had a good time yesterday."

Cole nodded. "We drove in a ute. That means utility vehicle."

"Right. You mentioned that earlier."

"I named the new dog too. Patch. That dog really likes me."

"That's nice." The sound of laces slapping against the sidewalk had Hope glancing down. "Cole, your sneakers are untied."

He kneeled down and tied them, then skipped a few steps to catch up with her.

Cole skipped. This was the happiest she'd ever seen him, except when his mother showed up after disappearing for days. Eventually, Anna would recall that she'd left her son at Hope's house. In she'd waltz, with presents and kisses, and everything would be forgiven.

A sigh slipped from Hope's lips at the unfairness of it all. Her nephew had no idea what consistency and security were. She suspected that he wasn't accustomed to any sort of routine. He'd spent most of his life as a mini adult to a sweet but chaotic mother.

Hope did her best to ground him in the security of routine while not stripping him of his past. Which explained why she hadn't insisted on new clothes and a haircut. Her goal for now was to prove she would never let him down and to retrieve his lost childhood. An overreach for sure. But she had to try. Cole deserved as much.

If someone had done that for her when her mother died, perhaps she would have grown up with fewer walls erected.

Ahead of them, a group of middle-aged women walking on the sidewalk approached. Carrying bright-colored shopping bags on their arms, they chattered and laughed, offering nods of greeting.

Hope smiled in return. When another group of shoppers passed, she grabbed Cole's elbow and pulled him out of the way. "Watch where you're going, sweetie."

The sidewalks of downtown Homestead Pass were certainly busy. Tourist season, she supposed.

"Trevor says that I'm really smart," Cole said.

"You are," Hope agreed.

She'd heard "Trevor says" at least a dozen times since yesterday's tour of the ranch. The grumpy cowboy had made more progress with Cole in thirty minutes than she had in a month. It had surprised her to learn that Trevor had a soft spot for children, but it worked in Hope's favor because now he had a son. And he needed to know the truth. Hope had lost more than a few hours of sleep when she'd recognized that she would be the one to break the news to him. It was time, and her stomach was in knots. She'd need to talk to him next week at the ranch.

"Right here," Hope said as she and Cole reached the local bookstore near the end of Main Street. The black awning said The Book Nook. She held open the door and let Cole step inside first.

"This looks like a fun place, doesn't it?" she asked quietly.

Cole nodded, his eyes fixed on the colorful posters and the tall rows of books.

Hope tucked a twenty-dollar bill into his palm. "I'm going over to the drugstore to pick up some things. Wait for me inside the bookstore, please."

"Is this all mine?" Cole stared at the bill in his hand, his mouth gaping with awe.

"Yes. All yours. Buy some books. It's going to be a long summer."

Again, he nodded, his gaze returning to the bookshelves.

"Did you hear what I said about waiting for me in the store?" When he didn't answer, she put a hand on his shoulder. "Cole, are you listening?"

"Don't worry. I'll keep an eye on him." A pretty, middle-aged woman with silver-blond hair came around from behind the cash register. "I'm Eleanor Pickett. Oops. I mean Moretti." She laughed, her eyes twinkling with delight. "I'm a newlywed. Still getting used to my new last name."

"Congratulations," Hope said. "Nice to meet you. This is my nephew, Cole, and I'm Hope."

"Wonderful to meet you." Eleanor smiled. "Go ahead and run your errands. I'll be here if this young man has any questions."

"Thanks so much," Hope said. "I won't be longer than fifteen minutes."

"Oh, take your time. Have a cup of coffee at Brew's. It takes some time to find the right book. You don't want to rush him." Eleanor gave Hope a conspiratorial wink.

"Are you sure?" Hope knew she had to learn to give Cole a little freedom, even though she was terrified of the prospect.

"This is Homestead Pass. He'll be fine," Eleanor said. "And I won't let him out of my sight."

Hope pulled her business card from her purse and handed it to Eleanor. "My phone number is on this. Just in case."

Eleanor examined the card. "A nurse. How nice. Welcome to town."

"Thank you." Hope stepped outside and stood on the sidewalk for a moment, peeking into the window of the bookstore.

Eleanor Moretti was chatting with Cole as she guided him down an aisle of the store.

Hope sent up a prayer of thanks for the kind woman before turning and assessing the charming town. Overhead, a festive "Welcome to Homestead Pass" banner stretched across Main Street. Smaller pink-and-green flags hung at intervals outside the shops, while pots with red geraniums, pink petunias and trailing ivy, placed at intervals on the sidewalk, contributed to the town's welcoming appeal.

Taking Eleanor's advice, Hope turned left on Edison Avenue, waited for the light and crossed the street. Though Brew's Coffee Shop was three doors down, she already smelled fresh coffee and began to smile with anticipation at the luxury of a few moments of quiet time.

The shop was a surprise. It would fit in nicely in an urban neighborhood. Comfy-looking cushioned chairs surrounded a low black table. Black pleather booths lined the storefront window, and a few cozy tables filled the rest of the room. Overhead, exposed beams and industrial hanging lights gave the store the illusion of spaciousness.

"How can I help you?" a smiling young woman asked.

"I'd like a vanilla latte."

"Hot or iced?"

"Hot, please."

"Coming right up."

When she received her drink, Hope carried it to a booth tucked into the far corner of the shop. She pulled a wrinkled white envelope from her purse and glanced around to be certain of privacy before taking out the folded birth certificate, which she'd reviewed over and over again in the last thirty days. Why hadn't Anna mentioned Trevor Morgan if he was the father of her son? It didn't make any sense. Anna always refused to discuss Cole's father. Hope realized she should have pushed harder and maybe she wouldn't be in this mess.

There had always been a fine line that stood between herself and Anna. Hope knew if she crossed it, her stepsister might not return. At least if the door was open, she could help when Anna made yet another poor decision.

Hope massaged her forehead with her fingers. A headache threatened to take over, as it always did when she thought about the past.

At age ten, Hope hadn't even processed her mother's death when her father brought home little Anna and her bitter and jealous mother. He'd remarried without so much as a heads-up and moved his new family to the country because Anna wanted a horse.

So Hope was uprooted from her friends without a vote. She'd adjusted and even came to enjoy rural life and learned how to ride a horse.

Her father wasn't warm and fuzzy, but she had Anna, and Hope loved her little sis. Things were tolerable for a while. Around the time Anna became a teenager, the household began to fall apart. Hope could no longer pretend she had a happy home. When arguments became the norm—mostly about money and Anna's wild and reckless antics—her father simply didn't come home one night. While she'd never had the close relationship with her father that she had with her mother, Hope hadn't expected him to walk away without looking back. By then, she was eighteen and Anna was fifteen. Hope couldn't stick around, not even for Anna.

She'd failed her stepsister. She would not fail Cole.

"Mind if I join you?"

Hope blinked and nearly fell over at the sound of Trevor Morgan's voice. Heart hammering as though she'd been caught doing something illegal, she scrambled to shove the birth certificate back into the envelope and slip it into her purse.

"Sure," she said on a shaky breath. Hope met his gaze and then glanced away, praying he hadn't noticed her hands trembling.

He wasn't wearing a Stetson today, further emphasizing how much he looked like Gus. Trevor's hair was also the color of caramel, and both had the same thick unruly waves.

No doubt about it, Trevor was very handsome, and she could see why Anna was attracted to him. Yes, it was a good thing that she was nothing like her stepsister. She had zero interest in rodeos, or cowboys, and even less interest in becoming a buckle bunny. And she definitely would never get involved with an emotionally unavailable man like this one. Handsome cowboy or not, Trevor Morgan was a complication she could do without.

He slid into the other side of the booth and placed a mug of coffee on the table. The once cozy spot now seemed far too intimate.

Tell him. Tell him now.

The words started as a chant in her mind.

She couldn't. No. No. No. She couldn't. What if he rejected Cole? Hope didn't think her nephew could handle another loss.

Cole was more than excited about the ranch and the dog he'd named. If she told him now, Trevor might call the home health agency and have her replaced. Then where would she be? Right now, everything was about Cole's future.

Her plan was unfolding nicely. It was best not to rock the boat yet. Maybe if Trevor got to know Cole, he'd come to love him as she did, and then he couldn't walk away. Hope knew only too well about walking away. She couldn't—wouldn't—let that happen to her nephew.

"Where's Cole?" he asked.

"In the bookstore." Hope studied a tiny fissure in the wood laminate tabletop. "Mrs. Moretti is keeping an eye on him." She glanced at her watch. "Maybe I should check on him."

"Mrs. Moretti is married to my sister-in-law's father. He's in good hands."

She gave a short nod at the information and tried to relax.

"You're not working today?" Trevor asked.

"I'm off on Friday and Sunday." Hope dared to look at him and immediately regretted the decision. She was probably the most transparent person on the planet. Could he tell she was hiding something? She feared her pale complexion was pinkening with the warmth of her deception as he met her gaze.

Trevor nodded slowly, as if mulling her answer. "We may have gotten off on the wrong foot this week."

She straightened at the words. "You mean when you asked me if I was qualified to take care of your grandfather?"

Trevor grimaced. "Yeah. That. I apologize. I've been known to bust out of the gate before my brain is engaged."

Hope bit back a sarcastic remark. Now was not the time to air grievances. She had to make nice with this man until she could figure out what to do next.

"Anyhow, I hope we can put that behind us."

"Yes, Mr. Morgan. I'm sure we can. We both have the same goal. Your grandfather's complete recovery."

"Absolutely right." He turned the mug in a circle and then studied her. "I'd like to talk to you about something."

"Oh?"

"I'd like to teach Cole to ride. Maybe one of the days that you're with Gramps at the house, and then a few Sunday afternoons as well." He paused. "I'm thinking this Sunday to start."

Despite having learned to ride as a kid, horses brought back memories of Anna injuring herself on the circuit. "I don't know..."

Trevor looked at her. "Do you have an issue with horses?"

"No. It's not me I'm concerned about. I can ride." She twisted her hands in her lap. When she opened her mouth to speak again, Trevor held up a palm.

"Hold on a minute. Let me plead my case before you shut me down."

"Go ahead," she said.

"I like Cole. He's a sharp kid. He's also bored."

Hope frowned at the jab.

"Now don't get all worked up." Trevor ran a hand over his jaw as though hesitant to proceed. "I'm not condemning you. The situation is what it is."

Not a condemnation? On what planet? Hope lifted her own mug to her lips and took a sip.

"I know you don't think much of me, but I'm happy to provide references. Pastor McGuinness can vouch for my integrity." He paused. "I'll be sure he wears a helmet, and I can promise to treat him like he's my own."

At the words, Hope inhaled her coffee and began to cough.

"You okay?" Trevor rose and came around to pat her on the back.

This time it was Hope who raised a palm. "I'm fine," she squeaked.

"Whew. First time a woman choked on me."
He chuckled. "Probably won't be the last."

She cleared her throat, noticing the patrons around them craning their necks to see what was going on. Hope reached for her latte and took several sips. Then she looked at him. "I think that's an incredibly generous offer..." The words were a hoarse wheeze.

"But?" He arched a brow. "I hear a *but* on its way."

Again, she cleared her throat. "Cole's on the small size for his age and he's timid. I'm not certain he could handle a horse."

"Size has nothing to do with it. But you are correct. Confidence is what matters, and you can trust that he won't go anywhere near a horse until I've given him the training he needs."

He looked at her expectantly, his blue eyes clear and sincere. Like Cole's. In that moment, Hope knew that she had to agree.

"You've become a bit of a hero to him." She paused. "He's had a rough time of it, so I hope you won't let him down."

"No, ma'am. I'll never let that boy down."

"All right then, Mr. Morgan. I'm going to say yes."

"Trevor. The name is Trevor. And I appreciate that."

Hope nodded. The man had no idea how prophetic his words might prove to be.

CHAPTER THREE

"WHAT DO YOU mean I can't watch?" Hope sputtered.

Uh-oh. Trevor stepped back when she removed her sunglasses and jammed her hands on her hips. Her hazel eyes were hot with annoyance.

Trevor glanced over to the area outside the stable doors where Cole stood, head down, kicking at the red dirt with his brand-new boots. Today he wore Wranglers and a navy T-shirt like Trevor's. He hadn't even mentioned proper gear on Friday, yet Hope had wasted no time outfitting the boy in essential clothing. Once again, he noted her devotion to her nephew.

"Mr. Morgan, I don't think you understand." The words were spoken in a low voice, for his ears only. "Except for the bookstore, Cole hasn't been out of my sight for the last thirty days. He's suffered a devastating loss. His mother died a month ago."

She stood on the gravel path between the house and the stables. And Trevor stood in her way. Sunday had delivered a beautiful afternoon, and the June sun beat down on them as he scrambled to defuse the situation. Hope glanced from Cole to him, her lips tight. He gave her credit. The woman cared about her nephew.

"I am sorry for your loss," he said. "But I do understand, as I've been where he is. I'm probably one of the few people who truly gets what he's going through."

Trevor took a breath. He didn't share often, and it was never easy. "My fraternal twin, Lucas, and I were thirteen when our parents were killed in a car accident. A truck driver fell asleep at the wheel."

Hope released a soft gasp and covered her mouth with her fingers. "Oh, that's terrible. I'm so sorry."

"Life isn't fair, is it?" he murmured.

"No. Not at all."

"Thank you for providing boots for Cole," Trevor said. "And for driving him here on a Sunday afternoon. However, I believe it would be best if he and I worked one-on-one. I don't want him to feel like he has to perform. Besides, as I mentioned Friday, it will be a few sessions before he actually rides a horse." Trevor gestured around the ranch. "He's got to get comfortable in the stables and around the animals. Riding isn't solely about getting in the saddle. It's about cleaning stalls, feeding and grooming the animals."

He paused. "Cole is very sensitive. I mean that in a good way. I'll want to pair him with an animal as intuitive as he is. That might take time as well."

"I see." She'd listened quietly, her face expressionless. Trevor couldn't gauge what was going on in her head. Friday, she'd deemed his offer to teach Cole to ride generous. It was clear she'd revised her opinion now that she'd heard about his rules.

Out of her scrubs today, she wore jeans, cowboy boots and a pretty peach-colored T-shirt. The color favored her fair skin, and the dark hair that touched her shoulders like a silk curtain. All facts that he shouldn't have noticed.

"That work for you?" he asked.

"What time should I pick him up?" The response was curt, but the steam had stopped rolling out of her ears.

"How about three hours from now."

"Fine. I don't agree with your process. However, I will respect it." She plunked her glasses back on her nose—a lightly freckled nose, like her nephew's.

"Aw, come on. I'm not holding Cole hostage. Think of it as time off for you. Maybe you can go shopping. Or chat with Pastor McGuinness about my character."

"I don't go shopping." She narrowed her gaze. "And I already checked with the good pastor this morning after service."

Of course, she had. He worked not to laugh. "And was his response to your satisfaction?"

"You'll be relieved to know that Pastor McGuinness thinks you qualify for citizen of the year."

Trevor's eyes widened at the words. "That might be an exaggeration."

"Not at all." Hope shrugged, looking perplexed. "Trust me. I was as surprised as you are."

"Are you guys done yet?" Cole called.

"Yeah. Be right there," Trevor hollered back. He turned back to Hope. "Three hours?"

"Fine." She dug in her purse and pulled out a card. "Do not hesitate to call me if Cole has any problems."

"Thank you for entrusting your nephew's care to me."

She didn't answer. Merely turned on her heel and left. Unspoken words hung in the air between them. *Don't blow it.*

Trevor had high hopes she'd mellow once she saw Cole gain confidence. He'd credited the good Lord, his grandfather and the ranch with saving him. Now, he'd return the favor.

As Hope drove off, another pickup pulled up to the house. It was his older brother Drew. He got out of the vehicle, went to the rear passenger door and lifted his three-year-old daughter, Mae, to the ground. At the same time, his wife, Sadie, slipped out of the truck and unbuckled their one-year-old son, Andrew. They were here to visit Gramps and give Bess an afternoon off.

That was a good thing. Since Gramps had come home from the hospital, Bess had been at the Morgan ranch for seven straight days. She'd willingly volunteered, but Trevor came by as often as possible to ease her load. Lucas had come off the rodeo circuit for Gramps's surgery, but had had to head out again for the upcoming busy season. Most of the load fell to Trevor, as he lived at the big house with his grandfather.

He had a house on the ranch—the one he'd built for his wife. Though, she'd never lived there. He and Lucas had for a time. But he'd moved in with Gramps and now the place sat empty.

They were going to have to find a solution soon, because Bess had already booked herself a plane ticket to visit her newest grandbaby. She would leave in one week and there was no way Trevor could manage the ranch and Gramps.

Drew and Sadie waved to Trevor before they headed into the house.

He offered a wave in return. His big brother had it all. A wife, a family and a life on Lazy M Ranch. It hadn't escaped Trevor, when he looked at the calendar this morning, that today was the seventh anniversary of his wife's death. Married just shy of six months, they hadn't even completed building their home on the property. Alyssa had collapsed at her parents' house. Aneurysm, the autopsy revealed.

The pain never went away. It simply changed from deep, hopeless mourning to an ache in the middle of his chest that rose to clog his throat when he dwelled too long on the past.

"You okay?"

He turned to find Cole at his side. Head cocked, the boy stared at him with concern in his blue eyes.

"I'm good." Trevor smiled. "Got something for you." He pulled a plastic bag from his back pocket. Inside were two neatly ironed and folded red bandannas. "Put one around your neck and the other in your pocket."

"Handkerchiefs?"

"Bandannas." Trevor shook one out and folded it into a triangle. Then he tied it around Cole's neck. "Pull it up when you go into the stables. It will help with the smell until you're acclimated."

Cole grinned. "I can do that."

"When you're on mucking duty, I'll give you a dust mask." He nodded toward the stables. "Now let's get to work. First order of business is a tour of the facility. Then you'll be scrubbing the stall water buckets."

To his credit, Cole didn't complain about the task. The horses were turned out for the day, making it easier for Cole to gather the buckets. An hour later, they were clean, and Trevor had Cole fill them with water. Together, they replaced the buckets.

"Nice job." Trevor handed a dry-erase marker to Cole. "Now you can mark the job complete on the board outside each stall."

"Yes, sir." Cole offered a crisp nod as he accepted the marker.

"Come on into my office when you're done." Trevor headed there and stood in the doorway for a moment, enjoying the cool air of the oscillating fan. He then pulled two bottles of apple juice from the refrigerator and grabbed a couple of granola bars from his desk drawer.

Cole entered a few minutes later. He pulled his bandanna from his nose and sank into a chair. A fine layer of red dust covered his clothes, and his hair, wet with sweat, had been pushed up from his forehead in spikes. To his credit, he was smiling.

"What's next, Mr. Trevor?"

"Break time." Trevor tossed Cole a juice and then a granola bar. "You're doing a great job, Cole."

"Thanks. It's fun. I like it. Maybe I can work on a ranch someday."

"I don't see why not."

They sat silently, enjoying the respite. Trevor

had to admit that he liked having Cole around. The kid was smart, well-mannered and eager to learn.

"Were you arguing with Aunt Hope?" Cole asked moments later.

"Naw. We were exchanging opinions."

Trevor narrowed his gaze, trying to put together pieces of the puzzle that was Hope Burke and her nephew. "Do you and your aunt live close by?"

"Aunt Hope has an apartment in Oklahoma City, but we're staying at the inn. I lived with my mom until..." He sucked in a shaky breath.

"I'm sorry to hear about your mama." Poor kid was still mourning.

"She's in heaven now. That's a good thing." The words sounded rehearsed, and the shrug of Cole's thin shoulders didn't convince Trevor he believed what he said. The kid missed his mama, and it hurt. Hurt all over. Trevor didn't want to be the one to tell him that it would be a very long time before that feeling eased.

Trevor took a long pull of his apple juice and frowned. "So if your aunt has an apartment in Oklahoma City, what's she doing in Homestead Pass?"

Cole peeled back the wrapper on the granola bar and took a bite. He finished chewing and met his gaze. "She's looking for my father."

"Your father?" Trevor froze.

"Uh-huh. I heard her talking on the phone. She said that my father lives in Homestead Pass."

Everything around Trevor became very silent.

His father?

Someone in Homestead Pass was the father of this sweet kid?

A thousand scenarios raced through his mind. None comforting. Twelve years ago, Cole's mother was pregnant with her son. That was a time Trevor remembered little of. His best friend, Wishard Mason—a man as close to him as his own twin brother—had been trampled to death by a bull in the arena. The accident had been Trevor's fault. Not a day went by that he wasn't reminded of that.

Trevor shivered, then shoved a hand into his pocket and touched his sobriety chip. Sometimes just touching the plastic disk helped anchor him and remind him that he'd given all that to the Lord a long time ago and he had to stop taking it back again.

"Are you okay?" Cole asked, alarm in his voice. "Maybe I wasn't supposed to tell you that."

"Hmm?" Trevor realized he had crushed the empty juice bottle in his hand. "Naw, it's fine. I was just thinking."

This was the second time Cole had asked if he was okay. The kid spent more time concerned about those around him than seemed normal. Most kids his age were much more self-focused.

Trevor glanced at his watch. "Finish up. We've got just enough time to show you around the tack room and teach you about saddles before your aunt returns."

Forty-five minutes until Hope arrived. Trevor tossed his container in the trash can, then pulled up his phone and sent a quick message to Drew. He would need some assistance because he and Cole's aunt were going to talk.

The woman sure had fooled him, looking all sunshine and smiles. Hope Burke had an agenda, and Trevor prayed it didn't involve anyone on the Lazy M Ranch.

HOPE COULDN'T SHAKE an ominous feeling as she drove up the ranch drive three hours later.

Trevor was sittting on the porch of the Morgan homestead. Was he waiting for her? As her car crunched on the gravel in front of the house, he stepped down the stairs, slow and steady, like he had all the time in the world.

Panic edged its way around her heart as Hope looked around for her nephew. Where was Cole? She fumbled to grab the keys from the ignition and quickly jumped out of the vehicle. "Is Cole all right?"

"He's fine. My brother Drew took him to the west pasture with the dogs. They'll be back shortly." Trevor met her gaze. His was hard and intense, once again assessing. Why did it seem that the man was constantly sizing her up and finding her lacking?

He cocked his head toward the outbuildings. "I've got an office in the stables. We need to talk."

Hope shivered. This couldn't be good. "Do we?"

"Yeah."

Her nose tickled when she stepped into Trevor's world. She barely heard the neighs and snorts of horses in their stalls as she followed him down the stable aisle to his office. It was like the walk to the principal's office in elementary school.

They stopped at a glassed-in room that provided a view of the facility. The small space held a desk, file cabinet and two chairs. "Did Cole do something wrong?" she asked.

"Nope." He waved a hand toward one of the chairs before he sat down behind the desk and folded his hands on the surface. "Cole tells me you're in Homestead Pass to find his father. Is that why you're here?" His stare became hard. "Is his father on the ranch?"

Hope gripped the arms of the chair tightly. She hadn't done anything wrong. "I'm a home health nurse here for the summer. Your grandfather happens to be one of my patients."

"Yeah. That doesn't exactly answer my question. Who are Cole's parents?"

"His mother was Anna Burke." Hands shaking, Hope rummaged in her purse and pulled out her wallet. She extracted a faded photo of her stepsister on a horse and handed it to him. "Anna was a barrel racer at one time."

"Barrel racer," Trevor murmured. His expression as he examined the photo revealed only curiosity. He turned the picture over. "This date says this picture was taken more than fifteen years ago."

"Yes. That's correct."

Trevor rubbed a hand over his face. "I remember her from the circuit. Hung around more than she rode. Fact is she was broke most of the time. A time or two, I gave her money. Once for a bus ride home. Maybe a couple times for a meal. No strings attached."

When he met her gaze, Hope searched for indications that he wasn't being truthful but found none. His story sounded too familiar. Anna was always a day late and a dollar short.

"Okay, now maybe you can tell me who Cole's father is."

She closed her eyes for a moment and then opened them. "You."

Trevor jerked back, his jaw slack, face pale. "Whoa. That's a leap."

Once again, she dug in her purse. This time she pulled out the envelope with Cole's birth certificate. Hope stood and placed the neatly folded paper on the desk before sitting down again and clutching her bag to her tightly, praying she wouldn't throw up. She wasn't good with confrontation. She'd never be compared to Nurse Ratched. Hope Burke, RN, was more like Nurse Pushover.

Trevor unfolded the paper and stared at it for a long minute. "If she thought I was her son's father, why didn't she say something, oh, I don't know, twelve years ago? And why isn't Cole's name Morgan?"

Those were million-dollar questions. Ones she'd asked herself over and over.

"I have no idea," Hope said. "Perhaps she thought you'd deny her custody since she was a single mother with nothing, and you're a rich rancher."

"Rich?" Anger flashed in the man's eyes. "The Lazy M Ranch is not run by any rich ranchers. We're a family operation that puts in long, hard days to turn a profit in a good year."

For a moment, he sat very still and seemed to study her. "Were you hoping to gain something from my family or me?"

Hope inhaled sharply at his words. Did he just say what she thought he'd said? "I…" she sputtered, then paused, working to compose herself. "Are you insinuating that I'm here to extort you?"

Trevor raised a palm. "I'm trying to figure out why you didn't just tell me. Why all the sneaking around?"

"I wasn't sneaking around. After locating you online, I came here to figure out what sort of person you are."

"Didn't your internet sleuthing tell you that?"

She bit back her frustration. "It told me that you don't have much of a footprint. Just rodeo articles about you and the rest of your family. I didn't do an exhaustive investigation." She swallowed. "As such, I don't know much. Maybe you already have a family. Maybe you have a criminal record."

Or maybe, like her stepmother, he had no room in his heart for a child who'd just lost his mother.

"I don't." His jaw tightened and he stared at her. "To all of that."

"Look, there's no need to be angry. Put yourself in my shoes. I'll do anything to keep Cole from getting hurt again. I'm the only thing that stands between him and the world."

Silence stretched between them. Trevor pushed back his straw cowboy hat and studied the photo and the birth certificate on his desk. His expression gave away nothing. Finally, he took a deep breath and met her gaze. "So Anna passed a month ago."

"That's right. Driving while impaired. Fortunately, no one else was involved."

"Again, I'm sorry for your loss."

Hope nodded and looked at her lap. She loved Anna despite the many nights she'd found herself on her knees praying for her stepsister, fearing things would not end well.

"Cole isn't aware of the circumstances of her death. I got a call from the Tulsa coroner and medical examiner's office and drove to Tulsa to claim her belongings." She pulled the faded envelope out and put it on the desk. "Anna had these clippings as well."

"So not only is Cole dealing with the death of his mother, but he's processing the fact that you're looking for his father." He released a breath. "That's a lot for a kid, isn't it?"

She grimaced, her stomach uneasy. "I wasn't aware that Cole knew what I was doing. But you're correct. It is a lot. More than any little boy should have to deal with."

Trevor nodded, then picked up each clipping and studied them. He gave a low whistle. "I don't get it. Where has your sister been all this time?"

"Stepsister. Her mother and my father were married for a time. In truth, before Cole was born, I hadn't seen her in a few years. Then she showed up nine months pregnant. She's been in and out of my life since. Usually dropping off Cole on her way to somewhere. Often a rodeo, though she hadn't ridden in years. So, no, I don't know exactly where she's been all this time."

"You didn't ask?"

"All I cared about was Cole." The question left her rethinking her decision, and she didn't like the unspoken accusation. "Look, I didn't push because I wanted the lines of communication to remain open, so she'd continue to drop him off with me. It was the only way to ensure I would be part of his life."

The words sounded lame to her own ears, but they were the truth. If she attempted to guide Anna, her stepsister complained she was judgmental, and Hope wouldn't see her or Cole again for months as penance.

Hope pinned him with a look. "You're his father. Where have you been all this time?"

A flash of anger came and went in Trevor's blue eyes. He leaned closer across the desk. Hope almost regretted asking. Almost.

"Now, just a minute here," he said, his voice low and husky. "I want to clarify a few things. First, twelve years ago, I was a young, stupid bulldogger on the circuit. I was a different man. I'm not making excuses, but I'm not ashamed to tell you like it is." He took a deep breath. "I am nothing but a sinner saved by grace. Again, that's not an excuse. It's a fact. If Cole is my son, I will do right by him."

The admission left Hope without words. Was Trevor Morgan as honest as he seemed?

He released a ragged breath and continued. "When were you planning to tell me?"

"I've already explained that. I've been the fallback person for my nephew. Whenever his mother took off, he was in my care." She met his gaze. "I wanted to find out what sort of person you were."

"What if I don't live up to your expectations? What are you planning to do? Run away with Cole?"

"I don't have a plan," Hope admitted. She'd planned for everything but this moment. Ridiculous excuse, and he wouldn't believe her if she told him that she'd been acting on an inner unction. A gut feeling that this was the path. One foot in front of the other. A walk in the dark and believing that the Lord had His hand on the situation.

Trevor leaned back in his chair and folded his arms. The stubborn man she'd met last week returned. "If Cole is my son, I think he should stay on the ranch."

Hope gave an adamant shake of her head. No.

She could never leave Cole. "I can't leave him here with you. You're a stranger."

"You said I'm his father."

Hope stood and gathered the papers on his desk, carefully folded them and put them back in the envelope. "Maybe."

"More than maybe, or you wouldn't have gone to the trouble of leaving your job and your home to come here for the summer. That was a bold move for a maybe."

He was right. It was a bold move, and remorse would keep her awake tonight. She should never have come here.

"I want Cole to stay on the ranch, at least until we figure things out," he pressed. "I'll need to contact my lawyer."

"I'm not leaving Cole with you." This was a battle Trevor Morgan would not win.

"Surely you realize that if I am his father, you'd be forced to leave him."

Hope licked her dry lips while her heart pounded an endless beat. *He's right.*

How did she get here? A slip of the tongue by her nephew and now the possibility of losing the only family she had left loomed. In the back of her mind, she thought she'd find his father, and they would agree on a plan to keep Hope in Cole's life. Was she fooling herself?

"You're thinking with your heart and not your head," Trevor said quietly. "Paternity claims aside, I like Cole, and he deserves more than the summer you've offered him."

Once again, Hope sucked in a breath. "You don't know me at all, Mr. Morgan. All this…" She waved an arm. "All this 'sneaking around,' as you call it, has been for Cole, because I want him to have a better future. I love Cole."

Trevor lifted a hand. "I'm not maligning your character. Just trying to figure things out, like you are."

Hope eased back into the seat as her heart pounded, regretting that she'd come to Homestead Pass.

"You can stay on the Lazy M too." Trevor's voice had gentled, and he looked at her as if he understood the war waging inside.

"No. I can't. I'm your grandfather's home health nurse."

Trevor shrugged. "Quit."

"I can't quit. I have bills to pay." The tenuous line she was walking with her finances was enough to keep her awake at night. "Besides, the agency doesn't look kindly on nurses who walk off the job. They might blackball me."

"We could hire you as a private duty nurse, through the agency, to work nine to five, five days a week with Gramps. Take him to physical therapy three days a week. That would relieve my brothers and I from leaving our jobs in the middle of the day." He paused. "And Bess is about to take some time off, and I can't have an eighty-two-year-old man recovering from hip surgery alone at the house all day." Trevor shrugged again. "We genuinely could use your assistance."

"Private duty nursing is expensive."

"We aren't rich—" He gave her a pointed look though his eyes seemed amused. "But my grandfather saved my life once. I'm more than happy to do what I can to ease his, and I know my brothers would agree in a heartbeat." He fiddled with a pen on the desk, brow now furrowed in thought.

"I've got a house on the ranch," he continued. "It's empty. You and Cole can stay there."

Hope frowned. "Why do you have an empty house?"

"My plans changed. Now the house is empty.

You can even take that pup Cole is fond of with you."

"Oh no." She shook her head. "I don't think it's wise for Cole to get attached to a dog, especially since I don't have any idea what the future holds or if there's room in that future for a pet."

"Cole is hurting, and a dog can fill that empty spot he's got in his heart."

Hope opened her mouth to speak and found herself without words. All the while, Trevor stared at her expectantly.

"What about Cole?" she asked. "What will he do all day? You have a ranch to run."

"No reason why he couldn't be with me during the day."

"You'd want him tagging along?" Was he really offering that?

"He's not a baby. I was doing ranch chores at his age. Cole can learn a lot, and I enjoy his company."

She couldn't help but stare at Trevor. So many thoughts were running through her mind. This was an answer to a prayer financially, and it would give her time to deal with the whole paternity issue. Still, it was a huge leap of faith.

"I'm going to need some time to think about

this," she said slowly. "Everything is moving so quickly."

That was an understatement. Trevor had not only turned the tables on her, but he had also pulled the rug out from under her. Sure, she'd planned to tell him soon, but she thought she'd have a bit more time—the weekend, at least—to figure this out.

"What was the pace you expected when I found out?" he asked.

"I keep telling you. I didn't expect anything. I wanted to do what was best for Cole. It seemed I at least owed it to him to find out if you were his father since you were only a few hours away. I decided to see if you were the kind of man who would appreciate what a great kid Cole is before I took further action."

"Look, I've only spent a few hours with him, but already it's clear that, yes, he is a great kid who deserves a break."

"I'll agree to this arrangement..." She met his gaze as a worrisome thought crept in. "But only if you promise not to tell him that you're his father. For now."

He seemed exasperated for a moment. "Make up your mind. Am I his father? Or not?"

She stared at Trevor. The man certainly knew

how to push her buttons. "Do you think any of this has been easy? All I'm asking is that we not talk to Cole yet."

"What about my family?" he asked. "I won't lie to them."

"I'm not asking you to. I'm asking you to avoid offering information until we figure things out."

"Figure things out." He nodded slowly. "The Lord brought both of you here for a reason. I guess we're about to find out why."

Hope's heart was heavy as she realized that, once again, he was absolutely correct. She prayed she hadn't made the biggest mistake of her life coming to Homestead Pass.

CHAPTER FOUR

THE CHAIR CREAKED when Trevor eased back into the soft leather, aged from seasons of use. The office used to be Drew's, and before that, it was his father's. Now it was his.

While he had a small office in the stable, this was where he could work surrounded by the comforting memories of the past. A photo of his parents, which included all four of the Morgan siblings, sat on the big cherrywood desk, just as it had when his father was alive.

Some days he felt ill-equipped to be the manager of the Lazy M Ranch. Today was one of those days. His brothers believed in him, so he'd do his best to believe in himself.

Trevor swiveled around and sighed as he stared out the bay window that provided an unobstructed view of Bess's garden and the pasture all the way to the horizon. He had so much to be grateful for. Yet, as always, it seemed that something was missing from his life.

He glanced at the oak mantel clock ticking away the hours on the bookshelf, his thoughts drifting to the events of earlier today. He'd invited Hope and Cole to stay in his house for the summer. Why? Because...well, because he'd been dumbstruck at the facts she'd presented to him. And in a very short time, he'd found himself very fond of her nephew.

Was he Cole's father? Could he even be worthy of such a title? Shame mixed with confusion as Trevor wrestled with the question.

A question that he couldn't deny with certainty. Twelve years ago, life had been dark and cloaked in despair after the death of his buddy, Wishard. He should have been in the arena that night. Chunks of time were missing after Wish's death, leaving Trevor ashamed of himself. One thing he did recall was the night his grandfather drove to the Okmulgee rodeo and brought him home. Gus and the good Lord had saved him. Gotten him dried out and put him in AA. Turned his life around.

"You coming to dinner?"

His ears perked at the sound of Drew's voice in the kitchen.

"On my way," Trevor called. He eased up from the chair and picked up the family photo, running a thumb over the surface. What would his father have done if faced with today's dilemma? Trevor liked to think he'd have done the same thing.

"I'll make things right, Dad," he murmured.

The aroma of something delicious greeted him as he walked down the hall. Savory and buttery with a hint of garlic. Was that roast turkey? And it wasn't even Thanksgiving.

Trevor stood in the kitchen doorway for a moment as the Morgan Family 2.0 laughed and jockeyed for seats at the oak table. Just a few years ago, there were only the Morgan brothers and Gramps around this same table.

It was difficult not to be a little envious. Drew and Sam had found happiness, and it showed on their faces. Trevor longed for what they had, but at the same time, he was hesitant to go after it. He'd finally made peace with the journey that had gotten him to today, and life was pretty good. Why go looking for trouble?

"We need to discuss how we're going to handle Bess's vacation," Sam said when he spotted Trevor. The number-two Morgan son pulled two trays of ramekins from the oven and placed them on the counter.

"Can we eat first?" Drew asked. "I'm starving. All I've had today is baby oatmeal."

"Daddy, silly!" Three-year-old Mae laughed, her blond curls dancing around her head as she moved. Drew buckled his daughter into a high chair that matched the one on his other side, which held one-year-old baby Andrew. Trevor's brother juggled both babies effortlessly before sliding into a chair between them.

"How can I help?" Trevor asked, with a nod to Olivia, Sam's wife.

"We're set." She placed a large tossed salad on the table while Drew's wife, Sadie, handed Trevor an overflowing basket of garlic bread.

"Good to see you, Trevor," she said.

"You too." Sadie held a special spot in Trevor's heart, as this particular sister-in-law had triumphed over a challenging childhood. Another reason Trevor felt driven to support kids in crisis with mentoring and the end-of-summer event he had launched.

"Something sure smells delicious. What's for dinner?" Trevor asked. He put the bread on the table and pulled out a chair beside his grandfather.

"Olivia Moretti Morgan's famous turkey potpies," Sam said. A note of pride and love was evident in his voice. Sam took a moment to plant a tender kiss on his wife's cheek.

"Enough with the mushy stuff," Gramps said. "Let's pray. I'm hungry."

Voices quieted and heads bowed as the Morgan patriarch led the family in prayer. Once "amen" sounded around the room, smiling faces popped up, and eager hands reached for serving dishes.

Sam nabbed a breadbasket away from Drew and chuckled. "Come to papa."

Drew rolled his eyes and ignored him. "About Bess's vacation."

"Bess and I have already figured out lunches for the ranch wranglers," Olivia said. "Everything is labeled and in the freezer." She looked at Trevor. "All you have to do is follow the instructions on the containers."

"I can do that. Sure appreciate you, Olivia." Trevor shook his head. The woman kept busy. She was pregnant with twins and ran Moretti's Farm-to-Table Bistro in town.

"When's Bess leave?" Gramps asked while focused on dipping his spoon into the golden crust of his potpie.

"Next weekend," Trevor said. "Her last day is Friday, and she'll be back beginning of August."

Sam glanced at the calendar on the fridge, and his eyes widened. "That's more than a month. I don't think we've ever gone that long without Bess. I'm sorry for Trev and Gramps. They'll be living on Trev's cooking in the evenings."

"Hey, I can cook," Trevor protested.

"Says who?" Sam laughed.

Trevor turned to his grandfather. "Tell him, Gramps."

"Yep," Gus said with a nod. "The Homestead Pass Volunteer Fire Department agreed when they arrived. Best burnt ends ever."

"That's not funny," Trevor said.

Even Drew chuckled. "It is a little," he murmured.

"It wasn't a fire. It was smoke." Trevor groaned. "Mrs. Pettersen saw the smoke and called the fire department."

"Gentlemen, could we focus on Bess?" Sadie asked gently, while scanning the table.

"You're right, sweetheart," Drew said. "Bess hasn't had a real vacation in years. She has a grandbaby coming, so she's flying to Texas."

"Texas?" Sam jerked back, his face screwed up like he'd bitten into a lime. "Texas is no place for a vacation. Those Longhorns think they're going to whup the Sooners. Not this year."

Drew laughed. "She's not pledging allegiance to Longhorn football. Just visiting her youngest son and his wife."

"So you say." Sam pointed toward the end of the table with his fork. "What about Gramps?"

Startled, Gus looked up from his meal, "What about me?"

"You're only a week post-op," Sam continued. "You'll need someone here during the day in case you need assistance."

"I've got it covered," Trevor said. "I made an executive decision."

All eyes turned toward him, and Trevor met them all, determined not to back down.

"Good for you. You're the boss now. That's your privilege," Drew said.

"Thanks. But you haven't even heard my decision."

"Doesn't matter," Sam chimed in. "You're doing a great job managing the ranch. We should have put you there years ago."

"Hear! Hear!" Drew said.

Trevor tucked away the praise for later, silently honored at the words from his big brothers, whom he'd idolized. He prayed they were right. He adjusted the napkin on his lap and sat straighter. "I've convinced Hope Burke to come on board as a private duty nurse."

"What's that mean?" Gramps asked.

"It means she'll be here nine to five Monday through Friday instead of two days a week. She'll be here while Bess is gone or until Gramps is released by the doctor. Whichever comes first."

"That's brilliant, Trev," Drew said.

Gramps grabbed tongs from the salad bowl and added salad to his plate. "What's she gonna do all day?"

"Get you back into the swing of things," Trevor said.

"Like fishing?" His grandfather perked, a grin sliding onto his face.

"Possibly," Trevor said. "Oh, and she's moving into my house with her nephew."

Silverware clattered, followed by an awkward silence that hung over the table.

"You sure you want to do that, son?" Gramps murmured.

"It's a house, Gramps. And it's been seven years. I'm thinking maybe it's time for me to stop reading the same chapter over and over. Time to start a new one."

Trevor stared at his plate, becoming uncomfortable with the discussion as well as the silence. "Pass the salad," he said.

Gramps handed the large bowl to Trevor and leaned close. "Proud of you, son," he said quietly.

"Thanks, Gramps."

"Quit hogging the bread, Drew," Sam groused. He snatched the breadbasket back and out of the reach of his brother's long arms.

"Save room for dessert," Sadie said. "Bess taught me how to make her Texas sheet cake."

With that, the conversation started again. Trevor couldn't help but smile. He was fortunate to have such a caring family. They gave him space when he needed it and never pushed him.

A short time later, Sadie and Olivia cut the cake and began to pass out servings.

Trevor looked at his watch and then stood. "I have to get over to the house. Hope and Cole are moving in this evening, so she doesn't have to pay for another night at the Homestead Pass Inn."

"Nice way to get out of dishes." Sam arched a brow and shook his head.

"I'll take your turn next time," Trevor said. He slipped out of the kitchen toward the pantry and opened the large freezer. Bess kept frozen oatmeal cookies in the freezer. Trevor grabbed a package of those and a frozen lasagna as well.

He detoured to the barn and greeted Patch, who dozed on a blanket in his wire crate. The pup looked up, excited to have a visitor. The animal's tail trembled with anticipation as Trevor unlocked the door, and he shot out of the crate the second it creaked open. Eager for adventure, Patch followed Trevor to his truck, where he put the crate in the flatbed and opened the passenger door for the pup.

"Sit," Trevor said. Patch obeyed.

All the Morgan boys had houses on the ranch except Lucas. Drew's was farthest away, at the top of the ridge, near the creek. Sam's overlooked the east pasture. Trevor's was a fifteen-minute walk or a short drive away.

Five minutes later, he pulled the pickup in front of a two-story dwelling, half brick and half gray clapboard. The plan had been to add on as needed.

There was no need. Alyssa died before the Sheetrock went up.

Patch eagerly followed him up the steps to the wide porch. The minute the key was in the lock, the pup shoved his nose close, ready to investigate.

"Sit," Trevor said.

The dog sat and whined with fervor.

Once the door was open, he raced in. The echo of his nails clicking on the floor filled the house.

The furniture in the place was covered with sheets. If he'd thought about it, he could have come by earlier and dusted. Trevor walked through the area, inspecting, then stopped in the kitchen to put Bess's food in the fridge.

For a moment, he stared out the kitchen window at the view. Maple trees created a border at the back, and conifers lined the left and right. Seven years later and they were already tall and sturdy against the sky. The sun had begun a slow descent, though it wouldn't be dark for a few more hours.

This was a good house. However, it held no memories. Alyssa never lived here. They'd met at a wedding of friends. She was from outside Seattle, in town for the weekend. The weekend turned into two weeks, and soon after that, he proposed, then they'd gotten married in her parents' backyard in her hometown. The plan was to have another wedding in Homestead Pass. That never happened.

He often reflected on that time in his life. How quickly he'd fallen in love and proposed. Had he rushed because he was afraid Alyssa would change her mind if she knew the shameful secrets of his past? The question haunted him.

A knock on the door had Trevor turning. Hope stood on the porch. He made the mistake of opening the screen before securing the pup. Patch once again took off like he was fuel-injected, nearly knocking Hope over. She reached for the door frame while Trevor grabbed the box in her arms before she dropped it.

"Patch," Cole called with excitement from the car. "I'll get him."

"Thanks, Cole," Trevor called back. He turned to Hope. "You okay?"

"Fine," she said, looking somewhat dazed. "I didn't realize the dog would be here."

"He's crate-trained. Just put him in his crate after he does his thing outside tonight. You'll both get a good night's sleep that way." He nodded for her to come in. She did, and the scent of vanilla teased his senses as she passed.

"What will I feed him?" Hope frowned,

her hazel eyes full of genuine concern. Trevor found himself wanting to rub away the wrinkle between her eyes. He shoved his hands in his pockets.

"I brought you everything you need," he said carefully. "This is Cole's responsibility. I'll have a chat with him before I leave."

"That would be appreciated." She released a breath. "I spend most of my time worrying that I'll harm Cole's psyche. I don't want to mess up a dog too."

"Don't overthink this."

Hope offered a brief laugh. "I'm sorry. We haven't known each other long. Overthinking is my middle name."

"Okay, then." He bit back a smile, realizing they had a lot in common. He'd messed up plenty in his life. Now he spent a significant amount of time overthinking as well.

Hope stepped farther into the entry and looked around. "Who lived in this house?"

"I did, with my brother Lucas for a time. Sam was alone in his house. Seemed like a waste of electricity, so we moved in with him." He walked around the open living room and removed sheets from the love seat and two chairs facing a stone fireplace. He tucked them under his arm, taking in the muted Southwest colors of the space.

"It's very nice," Hope said.

"Needs dusting."

"Dusting, I understand. Dogs are another story."

"Aunt Hope, do you want me to bring your suitcase in?" Cole called. Patch stood beside the boy on the walkway, his tongue lolling with joy.

"Yes, please," she replied.

Cole skipped back out of the house toward the car, with Patch trotting behind.

"That's a happy kid," Trevor observed.

"Yes. You may have been right about a few things."

"I am on occasion," he murmured. "Come on. I'll show you around."

Trevor opened doors and cupboards, explaining where things were located, until they ended up in the kitchen.

Hope glanced around at the appliances. "I've only ever dreamed of a stove like this. Convection, right?"

"Yeah. It has an air-fryer option and, go figure, it's called a smart oven."

"Wow."

Wow? He'd tossed a couple casseroles in the thing when he lived in the house, but that was it. From the look on Hope's face, he should have given the appliance more attention.

"I take it you cook," he said.

"Yes, it's a bit of a hobby."

"Good to know." Trevor nodded. "There's a couple of things I should mention."

Hope frowned. "Oh? Is this the boot-drop portion of our tour?"

Surprised by her response, he crossed his arms and assessed the woman before him. "Funny, I took you for an optimist."

She chuckled nervously and pushed her dark hair behind her ears. "Yes. Normally, I'm an annoying optimist. This has hardly been a normal day."

"You can relax for now. I'm only sharing the schedule."

"The schedule." She gave a short nod. "Okay."

"Cole and I will start at about nine tomorrow."

"Is that when you begin your day?"

Trevor nearly laughed aloud at that. If only ranching was a nine-to-five job. "No, ma'am. I start at daylight and end at dusk. However, while Bess is gone, I'll be home by five."

"What about your grandfather? Does he manage the ranch too?"

"Gramps was an electrical engineer before he retired. He moved to Lazy M when our parents passed and became our guardian. Gramps dabbles in ranching. Does a bang-up job of being our social ambassador. For that, all the Morgan boys are grateful."

"So besides physical therapy three times a week, is there anything else on your grandfather's schedule I should know about?"

"I'll leave that between you and Gramps, but normally he likes a few hours in town, and he's got regular functions that he attends. Like I said, my grandfather is very social."

"I'll talk to him. There's no reason why he can't slowly return to his usual activities."

"That would be great." Trevor paused. "Bess's last day is Friday, and she'll give you the rundown on the household."

"What about meals?"

"I'll be sure Gramps has breakfast in the morning. We have a routine for lunch. Bess will explain the plan. As for dinner, I'll be home in time to get it on the table."

"Got it," she said quietly, as though thinking. He eyed her, uncertain if things were all right. The woman was hard to read. Not that he had any real experience with women. Before Alyssa, well, he hadn't dated much. Lucas was the outgoing one. "Any other questions?" he finally asked.

"Oh, I'm sure I'll have a dozen. Tomorrow."

"I'll leave you then." Trevor held out the keys, and she took them. "There's a frozen lasagna in the fridge thawing, along with a bag of frozen oatmeal cookies. Courtesy of Bess and the Morgan pantry."

"That was very nice of you. Thanks." She looked at him for a moment. "We're still on the same page regarding…um, Cole. Right?"

"For now." He glanced at his watch. "I'm going to go and give him instructions on Patch. Then I'll be heading back to the house."

"Thank you, Mr. Morgan."

"Trevor."

"Trevor." She hesitated. "No matter how this turns out, your kindness to Cole is appreciated."

"I'm only paying it forward. Not a big deal."

"But it is," she said. "A very big deal. You've changed the course of Cole's life, and we haven't even taken a DNA test yet."

"That might be a bit of an exaggeration," he said. He didn't want anyone to think he was some kind of hero. Far from it. "Think of the Lazy M Ranch as a rest stop on the road to tomorrow."

"That's a poetic take on things," she said. "But I firmly believe that nothing occurs by happenstance, Mr. Morgan."

"Trevor. And I'll see you tomorrow." Turning, he walked out the door, mulling Hope's words. Could a few weeks on the ranch make a difference in the boy's life? He hoped so.

HOPE RESTED HER hands on her hips, catching her breath. *Wow, I'm out of shape.* An early Monday morning spent chasing Patch all over the yard behind the house had proved that. The energetic dog thought it was great fun to outsmart the humans. Hope had planned to walk to the main house, as it was only half a mile down the road. However, Patch changed those plans.

"I've got his leash on, Aunt Hope," Cole panted as he led the pup toward the car.

Hope laughed aloud. The dog had bested them both. She didn't feel so bad after seeing her nephew out of breath too.

"Wonderful. Why don't you sit in the back with Patch? Keep your hand on that collar. We cannot be late today."

"Yes, ma'am." Cole's gaze searched hers. "I'm real sorry he wouldn't come when I called."

"Sweetie, there's no need to apologize. We're both new to this dog game. Tomorrow we'll take him out with a leash." She smiled at the mischievous puppy, who cocked his head and looked at her with an expression that said, "I'm adorable. Let's play again." And he was adorable. He was also in serious need of obedience training.

Hope slid into the driver's seat and took a moment to collect herself. She ran her fingers through her bangs and checked her ponytail in the mirror.

Trevor Morgan was a contradiction she couldn't quite figure out. Never in a dozen years would she have expected him to offer the little house to them. And what a blessing it was. Though if it were her place, she'd paint the front door a cheery blue and add pink flower boxes with white petunias and crimson begonias spilling over the sides. Maybe a few hanging Boston ferns.

But it wasn't her house, so there was no point in dreaming. She put the key in the ignition and backed out of the gravel drive.

They pulled up to the main house at one

minute after nine. Hopefully, Trevor wouldn't notice that she was tardy. No need to get him grumpy again.

"Look," Cole said. "The horses are out."

She turned, and he was right. At least a dozen horses grazed in a grassy field, enjoying the sunshine and sweet spring grass.

"They're beautiful." Hope grabbed her equipment. "We have to hurry, Cole."

Her knock on the front door elicited a holler of greeting and an invitation to come in.

"What about Patch?" Cole asked.

Hope groaned. "Have a seat on the porch. I'll figure out where Mr. Trevor is."

She peeked into the kitchen and found Gus at the kitchen table reading a newspaper while Bess flipped pancakes in a skillet at the stove.

"Morning, Miss Hope," Gramps said. He glanced behind her. "I thought Trevor said you were bringing your nephew with you."

"Yes, sir. He's outside on the porch taking care of his new dog."

Bess chuckled, her gaze moving to Hope. "You've got your hands full with that pup."

"You don't know the half of it," Hope murmured.

A moment later, Trevor appeared in the

kitchen doorway. "May I speak with you for a few minutes?" He tilted his head. "I've got an office down the hall."

"Sure." She searched his face for a clue as to what was going on. As usual, he gave away nothing. Had he noticed she was late? Was there a problem? Maybe he'd decided to rescind his offer.

"Where's Cole?" he asked.

"On the front porch with Patch." She frowned. "I should check on them."

"I can do that," Bess said. She turned down the flame under the skillet. "You go take care of your business."

She nodded. "Thank you, Mrs. Lowder."

Hope followed Trevor down the hall to a spacious office. He gestured toward a set of wing chairs. She eased into one, and he sat in the other.

"What's wrong?" she blurted.

"Nothing is wrong." Trevor clasped his hands together. "I called Child Support Services this morning."

"And?"

"They were very helpful. Provided more information than I probably need." He looked at her. "Bottom line is that I'd like you to call and open a child-support case to establish paternity."

"I considered doing that a few weeks ago, when I first saw your name on the birth certificate."

"And?"

"I decided to check you out first, and I figured it would be simpler to ask you to consent to lab work for testing. It's a lot quicker than all that government red tape."

"While it's possible that Cole is my son, I'm functioning on the likelihood that he's not."

That gave her pause. What was his rationale here? "That makes no sense," she finally said.

"It does to me. Whether he's my son or not doesn't change our plans."

Hope stared at him. Was he afraid of the results of a DNA test?

"Besides, the fella I talked to told me that if I'm not Cole's father, this route will assist you in getting benefits for Cole, like health insurance."

"What happens after I open a case?"

"You'll meet remotely with a caseworker. Once we're in the system, then we'll have DNA testing done."

Hope put a hand on her knee to stop the nervous tapping. Yes, she wanted to move forward with finding out if Trevor was Cole's father, but a part of her was terrified. Of what, she wasn't completely certain. Losing Cole? Or maybe it was the idea of change. She functioned best with well-defined parameters. "How long does testing through child support services take?" she finally asked.

"A few weeks, give or take."

She blinked, doing the math. "You're talking two months. School starts right before Labor Day."

"Yeah." He shrugged. "That's nine weeks away. You agreed that Cole could stay for the summer."

"No, I did not. And your grandfather isn't going to need a nurse for more than another four weeks."

He blinked. "I don't see the problem."

Hope stared at him. Was he being dense on purpose? "I can't stay without a job."

"Sure you can. But if that bothers you, then go back to the home health agency and leave Cole with me during the day. Let the boy have his summer."

"I—I…"

"Or how about if we take it one step at a time?"

"I don't usually function one step at a time." Which was not entirely the truth, as it seemed that ever since she'd started on this journey to find Cole's father, she'd been functioning that way, and she didn't like it one bit.

"Yeah, I noticed you've got control issues."

Her jaw nearly dropped. "Excuse me?"

"Nothing wrong with that. I'm sure it's a trait that's served you well in the past." His expression turned thoughtful. "But the thing is, this is all about Cole. Not about you or me."

"I'm aware of that. I've been aware of that for nearly twelve years."

"Great. Then we agree. One step at a time."

Hope opened her mouth and closed it. She was accustomed to being in charge, but Trevor Morgan seemed to challenge her at every turn. The galling part was that his arguments were difficult to refute.

He smiled. "Aw, come on. We can work together, you know."

Work together his way is what he means. She shook her head. "Fine. We do it your way for now." She paused. "Is there anything else?"

"Yeah. He needs a haircut. The kid can hardly see with that hair in his face. I'll take him on Saturday when I go into town."

"I'm perfectly capable—"

Trevor raised a hand. "You've got to stop taking everything personally."

"Am I?" she shot back.

"Yeah. Cole is eleven. He doesn't need his auntie with him to visit the barber. I'm getting a haircut on Saturday. He can come with me. Good for him to have other influences in his life."

"You mean men."

"No. I mean 'other.' Gramps, Bess, Pastor McGuinness. His whole life has been you and his mother. Maybe he could learn something from others."

"Wait." She did a double take. "Are you calling me a helicopter aunt?"

"If the propeller fits."

Hope scoffed, unable to come up with a response but knowing he was right. Anna's wayfaring lifestyle hadn't helped Cole establish much of a support system.

Trevor stood. "This has been a good talk. I appreciate it."

Hope blinked. A good talk? He'd done all the talking and the decision-making. She followed Trevor back down the hall. Bess was alone in the kitchen loading the dishwasher.

"Hey, Bess. Where's Gramps?" Trevor asked.

"On the front porch. Eating second breakfast with Cole."

"Second breakfast?" Hope asked. "Like the hobbits?"

"No, like the ranchers," Trevor returned. "We don't have much of an appetite at four a.m., so we eat second breakfast around nine."

The screen door gently swooshed behind them as they went out to the front porch.

Gus and Cole were sitting at a wicker table eating pancakes. Patch was stretched out on the floor next to Cole's chair, obviously tired from his morning romp. When the Morgan patriarch leaned over to Cole, said something and chuckled, her nephew's face broke into a wide grin.

Hope's heart stuttered at the sight. Cole deserved more moments like this. Maybe a summer on the Lazy M Ranch wasn't such an outlandish idea.

"What are you two up to?" Trevor called as they walked toward the table.

"Nothing much. I was telling Cole here about the time you sat on that red anthill."

"An anthill?" Hope murmured, pinning him

with her gaze. "And you wonder why I'm protective of my nephew."

"Hey, no need to look at me like that," Trevor said. "That was a long time ago, and to be fair, I didn't realize it was an anthill."

"Yep, you were about Cole's age." Gramps grinned, his blue eyes crinkling at the corners.

Trevor grinned back. "Cole is a lot smarter than me."

"Can't dispute them facts." Gus laughed.

Bess stepped outside, flipping a dish towel over her shoulder, and assessed the table. "All finished here?"

"Yes, ma'am," Cole said. He wiped his mouth with the cloth napkin on his lap. "Thank you. Best pancakes I've ever had."

"What a sweet boy you are," Bess said as she began collecting dishes.

"I'll help you with that," Hope said, stepping forward.

"Oh, you'll have plenty of opportunities while I'm on vacation." Bess looked at Trevor. "What do you two have planned for today?"

"Cole and I have mucking class," Trevor said.

"Mucking class?" Cole repeated, his eyes widening. "You think I'm ready?"

"Sure you are. I've got a mask for you, just like I promised."

"Are you sure—" Hope began, looking from her nephew to Trevor.

The cowboy met her gaze. "I'm very sure."

She offered a tight nod and worked to tamp down her concern. How dangerous could mucking be? The horses were already out in the pasture.

"The boss man is going to muck stalls?" Gramp asked with a laugh.

"Yes, sir. No one on this ranch is too big to muck. After lunch I have a meeting. Cole will be with Jim to observe horse training for the afternoon."

Hope glanced at her watch. "We better head into Elk City, Gus. Physical therapy is at ten thirty."

"Yes, ma'am. I can see you run a tight ship like my grandson."

"Not quite that tight." Hope looked at Cole. "If you need me, have Mr. Trevor give me a call. For anything. Okay?"

"He'll be fine, Auntie." Trevor arched an eyebrow.

Heat warmed Hope's face. She opened her mouth and then closed it again, crossing her arms in exasperation.

This rancher knew how to push her buttons and she was determined not to allow him to best her. Not today, at least.

CHAPTER FIVE

"ARE YOU SURE you don't mind?" Bess asked. "I don't want to take advantage of you."

Hope smiled at the housekeeper. It had only been two weeks since she'd arrived on the Lazy M Ranch, yet it felt like she'd known the caring woman all her life.

"Bess, you've been wonderful showing me the ropes this week." She glanced around the spotless kitchen. "But it's Friday. Lunch is over. Gus is taking a nap. Dinner is in the refrigerator. There really isn't much left to do around here. Go run your errands and have a wonderful vacation."

Bess gave a little wiggle of her shoulders. "You're right. I'm going to do that." Then she paused. "Sadie and Liv know the routine. Give them a call if you have problems. All the numbers are in that notebook in the drawer. And promise me you won't let Trevor get to you. I know he can be a bit intimidating."

"Trevor? Oh, no, I won't. In my line of work, I deal with a range of personalities. I think of myself as Switzerland. I stay neutral at all times with my clients." Her eyes went to the refrigerator, where a sweet photo of Drew, Sadie and their children slid from the magnets to the floor. She picked it up and placed the picture next to several others of the Morgan brothers. All were represented, except Trevor.

"Bess, may I ask you a quick question?"

"Sure, honey."

"Why aren't there any photos of Trevor on the fridge?"

The older woman sighed. "There used to be. They were all of Trevor and Alyssa. When Alyssa passed, I tucked them away. It seemed every time he looked at them he got that woeful face."

"Alyssa?" A knot of dread tightened in Hope's stomach.

"His wife. We lost her about seven years ago. She was up in Seattle when it happened."

Trevor is a widower. How did she not see that in her internet searching? Hope's heart ached at the information. He'd found love and lost love.

The next time she had a pity party for her own life, she'd remember this moment. Perhaps she was fortunate to have never fallen in love.

"Didn't he tell you?" Bess asked.

"We haven't really talked about much except Gus and Cole and Patch."

"And he's not that talkative anyhow. Is he?" Bess added.

"Not exactly." A sudden thought crossed Hope's mind, and she couldn't help but ask the question. "Am I living in their house?"

"Technically, yes. Though the house wasn't finished before we lost her." Bess patted Hope's arm. "Trevor must like you because he's never invited anyone else into that house, except his brothers."

Hope nodded absently. She doubted that Trevor liked her. Aside from his assessing looks, which she interpreted as her not measuring up, it was Cole who was the cowboy's focus.

"Anything else?" Bess's gaze swept the kitchen in a final check.

"There is one more thing. Would you mind if I used your oven?" Hope asked. It would only be proper to get the cook's permission before she infringed upon her territory.

Bess laughed at that and pointed toward the

hallway. "The kitchen is yours. Consider me out that door."

"Thanks, Bess."

"No. Thank you, dear. I am relieved to know you'll be here in my absence."

Thirty minutes later, the scent of chocolate wafted through the room as the first batch of cookies baked. Hope turned on the oven light and peeked at them.

"What are you doing?"

She whirled around at the sound of Trevor's voice. The perpetual frown was on his face as he stared at her. With his straw Stetson perched on the back of his head, and a black T-shirt and Wranglers, the man was formidable as he filled the doorway. Hope wasn't accustomed to so much testosterone and took a step back.

"I'm making cookies. Secret recipe." A smile escaped at the admission. Baking and cooking brought back memories of her mother, who had invited Hope to experiment with recipes from an early age.

Trevor seemed annoyed at her cheerful response. But she refused to let him get her down. Especially since the cookies in the oven were some of her finest if she did say so herself. Double chocolate white chip. Her absolute favorite.

Not an heirloom recipe, but a recipe perfected with love over the years.

He looked around the kitchen, his gaze returning to her.

"You're awfully grumpy," Hope said.

"I get that a lot." Then he strode to the kitchen sink, pulled the disinfectant wash from the lower cupboard and turned on the water. That was when she noticed a dusty, blood-stained gauze bandage on the palm of his right hand.

Hope's medical training kicked in, and she moved closer. "Did you cut yourself?"

"Cut it last week and I accidentally opened the wound again. I need to pick up a different pair of gloves."

"Isn't there a first-aid kit outside? You really should have one in the barn and the stables."

"We do. I didn't want anyone to make a big deal out of it." He stared pointedly at her. "That's why I came inside to wash up."

"Oh." Standing straight, she refused to allow him to browbeat her. This was her territory now. "Is your tetanus up-to-date?"

"It is."

"In case you forgot, I am a registered nurse.

That means I'm qualified to assist you with that dressing change."

"I got it." He pulled out the trash can, then unwrapped the gauze and ran the cut under a stream of water.

"You're right handed."

"So?"

"It won't be easy to clean the area, apply antiseptic and secure a dressing." He glanced over at her, and she returned the same pointed look.

"Okay, fine," he muttered.

"Have a seat at the table." Hope covered the kitchen table with a protective pad and placed her tackle box on the material. She laid out all her supplies, carefully opening packages to maintain a sterile field, then donned nitrile gloves. "Could you put your hand on the table, please?"

He complied. "Sorry for all the dust. Job hazard."

"Not a problem," Hope said.

Silence stretched as she assessed the cut.

Trevor pulled out his phone and checked messages with his free hand. "Have you heard from social services?" he asked.

"Just a confirmation email. I've reviewed the documentation online at least a dozen times, and my lay interpretation is that the caseworker should reach out anytime now. You'll be notified, and then you can file an appeal denying paternity. We'll be sent instructions for genetic testing at some point in that timeline."

"The cogs of bureaucracy move slowly." He nodded. "What are you going to tell Cole regarding testing?"

"I don't know." She carefully concentrated on cleansing the wound. "Someone recently suggested that I take things one step at a time."

Hope lifted her gaze and met his. She smiled sweetly.

"Touché," he murmured. His lips twitched, and the half-lidded eyes offered a look of respect at her comeback.

Hope dried his palm and applied antibiotic ointment, followed by a loose dressing. "All done. It's healing nicely, though it's unfortunate that it's in an area that gets so much use. You should definitely get some gloves that will protect the laceration."

"Got it, Doc. I'll be in town tomorrow for that haircut. We'll make a stop at the Hitching Post." He paused. "You know what? I think we'll take Gramps with us too."

"That's a great idea." She pulled off her

gloves and began to roll up the pad containing all the used supplies. "It's only been a week, but I want to tell you that already I've seen a change in Cole. I mean, besides the fact that he practically falls asleep in his dinner and takes his shower without being told and is up to walk Patch at dawn."

Trevor nodded. "Ranching is good for him."

"Yes. Absolutely." Hope cocked her head. "How do you think he's doing?"

"He's a quick learner and he and the dog are good for each other."

"As you predicted." She hesitated. "I've been meaning to talk to you about that dog."

"That dog?" He raised a brow. "You don't like Patch?"

"Please. Who doesn't love Patch? He has a heart bigger than this ranch."

"Yeah, he does."

"However, while I've never had a dog of my own, I'm pretty certain they're supposed to be a little less independent than this one. He doesn't come when you call his name and wrangling him every morning is getting old. Aren't puppies supposed to have obedience training or something?"

Trevor stood and examined the dressing on

his hand. "I'll ask Slim Jim to spend some time with Cole training Patch."

"He trains dogs too?"

"Yeah, Jim's the ranch animal whisperer. He's been known to get the chickens to follow his instructions."

She grinned. "That I'd like to see."

The oven timer interrupted the conversation, and Hope washed her hands before pulling the cookies out of the oven and sliding in another sheet of unbaked dough.

Trevor's brow rose. "I'm still having a hard time believing Bess gave you free rein over her kitchen."

"She's on vacation." Hope tried to ignore the spark of irritation rising up. *Switzerland. Switzerland.*

"Yeah, but I saw you cooking with her yesterday too. Didn't you help her make that pot roast for dinner?"

"Actually, it was my recipe. Bess has been distracted preparing for her trip, so I offered to make it before I left for the day." She narrowed her gaze. "Why do you sound so surprised? And why all questions?"

"It's been my experience that Bess doesn't let anyone in her kitchen unless she's instructing."

"Instructing?"

"Yeah. Sadie needed training, and Bess obliged. Other than that, she's fairly possessive about that new stove. Gave me a list of dos and don'ts before she left."

"Sure, I understand. It's a very nice stove." Hope assessed the black, stainless-steel-and-porcelain appliance with its shiny black glass oven door. "However, I don't know what to tell you. I asked if she minded if I used her stove and she was fine with it." She paused, unable to resist a little dramatic effect. "Maybe she likes me. Some people do."

"I guess," Trevor muttered. He looked around. "Where is Bess?"

"She took off early since everything was done here and was headed to Elk City to pick up a few more things for the grandbaby."

"More stuff for the grandbaby? Is she having triplets or something?"

"No, but it's her first grandbaby. Grandmother's nest, just like mothers-to-be." Hope pulled a plate from the cupboard and transferred the cookies from the cookie sheet.

Trevor wandered closer. "You know this from experience?"

"No, not from personal experience. I've spent

much of my career supporting families. I can tell you that the birth of a grandchild can be one of the most anticipated events of a grandparent's life, often surpassing the birth of their own children."

"What about you?"

"What about me?" She blinked at the question.

"You support other families. Ever think about a family of your own?"

Hope stared at him, her mouth dry. Two weeks and he'd said six words of a personal nature. Today, he decided to be chatty and ask a question straight out of Random City.

"I have Cole. I don't need anything else." Or any*one* else. As a young girl she hadn't seen beyond the loving bubble of care her mother provided. She hadn't recognized her father's coldness. When her mother passed, everything changed. That was when she learned not to need anyone. Life was much easier that way.

She glanced at the big clock on the wall, eager to change the subject. "Where is he, anyhow?"

"He's observing Slim at the corral. That's code for making him take a break. That boy never stops, so I have to create opportunities for him to rest. He wants to please everyone."

Trevor was right. Cole expended a lot of energy trying to please the adults in his life. He probably should see a therapist at some point. Right now, what the cowboy was offering him was even better. Consistency and friendship. She had to admit that while his approach was similar to hers, he'd had faster results. Trevor *was* good with kids.

"What's Gramps up to?" he asked.

"I convinced Gus to take a nap."

"A nap? Like he's a five-year-old?"

"Would you please lower your voice?" She grabbed a spatula and removed the cooled cookies from the sheet, placing them on a plate. "He's eighty-two years old, recovering from hip-replacement surgery. I'm a little concerned about him."

"You are?" The cowboy's face paled.

"He's a bit depressed. Not clinically depressed. More like…sad. Having to slow down has been hard on him." She lowered her voice. "I can't help but think that maybe he feels like he's let his family down."

"Whoa. Maybe you could explain that last part."

"Your grandfather carries a rather large burden. He feels the obligation to keep all the

plates spinning for you and your brothers."
Hope often found herself in awe of the Morgan patriarch, wondering if things would have
been different if she'd had a Gus in her life.

Trevor scrubbed a hand over his face. "He
told you that?"

"Not in so many words. But it's obvious
your grandfather is a very social person, and
he's missing his interactions on the ranch and
in town. Before surgery, he was able to quietly
check on all his grandsons and those he cares
about. Now, he's isolated, a little lost and feeling guilty about it as well."

He stared at her, his expression soft and his
eyes warm.

"What?" Hope asked.

"I'm impressed at how well you understand
my grandfather."

"He's a very intuitive and kind person. You
and your family are fortunate to have him in
your life."

"I agree," Trevor said. "So tell me. What do
you suggest?"

"He's agreed to start joining the ranch hands
for lunch like he used to, starting on Monday.
I've called and rescheduled his physical-ther-

apy appointments. From now on, they'll be an hour earlier."

"Great. Great."

"There's a meeting of the town council next week. Gus and I will have dinner in town and stay for that. If you don't mind keeping Cole."

"No problem." He looked at her. "I sure appreciate this."

"It's my job."

Trevor eyed her. This time his gaze seemed oddly gentle. "You love your job."

"Of course, I do."

"I don't get it. People die. That has to be hard."

"Death is a part of life." She cocked her head. "It's a reality you face on the ranch every day."

"Yeah, but it's different with people." Trevor turned and looked out the window toward the pasture, his expression unreadable. "You aren't afraid of death, or the death of people you care about?"

Her heart clutched at the question, but she had to be honest. "I have comfort in knowing where I'll spend my everlasting and I try to make sure those I care about do as well."

"Good answer," he said softly. "Except I don't buy it. Everyone is afraid of death."

"I disagree. Everyone is afraid of losing the people they love. That's the scary part."

"Maybe so," he murmured. "Once you lose it all, it does make you gun-shy."

"Yes," she said with a nod. Gun-shy. That was exactly right.

He turned to face her. "I have a hard time wrapping my head around the fact that you do this job on purpose."

"I don't know what to tell you. I consider what I do to be more than a job. It's an honor." Hope raised a shoulder and dropped it. "Maybe it's a calling. Like your calling."

"I don't have a calling," he scoffed. "I manage a ranch."

"Your grandfather thinks you do, and I agree. You have a calling to kids. Your heart feels their needs and their pain. It's your ministry. That's why you invited Cole to stay."

"I invited you as well."

"Not that you had much choice."

He smiled, and Hope lost her train of thought. *That smile.*

She was right in her original assessment. It was his secret weapon.

"What's wrong?" he asked.

"Nothing. Nothing." She fiddled with the

edge of the plate, avoiding his gaze as her pulse returned to normal.

Silence stretched between them for a moment. Finally, she looked up to see him watching her. "Bess calls you a bit of sunshine," he said quietly.

Her heart warmed. She enjoyed being around Bess. "You say it like it's something bad."

"No. I just don't get it. You deal with death and dying. Why are you always smiling?"

"It's a choice. I choose to be happy." She offered him the smile he'd commented on.

"How can I choose to be happy, Miss Sunshine?"

"Oh, it's as simple as that smile you brought out of hiding a few minutes ago. You could do it more often."

The cowboy opened his mouth and then closed it.

Hope nearly laughed aloud. She'd rendered the big man speechless. She picked up the plate of cookies and offered them to him. "Have a cookie."

He frowned and took several with his unbandaged hand. "Uh, thanks." He held up his other hand. "And thanks for this."

"Anytime."

He looked at her, and once again, she had the feeling he wanted to say more but held back.

Hope's eyes followed him as he walked out of the kitchen. She didn't know how it happened, but it seemed that the gap between her and the cowboy had narrowed.

They weren't so different after all. Both had had the rug pulled out from under them, and now, in their own way, they were simply doing their best to carry on.

As SOON AS he finished off the last cookie, Trevor texted Jim to send Cole to the office. Delicious cookies. Nice big chunks of white chocolate. Hope knew her way around an oven. He'd give her that.

Still, he couldn't help but notice that she was the second woman of late who seemed to think he needed sweetening up. Hope had practically shoved those cookies at him.

It occurred to him that maybe, in another lifetime, he might have been interested in someone like Hope Burke. She wasn't anything like Alyssa. That was for sure. Alyssa was sweet and a bit lost in an adorable way. When he'd met her, he'd felt lost too—they'd needed each other.

Hope didn't need anything except her nephew. She was like a tree that withstood the storm. Or maybe she *was* the storm. For now, he figured he ought to maintain his guard around the ridiculously cheerful nurse. Something inside him whispered that she could be very dangerous to his well-being.

"Jim said you wanted to talk to me, Mr. Morgan?" Cole stood in the doorway, his shirt damp with perspiration and his face streaked with dirt and sweat.

"You can call me Trevor or Mr. Trevor. Okay?"

"Yes, sir."

"That works too." Trevor waved him into the office and pulled a couple of bottles of water from the mini fridge. He put one on the desk and tossed one to Cole, who easily caught it. "Have a seat."

The boy cracked the seal on his and took a swig before he settled in the chair.

"Be sure to stay hydrated. It's hot out here. Keep your water bottle close."

"I will."

Trevor opened his desk drawer and handed Cole a phone. "This is yours. Here's the box. It has the charger cord and stuff inside."

Cole's jaw dropped. "A phone?"

"This is a business phone. Do you know what that means?"

"It's for business?"

"That's right. Only business. The phone belongs to the ranch. It's a tool for you to use to do your job here. It's not a toy. All the ranch wranglers are assigned one. You're a member of the Lazy M team, so you should bring yours to work every day, fully charged. Like your boots and your work gloves. This phone is part of the job."

Cole nodded, straightening to his full height at Trevor's words. "Yes, sir."

"I don't have to tell you that the Lazy M is a big ranch, and I have to be able to reach you. You have to be able to reach me as well. This phone is your lifeline in an emergency. I programmed important ranch numbers and the nonemergency number for the Homestead Pass Police Department. You can use it as an alarm clock as well. Come Monday, we'll be starting our day earlier to avoid the heat of the day." Trevor paused. "Any questions?"

"No, sir."

"A word of advice. Keep it in your back pocket. And always take it out when you drop your drawers."

"Yes, sir." Cole looked at the phone in his hand with a mixture of awe and delight. "Thank you, Mr. Trevor."

"You're welcome." Trevor stood. "That's it. We're all done for today. You can head on down to the main house."

"But it's only three o'clock."

"Occasionally, we get caught up around here. Not very often, so don't get used to it."

Cole offered a solemn nod and looked at Trevor. "Am I doing a good job?"

The unspoken question filled the silence. The kid was concerned he was going to be asked to leave if he wasn't up to snuff. The thought nearly broke Trevor's heart.

"You're the best wrangler trainee we've had around here in a long time."

The boy's face lit up at the words.

"By the way, I'm going to talk to Jim about obedience class."

"For me?" Cole reared back in stunned surprise.

"No." Trevor started laughing. "For that wily pup of yours. Jim will teach you how to follow up on training." He looked around. "Where is Patch, anyhow?"

"I cooled him down with the hose. He's sleeping in the shade."

"Great. Now about that obedience stuff."

"He needs it. My aunt gets pretty annoyed when he plays hide-and-seek while she's trying to leash him."

"Between you and Jim, Patch will soon be a little gentleman. No worries." He chuckled. "Oh, and Gramps and I will pick you up tomorrow around ten a.m. to take you to town. We're heading to Ben's."

"Who's Ben?"

"Ben? Why Ben is a legend in Homestead Pass. He's the barber."

"I'm getting a haircut?" Cole pushed sweaty strands of hair away from his face. "My hair isn't long."

"It's summer in Oklahoma. Short hair keeps you cool. It's a health issue."

Cole sighed.

"It's hair, son. The thing is...it grows back." He glanced at the clock above the door. "You best get up to the house. Your aunt made cookies, and they're really good."

"Yes, sir!"

Trevor heard Patch bark and the fading voice of Cole as he raced away from the stables.

Maybe he'd call it a day as well. He'd check his email and review the upcoming schedule for the holiday week first. Ten minutes later, Hope appeared in his doorway.

She was mad. Her cheeks were a fiery pink, and her bangs were askew, as though she'd hustled to get to his office. It occurred to him that she was even prettier than usual. He pushed away the thought and prepared for the storm.

Hands on hips. Uh-oh.

"Can I help you?" he asked.

"Who gave you permission to give Cole a phone?"

"It's required for the job."

"A phone? A phone is required?" She all but rolled her eyes and gestured toward a chair. "Do you mind?"

"Can't say that my minding would make any difference."

Hope dropped into the chair. "I'm going to take the high road here and give you the benefit of the doubt. You've never had a child of your own. There are certain unspoken rules."

Trevor raised a palm. "I hate to start this discussion by contradicting you. I work with kids. I understand the rules. They don't apply here. The reality is that Cole is shadowing me on the ranch this summer. That makes him like staff, and all the staff are provided with phones. There are more hazards than you might imagine around here. He needs a way to reach out in case of an emergency."

"I assumed he'd always be where you can see him. I've entrusted my nephew to your care."

"He's not a baby, and I'm not babysitting." He sighed. "And he might be my son. Of course, I'm looking out for him. But Cole is nearly twelve. Boys are curious and they wander off. We can't cover them in Bubble Wrap. Stuff happens."

Hope leaned back in the chair and crossed her arms, her lips a thin line.

"I apologize," he said. "It was never my intent to disrespect you. As I said, all the Lazy M Ranch wranglers get a phone when they're hired on. It's a system we put in place when I took over as ranch manager."

She nodded. "I appreciate the explanation. It does make sense. However, I would like you to discuss things that involve Cole with me ahead of time."

"Yes, ma'am. I can do that."

"Thank you." She stood. "Have a good weekend."

She moved out of his office as fast as she'd

entered it, nearly sideswiping Jim on her way. "Oops, sorry."

"No problem." Jim eased into the chair Hope had vacated. "I thought tornado season was over."

Trevor chuckled. "Apparently not."

"Takes quite a gal to stand up to the boss. Half the wranglers wouldn't have the guts to come in here and give you grief. The other half aren't that smart." He raised his brow. "You may have met your match."

"Were you eavesdropping?"

"God blessed me with superhuman hearing." Jim put a hand to his spectacularly large ears that stuck out from beneath his battered, straw cowboy hat. "Nothing I can do about it."

"I'd appreciate it if you'd zip your lips."

"About the phone or the part where you said Cole might be your son?"

Trevor grimaced and ran a hand over his chin. "Did anyone else hear that?"

"Only a few horses, and they're discreet."

"She thinks I'm Cole's father."

Jim clucked his tongue. "And?"

"You know that I went through a rough patch a long time ago. Turns out, there are a few empty hours I can't account for." He looked at the other cowboy. "Under the influence or not, I don't believe I'm the father. I'm ashamed to admit that I was a quiet drunk. Drank myself into oblivion all alone to escape my problems."

Warmth shone in Jim's eyes. "It was a tough time for everyone. Lots of folks were concerned about you, Trev." He paused. "But if you don't think you're the father, then why is Cole here?"

Trevor thought about the question for a moment. How could he adequately explain the connection he felt for the boy? He couldn't.

"Is that a hard question?" Jim queried.

"Yeah, maybe it is. I invited Cole to stay because he's a good kid who lost his mother recently. He never had a father and he's got nowhere else to be this summer." Trevor smiled. "Plus, he's a *Space Knights* nerd."

"Well, hey. That's all I gotta hear. Knighties, unite!"

"Thanks, Jim."

"No problem." He glanced around and then leaned closer. "Does your family know?"

"Nope. I'd like them to welcome Cole to the ranch because he's a great kid and nothing more for now."

"I guess you thought about a DNA test."

"Sure, and we'll get to that. But when it

comes back negative, Hope will head back to Oklahoma City with him. I think he needs Lazy M Ranch in his life right now." He sighed. "The ranch is what saved me when I lost my folks. Hard work is a balm for the heart, and the ranch gives you a sense of purpose when life is confusing."

"I hear you," Jim said. "I'm grateful for the Lazy M, myself." He looked at Trevor, a question on his face. "And if the test is positive?"

"Then I'll gladly accept the responsibility and my family will be the first to know."

The lanky cowboy gave a slow nod, his lips pinched together in thought. "Okay, then. Mum's the word."

"Thanks. I appreciate that. Was there something you needed?" Trevor asked.

"I figured you'd be doing the schedule, and I wanted to remind you that I'll be visiting my sister and her family in Okmulgee over the Fourth of July holiday. You said I could take off next Thursday through Sunday."

"Yeah, sure. I have it down."

"When you get back, can you put Patch on your to-do list? Work with Cole and give them both some obedience training."

"You got it." Jim unfolded his frame and

stood. "What are you doing for the Fourth of July?"

"Give me a break. You know that ranchers don't have holidays."

"No. *You* don't have holidays." He eyed Trevor. "Okay, after you finish chores, what are you going to do?"

"Requisite picnic at Drew's."

"Don't make it sound like the death penalty. You have a great family, and Sam married a chef. Doesn't sound like torture to me."

"Yeah, you're right." Trevor took a deep breath and released it slowly. "It just gets tedious with all that love in the air. Lucas isn't around to provide a distraction."

Jim laughed and nodded toward the door. "Your tornado friend going to the barn dance?"

"I heard Gramps mention it. But I don't know."

"Invite her yourself. That would provide plenty of distraction."

Yeah, that was an understatement. Hope, with her long straight dark hair and those bangs, always tousled, and her clear hazel eyes. A distraction, all right.

Trevor stood. "Well, would you look at the time. Sorry that you have to be going."

Once again, Jim's laughter rang out. "You can't run from life forever, my friend."

"Sure, I can. Watch me."

CHAPTER SIX

SWITZERLAND. TALK ABOUT eating your words. Hope pulled into a parking spot in front of the Homestead Pass Inn.

She'd lost her temper with Trevor yesterday. Not cool. Not Switzerland either. She was in the right, but she could have handled things more diplomatically.

Stepping out of the car and into the humid embrace of summer, she glanced up and down Main Street. No sign of Trevor's truck. Maybe it was around the block.

The barbershop was on the same side of the street as the inn, on Main, but at the other end of the block, next to a law office. All she had to do was casually make her way down the street, window-shopping. Yes, that was what she was doing. Window-shopping her way toward the barbershop because she couldn't resist a peek at Cole on male-bonding day.

As she started up the street, Hope heard her name called and turned around. Sadie and Liv Morgan were walking toward her with smiles on their faces. She'd gotten to know the two Morgan wives from when they'd show up at the house to visit Gus. Both were gracious and welcoming.

"Hi," Liv called as she approached. In jeans and a T-shirt, her red cowboy boots clicked on the sidewalk. The vivacious brunette offered a smile.

"What are you up to today?" Sadie asked. Drew's wife seemed the more subdued of the duo.

"I'm running a few errands." *Not untrue.* "I see you're having a mom's day out," Hope said to Sadie.

"Yes. Drew has the kids, and I'm catching up on my life. Liv and I have hair appointments at the salon in a few minutes."

"I wasn't aware of a salon in town."

"Oh yes. Turn right at the corner of Main and Edison," Liv said. "It's next to the Hitching Post. The Rancher's Wife Salon. Wonderful place. They have cucumber water on tap and the best fashion magazines. Just like the city."

As they stood on the sidewalk, Eleanor from

the bookstore hurried toward them, clipboard in hand. "Yoo-hoo! Hello to my favorite girls." She gave Liv, her stepdaughter, a kiss and hugged Sadie. "Miss Hope, how are you?"

Liv looked at Hope. "You two have met?"

"Yes. We met in the bookstore."

"Fundraising barn dance is two weeks away." Eleanor flipped through the papers on her clipboard. She arched an eyebrow. "Hmm. I don't see that any of you have bought tickets."

"You're right," Sadie said. "And it's for such a good cause." She pulled a few bills from her purse and handed them to Eleanor.

"Olivia?" Eleanor tapped her clipboard.

"I wouldn't miss it. My aunt is catering. Two tickets and hit my husband up for the bill."

"And you, Ms. Hope?" Eleanor shot her an expectant look.

"I don't think so. I don't even know anyone in town."

Liv put her arm through Hope's. "That's why you should attend. Besides, Colin Reilly doesn't open his ranch to the public often. The event will be outside, but you can be sure it will be fabulous."

"Colin Reilly?"

"Reilly pecan empire," Liv said.

"Doesn't ring a bell."

"His daughter, Harper, is best buds with Lucas Morgan," Liv said. She patted Hope's arm. "It will all make sense once you meet everyone. Another reason to attend."

Hope considered mentioning that she was only here for the summer. If that. But resistance seemed pointless.

"Okay. Sure." She reached for her wallet.

"No. No. My treat," Liv said. "Eleanor, we'll take two more tickets. You can charge my husband for those as well."

"That's what I like to hear." Eleanor laughed as she handed out the tickets. Then she looked across the street, where two women stood looking into the Glitz and Glam boutique window. "I see customers. Toodle-loo, my dears. Must sell more tickets."

Hope stared at the bright pink tickets in her hand. "Why two?"

"One is for your date, silly," Liv said with a smile. "We can discuss it at the Morgan Fourth of July family picnic. Drew and Sadie are hosting this year." She paused. "Gus invited you to the picnic, right?"

"Yes, but I don't want to intrude on a family event." Though she'd been touched by the older man's invitation, Hope still wasn't certain about attending.

"You're family for the summer," Liv said. "Besides, the men who work on the Lazy M adore Cole. All I hear from Sam is 'Cole this' and 'Cole that.' You have to bring him."

"I didn't realize your husband works on the ranch as well," Hope returned. "I haven't seen him."

"Ranch accountant. He mostly hides in his office and comes out for events that require all hands on deck. Actually, all the Morgan men have their fingers in the ranch activities somehow," Liv said.

Sadie put a hand on Hope's arm. "Listen, I was new to town myself two years ago. The Morgans are the-more-the-merrier type, and they mean it. Besides, it's at my house, making me the boss."

"It's a ton of fun," Liv said. "We bring out the horseshoes, and my father sets up the bocce balls. My family is coming, including my aunt Loretta. They're Morettis not Morgans." She chuckled. "The more-the-merrier theme continues."

"All right. We'll be there. Thank you so

much." A warmth settled in her chest at the kindness.

"Oh, and it's a potluck," Liv said. "Bring your favorite side dish."

"I make a yummy spinach salad. Would that be appropriate?"

"Nutritious food. What a novelty. Yes, please." Liv patted her abdomen. "Our little baby Morgans would like that."

Sadie checked her watch, and her eyes rounded. "We better hustle, Liv." She smiled at Hope. "See you for the Fourth, if not sooner."

"Yes," Hope returned. "And thank you."

"Nice to see you again," Liv echoed as they headed in the other direction.

"You too."

Hope continued down the street buoyed by the conversation with Liv and Sadie. What would it be like to be part of a large loving family like the Morgans? She couldn't even imagine, but for now, she'd enjoy the hospitality and do her very best to avoid any further discussion of dates.

She stopped just before the barbershop and planned her casual stroll past. When the glass storefront came into view, she took a quick side-eyed glance inside. Her heart melted at the sight of Cole sitting in the barber's chair next to Gus. Both males had black capes around their necks as barbers attended to their hair.

Anna's boy was growing up. The moment was bittersweet.

"Hope!" Trevor's voice rang out.

Busted.

She turned. "Oh, Trevor. Hi there. I was just…"

"Helicoptering?" His lips twitched in that annoying know-it-all way.

"As a matter of fact, I'm on my way to the coffee shop."

He pointed a thumb behind them. "It's the other direction. Take a left on Edison."

"I've been there before, thank you. Getting my steps in by going around the block."

"Right." The single word conveyed his skepticism.

"Where's your truck?" she asked.

"I borrowed Drew's sedan. Easier for Gramps to get in and out of than my dually."

"Of course. I should have suggested that." Hope cleared her throat and absently removed a white piece of dog hair from her T-shirt. Courtesy of Patch.

"About… About yesterday," Hope began.

"Yesterday?" He shook his head as if confused.

"The phone thing." *Could this get any more awkward?*

"Have you changed your mind? Do you want me to get the phone from Cole?"

"No. I'm trying to apologize for overreacting before I heard your side of the story."

"Not a big deal."

"It is to me. You've been nothing but generous with your time and expertise and, well, the whole house thing." Now she was babbling.

As they stood there, a breeze moved past, bringing a fresh, clean, powdery aroma from the cowboy. His thick caramel hair ruffled, calling her attention to his head.

"Nice haircut," Hope said. Trimmed neat and short, the curls on his neck were gone, which was too bad. He'd gotten a shave too. The effect emphasized the angles of his face, though truthfully, she was partial to the stubble.

"You don't think it's too short?" He ran a hand through his hair.

"It's hair. It will grow back. I think it looks great." Hope glanced away, adjusting her purse on her shoulder.

Trevor laughed, and she looked up. "What's so funny?" she asked.

"I told Cole the same thing about hair growing back. I guess we're on the same wavelength."

That, she doubted.

"Did you see Cole?" he asked.

"Yes. I've never seen him happier. He looked like he was having a great time. Thank you."

"Nothing I'm doing. Just let him be a kid."

"It's not just that. You're not treating him like a kid. You treat him with respect, and you listen to him. You have expectations, and you're confident he won't disappoint you. He senses that."

Trevor's blue eyes flashed with surprise. "I think that's the nicest thing you've ever said to me."

"Don't let it go to your head."

"I just might." He offered a small smile.

"What kind of haircut for Cole?" she asked. "I mean, how short? One or two inches." Hope nodded, waiting for his agreement.

"Oh, he's getting the summer special."

Hope looked at him. "Summer special?"

"Buzz cut."

"A buzz cut?" She was more than a little surprised. Cole liked to hide behind his hair. "He's okay with a buzz cut?"

"Sure. It'll keep him cool."

"He agreed to a buzz cut?" That didn't sound like Cole at all.

"We discussed the pros and cons, and he made his own decision." Trevor shrugged. "I might have sweetened the deal with the promise of a straw hat like mine after the haircut."

Her jaw sagged. "You bribed him?"

"Not at all. Cole needs a hat regardless." He shrugged once again. "I like to think of it as synchronicity."

Synchronicity. That was a stretch. "I could have gotten a hat for Cole," she said.

Trevor narrowed his gaze. "Have you ever shopped for a cowboy hat before?"

"No."

"Then why not leave it to the experts? Besides, Gramps is looking forward to giving his opinion. He's also looking forward to restocking his horehound candy supply while we're there. You don't want to disappoint my grandfather, do you?"

"No." Hope paused. "Thank you," she said softly.

"My pleasure. We plan to stop at that new burger place outside town for lunch. Care to join us?"

"Oh, no." She raised a hand. "I don't want to intrude. Enjoy your day."

Trevor raised a brow. "You enjoy your walk."

Her walk. It was a long one. Around the block and up Parker Road, before turning left on Edison.

As she was about to walk into the coffee shop, Pastor McGuinness walked out. The tall, gray-haired pastor offered a bright smile.

"Ms. Burke," he exclaimed. "Good to see you. I tried to catch you on Sunday, but you walk much faster than I do."

She stepped aside to let customers enter the coffee shop. "I'm sorry, Pastor. What can I do for you?"

"The church is looking for a few youth volunteers to help with vacation Bible school next week. It's only a few hours each morning. Do you think Cole might be able to help us out?"

"Sounds like a nice change of pace from the ranch. I'll ask him and give you a call."

"Thank you so much, my dear." He turned to the door. "Let me get that for you."

A welcome blast of cool air greeted Hope as she entered the shop. She stepped up to the counter, and the same young barista as her last visit greeted her with a smile.

"Vanilla latte, right?"

Hope blinked at the woman. "You remembered."

"I did." She laughed.

"May I have it iced today?"

"Absolutely."

Hope carried her order to the same booth as last time and settled close to the window, where she could people-watch. Across the street, several women she'd met at church entered the library with their children. She found herself pleasantly surprised at how many of the folks strolling up and down the street she recognized.

Homestead Pass was a lovely town. It was a town to settle down in and raise a family, like the Morgans had. She often wondered how different her life might be if her mother hadn't died. All the rituals of everyday family life disappeared when her mom passed. Holidays were just another day. And if she didn't remind her father, he'd forget her birthday as well. When he remarried, holidays resumed, except now she was the odd person out, on the outside looking in. Once her father officially adopted Anna, it was as though Hope didn't exist.

It was fine. All good. She'd gotten by and had a satisfying life now. Her job blessed her beyond measure. She had a nice little apartment and friends from work. The home health company and her patients were her family.

Still, deep inside she was only too aware that it wasn't the same as real family.

Hope wanted so much more for Cole. The Morgans offered him more. Trevor was a good man, despite his gruff exterior. A good man who had already lost so much.

Her opportunity for a happy childhood disappeared once her mother died. Was she foolish to hope for a happy ending for her nephew? An ending she'd never had?

She'd gotten to know Trevor well enough to realize that she'd be okay with Cole living permanently with the cowboy. She could visit regularly, which would be more than she had when Anna was alive.

But what would happen if the testing was negative? Now that Cole knew why she was in Homestead Pass, how would she explain things if she didn't find his father? The conversation about finding his father had been difficult. Explaining that she'd failed would be even harder.

Hope rubbed her temple. One step at a time,

she reminded herself. That's what Trevor said. She wasn't on this journey alone. The Lord had her back.

"NEED ANY HELP?" Trevor called to Drew.

"Naw, I've got it." Drew dumped a bag of charcoal into the grill and stepped back from the flying cinders. He dusted off his hands and turned to Trevor. "I won't start cooking until Gramps declares himself the horseshoe champ."

Trevor couldn't hold back a laugh. Gramps held strong opinions regarding horseshoes. A glance overhead confirmed a brilliant blue sky with fluffy cumulus clouds. Perfect weather for the Fourth of July.

He grabbed a can of soda from a big tub stocked with ice and beverages, then pulled the tab. As he downed a swig of the cool liquid, snatches of conversation drifted to him, and his ears perked.

"Find you a date…" That came from Liv.

A date? Who was she talking to? A niggle of concern had him walking closer to the house where Liv, Sadie and Hope were seated on Drew's deck beneath large, colorful, sun-blocking umbrellas. Even little Mae sat in a miniature lawn chair with the ladies.

"It's going to be a wonderful event. I'm so glad…" That was Sadie chiming in. Except he couldn't hear all her words.

The clang of metal rang out, and Trevor turned. Across the yard, Gus offered Cole instructions on how to toss horseshoes as they warmed up for the annual family competition.

"The secret is in the wrist," Gramps said, holding a horseshoe. He stretched out his arm and narrowed his gaze, preparing to pitch as he focused on the stake in the pit. "You want to hit that stake. It's great to get a ringer. Three points. But touching the stake is good too. That's one point."

"How many times do we do this?" Cole asked.

"Twenty-five innings in a game."

Cole jerked back. "That's a long time, Mr. Gus."

Gramps put a hand on Cole's shoulder. "Nah. Time flies when you're winning. You'll see."

Trevor chuckled. The real secret was keeping an eye on his grandfather's foot action. Gramps had some stealth moves involving the foul line that might not exactly be legit. They'd spent many a fine afternoon loudly discussing dead ringers. But he'd let Cole figure that one out himself.

"How's it going, Trev?"

He did an about-face and found Sam approaching with a mischievous look on his face. "What do you mean?" Trevor asked.

Had Hope mentioned the paternity thing? Surely not. She was the one who had insisted on keeping things quiet. Maybe Jim had leaked the information. He sure hoped not, as it wouldn't help his overtures to become friends with Cole's aunt.

"Ease up there, buddy." Sam grinned. "That was a friendly conversation starter. No pressure."

"In that case, it's going fine." He looked at Sam. Really looked at him. His brother was always smiling these days. The crinkle lines at the corners of his eyes were permanent fixtures.

"What?" Sam raised his hands in question.

"Can't help but notice how happy you are."

"Oh yeah. Got me there. True love." Sam paused, his face stricken. "I didn't mean… Aw, Trev, that was inconsiderate of me."

"Cut it out. You can't go around walking on broken glass with me. I'm happy for you. You deserve this."

Sam's eyes softened. "Thanks."

"Excited about becoming a father?"

"Terrified. My heart starts thumping a mile a minute when I think about bringing a child into the world. At the same time, I thank God every single day for this blessing."

"How come you're terrified?"

"Aw, come on. Drew herded you and Lucas when we were growing up. I wasn't much help. What do I know about parenting?"

"It's all common sense."

Sam chuckled. "According to Gramps, common sense isn't all that common these days."

"True. However, you are aware that Sadie has an entire library of baby books, right? Borrow a few."

"Are you kidding? I already have." Sam cocked his head. "I don't know how you find it so easy working with kids."

"Maybe because I'm a big kid."

"Nah, that's not true. You've been an adult all your life. Independent and bossy. Gramps told me you walked to the nursery from the delivery room."

"Gramps may be exaggerating," Trevor said.

"I don't think so. I can't remember a time you weren't responsible."

Trevor could. He remembered a time, and it still haunted him. He cleared his throat. "Look, the truth is I was plenty nervous last year when the school bus showed up for the first Kids Day event. Then I remembered two things. I've worked with kids before. At church. We all have. The most important thing is that I'm doing what the Lord put in my heart." Trevor gave Sam a soft shoulder punch. "Same is true for you. You and Olivia are right where the good Lord wants you to be. All you have to do is trust that He will equip you for the job He called you to do."

"I'll try to remember that," Sam murmured.

Women's laughter rang out, and both men glanced over at the deck area. "Hope has sure stepped up to help in Bess's absence," Sam observed. "Hiring her full-time was a smart move, Trev." That mischievous look he'd come over with was back.

"Thanks." He'd had the same thoughts of late.

"I like Cole too. Good kid."

"Sam, we're starting," Eleanor called from behind them.

"Want to join us for bocce?"

Trevor counted heads. Eleanor. Olivia's father and her aunt, Loretta. "Nah, you've got your teams."

"You could take my place." Sam raised his brow. "I'd do that for you."

"No way. Those Morettis take their bocce way too seriously. Last time I played, your wife's daddy made me glad looks couldn't actually kill."

Sam laughed. "Anthony is all bark."

"So you say."

"Trevor," Olivia called. "Could you come here?"

"What do you know?" Trevor grinned. "I'm being summoned."

"Once again, your timing is excellent, little brother."

"It's a gift."

"Trevor?" Sam's wife called again.

He headed toward the deck and saw panic on Hope's face. *Uh-oh. Better come to her rescue.* Though he wasn't anybody's knight, it was his duty to step in as she was new to Morgan-family dynamics.

"Coming." He hurried toward the women and climbed the steps to the deck.

"We need to find Hope a date for the barn dance," Olivia announced.

We? He rubbed a hand over his chin. "Is that right?"

"Yes. You're a guy. You know guys," she continued. "Who's a good candidate?"

There wasn't anyone in Homestead Pass equal to the task. Though it wouldn't be wise to say that aloud.

Trevor snuck a peek at Hope, whose worried gaze moved between the Sadie and Oliva. Yeah, he'd be worried too, if his fate was in the hands of his brothers' wives.

"What about Jim?" Sadie asked. "He's such a gentleman. And look how good he is with animals."

A horrified expression crossed Olivia's face. "Jim lives with his mother."

"To be fair, his mother lives with him," Trevor said. "He bought that house and has already paid it off." Trevor felt obligated to defend his buddy, though there wasn't a chance he'd let Jim date Hope.

"Trev's right." Drew had joined them on the deck. He leaned against the rail and nodded. "You can't discount a man who owns real estate."

"I agree," Sadie chimed in. "In this economy, living with your mom is not a reason to cross him off the list. Besides, Trevor lives with his grandfather. Same thing."

Whoa! Not the same thing. Trevor opened his mouth to defend himself and thought better of the idea. Best for him to stay on the sidelines of this conversation. He didn't want anything to do with setting up Hope with one of his buddies. For some reason, the thought only irritated him.

"Steve Keller is single," Sadie said. "A man in uniform has universal appeal."

"The police chief?" Drew shook his head. "No, he's hung up on Melissa from the post office."

Sadie looked at her husband. "Oh? Surely we can help the situation along."

Drew cringed. "Maybe we can talk about it later."

"What about Hank Garrett?" Olivia gave a dramatic sigh. "He's awfully cute."

Handsome Hank. Trevor barely resisted rolling his eyes, and Drew offered a snort of disgust.

"I don't think Hank is in town anymore," Trevor said. "He got a position in Arkansas at a bird sanctuary."

"Really? Okay. No Hank..." Olivia pursed her lips in thought. "What about Lucas?"

"Luc won't be home until August," Drew said.

Lucas. Not a good idea. Sure, his twin would have taken Hope to the barn dance in a heart-beat. His brother was a charmer. Women swooned in his presence, and he enjoyed his title as one of the most eligible bachelors in Homestead Pass. Oh yeah, Luc would gallantly offer to take the prettiest single woman in town to the dance. Trevor tensed at the thought as he glanced at Hope.

Her silky straight hair touched her shoulders, and the red, white and blue sleeveless blouse she was wearing with navy shorts showed off golden skin, tanned from outdoor excursions with Gramps. A smile touched her lips as her gaze moved between Sadie and Olivia. And though she appeared calm, he recognized the little wrinkle between her eyes that signaled anxiety.

He didn't blame her. His brothers' wives were playing roulette with her life.

"Trevor, did you hear me?" Olivia asked.

"Ah, sorry. I was thinking."

"Why don't you accompany Hope?" She smiled sweetly, pleased with herself. "You know. As friends. It's the perfect solution."

Fear shot through Trevor. He tugged on the

neck of his T-shirt, then took a long swig of soda. Hope sat very still, her fingers tracing the webbing on the arms of the aluminum beach chair. Any answer except "yes" would humiliate her.

Head down, Trevor studied the ingredients on his pop can. "Uh, yeah. Sure." He raised his head in time to see the nonverbal exchange between his sisters-in-law. For a moment, everything froze, and then he put the pieces of the puzzle together.

I've been set up.

Set up by his brothers' wives, and he'd fallen for it like a rookie.

"You don't have to escort me," Hope said quietly.

Trevor raised a shoulder, as nonchalant as can be. "Happy to do my part for charity."

Olivia gasped, while Hope's hazel eyes flashed with surprise.

"The barn dance." Trevor's tongue tangled as he worked to get the words out. "It's a fundraiser for charity. I'm happy to do my part for the clinic."

Hope stood, her face pink. "I think I'll check on Cole." She moved right around him, down the deck steps and across the yard, her back straight.

"Way to step in it," Drew murmured.

All Trevor could do was groan. This. This was yet another reason he preferred to sit out social gatherings. His boots always jumped into his mouth.

Now he had become the bad guy. Trevor raced to catch up with Hope. "Hey, you okay with this?"

"Oh, sure. I haven't had a pity date in a long time." She didn't break her stride.

"No. No. It's not a pity date. We're both going, and I think we're friends, right?"

She kept her eyes ahead. "Technically, you're my boss."

"Nope. Not your boss. Your checks come from the Lazy M Ranch corporation."

Hope jerked to a stop and looked at him. A grimace touched her mouth before she glanced at the deck, where the Morgan family worked to pretend they weren't watching. "That is not what you said."

When she didn't respond, he released a breath of frustration. "Look, this caught me off guard. I haven't even thought about the word *date* in a very long time. I'm talking years."

Her eyes softened as though she understood. Did she? Had Gramps talked to her about his past? Suddenly it occurred to him that maybe he was the one who'd be the pity portion of any date with Hope.

"What are your thoughts on going as friends?" Hope asked.

His gaze skimmed her heart-shaped face, the tiny overbite and her full lips, and he felt the pull of attraction. And why not? Hope was lovely and nice. He'd noticed that, of late, he'd even begun to let down his guard around her.

It was as though he was waking up after a long slumber.

"Friends," he finally said with a slow nod. "I would like to go to the barn dance with you as friends, Hope."

"Okay. I accept."

She'd said yes, which meant that he now had his first date in over seven years, with a beautiful woman, to a dance that he'd insisted he wasn't going to attend.

Who'd have thought?

He could only pray that Jim didn't find out, or he'd find himself the punchline of his friend's jokes for weeks to come.

HOPE LOOKED AROUND the kitchen, satisfied that everything was in order. With Gus gone for the morning, she'd had time on her hands. Plump oatmeal-and-raisin cookies were piled on a plate, covered with foil. She'd baked a chicken-and-rice casserole and tucked it in the refrigerator for Trevor and Gus's dinner.

The kitchen was spotless, and she'd even washed and dried a load of towels. It was noon, and there wasn't anything else to do except let Trevor know she was leaving.

Heading down the hall, she stood outside his office, hesitant to knock. He'd been unusually quiet since the Fourth of July picnic a week ago, and he'd been strong-armed into taking her out.

Pushing past her anxiety, Hope swallowed and gently rapped on the closed door.

"Come on in."

She turned the handle and peeked inside. His back was to her, his broad shoulders stretching the fabric of a navy T-shirt as he stared at a chart pinned to the wall. He turned around and flashed a quick smile. At the unexpected gesture, her heart, normally so restrained, responded with a little skip, and her breath caught in her throat.

"I'm leaving now," she blurted. "Gus is at that

book-club luncheon at Jane Smith's. He made it clear I wasn't needed, and he has a ride home."

"A solo outing. So you think he's ready for that?"

"Your grandfather was quite adamant. I gave Jane my number, just in case."

Trevor nodded slowly. "Jane Smith? She used to be the librarian when I was in school." He paused. "Great to see Gramps being social, don't you think?"

"Just so you know. I think it might be a little more than being social."

"Really?" His brows shot up with surprise. "Gramps?"

"Yes." She smiled, amused at the expression on Trevor's face. The man clearly hadn't considered the possibility that his grandfather had a personal life.

"Okay, my grandfather is dating. This is good. I think." He stood and added a sticky note to the chart. "Where did you say Cole is?"

"Vacation Bible school at the church. He's a teacher's aide. I'll pick him up soon."

"Yeah. Yeah. That's right. Good for him. He's paying it forward."

She glanced at the chart. A closer look showed

it to be a colorful map of the ranch. "What are you working on?"

"It's a topographic map of the layout for Kids Day."

"Oh yes. I noticed signs in church on Sunday. Coming up, isn't it?"

"Coming up way too fast. It's in August. This is the second year, so hopefully, all the glitches are behind us. Volunteers from the church signed up long ago. Olivia's restaurant donates box lunches. I have wranglers signed up for different ranch events with the kids. Sam and Drew are my ground team, handling generators, portable restrooms and such. Sadie is the point of contact for the few vendors we have. And the church staff is taking care of the crafts tent."

"Vendors?"

"The kids get tokens when they arrive, and they can earn them at each event. The tokens can be turned in at a vendor booth for prizes like books, games, treats."

"What a fantastic idea."

"Yeah. I can't take credit for that. It was Lucas's idea. This is the first year to implement that system."

"I think it's genius."

"Luc saw something similar at a kids' rodeo up in Montana."

Hope nodded and pointed to the wall. "What are all those colorful squares?"

He glanced between her and the map. "Each of these squares represents an event. This red cross is the medical tent. I have a nurse from Homestead Pass Elementary School coming and the local ambulance service is on standby."

"Having a medical tent is very wise." She nodded with approval. "Tell me more about the events."

"A couple down the road will bring miniature horses for rides, and I'm working on a petting zoo." Trevor pointed to different squares. "There's fishing in a barrel. Rubber-dart archery. We even have a hay maze race." He grinned, obviously excited to share the details. "Oh, and Jim teaches roping using a dummy steer. We even have a class on how to feed chickens and collect eggs. They love that."

"That sounds like fun...and a lot of work."

"Yeah. I'm spending a significant time in prayer because the reputations of the event, the ranch and even Pastor McGuinness are on the line. I can't let anyone down. Especially the kids."

Her heart warmed at his determination. The man really cared. "That's a lot of pressure."

"Tell me about it. Turns out I can't rest on the success of last year. So, yeah. I'm more than a little nervous, which is why this year's prep work started months ago."

"I'm sure it will be wonderful." If there was one thing she'd learned about Trevor, it was that he was organized. "How did all this come to be, anyhow?" she asked.

"A few years ago, we had a pulpit guest from a church in Elk City. They had an event like this." Trevor eased onto the corner of his desk as he spoke. "Pastor and I got to talking, and he took it to the church board for financial approval, and we launched last year."

"How do you decide which kids to invite?"

"That, I leave to the good pastor."

"Any child would be thrilled to be part of this. It's an amazing outreach, Trevor. I know that I could have used something like this after my mother died. An opportunity to simply be a kid for the day."

A crease appeared between his eyebrows. "I didn't realize your mama passed. I'm sorry for your loss. I take it you were pretty young?"

"Yes. I was ten, and my father remarried an

unpleasant woman. Anna's mother became my stepmother." She laughed at herself. "I sound like I'm poor little Cinderella."

"Not at all," he said slowly. "It sounds like this is why you empathize so much with Cole. You've literally been there."

"And so have you," she said softly.

He nodded, his gaze on the chart.

Silence stretched between them, the only sound the soft buzz from the air-conditioning vents.

Trevor's phone pinged, breaking the silence, and he looked down.

Hope gestured toward the door. "I should go."

"Sure." He raised his phone. "Confirmation for the lab appointment. Did you get yours?"

"Earlier today. Elk City."

"Mine is in OKC." He frowned. "Different locations?"

"Yes. I was told that's the protocol. You're voluntarily doing this, but many situations are contentious, so assigning different locations is appropriate."

He nodded and cleared his throat. "Are we still on for tomorrow night?"

"Yes. Of course. I hadn't planned to stand

you up." She paused. "But if you need to cancel, I understand."

"Cancel? No. I wouldn't do that to you."

She nodded, searching for something to say. "There are cookies on the counter and a casserole in the fridge."

"Aw, you didn't have to do that. You're supposed to be a nurse, not a housekeeper. I mean, not that we don't appreciate it. We do. I'm getting mighty tired of my own cooking."

"You realize my nursing services may not be needed much longer, right? Your grandfather is progressing nicely," she said.

Trevor glanced at the wall calendar. "It's just over two weeks until his follow-up appointment."

"Yes, and I'm committed until then."

"Great, because it's been a huge peace of mind knowing you're at the house during the day." Trevor tilted his head and looked at her. "So if you have to bake more cookies because he's doing well, then so be it."

Hope laughed as she reached for the doorknob. She headed back down the hall, her steps light. Once she was outside on the porch, she stopped and glanced around at the bustle of ranch activities. The air smelled of the musky scents of animals, dirt and the Oklahoma sun.

In a heartbeat, she realized how much she enjoyed the Lazy M. Yes, living here was something she could get used to.

And that concerned her because this was only a temporary stop on the road. She needed to remember that.

CHAPTER SEVEN

It had been more than a week since the picnic, and Trevor had spent every day since dreading tonight. Tonight was the charity barn dance at the Reilly Ranch.

He scowled as he looked at himself in the mirror.

Blue oxford shirt. Check.

New Wranglers. Check.

San Antonio trophy buckle. Check.

Lousy attitude. Check.

What am I doing? He glanced at the picture of himself and Alyssa on his dresser. Was he moving on? Was that what this was?

Emotion clogged his throat, and he swallowed hard. Would Alyssa understand?

Hope was a friend. This really wasn't a date. Yet, it seemed a monumental turning point.

And he was scared.

He picked up his wallet, and it slipped from

his fingers. For a moment, he simply stood and stared at his shaking hands. Then he took a deep breath and retrieved the leather.

"Trevor, you're gonna be late, son." Gramps's voice echoed from the bottom of the stairs.

"On my way." He strode toward the door, flipped off the light switch and double-timed his way down the steps and into the kitchen.

Trevor's heart warmed at the sight of Cole and Gramps eating cookies and drinking milk at the table. A half-eaten package of chocolate-sandwich cookies sat smack in the middle of the table.

"You have to open the cookie and eat the cream first," Cole said. "That's the best part."

"Naw," Gramps protested. "That's for amateurs. The proper method is dunking the cookie in the milk, and then you're supposed to put the entire cookie in your mouth."

Gramps demonstrated, and Cole started laughing, slapping a hand on his leg. He was still wearing his straw cowboy hat, now perched on the back of his head. Hope said he only took it off when absolutely necessary.

"So, Cole, what are you and Gus going to do tonight?" Trevor asked.

Cole shoved another cookie in his mouth and

chewed thoughtfully before answering. "He said to call him Gramps from now on."

"Okay, what are you and Gramps going to do?"

"Gramps is going to teach me to play chess."

"Wow, that's impressive."

"Quit stalling and get going." Gramps eyed Trevor and nodded toward the door. "You got this."

In response, Trevor leveled a gaze at his grandfather. "It's been more than seven years. Maybe I forgot how." Or maybe he didn't want to remember. Life was a lot safer if he didn't take risks.

"You never forget how to live life. Go get yourself back in the game," Gramps said.

"What are you talking about?" Cole looked between the two men.

"Nothing important," Trevor said. "I better go. Don't let Gramps get into the Dr Pepper while I'm gone."

Cole wiped his mouth with the hem of his white T-shirt and looked at him. "Why not?"

"Because he won't be able to sleep if he drinks too much caffeine. And if Gramps doesn't sleep, nobody sleeps."

"Aw, go on," Gramps muttered. "You're a party pooper."

Trevor chuckled as he left the duo and headed to his truck.

The setting sun cast a lavender-and-orange glow upon the horizon as he pulled up to Hope's house. Trevor paused. Hope's house? How had that happened? But it was more her house than it had been anyone else's. She'd put her mark on the place.

The woman loved pink. Pink flowers hung from baskets on the little front porch. She'd found two wicker chairs at a yard sale and painted them white and put pink flowered cushions on them. The place was welcoming now.

Trevor jumped out of his truck and took the steps two at a time to the porch.

"I was beginning to think you changed your mind," Hope said from the other side of the screen. The woman was clearly annoyed.

"Lost track of time. Sorry." He glanced at his watch. "Good not to be the first to arrive."

"I guess." Hope opened the screen and stepped outside, turning suddenly and nearly running into him. "Sorry," she murmured.

"Now we're both sorry," Trevor said.

She looked up at him and chuckled. "I'm cranky *and* sorry."

That got him laughing. "Nice to meet you."

Trevor noted her white peasant blouse, denim skirt and boots with appreciation. What was the protocol here? Should he tell her that she looked nice, or would that cross the friends boundary line? As tempting as crossing that line seemed, it meant letting his guard down and sharing the secrets of his past. He wasn't certain he was ready for that. He stepped back and gestured for her to lead the way to the truck. When she did, her scent wafted past. "You smell like vanilla." The words slipped from his mouth without asking permission.

"It's my shampoo, I imagine. I don't wear perfume. Too many patients with allergies or sensitivities to scents."

"I never thought of that."

A thump sounded, and he looked down at Hope's purse on the ground. They both reached for it, his head inches from hers.

"I've got it," Trevor said. He scooped up the bag and handed it over.

"I might be nervous," she murmured. "And a little grouchy because I agreed to this. Nothing personal, but social events aren't really my thing."

"I understand." He opened the door and offered Hope his hand to step up into the truck.

"Thank you."

It was impossible to ignore how her hand, soft and warm, fit nicely into his. He hadn't held a woman's hand in a very long time.

"You're nervous too?" Hope asked when he climbed into the driver's seat.

"Uh-huh."

Trevor pressed the ignition button. "You and I haven't chatted about much but Cole, have we?"

She nodded. "You're right."

"Full disclosure. Small talk isn't my strength."

"Mine either." She fastened her seat belt and sat quietly as the truck's engine purred.

"You should know that this is the first time I've been on a...whatever this is since I lost my wife seven years ago. Can't say I've been very social since then." Trevor chuckled. "Not that I was social before that." He met her gaze and looked away.

"I'm sorry for your loss, Trevor." Hope cleared her throat. "Since we're being honest, Bess mentioned your, um, situation a while ago."

"And yet you still agreed to let me escort you tonight?" He gave a slow nod of respect.

"We've all got history." Hope shrugged. "It's about how that history makes us or breaks us and dictates our tomorrows."

"Well said. So how come you're nervous?" he asked.

"As I said, I'm not very social either. I'm a hot mess in situations like this."

Trevor laughed. "I get it." He fastened his seat belt. "Now that we've ascertained that we're both socially challenged, let's relax and get through the evening." He looked at her, taking in the clear hazel eyes and the hesitant smile that touched her lips. "Can't say there's anyone I'd rather be awkward with tonight besides you."

She seemed to relax at the words. "Thank you."

It felt good, to be honest. Hope was easy to talk to, and conversation flowed. He was surprised when fifteen minutes had passed, and he guided the truck through the gated drive of the Reilly home.

"Wow," Hope said. She peered out the window. "Is that valet parking in the middle of farmland?"

"Yeah. The Reillys are Homestead Pass royalty. Only the Pecan King would build a mansion here in the middle of nowhere."

"The Pecan King. Who knew?"

Before Trevor could get out of the truck, a valet opened the passenger door and offered Hope a hand to the ground.

The raw high-pitched twang of a fiddle tuning up could be heard in the distance.

Colin Reilly greeted them as they strolled up a flagstone walkway. The older man wore an impressive Stetson, and a crisply starched white Western shirt and bolo, with creased Wranglers and shiny boots. He grinned and reached for Trevor's hand.

"Trevor Morgan. I thought I was hallucinating. My wife is going to regret missing this event. Harper as well."

"Good to see you, sir." Trevor turned to Hope. "This is my friend Hope Burke."

"Pleased to meet you, ma'am. My wife was unexpectedly called out of town. Her mama isn't well."

"I'm so sorry," Hope said.

"Hope is a nurse," Trevor interjected. "She's been taking care of Gus after his surgery."

"I see. Sounds like, not only are you dating

a pretty gal, but she's smart too." He grinned. "You and I should talk, Miss Hope."

"Oh?"

"Yes, ma'am. I've got some ideas you could help me with." Colin paused and shook his head. "Shame on me. My wife would be wagging her finger about now. Here I am, all ready to talk business." He gestured toward the other guests. "You two go enjoy yourselves. We'll talk another time."

"Nice to meet you, sir," Hope said.

"You as well. I'm pleased as can be that Trevor brought you."

"Sorry about that," Trevor said when they'd moved from Colin's hearing.

"What?" She looked at him.

He frowned and glanced around. "Colin assumed we're an item. Folks are going to think the same thing and I don't have the energy to explain otherwise to all of Homestead Pass. My plan is to nod and smile. That work for you?"

"Sure. We can break up tomorrow." Her lips twitched, and amusement lurked in her bright eyes.

Trevor laughed. He was beginning to suspect that Hope had a wicked sense of humor. "Yeah. Good plan."

He took her arm. "This way. Watch your step. The ground is a bit uneven out here." Glowing lights lining the pathway directed them toward the barn area, where the guests had gathered.

"Thanks," Hope said. "I'm glad I wore boots." She smiled.

"New boots?" he asked.

"Not at all. These are Ariats, and I have several others in my closet." She gave him a sidelong look. "I'm an Okie too, you know."

"I guessed you were a city girl."

"A little bit country and a little bit city. I was born in Oklahoma City, though after my mother passed, my father moved us to a dot on the map outside El Reno."

"Your father still around?"

"I'm sure he is, but he doesn't keep in touch. He took off when I was eighteen and headed back to the rodeo. He was a stock manager."

There was no emotion in her voice. No indication of how she felt about her father's defection, and Trevor couldn't help but ache for all Hope had lost. "I'm sorry," he murmured.

"There's nothing to be sorry about," she said. "That's my past. This is my present."

Somehow he doubted that was all there was

to the story, but he wouldn't spoil the evening with questions. He knew what it was like to be prodded about things he'd rather keep buried. Once again he couldn't help but notice that he and Hope had a lot in common.

The sound of country music and the hum of voices got louder and broke the silence as they approached the expansive yard behind the Reilly home.

The ground lights disappeared, giving way to overhead lighting. Large globe lights strung on poles lit up more of the yard. Even more lights crisscrossed overhead to illuminate a portable dance floor that backed up to a small stage, where a country band was playing a peppy number.

An ingenious decorator had placed bales of hay covered with quilts around the perimeter of the dance floor to provide seating. To the right, a row of pecan trees wrapped with tiny white lights set a romantic scene. All around, couples stood in groups, talking and tapping their toes to the music.

"This is beautiful," Hope murmured.

"Yeah. The barn has been set up for a buffet dinner. Olivia's aunt caters events like this. I heard there's a barbecue with all the fixings."

"I'm hungry already," Hope said. "I guess you've been here for parties like this before."

"A few times. The Reillys have four daughters. Three of them are married, and their weddings were held here. Impressive events, not unlike this one."

They kept walking until the Reilly house came into view.

Hope stopped in her tracks and tipped her head to assess the classic stone colonial mansion that provided a backdrop for the evening.

"I hear it has six restrooms," Trevor said.

"Wow, that's a big house." She lowered her voice. "I like your little house better," Hope said.

"Me too," Trevor agreed, though it was nice to hear someone say it aloud.

She looked around, her eyes round as more and more people appeared. "Is the entire town here?"

"Close to it." He turned to her.

"What's that tent over there for?"

He turned toward a white tent on the other side of the barn. "Silent auction to benefit the clinic. Do you want to take a look while I find us something to drink?"

"Yes. That would be lovely. Thank you."

Hope's gaze followed Trevor. Tall and handsome, he garnered more than a few appreciative glances as he wove his way around people. She sighed, grappling with the reality that she was having more than simply friendly feelings toward the man. It wasn't all about his good looks either. Trevor was genuinely nice, with a heart as big as the corral that sat outside the stables.

All good if she was looking for a complication. Looking to need someone in her life.

She wasn't.

Hope began to turn toward the silent auction tent, then stopped when she spotted Eleanor moving quickly in her direction.

"Yoo-hoo, Hope!"

"Eleanor, how nice to see you." The older woman had on a white felt cowboy hat with a turquoise feather. Her Western outfit, complete with high-wattage bling, would get a nod of approval from Dolly Parton herself.

"I'm thrilled that you made it tonight." The older woman assessed Hope from head to toe. "That peasant blouse is adorable. Love the skirt."

"Thank you."

"Are you here alone?" She glanced around. "Or did Olivia find you a date?"

"I'm here with a friend." Hope braced herself for an interrogation.

"How nice." Eleanor smiled. Her owlish eyes lit up. "Anyone I know?"

"Trevor Morgan." She said it casually and feigned interest in the auction tent she hoped to reach soon.

"Trevor?" Eleanor released a soft gasp. "Trevor!" The older woman's face lit up with delight. "Well, isn't that something? I had no idea you two were an item."

"We're not." She offered Eleanor a bright smile and gestured around them with a hand. "Isn't it heartwarming how the entire community came out in support of the clinic?"

The diversion tactic flew straight over the woman's hat. "I'm just tickled that Trevor is finally dating again. Wait until my Bible study hears this. We've all been praying for that boy."

"No. We—"

"Eleanor, Daddy's looking for you." Liv stepped between Hope and her stepmother.

"Oh, is he? Isn't that sweet? The man can't go five minutes without me."

Liv slipped her arm through Hope's as the older woman walked away. "I hope you aren't upset that Sadie and I finagled you into attending the event with Trevor." She chuckled. "We were sort of surprised that it worked, to tell you the truth."

Hope couldn't stay annoyed with Liv. She had a heart of gold. Although two hours ago, she wasn't feeling quite so generous. "Are you and Sadie considering new career paths?" Hope asked.

"You never know." Liv leaned close. "I saw you two walk in together, and my first thought was Beauty and the Beast."

"What?" She looked at Liv. "Which of us is the beast?"

"Trevor, of course. He had quite a scowl on his face. Trust me, I've been the target of his displeasure before."

"Why?"

"Long story short, the Morgans protect their own. He thought I was going to break Sam's heart." Liv held out her hand and admired her wedding ring. "Trevor had it all wrong. I wanted Sam's whole heart forever."

"Oh, Liv. That's so romantic."

"Yes. It is." Liv smiled, her eyes warm with emotion. "What about you? What do you think of Trevor?"

"He's very nice."

"That's all?" Liv laughed. "I guess you didn't notice that Trevor, like all the Morgan men, is tall, dark and swoony."

"The Morgans employ me. I don't think it would be appropriate to notice," Hope returned.

Liar. She was only too aware that Trevor was the most handsome of the brothers.

"Just an FYI. There are at least a dozen women here who have been waiting for Trevor Morgan to return to the bachelor market again." Liv paused. "You know, if he really didn't want to bring you tonight, he wouldn't have. I have a hunch that Trevor likes you."

"We're friends."

Liv's chuckle clearly said, "Nice try."

"No. Really," Hope insisted.

"He invited you to live in his house. I think it's a little more than friends."

"Trevor likes Cole."

Liv slowly shook her head. "Oh my. You are definitely underestimating yourself, Hope."

She shrugged. "I'll be gone in a few weeks. There's no time to think about anything except my plans when summer ends."

"That's a shame. You fit in so well here. Everyone loves you, and it feels like you've been here forever."

Hope smiled at the kind words. In a short time, she'd come to care about everyone in Homestead Pass too. So much so, that she didn't want to think about goodbyes. At least not tonight.

"I think all we have to do is help Trevor to realize that you need to stay."

Hope opened her mouth to refute the statement, but Liv kept talking.

"I'll let you in on a little secret. It's been proven that the way to a Morgan man's heart is through his stomach, so don't discount the power of a great recipe. I have a few I can share."

"Liv. Where's your husband?" Trevor asked, interrupting in the nick of time. He handed a glass of iced tea to Hope.

"I should go find him. Looks like the band is about to start a new set, and I've got my dancing shoes on." She gave Hope a hug. "Remember what I said, my friend."

Trevor watched Liv walk away and turned to Hope. "That sounds important."

"She offered to share a recipe." Hope snuck a peek at Trevor. Tall, dark and swoony for sure.

It had been easy to ignore how handsome he was until this evening because he was also a prickly thorn in her side.

Tonight, he'd revealed that he was vulnerable. Paired with his smile, it was a dangerous combination that left her a little weak-kneed.

Across the yard, Hope spotted a tall man waving and trying to get her attention. "Is that Jim?"

Trevor glanced over. "Uh-oh. Looks like." He nodded toward the dance floor. "Can you dance?"

"Yes," she answered, more than surprised by the question.

"Let's dance."

Trevor took her hand and swept her into the crowd. He moved them around the dance floor to a slow, sweet country song. *Swept*. That was precisely what he'd done because, as it turned out, he was a very good dancer.

"Where did you learn moves like this?" Hope asked. She cautiously raised her gaze from his clean-shaven chin to his blue eyes, heavy-lidded now, as he, in return, watched her.

It was disconcerting to realize she was close enough to smell the citrus scent of his aftershave and the mint on his breath.

"Gramps taught Lucas and me for our high-school prom. He gave Drew and Sam lessons when they were in high school too."

"Sounds like you were social once."

He shook his head. "No. I didn't attend. One of my favorite science-fiction authors was in Oklahoma City for a book signing, and I convinced Sam to drive me there."

"You were a bookworm?" She feigned shock.

"I still am, thank you very much. And proud of it. Another reason why Cole and I get along so well."

She nodded, though she knew it wasn't just books. Trevor and Cole had a connection she couldn't define.

Suddenly, Hope realized that the music had stopped. She looked around. "That was nice," she observed. Unplanned and nice.

"Very nice," Trevor said softly, his gaze intent.

"Miss Hope, you are the prettiest gal here. Though I imagine Trevor already told you that."

She spun around to see a smiling Slim Jim. "Hi there," Hope said.

The skinny cowboy glanced from her to Trevor, nodding and smiling.

Trevor frowned and offered a stiff nod of greeting. "Did you bring a date?" he asked.

"Aw, she canceled, so I brought my mom." Jim chuckled and looked at Trevor. "Guess you don't have to write that check now."

"Nope." Trevor glanced around. "Your mother is looking for you."

"Yeah. Okay. I better check on her." Jim offered Hope a short bow. "Good to see you."

Hope turned to Trevor. "Okay, what was that? I got the distinct feeling that I missed something in the subtext."

"Nothing much. Trust me." He paused. "I was remiss not to tell you how lovely you look."

"Oh, thank you," she murmured. Heat warmed her face at the words.

"You know, I just figured out something," he said.

"What's that?" Hope asked.

"When we're on the dance floor, I don't have to talk to anyone."

"Except me."

"That's right. Except you." Trevor smiled, causing a chain reaction in the vicinity of her heart.

She took the hand he offered and followed

him onto the dance floor as the first notes of a slow ballad began.

Tonight wasn't turning out as she'd expected. Weeks ago, she would have never believed that she and the cranky cowboy would find middle ground on the dance floor.

Oh, that God. What a sense of humor He had.

TREVOR LEANED BACK in his chair, the sounds of the stables around him a soothing white noise. Here it was Monday, and he was still thinking about that barn dance. Thinking about Hope if he was honest.

Hope was a good listener, and they had a lot in common. He couldn't help but notice that neither of them was afraid to laugh at themselves.

And it sure didn't hurt that she was easy on the eyes.

Twice this morning he'd started on paperwork and got distracted thinking about holding her in his arms on the dance floor. Each time, he'd gotten up and started for the main house, with a paltry excuse to see what she was up to today. Then he'd lose his nerve and sit back down.

"I am so lame," he muttered. He stood again and headed out of the stables, only to run into Jim.

"Hey, boss." Jim chuckled. His friend was obviously eager and ready to razz Trevor about taking Hope to the dance.

"Don't even," Trevor said while showing him a palm. "Not one word."

Jim laughed and kept walking.

"Keep an eye on Cole," Trevor called out. "He's in the tack room, cleaning saddles."

"Yes, boss. Sure will." He chuckled again.

As Trevor strode to the house, he realized Hope's car was gone. This wasn't a physical-therapy day, so maybe she'd gone into town. Just as well. He had no clue what he was going to say to her, anyhow.

He stepped into the front entry and was enveloped by cool air and the sweet aroma of cinnamon and butter. "Gramps?"

"Nobody here but us," Sam called out.

Trevor moved down the hall to the kitchen and found Sam and Drew seated at the kitchen table with coffee and cinnamon rolls in front of them.

"Hope took Gramps to Elk City today to visit the big sports store," Drew said.

Trevor nodded absently. His attention was riveted on the pan of cinnamon rolls on the counter. "Where'd you get these?"

"Cinnamon rolls?" Sam grinned. "Pulled them out of the freezer yesterday to thaw. I figured this was the perfect time to get them in the oven."

"I didn't even realize Bess had cinnamon rolls in the freezer," Trevor said.

"Yep. If everyone knew about it, they wouldn't last long, would they?" He offered a wink.

"True." Trevor grabbed a plate and helped himself to a plump roll. Then he glanced warily at the coffee maker. "Did one of you two make the coffee?"

"Yeah," Drew said. "You're safe."

Gus Morgan's coffee was legendary, and not in a good way. Gramps claimed that his coffee put hair on your chest, while Trevor and his brothers were pretty certain it burned a hole in your gut.

Trevor slid into the chair opposite his brothers.

Sam leaned back and eyed him. "Saw you on the dance floor Friday."

"So did most of Homestead Pass," Drew added.

"Uh-huh." Trevor bit into his cinnamon

roll, savoring the blend of butter, cinnamon and cream cheese. For a moment, he could forget his brothers were talking.

"You and Hope." Sam cocked his head, waiting for a response.

"We're friends."

"Trevor, we don't mean to butt into your personal business," Drew began. "I usually leave that to Gramps, but if you're under the illusion that you and Hope are just friends, you're mistaken."

"I don't want to talk about it." Nope. He wasn't going to discuss Hope with anyone. What was there to discuss, anyhow? It was too new, and he wasn't even sure what "it" was yet.

Drew looked at Sam and nodded. Dread pushed at Trevor.

"What's the deal with Cole?" Sam asked.

Trevor jerked up in his chair, alarmed at the question. "You two have a problem with Cole?"

"No. Of course not. He's a great kid." Sam shook his head. "But something's going on and we'd like to know what it is."

"What he said," Drew chimed in.

"You two sound like Gramps."

"We already asked Gramps," Sam said. "He said he doesn't know."

Drew crossed his arms and leaned back in the chair, until it rested on two legs. "You may as well spill the beans. We're not leaving until you do. You know we don't do secrets in this family."

Trevor stared at his cinnamon roll with longing. The sooner he got this over with, the sooner he could go back to enjoying his pastry. Besides, Drew was right. They didn't do secrets. He should have never agreed to Hope's request to keep this confidential. Somehow, he'd have to make her understand.

"Well?" Sam asked.

"My name is on Cole's birth certificate."

Drew's chair fell back with a bang. *"What?"*

Sam did a double take. "Cole is our *nephew?*" He beamed.

Trevor glanced around quickly. "Could you lower your voice?"

"Could *you* answer the question?" Sam asked.

"I don't know anything until the DNA testing is complete. Until then, you two are going to have to keep your mouths shut and keep your questions in your back pocket. I'm not going to discuss it further."

He should have known his brothers would be more excited about adding Cole to the family tree than about knowing the circumstances of any indiscretion he may or may not have committed.

"Huh. How about that?" Sam mused. "I knew there was something awesome about that kid."

Trevor glared at him. "Am I going to have to duct-tape your mouth?"

"What's the big deal?" Sam shot back. "I'm excited."

"This is a delicate situation. Cole doesn't know and I've already broken my pledge to Hope. That's the deal."

Drew shook his head solemnly. "I sure hope you know what you're doing."

"Let me assure you, I do not," Trevor admitted. "Feel free to add me to your prayers."

"Yeah. For sure," his oldest brother murmured.

"All right then." Sam stood, then took his plate and mug to the sink. "Carry on in the proud tradition of Morgan men who also have no clue what they are doing."

Drew stood and released a whoosh of air. He grabbed his Stetson from the wall hook and slapped it on his head. "Good talking to you."

Trevor nodded and stared at his plate, his appetite now gone.

Minutes after Sam and Drew left, Trevor heard Gramps in the front hall. His grandfather stepped into the kitchen, with Hope behind him carrying half a dozen shopping bags.

Trevor jumped up. "Let me help you with those." He took the bags from her, his fingers tangling with hers.

"Oh, sorry," she murmured.

"Cranky and sorry?" He bit back a smile, remembering Friday. When she met his gaze, Hope smiled too.

"What is this?" Gramps stood next to the counter, his eyes fixed on the pan of cinnamon rolls. "Am I dreaming?" He closed his eyes and opened them again, then turned to Trevor.

"Found them on the counter when I got here," Trevor said. "Where do you want these bags?"

"Could you take them to my room, please?"

"Sure."

Trevor headed down the hall and neatly placed the bags on Gramps's bed. By the time he returned to the kitchen, his grandfather was in a chair with a cinnamon roll and a cup of coffee in front of him.

"They're still warm." Gramps frowned. "And they taste like Bess made 'em."

"Yep… What did you get at the store, Gramps?" Trevor asked.

Gus took a swig of coffee and grimaced. "Supplies for the fishing derby. A man wants to look nice when he's winning the top prize."

"Who's on your team this year?"

"About that. Turns out Hope's got her own pole, so I invited her. She picked up a pole for Cole today." He looked at Trevor. "We need a fourth. That's where you come in."

"Gramps, the last time I was on your team, you became unnecessarily agitated when we didn't win."

"I've matured since then. Besides, I have to be on my best behavior for Cole."

Trevor nodded. "All right. I'm in. But I'll hold you to a higher standard of sportsmanship this year."

"Whatever," Gramps murmured. "Could you go into town and pay the entry fee?"

Trevor laughed. "Is that why you invited me to join the team?"

"'Course not. You're Cole's mentor, and I thought this would be a good experience for both of you."

"Fine. I'll get our team registered." He glanced at his watch. "I better get back. Cole has a riding lesson soon."

"How's he doing?" Hope asked, her gaze curious.

"That boy is amazing. Tell you what. Why don't you and Cole join Gramps and me for dinner next Saturday after the fishing derby? Afterward, we'll head out to the stables and have a little show. I think it's time for you to see for yourself."

"That would be wonderful." She eagerly nodded. "Do you want me to bring something?"

"Nah," Gramps said. "We'll have our prize-winning fish for dinner."

Hope smiled. "I'll bring dessert."

"Fair enough," Trevor said. He turned to leave.

"I've got mail in my car," Hope said. "We stopped at the post office on the way in. Do you want me to grab yours?"

"Sure." He nodded to his grandfather. "See you for dinner, Gramps."

"Yes, you will. Though I probably won't be hungry once I finish this pan."

Trevor chuckled as he followed Hope out

of the house to her car, where she opened the door, grabbed a stack of mail and handed it to him.

"This is the ranch mail."

"Thanks," he said, searching for something to say to fill the awkward moment.

"No problem." She paused. "Did I thank you for a nice evening last Friday?"

"You did. Maybe we could do it again sometime without the town watching."

"You want to go dancing?" Her eyes rounded.

"Naw, I thought maybe dinner?"

"How about if I invite you to dinner with Cole and me?" She looked at him, her expression hopeful as she played with the mail in her hands.

She's nervous. The observation surprised him. That she hadn't rejected him surprised him even more.

"Okay, that sounds great."

"Does Thursday work for you?"

"Sure." Trevor smiled, working to keep things cool and casual. Yeah, he could do this.

"About six?"

"Yes, ma'am." He tipped his hat. "See you then."

Trevor whistled as he headed back to the stables. He hadn't made a fool of himself, which was good. For a moment, he allowed himself to think about the future. About taking a chance again. Living life, as Gramps put it.

Then he reined in his thoughts.

Right now. Today. That was all he could handle. And that was okay.

CHAPTER EIGHT

GRAMPS TURNED FROM the sink, wiping his hands on his Wranglers. He eyed the self-adhering wrap on Trevor's arm. "Did you donate blood?"

Trevor removed the wrap and tossed it in the trash. "I forgot about that."

"Want some?" Gus asked as he poured a cup of coffee.

"Uh, no thanks."

Mug in hand, the Morgan patriarch stepped slowly across the kitchen and eased into a chair.

"Look at you, walking with that coffee in your hand," Trevor said. "Steady as can be."

"I've been practicing for two weeks. First time I didn't spill." He chuckled. "All thanks to Hope. The woman has a will of steel. She refuses to allow me to do things the easy way. Nope. Eye on the prize, she says."

Yeah, that sounded like Hope, all right. "Glad to see you recovering so well."

"Feeling great too. And my incision is a thing of beauty. Want to see?" Gramps stood and reached for his belt.

"No!" Trevor held out a hand. "I believe you. When's your doctor appointment? Coming up, right?"

"Yep. Shortly after the fishing derby. I expect to be cleared to drive then. Praise the Lord. I'm tired of being chauffeured everywhere I go."

Gramps pushed out a chair with his boot. "Sit a spell, and you can answer that question you sidestepped five minutes ago."

"I'm not sidestepping anything." Trevor sat. "I had lab work done in Oklahoma City first thing this morning."

"That right? Are you sick? You look fine." He leaned closer, peering at Trevor. "Why didn't you go to the clinic?"

"I am fine. It's all good." Trevor ran a hand over the vein where the tech had drawn blood.

"Seems to me that's not the whole story." Gramps narrowed his gaze. "Something is going on. Care to enlighten me?"

"What makes you think something is going on?" Trevor looked around the room. Everywhere but at his grandfather, as he silently prayed he wasn't going to have to have a heart-to-heart like he'd just had with his brothers on Monday.

"Because my big toe is twitching, which means either a tornado or trouble. Or, in your case, maybe both." Gramps shook his head. "Also, it's Thursday morning, and you're usually knee-deep in chores this time of day."

Any other time, Trevor would have laughed and distracted his grandfather. But after the trip to have his blood drawn for genetic testing, he was far from good-humored. Reality had sobered his thoughts on the drive to and from the lab. Negative or positive, he sensed that the results of the lab work would change his life forever.

Trevor took a deep breath. It was time. He'd kept things from his grandfather long enough. "I had an appointment at a lab in Oklahoma City first thing this morning for genetic testing."

His grandfather jerked back at the words, his blue eyes, so like his own, wide with surprise. "Come again?"

"My name is on Cole's birth certificate."

Gus stared in shocked silence. "I've got no words. Day and time. Put it on the calendar."

"Yeah. I hear you," Trevor said.

"When did you discover this?"

"In June. Hope told me about a week after she arrived. After I sort of stumbled on the information."

Gramps seemed to mull the words. "That's why she came all the way from Oklahoma City to take a job in Homestead Pass. Why didn't you tell me?"

"You had enough going on recovering from surgery. I didn't want to bother you."

"Have you told your brothers?"

"Drew and Sam wrestled it out of me on Monday."

Gramps snorted. "Can't say I appreciate you telling them and not me."

"It wasn't planned."

His grandfather glanced at the kitchen clock. "Son, I've got a million questions, as you may have guessed, but Hope will be back from town shortly, so I'll make it quick."

"Fair enough."

"Cole's mama. What's the story?"

"I barely knew her."

"You think you might be Cole's daddy?"

"Technically, anything is possible. You know what shape I was in back then." He tapped his fingers on the table and shook his head.

Gramps nodded, a frown drawing his eyebrows together.

"We won't know for a few weeks," Trevor continued. "The thing is, test results won't change how I feel about Cole."

It was important that he say that aloud. He wasn't mentoring Cole because he had to but because he wanted to.

"I wanted Cole to have a summer without any strings attached. The boy lost his mother. He needs to grieve and be a kid for a while, regardless of what happens." Trevor's heart clenched as he said the words.

"I guess you'd be the one to understand that firsthand."

Trevor nodded as he straightened the place mat on the table. Drew was twenty-one when their parents died. Sam, seventeen. He and Lucas were thirteen. They were anchorless and grieving until Gramps moved in. Yeah, he did understand.

"I kinda got the idea you might have feelings for Hope. Am I right?"

"Maybe. I'm taking that slow."

Gramps gave a slow nod. "Have you told her about AA?"

Trevor folded his hands and studied them. He had his father's hands—wide with blunt nails. "Not in so many words," he murmured.

"Are you scared?"

His head shot up, and he looked at his grand-father. "Sure, I'm scared. I'm terrified."

"Why? Alyssa didn't have a problem with it."

"I... I didn't tell Alyssa."

Gramps's jaw fell. "She was your wife."

"Yep. You're right. But it was a whirlwind thing, and I was scared that if I told her, she'd walk away. We got married, and six months later... She was gone."

"Aw, son. You need to tell Hope. Upfront and immediately."

He nodded, wrestling with the inevitability of what he had to do. For too long he'd hidden from the world, and from the secrets of his past and the truth of his battle with sobriety.

Gramps was right. There was no room for secrets. He'd been ashamed to tell Alyssa. His growing feelings for both Hope and Cole de-manded his complete honesty. "Yes, sir. I'll tell her tonight."

"Tonight?"

"That's the reason I came in the house. I'm having dinner at Hope's this evening."

His grandfather perked at the words. "Why, that's great."

"Sam and Olivia will be by to join you for dinner. Olivia is cooking."

"Again with the babysitter." Gus grimaced. "Why is it that once you reach your glory years, everyone treats you like you're feeble?"

"They *want* to come by. For some reason, people actually like you."

"Strangest thing." Gramps eyed him over the rim of his mug. "Have I told you lately how proud I am of you?"

"I haven't done anything remarkable."

"Sure you have. Look what you've done for Cole. You've got that children's event coming up again. You're touching lives, Trev. Your mama and daddy would be proud."

Trevor swallowed hard. "Pastor McGuinness brings them in. I entertain them. Not a big deal."

"Now, there you go again, short-changing yourself and downplaying your ministry."

"It's not—" His grandfather shot him a look that stopped further protesting.

"Don't be bad-mouthing God's gift." Gramps's

hands, weathered by age and arthritis, were wrapped around his mug as he leaned closer. "Let me ask you a question. What part of farming is the most important, do you suppose? Planting the seed? Watering? Sunshine? Or maybe harvesting?"

"Okay, Gramps. I get it." He'd heard this particular Gus Morgan parable before. Gramps always knew what to say to knock sense into him.

"Do you?" He shook his head. "You're a godly man, and you minister by example."

"I feel like a hypocrite."

"What part is hypocritical? The part where you were humbled and asking your Lord for forgiveness? Or the part where He forgave you?"

"Point taken, but I've got a long way to go before I can forgive myself for the past."

"You're wrong, son. Forgiveness for your sins is someone else's job."

Trevor shifted uncomfortably at the words and looked at his watch. "I've got to shove off."

"Okay, but you take my words with you."

"Yes, sir. I will."

As he strode down the porch steps, Hope's car pulled into the drive. Trevor waved, and she gave a friendly hit on the horn.

He stopped at the car and Hope rolled down

her window. "Everything okay?" she asked. "You looked concerned coming out of the house."

"All good." Trevor nodded. "Had my lab work done this morning."

"Cole had his blood drawn this morning as well."

"What did you tell him?"

"I told him the truth. That we needed to have his lab results on file in case we found his father."

"What did he say?"

Hope stared straight ahead for a moment before turning back to him, lifting her chin so she could meet his gaze.

"Trevor, he said that he prayed you were his father." She blinked, her eyes becoming glassy. "I'm only sharing that because if you aren't his father, things are going to get more complicated. You should be aware of how much he looks up to you. Be very careful with his heart."

He sucked in a breath at her honest admission. Another confirmation that he had to level with her about his past tonight.

"It's a huge responsibility, being close to someone. I get that. I won't ever hurt him. Or you. You have my word."

Hope's lashes fluttered and she glanced away while offering a slow nod.

"I better get moving. Are we still on for tonight?" he asked.

"Yes. I'm looking forward to it," Hope said. Her face pinkened with the admission, a sweet vulnerability evident in the hazel eyes.

Trevor's heart tumbled at the sight. He smiled. "Me too." He set off again toward the stables, with Gramps's words echoing in his ears.

Yeah, his grandfather was right. He should have told Alyssa.

His feelings for Hope were new and a little terrifying, but he vowed not to make the same mistake twice.

"Aunt Hope, are you and Trevor boyfriend and girlfriend?" Cole asked as he opened the refrigerator and stared at its contents with great focus and then closed the door.

Hope blinked at the unexpected question. She'd intended to be circumspect around Trevor. Cole was going through a lot. There was no need to add more complications to his life. He needed to be able to trust that she'd never let him down or fail to put his best interests first.

She turned and looked at him for a moment. He was wearing his straw hat, as usual, and she noted he'd added a few healthy pounds to his slight frame. Though he wore sunscreen at her direction, his skin had tanned a light gold and his freckles had multiplied since they'd arrived at the ranch.

"Trevor and I are friends." She grabbed a potholder, lifted the slow-cooker lid and stirred the chicken and rice. The aroma of wild rice and savory chicken had her stomach grumbling.

"Then why is Trevor coming to dinner?" He closed the refrigerator and looked at her. "And why did you put on your nice clothes and lipstick and all?"

Hope stared at her nephew. He was much too observant. Yes, she was guilty of taking a shower and putting on a sundress and sandals. She'd even put on lip gloss. Of course, he noticed.

"It's not a date. It's dinner. Friends have dinner with each other. Remember how you and Gramps and Trevor went for burgers?"

"Are you sure? I saw him talking to you at the corral, and Jim said he's sweet on you. That means he likes you." Cole gave her a knowing look.

"I like him too. I like you and I like everyone here on the ranch." It was time to change the subject. "So, Cole, tell me about your horse-back-riding lessons. Trevor says I get to watch on Saturday after we have dinner with Gus."

"I ride Storm. He's a Appa—Appa…"

"Appaloosa."

"Yeah. That. Storm is dark brown and white like Patch. I groom him and everything. No one else rides Storm except Trevor and me. He's like my very own horse." He grinned. "Trevor said I can bring him an apple sometimes. Can we buy apples?"

Hope stared at him, concern nagging at her. First the dog and now a horse. This would complicate leaving. And they'd know if that was their next move very soon.

"Storm. Wow, that's great. Yes. I'll pick up a few apples."

"Thanks, Aunt Hope."

She put a hand on his shoulder. "Cole, you know we're only here until my job with Gus ends, right?"

"Can't we stay until school starts?" He frowned, his lower lip jutting. "You said you're going to find my father."

The heavy weight of Cole's words nearly

crushed her. Hope prayed for guidance, knowing how important her response was. This was not the time to dismiss his concerns. She'd vowed honesty with her nephew, but hadn't expected it to hurt so much.

"I'm doing my best to find your father, but the truth is, we may never be able to locate him. Your mother didn't leave us with much information." She'd rather prepare him for a worst-case scenario than give him false hope about Trevor Morgan.

Confusion clouded his blue eyes.

"As for how long we stay, I don't have an answer to that yet. Oklahoma City is your home now. It's where you'll go to school. We can't stay in Trevor's house forever." Hope paused. "We have a few more weeks here. Plenty of time to enjoy Storm, right?"

"I guess," he mumbled.

She longed to tell him that Trevor might be his father, but if the results came back negative, Cole would be devastated.

"Did you know I used to ride when I was your age?"

Cole lifted his head at that admission. "You did? Did you groom your horse yourself?"

"Yes, but it wasn't my horse. Our neighbor

let me ride his horse." Cole's eyes widened at the information.

"Did you muck stalls? Trevor says I'm the best mucker he ever had."

"I don't doubt that. You're a hard worker, Cole, and I'm proud of you."

"My mom rode horses."

"Yes. I knew that. She had her own horse."

"My mom was a champion barrel racer. Did you ever see her race?"

"I did. Your mom was very good."

He nodded, seeming pleased with Hope's answer.

"Here." She handed him plates and silverware. "Why don't you set the table."

"Okay."

"Your room is clean, right? Trevor might want to see where you do all that reading."

Cole grimaced. "It's kinda clean."

"Set the table, and then make sure your room is tidy, please."

"Yes, ma'am." He started walking toward the dining room.

"You walked and fed Patch, right?"

"Yes, ma'am. Patch pulled weeds with me today. He's sleeping in his kennel."

"Perfect. I'm proud of the way you handle

your responsibilities, Cole. You've really stepped up to help me too."

"Aunt Hope?" He paused and looked up at her, the blue eyes wide and trusting. "Are you sure we have to leave?"

"Yes, Cole. Let's not give it too much thought right now."

He nodded and left the room, leaving Hope's heart aching for what she saw in those eyes. Cole longed for a forever home. Everything he wanted was on the Lazy M Ranch. However, she refused to make promises she wasn't certain she could keep. Lazy M was indeed a dream come true. That dream, however, was temporary.

Hope pulled out a big bowl from the cupboard. By the time she'd finished putting together a tossed salad, the doorbell rang.

Cole raced to the door before she could. Hope finished putting away ingredients, all the while listening to the conversation at the entrance.

"Why did you bring Aunt Hope flowers?" Cole asked.

"It's customary for the guest to bring a gift to the host," Trevor said. She could hear the amusement in his voice.

"Why?"

"As a thank-you for the hospitality."

"What does *hospitality* mean?"

Trevor chuckled. "Hospitality. Hmm. That's you inviting me to your home."

"Okay, I get it. So what did you bring me?"

"Cole!" Hope rushed to the door. "You didn't even invite Trevor in." She opened the screen. "Come on in. I'm so sorry."

"He's right. Cole is my host tonight as well."

Trevor handed Hope a large bouquet of bright, cheerful sunflowers. "Wasn't sure what kind of flowers you like, but these reminded me of you." He winked. "A little bit of sunshine."

"Thank you," she breathed. Her heart clutched as she caught his gaze.

No one had ever given her flowers before. She'd remember this moment for a long time.

Trevor kneeled down and pulled his back pack from his shoulder. "Got something for you right here, Cole."

Cole inched closer to the bag as Trevor unzipped the outside. He brought out five hardcover books. "The rest of the series."

"I can borrow them?" The blue eyes rounded with surprise as he eyed the stack like they were piles of gold.

"They're yours. My gift to you."

"Wow. Thank you, Trevor."

"Hey, my pleasure." He grinned. "Always good to have another friend who's a *Space Knights* fan. We Knighties have to stick together if we're going to save the universe."

Cole grinned back. "I'm going to put these in my room."

"That was really sweet of you," Hope said when Cole left the room. "Maybe you shouldn't buy him gifts, though."

His brow creased. "Hope, they're books. I didn't hand him the keys to a car."

"You're right. You're right," she said, backtracking.

"This is about you worrying that he'll get too attached to me?"

She nodded, emotion tugging at her again. The conversation earlier with Cole and now this kindness from Trevor overwhelmed her. What if the DNA test was negative? Where did that leave her nephew? Where did that leave her? Trevor had unwittingly scaled the walls of her heart without even knowing. She feared not just for Cole, but for herself.

"No matter what the future holds, Cole will

always be my friend. Always. And friends stay in touch. Right?"

"Yes."

Trevor's eyes were full of emotion, which did nothing to reassure her that she wasn't heading straight for the heartache she'd so carefully avoided for so many years.

A timer interrupted the conversation.

"Biscuits are done." She worked to sound cheerful and headed to the kitchen.

Trevor followed her. "Something smells good."

"Slow cooker chicken and rice. Nothing fancy."

"I've had your chicken and rice. It's fancy enough for this cowboy," he said.

Dinner went quickly, with Cole practically shoving his food down, eager to get back to his books.

"Let me help with the dishes," Trevor said. He finished off the last biscuit. "Least I can do after such a delicious meal."

"No. I don't believe in doing the dishes when there's a guest in the house. They're soaking in the sink. I'll toss them in the dishwasher later." She stood. "Let's sit on the back porch and enjoy the evening."

"Mosquitos don't bother you?"

"They haven't been too bad this year."

He followed her outside, where she turned on the ceiling fan, creating a breeze.

"You did everything right with this house," she said. "I sit out here almost every night, thanks to that fan."

"I can see why. Look at that full moon."

Hope glanced at the sky where the glowing moon with its hazy halo lit up a blanket of stars. She took a mental snapshot of the sight and tucked it away to remember when she was back in the city.

They each sank into cushioned rocking chairs, positioned at angles with a small table in between. For long minutes, Hope gently rocked, occasionally sneaking peeks at Trevor's profile in the semidarkness.

"I'm sorry you never got to live in the house as you intended," she finally said.

"Me too. But life doesn't turn out the way we planned for most of us." He turned his head and smiled. "Things are pretty good right now."

"Yes," she said softly. "They are."

A comfortable silence stretched between them. The only sound was the song of the katydid over and over. *Katydid. Katydidn't.*

"Time is moving quickly," Hope said. "August will be here before we know it."

Trevor nodded.

"How are things coming along with your event? Anything I can do to help?"

"Well, since you mentioned it. Maybe you can do me a favor."

"Sure. Whatever you need."

"I told you about the medical tent. The nurse from the elementary school called last night. She has to withdraw due to a family emergency."

"I've love to help you." Hope did a quick mental calculation. "Especially after all you've done for Cole and me. But your grandfather will certainly be given a medical release next week and won't need me. I'm in limbo until the DNA results come in." Hope paused. "I'd hate to commit and then find out I wasn't staying in Homestead Pass."

Trevor nodded as though he understood her quandary. "The event is the third Saturday in August," he said. "Why don't you take a staycation while you're in wait-and-see mode."

"A staycation?" Hope chuckled. "I can't remember the last time I took time off in my life." She did another quick mental assessment, this time of her finances. It was true she'd brought in more income as a private duty nurse than as a case manager, which meant her bank account had a cushion until the end of August.

"You know it would mean a lot to Cole," Trevor added.

"No need to pull out the violins," she said. "If you're willing to put up with me staying here until your event, I'm willing to volunteer."

"I really appreciate that. You won't regret it once you see how the kids enjoy the day."

Hope leaned back in the chair, surprised at herself. She couldn't believe she'd agreed to Trevor's proposal so quickly. That wasn't how she normally functioned. She usually took days to assess all sides of an issue before making a decision.

The exception had been coming to Homestead Pass. She'd arrived on a wing and a prayer, without a safety net.

Soon she'd go back to her orderly life. The thought was unsettling.

They sat silently rocking beneath a clear sky sprinkled with diamonds and lit by a full moon. "This is nice," Hope said. More than nice, her heart whispered.

"Yeah. You can see the lights of Drew's house from here, above those trees."

Hope stood. "Yes. I see them."

"What do you want out of life, Hope?"

She eased back into the rocker and looked at him. "Where did that come from?"

Trevor shrugged. "Since you came and I found out Anna named me as Cole's father, I've been reevaluating my life."

"I see. Well, there isn't that much I want. Someday, I hope to have enough money saved up to buy a little house. I'd like my own garden."

He nodded. "What about you?" she asked.

Trevor turned his head toward her, his blue eyes intent. "I'm not as certain about things as I used to be," he said. "To tell you the truth, I hadn't expected you and Cole to have such an impact on my life." He looked at the sky and took a deep breath. "I'm feeling things for you that I never thought I'd feel again."

Hope sucked in a breath at his words, her heart stuttering. There was no denying that despite her good intentions, she was falling for the cowboy.

Trevor cleared his throat and shifted in his seat, looking almost pained. "The thing is, I haven't told you everything about my past and I realize that I ought to."

"I'm listening." She'd learned to remain calm and nonjudgmental when listening as part of her job as a caregiver. Inside, however, she was anything but calm. Her chest was tight, and her heart thudded. Hope held her hands tightly in her lap.

"Twelve years ago, my best bud, Wishard Mason, died. And it was my fault." He ran a hand over his face and took a deep breath. "Small rodeo outside Okmulgee. I was supposed to be hazing for him that day, but I was hungover, so someone else took my place. Wishard hit the ground wrong and took a horn to the ribs. Freak accident, really. But I should have been there. It was my job. I let Wish down."

Hope knew enough about rodeo to understand hazing. It was the hazer's job to keep the steer in line. She opened her mouth to speak, but he held up a hand.

"The drinking got worse after that. I was a quiet drunk. Drank for breakfast, lunch and dinner. Didn't bother anyone. I wasn't the type to fool with women, which is why I've been skeptical about your stepsister's claim that I'm Cole's father."

He paused and looked at her, eyes bleak.

"One particular bender, Lucas called Gramps because he was concerned. Gramps came in the middle of the night and hauled me home." Trevor pulled a chip from his pocket. "Twelve years sober this year."

The chip fairly glowed in the light of the moon.

"That's a huge deal," Hope said softly. She respected him all the more for what he'd been through and the courage he'd mustered to tell her tonight.

"It is." He took a deep breath, as though a huge weight had been lifted. "I like you, Hope. Far more than I expected. I don't know where you and I are going, but I don't want to keep secrets."

"I appreciate that."

"Are you okay with the fact that I'm a recovering alcoholic?"

Hope placed her hand on his. "Trevor, if you're concerned that I'll hold that against you, you're wrong. You're a man of integrity who's been through a lot and turned his life around."

He sighed, releasing a long breath. "Thank you. That's all I expect. An honest answer."

She smiled before another thought occurred.

"Cole has been awfully quiet." Hope stood. "I should check on him."

"Mind if I tag along?"

"Sure." She walked quietly down the hall and peeked into Cole's room. He was asleep on the bed with a book in his hand. Patch was at his side. Hope sighed at the tender sight.

The dog looked up, his big brown eyes curious, and he gave a small sound as if asking "what?"

"That's beautiful," Trevor said.

"It is," Hope said. "We have you to thank for it. You've made a difference, Trevor. Don't ever doubt that you're right where the Lord wants you to be."

Hope turned her head, not realizing he was so close. She froze. Unable to move.

For the longest moment, Trevor gazed at her. Then he smiled. "Did you say there was chocolate cake?"

Hope smiled back. "Yes. Come on. I'll even put on a pot of coffee."

"Ever try Gramps's coffee?"

"I have. It's the most disgusting thing I've ever tasted in my life."

Trevor laughed. "Yep. That would describe Gus's killer coffee."

Hope entered the kitchen and moved a domed pink glass cake stand from the counter to the kitchen table. "Wait until you see this cake. I think it's the buttermilk that makes a difference."

"Where'd you get that cake stand?"

"At that home goods store inside Liv's restaurant." She lifted the lid, revealing a two-layer cake with swirls of shiny chocolate frosting. "Perfect. Right?"

"Yeah," he said softly. Trevor's blue eyes were tender as he watched her. "Perfect."

Hope nearly swooned at his words. Her face warmed. Oh, this wasn't good at all. She'd been concerned about Cole getting too attached to Trevor. Her heart whispered that she was falling for the man who might be her nephew's father.

CHAPTER NINE

"THIS IS LIVING," Gramps said with a happy sigh. He leaned back on his chair, his line in the water, and his feet propped up on a cooler filled with Dr Pepper. "Was that the prettiest sunrise you've ever seen, or what?"

"Yep. It was a nice sunrise," Trevor said without looking up. First, he'd stabbed himself with a lure. Now his line was tangled. He'd been working to untangle it for the last forty-five minutes.

"Nice? That was God's handiwork," Gramps said. "There were more colors in the sky than on the paint chips at the hardware store." He huffed. "You kids take it all for granted."

"Gramps, I roll out of bed at four every morning. I like a sunrise as much as the next guy. But we've been sitting here for four hours now without a nibble. I'll take cattle over fish every day."

Trevor shook his head. Nope, fishing was not his favorite sport. He wasn't even sure it was a sport. Crawling out of a perfectly comfortable bed at dark thirty in the morning to sit on the banks of the Homestead Pass Lake didn't make any sense to him. But he'd do it once a year if it made Gramps happy.

"Fishing is all about patience. Patience has never been your strong suit, Trevor. Relax and enjoy God's gifts all around you." Gus swept a hand through the air like a game-show host. "Hear that water lapping against the shore?"

"I do, and it's putting me to sleep."

"Did you notice that red-tailed hawk that soared across the sky?" Gramps shook his head. "I'm counting my blessings because, if it wasn't for Hope, I might not have been in shape to be here today. I'm mighty appreciative."

Trevor glanced around. "Where is Hope, anyhow?"

"She went over to the other side of the lake to visit your brothers' wives. They've got a fancy tent set up. That's another thing," Gramps continued. "What happened to man and the elements?" His eyes rounded with outrage. "And can someone tell me why there's a food truck in the parking lot?"

"Free enterprise, Gramps." Trevor chuckled. This might not be an opportune time to point out that man and the elements probably didn't include the six-pack of Dr Pepper Gramps had on ice in his cooler.

"I'm hungry," Cole announced over the conversation.

"You gotta talk soft, or you'll scare the fish," Gramps said.

"I'm hungry," Cole whispered.

Trevor dug in his pocket and pulled out a bill. "Here you go. Get yourself a hot dog and grab me one too, please."

"Sure. Thanks, Trevor. Will you watch my line?"

"Absolutely." Trevor glanced over at Cole's line, which was not tangled. Not a bit of movement. The water was clear enough to see to the bottom, but the fish had checked out. The number of anglers lining the shore today had probably sent them into hiding. Gramps was responsible for getting the word out about this event. He'd negotiated with the local press in Homestead Pass and Elk City. The derby had sold out, and the place was wall-to-wall anglers. There wasn't an empty spot on the banks of the lake. Gramps was no doubt having regrets.

"Need anything, Gramps?" Cole asked.

"No thank you, son." Gus patted the ice chest at his feet. "Got everything I need right here. Just like the good old days."

This time, Trevor did laugh.

When Cole was out of earshot, his grandfather stole a look around and then gave Trevor a nod. "You talk to Hope?"

"Yeah, Gramps. I did." His line was nearly untangled. Might be ready to cast again before it was time to head home.

"I appreciate that you are a man of few words, but could you be more specific?"

Trevor raised his head and looked at his grandfather. "It went fine."

"Ha." He slapped his leg, a gesture that Cole had picked up. "Told you so."

"Yes, you did. But let's not get all excited about *fine*."

"Well, sure I will. If I waited for *you* to get all excited, I'd be waiting a long time." He released a breath and smiled. "When do I find out if I have a new grandchild or not?"

"The test results?" Trevor glanced around. "We can't talk about that here."

"Answer the question and we won't."

"I don't know. There's a lot I don't know, to

tell you the truth. I don't know what will happen if the test is positive. I don't know what will happen if it's negative. Either way, Hope's headed back to Oklahoma City soon."

"I guess you'll have to figure out a way to get her to stay in Homestead Pass and let her think it was her idea."

"Gramps, that's a little devious. Even for you."

"*Devious* is a strong word." He offered a mischievous smile, his blue eyes sparkling. "You're a smart feller. Put that college education to work."

"I am a smart feller. I've convinced her to volunteer at the Kids Day event. She's agreed to take a vacation after you're released by the doctor."

"See, I knew you were smarter than you look."

Trevor rolled his eyes. "Thanks for the vote of confidence."

"Excuse me."

Both Trevor and Gus turned to see a pleasant middle-aged woman standing near their gear. She held a can of soda in her hand and peered down at Trevor. "Is that your son over there wearing that straw cowboy hat?"

Trevor's gaze went from the woman to Cole, who did indeed have his hat on, along with a striped tank top and cut-off jeans. Despite Hope's encouragement to wear shoes, he was barefoot.

"Yes, ma'am. That's him. Is there a problem?"

"Quite the opposite. You should be proud. I forgot my wallet, and he paid for my soda. He's a fine boy. I wanted to tell you that. You and your wife did a good job raising him."

"He is a good kid. Thanks for letting me know." He smiled as the woman left.

"Aw, that boy nearly breaks my heart," Gramps said. "You did a good thing taking him under your wing. I wouldn't be unhappy to find out he's your kin."

"That's one thing we both agree on," Trevor said. He still didn't fully believe Cole was...but part of him wanted it to be true.

Cole returned minutes later and handed Trevor a hot dog. "Where's yours?" he asked.

"Aw, I didn't really need one."

Trevor pulled out another bill. "Go get a hot dog. And, Cole, that was a kind thing you did, buying that woman's drink."

"I remembered that last Sunday, Pastor talked about kindness. He said we aren't supposed to let our left hand know what our right hand is doing."

"You got the gist of it, Cole." Trevor nodded. "But the Lord knows, and I'm sure He's proud of you. I sure am."

A grin lit up his face as he raced back to the beverage tent.

"What was that all about?" Hope asked as she approached, her gaze following Cole.

"Nothing," Trevor said. "Just your nephew being a great kid."

"He is, isn't he?" She smiled and sat down on her lawn chair next to her line and adjusted the rod. Trevor had noticed a few anglers stop and chat with her today. He couldn't blame them, though he'd gone out of his way to stand and stretch when they approached.

Just doing his part to keep the yahoos away. He was reminded of Bess's remark that Hope was a little bit of sunshine. Today she wore a yellow tank top and denim shorts with flip-flops. Her hair had been pulled up into a ponytail. A smile was never far from her lips.

Her life hadn't been easy either. It occurred to him that she taught him a lot by example. She'd left home at eighteen. Put herself through college. Gramps was right. Hope kept her eye on the prize. Slow and steady won the race.

"Fish biting on the other side of the lake?" Gramps asked.

"Nothing legal," Hope replied. "Drew and Sam have tossed back half a dozen. Liv and Sadie have pretty much given up. What they do have over there is ham-and-cheese quiche from Liv's restaurant and chocolate croissants." She frowned. "I packed peanut butter and jelly. I'll know better next time."

Next time. Trevor liked the sound of that, and he also liked the silent communication that had developed between them. A single move of her eyebrows or a twist of her lips and he knew exactly what she was thinking. Yep, life was good. Better than he would have expected or deserved.

"Any action on my line while I was gone, Gus?" Hope asked.

"Not even a jiggle. This is getting downright discouraging. Too many people and too much noise, I guess. Those fish are sitting at the bottom of the lake laughing at us."

Hope turned to Trevor. "How are you doing? Anything?"

"One tangled line, a punctured thumb and

six mosquito bites." He yawned and checked his watch. "Only four hours until this fun ends. Then I suppose we'll have to stop and get hamburgers for dinner."

"I haven't given up yet," Gramps said. "The day is young."

Trevor groaned and closed his eyes.

"Your arms sure are red," Hope said. "Did you put on sunscreen?"

"Yes, Mom. I did."

"Someone's a little cranky."

He opened one eye and peeked at her. "Yep."

"Aunt Hope, your line is moving." Cole stood behind them, eating a hot dog and pointing at her rod. "Hurry, he's trying to get away."

Hope jumped up, knocking her chair over. "Oh my. You're right, Cole."

"Keep that line tight," Gramps said. He stood and moved closer to Hope. "That's it. Use that drag. Woo-ee, that's a daddy. We won't be putting that fella back."

"He's fighting me," Hope said. "I've never had one this big."

"You want help?" Trevor asked. He stood behind her, trying to get a good look at the catch.

"Yes, please."

Trevor stepped behind Hope and put his

hands over hers. "All we have to do is hold on until we tire him out."

Around them, people had moved close to watch the scene, some cheering her on, others filming with their phones.

"Hang in there, Hope," Gramps said. "Trevor is right. No burgers tonight. We might even snag ourselves a trophy."

Hope grinned, her face close to his. "He's slowing down."

"Let's reel him in, nice and easy."

"I got the net," Gramps called, his voice triumphant.

Cole jumped up and down. "You got him, Aunt Hope."

"Here he comes," Trevor said. "Largemouth bass for sure." The fish flew up a bit, splashing water as his tail swished in protest. Gramps netted him and held their prize in the air for all to see.

The crowd that had gathered broke into applause. Hope laughed, her hazel eyes shining. Trevor was certain he hadn't ever seen a prettier sight.

"Let's get him weighed and on ice," Gramps said. He grinned and shook his head. "I knew it was a good idea to get you on our team."

By noon, Trevor was certain Hope had brought their team to victory, as not a single angler had pulled anything out of the lake that came close to her big boy. He was proved right when the mayor stopped by with a photographer from the *Homestead Pass Daily Journal*. He put a ribbon around Hope's neck and handed Gramps a trophy as the photographer snapped pictures.

"This is the best day I've had since I pulled that home run in the church softball league," Gramps said. He sat in the back seat of the truck staring at the trophy, a silly grin on his face. "They said they'll send us a nameplate with our names on it."

"Can I hold it, Gramps?" Cole asked.

"Of course. It's going home with your aunt."

"Oh no," Hope said. She wiped her face with a towel and fastened her seat belt. "It was providence that fish grabbed my lure instead of yours. They were sitting right next to each other. We're a team. We're the Gus Morgan team. That's what the registration card says. The trophy goes on your mantel, Gus."

"Aww, thanks, Hope."

Minutes later, Trevor pulled the truck in front of the main house, and everyone piled out.

"Whose gonna clean the fish?" Gramps asked.

"Who do you think is going to clean the fish?" Trevor pointed a finger at his grandfather. "Hope caught it. I'm going to fry it up. Cleaning is all yours."

"That's what I was afraid of. You want to put that ice chest on the back porch for me?"

"I can do that," Trevor said.

"Cole and I are going to head home and get cleaned up ourselves," Hope said. "We'll be back later to help with dinner."

"Sounds like a plan."

Cole grabbed his rod-and-tackle box and started walking down the road toward home. "This was the best fun ever."

"Yeah, it was," Trevor called after him.

"What are you talking about? You complained the whole time," Gramps said.

"Except for getting up way too early and sitting for hours without a nibble, it was fun."

Hope laughed. "That makes no sense whatsoever."

Trevor's gaze skipped over her. Her hair was a mess, tucked up into a ball cap that hadn't kept her nose from turning pink after hours in the sun. The tank top she was wearing had a peanut-butter-and-jelly stain, and her legs were splashed with lake mud. Yep, she was beautiful.

He was certain that he could learn to tolerate fishing if Hope was by his side each time. She made everything more interesting.

Gus released a sigh. "What my grandson is trying to say is that he enjoyed himself in spite of himself."

"Yeah. What Gramps said." It was as though he was waking up from a long sleep. Today he felt more like his old self than he had in a very long time, and he didn't want it to stop.

More and more, he was beginning to think that maybe Gramps was right. He ought to start giving Hope reasons to stay in Homestead Pass.

THE AFTERNOON SUN warmed Hope's shoulders as she perched on top of the corral fence, waiting for Cole to come out of the stable door. Another first for her nephew. This morning it was fishing. Hope smiled as she thought about the derby. Trevor's hands on hers, his encouragement in her ear as she reeled in the bass. Cole had ended up catching a few as well. Too small to keep; nonetheless, they'd created memories today that would not soon be forgotten.

"What's taking them so long, do you suppose?" Gramps said.

"Trevor said Cole needs to tack up Storm all by himself in order to ride. Those are the rules." She pursed her lips. "You know, Cole hardly touched his fish, and he passed on dessert. I think he's having second thoughts about riding in front of us."

"They better play ball or go home, 'cause I'm about to fall asleep standing up. That fish supper was delicious, especially since you caught it. But it's been a long day and I'm ready for a nap."

The approaching sounds of a horse's hooves and tack jingling had both Hope and Gramps turning toward the stable door.

"Sounds like they're coming," Hope said.

"Oh yeah. There's our boy," Gramps said.

Hope released a small gasp. "Oh, look at him. He looks just like his mother." She couldn't contain her pride. Cole had achieved so many milestones since they'd arrived in Homestead Pass. This might be the most memorable one.

Her nephew seemed smaller and younger astride the Appaloosa. Helmet in place, heels down in the stirrups, Cole sat tall in the saddle with his shoulders back. Tension had his hands a little too tight on the reins, instead of being easy and relaxed, and he didn't look at her or Gramps.

Poor kid was nervous. His gaze remained laser-focused on each step, and he nodded stiffly in response to Trevor's gentle guidance. Trevor continued to reassure Cole while walking next to Storm. The horse and rider moved around the perimeter of the corral in a clockwise circle.

Come on, Cole. You can do this, buddy.

Hope remembered the first time her father came to watch her ride. She'd been nervous and awkward. Anna, on the other hand, was a natural, confident and relaxed. Her stepsister had been born to ride.

After a few laps around the corral, Trevor led Cole and Storm back toward the stables.

"Way to go!" Gramps hollered. He turned to Hope. "He'll be comfortable in the saddle soon enough. It's wise of Trevor to take things slow."

"I agree," Hope said. There was no rush. Cole had to learn to trust the horse and himself, which might take some time. Trust was the first thing someone lost when adults didn't keep their promises. When that happened, a child learned to be wary and to closely control the few things that they did have control over.

Poor Cole. She'd been there. It was the reason she didn't like to depend on anyone but herself.

"I'm heading back to the house," Gramps said. "They'll be a while."

"Need any help?" Hope asked.

"Naw, I'm good. Tired and old but good."

Hope jumped down from the fence, kicking up a small cloud of red dirt, then started toward the stables to watch Cole groom his horse. Trevor met her at the entrance. He grimaced.

"That didn't go as planned. We even practiced a few fancy steps," he said. "The horse was willing, but Cole was nervous. I couldn't get him to relax. It was like his first time on the horse."

Trevor shook his head. "He's come a long way. I know he talks a good one about the horses, but it's been slow going, building his confidence." He shrugged.

Hope put her hand on Trevor's arm. "You don't need to convince me. I know Cole. Anna has dragged him all over the country. He's been in and out of a dozen different schools. That contributes to his shyness and lack of confidence."

She smiled up at him. "But my heart nearly

exploded seeing him on that horse. It's a huge step, and you made it happen."

At that moment, Cole burst out of the stables. He adjusted the red bandanna around his neck and raced up to Hope. "Did you see me, Aunt Hope? Did you see me?"

"Cole, you were like a professional cowboy on that horse," she said. "I'm so proud of you."

"I looked just like Trevor, didn't I?" He searched her face for confirmation that he was just like his hero.

Hope's heart lurched at the words, and she quickly looked at Trevor and then away before nodding.

She sent up a silent prayer. *Lord, whatever happens, don't let this little boy's heart be broken.*

As THE NEW week began, Cole's words continued to play over and over in her head, haunting her waking hours and keeping her up at night. Everything rested on the results of the DNA test, and she wasn't prepared for either result. Once again, she found herself wondering how she'd gone from having a tight lid on her life to it becoming out of control.

On Monday, she and Gus headed to Elk City

for his doctor's appointment, and Hope continued to mull that thought.

"Are you absolutely sure you don't want to let me drive home?" Gus said. "You heard that doctor. I've been cleared. I feel like I should celebrate."

"Congratulations. You put in the work, Gus. I'm proud of you." She signaled and pulled into traffic. "How about an extra Dr Pepper today instead of driving my car?"

Gus frowned. "Is that a bribe from a medical professional?"

"Why, yes, it is."

He screwed up his face in disgust. "I guess we know who doesn't trust me with her vehicle."

Hope chuckled, momentarily distracted from her thoughts.

"Used to be an old-fashioned soda shop on that corner," Gus said as they headed down Route 66. "Trevor's daddy would fit the boys into the pickup and take them for a drive to Elk City. Then he'd take them bowling for the afternoon. It was his way of giving his wife a break."

"That's a wonderful memory," Hope said.

"Yep. Lots of good memories. Do you have some tucked away?"

"My mother… She made me believe I could do anything. When she died, and I was pretty much on my own, it was those lessons she taught me that helped me make it through." Hope sighed, remembering those good times.

"You've been sighing an awful lot today. Everything okay?" Gramps asked.

"Oh, sure—I just have a lot on my mind." She gripped the steering wheel tightly. That was an understatement.

"Something to do with that paternity test?"

Hope hit the brakes and nearly swerved. "What?"

Gus jerked forward and braced a hand on the dash. "Woo-ee. Opening my mouth may have been ill-timed."

"Sorry, Gus. Maybe you could drop further bombshells when the car is parked."

"Yeah, I will surely remember that." He released a breath for dramatic effect. "My life flashed before my eyes, and I realized I forgot to make my bed this morning."

Hope shot him a glance. "I wouldn't qualify that as a near-death experience. Trevor, on the other hand, may experience one when I get back to the ranch." She shook her head. "He promised not to tell anyone. I can't believe he told you."

"Aw, don't blame Trevor. I pretty much beat it out of him."

Now she had to wonder who else knew. Was everyone whispering behind her and Cole's back? Was all of Homestead Pass laughing at them?

"My lips are zipped," Gus reassured her.

"Thank you, Gus. I appreciate your discretion."

"Happy to keep my mouth from running," he said. "No need to be concerned."

"I am concerned," she said. "Very concerned."

"Are you worried Trevor is Cole's daddy, or are you worried he isn't?"

Hope offered a begrudging smile. "You pretty much nailed it." She slowed for a traffic light, which turned green, and shot him a quick glance. "When I first arrived, I would have said with complete certainty that I had no plan other than finding Cole's father. When I met Trevor and realized how he and Cole hit it off, I realized that I might lose Cole. It was all I could do not to run in the other direction."

She sighed. "Now? Well, now I think my heart might break if Trevor isn't his father. That boy loves him, and I think Trevor feels the same way."

"Well, sure he does. Trevor has mentored a few boys over the years. Cole is different. I believe Trevor sees himself in that boy."

She swallowed back the emotion threatening to bring her to tears. "Trevor has helped Cole to heal and to grow. It's been a transformation that could only be divinely orchestrated."

"And you might say the same is true of Trevor. Don't you think?"

"Yes. You're right. Trevor is changing."

"I don't see the problem," Gramps said. "Stay. It's clear as the nose on your face that Trevor cares about you as well."

"He hasn't dated in seven years, Gus. I'm not willing to be the rebound girl who helps him get over his first love. That never ends well."

Hope had spent more than a few nights wrestling with the realization that she was falling for Trevor. That didn't mean she was ready to let go of the roadmap she'd carefully drawn for her future.

"Is that what you think?"

"It's classic. I know Trevor is in AA, but has he had any sort of counseling since his wife died?"

"Can't say that he has."

She nodded. "Trevor is finding Trevor again, and that's a wonderful thing. He'll be ready for a relationship eventually. Maybe even soon. But I'm not convinced that he's ready now." Or maybe she wasn't convinced that *she* was ready. She'd learned to keep her heart guarded a long time ago.

"I'd argue with you, except you're giving me a perspective I haven't considered. It's clear you care for Trevor too, which makes me think that you're a selfless young lady."

Hope grimaced. Gus had it all wrong. She wasn't selfless. More like self*fish*, because so far the only person she'd ever really trusted was herself.

"Don't give me too much credit," she finally said. "If I have any insight at all, I gained it all the hard way."

"Sounds like you graduated from the school of hard knocks too." He cocked his head. "I was at the top of my class."

She smiled. "Oh, Gus. The Morgan men are so blessed to have you as their guardian. I only hope that I can do for Cole what you've done for them."

"Now you're going to make me blush."

She put her hand on his and squeezed. "I mean it."

"I appreciate that. Now let me give you something to chew on, because you don't get to be my age without learning a few things."

"What's that?" Hope asked.

"Don't discount the hand the good Lord plays in our lives. There's a plan bigger than you and Trevor. We make plans, and the Lord laughs and offers a better way. A way we couldn't even see, because sometimes, we can't get out of our own way."

She nodded as he continued.

"You never know." He shrugged. "My advice to you is to stay open to detours. We get so fixed on the map, that we miss what's right in front of us."

Now Hope chuckled. "My life has been nothing but detours. I always get to point B courtesy of point Z. But, yes, I will keep an open mind."

"That's all I ask."

Was Gus right? Was it time to turn it all over to the Lord? The thought of letting go was almost as difficult as the thought of saying good-bye. Once again, she found herself praying.

Lord, please guide me. Because I've got some hard decisions to make.

CHAPTER TEN

THE RUMBLE AND clang of a dually and horse trailer approaching the house caught Trevor's attention the following Thursday and he stopped in his tracks. He'd been about to take Cole out in the ute to check the herd when he turned to see who it was.

"Well, what do you know?" Trevor grinned.

"Who is it?" Cole asked absently. He threw a stick, high and far, and Patch chased.

"The long-lost Morgan brother. Mr. Lucas Morgan."

The truck's horn blasted a staccato beat, and his brother stuck his head out of the driver's window, waving his hat. "Woo! Hoo! Good to be home."

Moments later, Lucas parked the dually, jumped out and raced up to Trevor, grabbing him in a bear hug. Trevor had more muscle, but Lucas had the height, and Trevor was unable to wrestle free from the embrace. Luc laughed like a kid, then finally released him.

"Hey, Trev. Looking good," his twin said. "I see you got your summer haircut."

"Yeah, one of us has to maintain some decorum." Trevor reached for his brother's hat, knowing his brother hadn't trimmed his shaggy hair in months. In response, Lucas laughed and stepped just out of reach.

"That would be you," Lucas said. "The lone ranger. Lazy M boss man. My brother."

"Hilarious, as usual," Trevor observed dryly. "Welcome home, prodigal son. How long are you staying?"

"I'm here at your request. Remember?"

Trevor frowned. "Come again?"

"I came to help you with your summer kids thing. It is next weekend, right?"

"Close. Two more weeks."

"Really? Well, I sure got that wrong." He shrugged. "That's okay. Between you and me, I could use a little break from the circuit. Had a bad spill last week. Ended up with a concussion and managed to bang myself up." He rolled up the sleeve of his cotton shirt and held up his right arm, where a row of fresh stitches trailed from his elbow to his wrist. The arm itself showed signs of fading bruises.

Bronc busting was an accident waiting to happen. Yet, Luc hadn't figured that out yet. With each accident, Trevor prayed his brother would get out of the sport that all the Morgan boys had dabbled in.

Trevor eyed his brother. "I assume you had it X-rayed."

"Yeah. Nothing broken but my bank account." Luc grinned. "Don't tell Gramps, would you?"

"You know Gramps. He finds out whether we like it or not."

"Yeah. Just don't give him any hints. I don't want to worry him." Lucas looked around. "Where is our faithful leader?"

"In the house. He'll be glad to see you."

"How's he doing?" Luc's gaze searched Trevor's, worry evident in his eyes. "I call him whenever I can, but you know Gramps. Cards to his chest."

"He was cleared by the doctor last week."

Luc nodded. "Good. Good. Don't know what I'd do without the old man."

"I hear you," Trevor said.

His brother frowned and looked behind Trevor. "Hi there, little man."

Trevor turned and put a gentle hand on Cole's shoulder and urged him forward. "Cole, this is Lucas. He's my fraternal twin."

Cole's eyes widened and he looked from Trevor to Lucas. "You don't look the same."

"Nope. We don't," Trevor said. "I'm handsome and Lucas isn't."

Cole laughed. "That's not what I meant."

Trevor smiled. "Some twins are identical, and some are not. Lucas and I are in the *not* category. I'll explain how that works when we feed the chickens tomorrow."

"Nice to meet you, Cole," Lucas said. "Is that your dog?"

"Uh-huh." He patted the energic pup on the head. "This is Patch. Trevor gave him to me."

"Did he?" Lucas raised his brows at the words.

At the mention of his name, the dog barked, did a circle dance and sat down.

Lucas laughed. "Whoa. Look at that. What a neat trick."

"I taught him." Cole grinned.

"Very good."

"Cole, would you take a run up to the stables and see if Jim has any chores he needs help with?" Trevor asked.

Cole furrowed his brow. "We're not going to check the herd?"

"We will. As soon as I visit with my brother."

"Yes, sir." Cole nodded. "Come on, Patch. Come on, boy." The dog eagerly raced his master to the stable.

"'Yes, sir,' huh?" Lucas murmured. "When did you start recruiting ranch wranglers from the elementary school? I knew you were short-handed but come on."

"Funny guy. Cole's here for the summer."

Lucas cocked his head. "I sense a story here."

As they spoke, the door to the main house creaked open, and Hope stepped outside. She waved. Trevor waved back but didn't stop her before she got in her car and headed home. He'd introduce her to Lucas. Just not right now.

It occurred to him that he'd never concerned himself with introducing Luc to a woman before. It was a given that young or old, they swooned over his brother.

But this time, it was different. Trevor wanted to keep his friendship with Hope private for a little longer.

"Who's that?" Lucas asked.

"Gramps's nurse. She came on board so he wouldn't have to go to a rehab facility after surgery."

Lucas gave a slow nod of interest. "Doesn't look like any nurse I ever met, and I've seen my share of late."

"Hope has been a huge help to Gramps this summer. Cole is her nephew. They're staying on the ranch for the summer."

"Looks like I missed all the excitement." He looked at Trevor. "So where's she staying?"

"I invited them to stay at my house."

Lucas jerked back at the news. "Are you kidding me? That's a huge step, isn't it?"

Trevor shrugged. "It's been seven years and the house is empty. I'm not sure why everyone thinks it's a big deal."

"Cut it out, Trev. It *is* a big deal. We both know that." He glanced in the direction of the departing vehicle. "When do I get to meet her?"

"She's in and out at the main house. I'm sure you'll run into her, eventually."

"Eventually, huh?" He paused as if speculating. "I mean, unless you don't want me to say hello to Gramps's nurse."

"Don't be ridiculous."

Lucas assessed him. That was the trouble with being a twin. You couldn't get away with much. It would be nearly impossible to hide how he felt about Hope from his brother for long.

"Where's your partner in crime?" Trevor asked, trying to change the subject.

He was surprised Harper Reilly wasn't here, following him around. Though in truth, while Harper acted like she barely tolerated Lucas—and in return, he treated her like she was one of the boys—Trevor was certain she was secretly in love with his brother.

"Harper? She followed me all the way from Oklahoma City. Turned off at her daddy's ranch."

"How's the champion barrel racer?"

Lucas scoffed with disgust. "That woman bested me at every turn. She came out in the top three at nearly every stop. Harper is good, Trev. Better than good. Which is why she always buys lunch."

"How about you? Did you stay on the leaderboard?"

"I refuse to answer on the grounds that I'll look like a fool."

Trevor clapped his shoulder. "Come on. I'm

the last person to give you a hard time. I washed out of rodeo a long time ago."

"All I can admit is that I'm still in one piece, except for the stitches."

"Make any decisions about retirement?"

Luc nodded, looking contemplative. "I've set a deadline. Next summer, I'll be home for good. Maybe." Trevor's heart perked at the thought. He'd love to have his brother home with him.

Lucas took off his hat and then slapped it back on. "What's for dinner, anyhow? I'm starving. Haven't eaten in hours."

"I'm not sure. I'm cooking tonight."

"You?" He grimaced. "Where's Bess?"

"You're way behind on the news. Bess has been gone for a little over a month, visiting her new grandbabies in Texas. She'll be back some-time tomorrow."

"Texas." Luc raised both palms. "My favor-ite woman left us for Texas? What's this world coming to? I'm bereft. I got through the last leg of the drive dreaming about warm cinnamon rolls slathered with cream-cheese icing."

Trevor lowered his voice. "Sam might be able to hook you up. Ask him when no one is listening."

"I'll do that." Luc nodded toward the house. "You going in?"

"I will, shortly. Got a few things to take care of."

"Okay, I'll see you later."

"And, Luc?"

"Yeah?"

"Take a shower before dinner."

Luc laughed. "Good to see you too, Trev."

Trevor smiled. It was good to have Lucas home. Seemed like everything was complete when the whole family was at the Sunday dinner table.

Lucas paused and looked Trevor up and down, his gaze penetrating. "You're different, Trev."

"What?" Trevor frowned. "I'm not different. I'm tired."

"No." Lucas shook his head. "It's something else. What's going on?"

"Nothing. You're dreaming."

"Am I?" Luc narrowed his eyes. "I'll figure it out eventually. Twin mind meld and all."

Trevor mulled his brother's words for a moment. Was he different? Maybe so. A lot had changed since he'd last seen Lucas. The last time all four of them had been together was in the hospital waiting room, praying, while Gramps was under the knife with hip-replacement surgery.

Yeah, that was early June. A lot *had* happened since then.

Trevor ran a hand over his face and looked at Lucas. No denying it. His brother was right—he would figure it out eventually. He'd already let things slip to Gramps and his older brothers.

"Hope is here because she thinks I'm her nephew's father." The words tumbled out, and he stood back and waited for the fireworks.

Lucas opened his mouth and closed it. Then he grinned and reached out to hug Trevor again.

"Nope." Trevor jumped back. "Get away from me. You smell like old socks and burnt coffee."

"I can't believe my little brother is a father." Lucas whooped loudly.

Trevor shook his head. It was a good thing they were outside and no one was in earshot. "I'm not your little brother."

"Two and a half minutes, Trev. That makes me your big brother."

"Whatever." He paused. "I know I'm asking

the impossible, but could you keep your mouth shut about this?"

"I suppose I could, except that doesn't sound like any fun. Aren't you excited?"

"I haven't let myself get excited." Trevor's throat became tight. In that moment, the truth hit. He was going to be devastated if Cole wasn't his son.

"YOU'VE GOT MAIL."

Hope dropped her coffee mug into the soapy dishwater and turned to see Bess step into the kitchen. She had mail in one hand and the newspaper in the other.

"Oh, thanks," Hope said. "I didn't realize you were back from the post office already."

"You've got certified mail," the housekeeper said. Her voice reflected curiosity. "Trevor got one too. I signed for them."

"Thanks, Bess." Hope wiped her hands on a towel and reached for the official-looking envelope. She examined the outside, her heart catching at the return address. DNA testing results.

A shiver raced over her. This was it. She'd waited weeks to find out what Cole's future held. What *her* future held. Now that the answer was in her hand, Hope was hesitant to open the envelope.

Thankfully, Cole was gone for the day. Drew and Sadie took him to Elk City to the farmer's market, along with Mae, while Liv babysat little Andrew. It was a nice treat for Cole, and she was appreciative of how the Morgans went out of their way to include him.

"Bess, I'm going to head home. Now that you're back, there's not much for me to do around here."

"You're like me," Bess said. "You have a hard time sitting still. Thanks for weeding my garden this morning."

"I was happy to."

"Trevor says you're on vacation. That means you're not supposed to find anything to do except relax. Go read a book or something."

"Maybe I will." She looked at Bess. "It's really great to have you back."

The older woman offered a kind smile. "Great to be back. I don't mind telling you, I was a little nervous about what kind of disaster the boys might have left me. Wasn't I pleasantly surprised to discover that this place is cleaner than when I left? You might put me out of a job."

"Never. You don't replace family. The Morgans have made it clear that you're one of them."

"Aw, what a lovely way to put things." She smiled. "By the way, I'm going to need that recipe for your chocolate cookies. White chocolate, is it? All I've heard is how delicious they are. You're giving my cinnamon rolls some competition."

"I'm happy to share. However, your cinnamon rolls remain the blue-ribbon winner around here." Hope tapped the letter against her hand. "I'll head out." She scooped up her car keys from the table and turned.

"Oh, and, Hope. Everyone is coming for dinner on Sunday. A little reunion. I'm cooking. Will you and Cole join us?"

"Um, I don't know." Hope hesitated, knowing that the more time she spent with the Morgan family, the more attached to them she became. She glanced at the envelope again, her stomach sinking.

Bess peered at her. "Everything okay, honey? I don't want to be nosy, but is that letter bad news or something? Is there anything I can do?"

"No. No. I'm just tired."

Tired of waiting. Tired of life in limbo. Everything was out of her control right now and that was the cruelest part of this situation.

Hope drove home slowly, dreading the moment she'd find out what was in the letter. The climb up the stairs to the door seemed the longest of her life. She grabbed a bottle of water, went to the back porch and turned on the ceiling fan before sinking into a rocker.

All the scenarios that kept her awake at night now rolled through her head. Cole was Trevor's son and she'd be forced to leave him behind. Yes, she'd visit him, but that wouldn't be the same. Or there wouldn't be a match and she and Cole would return to Oklahoma City.

Her hands trembled as she turned the paper over. It slipped from her fingers to the wooden planks of the porch floor. She took a calming breath and picked it up.

After slipping her finger beneath the gummed closure, she pulled out the letter.

She skimmed the document, her heart racing. Until she saw the words.

The data does not support a paternity relationship. Probability of paternity is 0%.

The rest of the sentences in the letter became hazy as tears clouded Hope's eyes.

Her breath stuck in her throat and her heart hammered in her chest.

What was she going to tell Cole? *I thought I found your father, but I was wrong?*

Why had Anna put Trevor's name on the birth certificate? Anger at her stepsister bubbled up from deep inside. She closed her eyes tightly as tears slipped down her face.

Hope had so believed that things were going to turn out all right, which was ridiculous as there was no scenario where the word *right* fit. None.

"Hope? Are you back there?" Trevor called. His voice traveled from the front yard.

"Yes. The front door is open." She took a breath and quickly scrubbed the moisture from her face.

"Mind if I come in?"

"Trevor, it's your house." The words came out a little sharper than she intended.

Minutes later, he stepped onto the porch. His gaze took in the letter in her hands. Today, his eyes were bleak with pain. "I'm sorry I'm not Cole's father."

The words nearly gutted her. He was apologizing for a negative paternity test.

Hope blinked hard. *You will not cry.*

Trevor crouched and took her hands in his. Hope concentrated on the feel of his hands, trying not to think about the day when he wouldn't be in her life. Trevor was a good man. He had come alive since Cole entered his life. Maybe they both had come alive since they'd met here on the Lazy M.

What would happen now? She couldn't just hang around because there was a stirring in her heart when Trevor was near. It was time to move on.

"I care about Cole," Trevor murmured.

"I know you do."

"I care about you as well, Hope."

She took a deep breath. "You're a good friend, Trevor."

"What if I want more than being your friend?" He searched her face and she had to look away. "Am I imagining that you and I have something?"

He paused. "I know what I want and I'm not afraid to go after it. What about you? Are you willing to put aside the fears of the past and go after what you want?"

Then, she dared to meet his eyes. Big mistake. Hope longed to put a hand on his stubbled jaw and tell him how much she cared, but the words were locked inside. Falling for

Trevor was a risk. He was right. She was afraid to love him.

"I'm confused, Trevor," she finally said. "I haven't even had time to process that I've spent weeks holding my breath about Cole's heritage only to find out I had it all wrong."

"Are you sorry you came to Homestead Pass?" He searched her face and she looked away.

How could she adequately explain how she felt? The town, the ranch, the Morgans—and yes, Trevor—were all a dream come true. Someone else's dream. This would all be a memory she unwrapped and looked at when she wanted to play what-if someday. But it wasn't her reality.

"Wow. I guess I have my answer. I had it all wrong too, didn't I?" Trevor stood. "What are you going to do?"

"Nothing has changed. I'll be here for your event. I'm looking forward to it." She worked to sound upbeat.

"What about finding out who Cole's father is?" he asked. "That kid deserves so much more. If I was smarter, I would have refused the test and simply claimed him as my own when he showed up. This way hurts. It hurts like I haven't hurt in a long time."

Hope winced at his words. Words that reflected her pain as well. She thought she was following a prayerful nudge to Homestead Pass. Instead, she'd found heartache for everyone.

"Anna never mentioned anyone else," she finally said. "I talked to Cole and asked him if his mom ever discussed a boyfriend, and he said no. I can't go randomly swabbing cheeks of every guy on the rodeo." Again, she tried to make light of things. "I need to get Cole enrolled in school and get back to my life."

"Don't discount this as your life. Your future," Trevor said.

"What does that mean?"

"I spoke to Colin Reilly the other day."

She looked at him with surprise. "Colin Reilly? What does he have to do with anything?"

"Remember that comment he made about wanting to talk business with you?"

"At the barn dance?"

"Yeah. I ran into him in town Wednesday morning."

Tension unfurled in her stomach. "You talked to Colin Reilly about me when I wasn't present?"

"It was casual. I wasn't going behind your back."

"Trevor, the fact that I wasn't there, and I

didn't give you permission to discuss me, is going behind my back." Now she was becoming cranky. "You did it when you shared about Cole to your grandfather as well."

Trevor ducked his head and then looked up with a grimace. "Yeah. Maybe this is the time to fess up. I told all of my family about Cole."

Hope gasped. "But we had an agreement."

"I apologize. It was an agreement I should have never agreed to. My family is everything and I found out the hard way that secrets don't work."

"And Colin Reilly?" she prompted.

"He's going to bring his mother-in-law to his home and needs someone he can trust to manage around-the-clock care. I told him what you'd done for Gramps. He was impressed and even mentioned salary and benefits." Trevor rattled on with numbers and specifics.

The more he spoke, the more upset Hope became.

"What do you think?" he asked.

"What I think is that you should have given him my phone number. You were way over the line." She shook her head, unable to believe what she'd heard.

Trevor leaned closer. "No. That's not it at all. This just sort of happened."

"Trevor, I don't need my life managed. I've taken care of myself since I left home. Before that, really. Up until I came here, I've been doing a pretty good job too."

He stood and paced back and forth, his boots echoing on the wood planks of the porch. "We're friends, Hope. More than that, really, and my intentions were all directed at helping you and Cole."

His gaze searched hers then fixed on her hands, held tightly in her lap. "Honestly, Trevor, I don't know what I want anymore."

"Maybe you could let me know when you do. I've made it clear I care about you and Cole. The truth is, I'm in love with you, Hope."

Hope swallowed at the admission. Fear clutching at her heart.

"You're determined not to need anyone," he said with a deep sigh. "I'm guessing I need to wake up and realize that we're not walking toward the same tomorrow."

She shook her head and searched for an answer. Except she didn't have one. Maybe that was the most telling thing. Cole would be more than happy to stay here, and he'd thrive. Somehow, she'd managed to connect her nephew with the man most likely to provide him with everything he needed.

What about her?

Trevor needed to hear that she was okay with an uncertain future here. Except she couldn't commit to a future in Homestead Pass if it meant giving up the security of life in Oklahoma City.

Needing someone was a risk she couldn't—wouldn't—take.

CHAPTER ELEVEN

"THIS IS SO COOL." Cole stared at the school bus unloading children for Kids Day.

Children ranging in age from six to twelve bounded from the bus and were led to the welcome tent by a volunteer. Trevor smiled, his heart warm with satisfaction as he glanced around the grounds, where white tents dotted the landscape. Kids Day banners in bright colors had been stretched between tents. Overhead, a blue sky confirmed the perfect weather he'd prayed for.

Trevor had prepared for this day for an entire year. Things were getting off to a good start.

"Where did all these kids come from?" Cole asked.

"They're city kids who have never been to a ranch," Trevor said. "Pastor McGuinness coordinates with city churches and I rent the buses."

"These kids are like me before Aunt Hope brought me here," Cole said.

"That's right." Trevor's heart stuttered at the mention of Cole's aunt. Too many long days and nights had passed since the DNA test results arrived, throwing his life into chaos.

Opening that envelope and seeing the results had been a punch in the gut. Seeing the real panic in Hope's eyes that day had shaken him to his boots.

Hope had managed to dodge him nicely since then. She'd politely declined dinner with the family and kept a low profile at his cottage. When he'd questioned Cole about his aunt, he only said that she was baking. A lot.

Gramps had nagged him at every turn about the situation, while Lucas accused him of trying to keep him from meeting Hope. Sam and Drew at least had the good grace to stay out of his business. Though on more than one occasion he'd caught his brothers giving him the side-eye and talking quietly. Bess kept silent about Hope's absence at the main house as well, the only commentary a clucking *tsk-tsk* when she didn't realize that he was within earshot.

Didn't matter. The situation was out of his

hands. He couldn't make Hope care enough to stay.

"What am I supposed to do today, Trevor?"

Trevor looked down at Cole, who wore a pint-size shirt that matched his own. A yellow T-shirt with the Lazy M Ranch logo on the back and the word *staff* on the front. The sight made him smile. He was so proud of how far this boy had come. As proud as if Cole was his own son. The thought only stabbed at his already tender emotions.

"You and Jim are my security team," Trevor said. "Stick with him and keep an eye out for any problems. Call me immediately if you see something that needs my attention."

"Yes, sir. Should I go find him?"

"He's in my office getting batteries for one of the walkie-talkies. But, yeah."

Cole turned and then looked up at him. "Mr. Trevor, can I ask you something?"

"Of course, Cole."

"Why do we have to leave the ranch?" He kicked the dirt. "Don't you want us here anymore?"

Trevor released a breath. The topic most likely to make him grumpy. "Have you talked to your aunt about it?"

"Yes, sir. She says my home is with her now and that's in Oklahoma City."

"Why do you think I don't want you here?"

"Can't think of another reason why we're leaving. Aunt Hope is happy here. I figured you said it was time for us to go." He made a sour face. "Patch won't like that. You know he won't. He'll miss Cooper. Cooper is like his brother."

Trevor nodded. The despair in Cole's eyes was shredding him.

"Who will give Storm apples if I leave?" Cole asked quietly. His quivering voice begged Trevor to throw him a lifeline. "Maybe my aunt is mixed up. Can you talk to her?"

"Sure," Trevor said quietly. What else could he say? The kid's heart was breaking, and with each plea, his was as well.

The boy shot him a grateful glance. "Thanks, Mr. Trevor. You'll have the right words to make her understand we gotta stay."

Trevor nodded absently, though he knew for a fact that he didn't have a single word that could fix things. For the kid's sake, he'd take one more shot even though he'd probably fall on his face again. How could he convince a woman who'd done everything by herself all her life to let him in?

He didn't know.

"I hope so, buddy," Trevor finally said. He glanced at his phone. Time to do another check of all the activity stations. "Okay, Cole. Remember, you're staff today." He pointed a thumb toward the stables. "I'll check in with you later."

"Yes, sir."

Trevor started toward the corral, where Drew and Sadie were assisting, offering miniature pony rides to eager children.

Both Drew and Sadie waved at him, and he returned the gesture. "Helmet on?" Sadie called to the next child in line.

Trevor moseyed up to the fence to watch, pulling his hat down to protect himself from the morning sun. He'd applied sunscreen. Even that simple act reminded him of Hope.

A moment later, his grandfather joined him, resting his arms on the top rail.

"You continue to amaze me, son."

"Are you complimenting me or insulting me?" Trevor asked. He wasn't in the mood for whatever lesson Gramps was about to teach.

"Both, of course. This event is nothing short

of amazing. I'm thinking next year we oughta bring in the press."

"No way, Gramps. It's supposed to be a homegrown event. I don't need press. The only people I want to impress are the kids. That's already been checked off my list." He kept his eye on the corral while he spoke. "We've got six or seven kids at each activity, with two volunteers. Every child gets the attention they deserve. It also ensures that no one gets lost or hurt."

"Fine by me, but I'm thinking you could get a sponsorship and expand. Bring in a few rodeo stars. Sell merch and such."

"Hard pass." He eyed his grandfather. "I appreciate the input. All excellent ideas, but not for the vision I have for this program."

Gramps nodded. "I respect your right to be wrong."

Trevor laughed.

"Remind me what your vision is for Hope Burke and her nephew."

Zing! There it was. Gramps never missed an opportunity to nudge him in the direction he decided was the right one.

"Gramps, Hope and Cole are in God's hands. I've done all I can do about the situation."

"I don't believe that for a minute."

The squawking static of his walkie-talkie sounded, interrupting the conversation with perfect timing. "Got to go. There's a problem at the medical tent."

Anxiety chased Trevor as he double-timed it over to the tent Hope was monitoring. Last year, there'd been only one incident—barely an incident at all. A sliver from the corral fence.

Trevor dodged kids and prayed that whatever it was this time would be benign.

He stepped into the tent to find Lucas seated in a chair with his arm on an exam table. His cowboy hat rested on the back of his head and the expression on his face said he was enjoying himself. Hope's head was bowed near his as she concentrated on her ministrations.

Lucas said something and she smiled, looking amused and relaxed. Trevor's gut ached, remembering a time when she'd looked at him like that. After a moment, Lucas saw him in the entrance.

"Hey, Trev. I finally got to meet Hope. I guess you forgot to tell me she's as pretty as she is nice."

He didn't forget anything. Trevor's gaze went to Hope. She looked much the same as the first time he'd met her. Pink scrubs, hair in a ponytail and a pink stethoscope around her neck. He grimaced, recalling how he'd messed up both then and now.

"What's going on?" Trevor asked.

She looked at him, then looked away. "Your brother prematurely lost a few of his stitches. There was a small amount of bleeding, which had a few of the children concerned."

"Not my fault. I promise," Lucas said. "One of the kids decided to climb up on the tractor. I grabbed him before he nose-dived and ended up running my arm into the machine. Totally not my fault."

"Sounds serious. I think you should go ahead and remove his frontal lobe," Trevor said. "I'm happy to sign the surgical consent."

"What?" Hope stared at him for a moment and then started laughing.

Her smile was a punch in the gut. He missed her.

"No surgery is necessary," she said. "I'll clean the area and apply sterile strips. He should check in with a physician on Monday."

Trevor nodded. It was good to see Hope smile in his direction.

When he moved closer to check out his

brother's arm, the sweet vanilla scent of her shampoo teased him.

"Am I done, Doc?" Lucas asked.

"Nurse Burke," Hope corrected. She pulled off her gloves. "You are officially discharged. Try to be careful when you're jumping off tractors."

"I'll do that," Lucas said.

Trevor nodded to Hope. "Thanks for taking care of him."

"That's my job," she said.

He turned to Lucas. "Come on. I have it on good authority that the snack tent is open. Let's get something to eat."

Minutes later, he and Lucas straddled a picnic table bench in the snack tent with half a dozen empty juice boxes and a bowl of circus crackers in front of them.

"Need anything else, boys?" Bess asked.

"No, ma'am," Trevor said. "This is great. Just like when we were kids."

Lucas popped an animal cracker into his mouth while closely watching Trevor. Then he shook his head.

"What?" Trevor asked.

"I'm your brother. You're supposed to tell me when you fall in love." He gave a shrug of his shoulders. "Though I have to say, you did a good job without me. Hope is sweet and kind and funny. I like her. I wouldn't object to her as a sister-in-law."

Trevor frantically scanned the room, then leaned across the table. "What are you talking about? And whatever it is, could you do it a little more quietly?"

"Got it bad too, huh?" Lucas sucked on his straw, making loud noises until Bess came by and snatched the box from his hand.

"I don't know where you got that random idea but keep it to yourself. Would you?" Trevor dipped his head and stared at the plastic tablecloth. He'd barely admitted to himself how he felt about Hope; he didn't need Lucas making an announcement.

"Do you need a character witness? Is that it? You're kind of a sketchy character."

Trevor gave a short bitter laugh. "Funny you should say that. I actually did two months ago when I was trying to get her to stay at the ranch for the summer."

"Summer is almost over," Lucas said. "She's been here all this time. That's got to mean something."

"She's leaving next week." Trevor stared

ahead, seeing nothing except the image of Hope's car driving away.

"What do you want me to do? Borrow her car keys, maybe? Or I could have Sheriff Steve arrest her for first-degree heartbreak." He shoved a handful of crackers into his mouth.

"You're real funny, Luc."

"It's all I've got." His brother shrugged. "Love is not in my repertoire. My theory is that if you don't fall in love, you can't get your heart broken."

"That advice would have had standing in June." Trevor ran a hand over his face and sighed. "Today? Not so much."

"What are you going to do, Trev?" Luc looked at him, compassion in his eyes.

"I don't have a clue, and I'm running out of time and ideas."

"When in doubt, pray." His brother reached into the bowl and chased the last cracker. "And ask for more crackers."

"As usual, you're a font of wisdom."

"You want wisdom, you go to Gramps. Everyone knows that."

Trevor scoffed. "Gramps is the last person I should talk to."

"Drew and Sam bit the bullet and took

Gramps's advice and look where they are. Smiling and at peace."

"I'm not desperate," Trevor said. "Yet."

"Look, Aunt Hope. That sign. Do you see it?"

Hope slowed the car and read the banner stretched across the Homestead Elementary School playground fence. "School enrollment."

"Uh-huh. It says all grades. Can we go check it out?"

"It's Sunday. School isn't open on Sunday."

"It will be open tomorrow." His blue eyes pleaded with her.

"Cole, you're already enrolled in Oklahoma City." She'd done that last week.

Cole crossed his arms and stared out the window. "I don't want to go to school in Oklahoma City. I want to stay in Homestead Pass." The words were spoken without emotion.

He was being unreasonable, and at the same time, Hope admired her nephew. No temper tantrum or acting out. Cole simply made his feelings known. Maybe it would be better if he had a full-blown meltdown. She certainly wanted to.

She'd come to Homestead Pass looking for Cole's father and ended up falling in love with the town, with the Morgans and with Trevor. Such foolishness.

"We don't always get what we want," Hope said quietly as she continued driving. "I know you think that stinks."

"Aunt Hope, I never get what I want."

Oh, what a stab to her heart those words were. Hope swallowed, fighting back tears. No crying. She'd learned when she was ten years old that crying didn't help, so she never cried. Until now. She had shed more tears in the last few weeks than in her entire life.

Tears for all Cole had lost. She'd promised him so much and instead she'd allowed his heart to break a little more.

Hope parked the car in front of the bookstore, got out and waited for Cole. He was being terminally slow. Finally, he reluctantly exited the car.

"What are we doing here?" he asked when he joined her on the sidewalk.

"We're going to buy a thank-you gift and a card for Trevor from you."

Cole perked up at that. "May I pick out the book?"

"The book. The card. Everything." She met

his gaze. "Pick out something that will make him smile."

"I can do that." He nodded. "I know what he likes."

"Yes. I figured you were exactly the right person for this job." She motioned up the street.

"I'm going to the coffee shop. I'll be back shortly."

"Okay."

Hope waited until he entered, and the door closed behind him with a final tinkling of the chimes. It was only a short time ago that she'd worried about leaving him in the bookstore.

So much had changed since then. Cole was no longer a little boy. He was a young man. Through the window, she could see Eleanor's wide grin as she welcomed Cole. They spoke and then Eleanor looked out the window and waved at Hope. She returned the greeting and started down the street, grateful that during tourist season all the shops were open on Sundays.

Bright yellow signs posted in the window of several shops caught her attention. She stopped and stared at one. The signs advertised a Labor Day sidewalk sale. Labor Day.

And that meant the swift entrance of Thanksgiving and Christmas.

Her chest tightened and she kept walking. The maple trees lining Main Street would change colors as summer transitioned into autumn and then to winter. What was Homestead Pass like at the holidays? She envisioned tiny white lights on the lamp poles with red velvet ribbons. The Lazy M Ranch covered with snow came to mind and she sighed. Liv and Sam's babies would arrive right around the holidays. More grandchildren for Gus to dote upon.

Standing outside the coffee shop, she wiped away the moisture that dampened her eyes, then pulled open the door.

"The usual?"

Hope smiled at the young woman behind the counter. "Yes, please. Iced. And to go."

She returned a few minutes later and handed the covered cup to Hope. "I saw your picture in the paper."

"The paper?" Hope frowned, and then remembered. "Oh, the fishing derby. Yes. Strictly the right place when that big boy was hungry."

The young woman held out her hand. "I'm Britt." She smiled. "I like to meet all my regulars."

"Hope. Hope Burke. Nice to meet you." A

regular. Funny how such a little thing could touch the heart. Being known as a regular at a coffee shop in Homestead Pass was the sweetest thing she'd heard in a while. She was going to miss this place.

"You too." Hope sipped the beverage before venturing out into the heat again. She walked beneath the awnings on Main to keep out of the sun, once again window-shopping as she made her way back toward the bookstore.

At the floral shop, she admired the blue distressed cart parked outside the door that held glass pitchers filled with sunflowers. Sunflowers were what Trevor bought her. It wasn't so long ago that they'd had dinner and sat on the back porch under a full moon.

Another memory to tuck away.

"Hey there, Miss Hope," someone called.

She looked across the street and spotted Jim waving at her as he came out of the post office.

"Hi, Jim."

The cowboy smiled. "Haven't seen you around much. Congratulations on that bass. Trevor's got that front-page picture on the wall in his office. But I guess you know that."

"Thank you, Jim."

"See you back at the ranch then."

Hope nodded. Yes, back at the ranch. She was going to miss the ranch most of all.

CHAPTER TWELVE

"COLE, ARE YOU READY?"

Hope walked through the house, assessing as she went. She'd worked hard on Sunday and Monday, dusting and cleaning to ensure she left Trevor's house just as she'd found it. The trunk of the car was packed. All she needed was Cole's boxes, then they'd go to the main house and say goodbye to Gramps and Bess. She'd promised Sadie and Liv she'd stop by their houses on her way out as well.

As for Trevor, there really wasn't much more she could say. Cole had given him his gift and the card they'd both signed on Sunday. Seeing him again would be a mistake.

"Cole?" she called again.

She'd heard the back door creak a while ago. Maybe he was outside with Patch. Hope stepped outside and was blasted with the heat. August in Oklahoma had a reputation for excess. The heat index had to be at least ninety, the humidity thick and stifling. She stood at the rail, her gaze scanning the empty yard.

Anxiety niggled as she stepped off the porch, walking farther into the yard and peering through the shade trees. When she walked back into the house and headed down the hall to his room, two boxes of his belongings were stacked in the middle of the room. Everything was as it was last night. A *Space Knight* book was on the bed.

Patch wasn't in his crate. The familiar red leash was missing from the hook on the wall.

A shiver raced up her arms. Something wasn't right.

She grabbed her keys from the counter and raced to her car.

In the short time it took for her to get to the main house, she'd worked herself up into a panic. She parked the vehicle, jumped out and headed to Trevor's office in the stables, taking slow breaths and working to calm herself. Cole had probably walked over to see Trevor and Storm one last time.

She'd promised they would visit. Not an unreasonable request and one she planned to honor.

Her sandals slapped against the floor of the stables as she moved down the center aisle, checking stalls but finding Cole in none of them. She'd passed half a dozen before Trevor's office came into view. He sat at his desk, eyes on a computer screen, a phone in his hand, talking to someone.

His eyes moved from the computer to her, and he frowned, surprise registering on his face. He said something into the phone, put it down and stood, just as she entered the doorway of his office.

"Is Cole here?" she asked.

Trevor frowned. "No. Is there a problem?"

"I can't find him anywhere and Patch is with him."

"He's probably taking him for a walk."

"I checked the yard. They aren't out there. I think he ran away." She let out a deep breath, the realization slamming into her.

"Don't get ahead of yourself. I'm sure he's around here somewhere."

"Trevor, he's not. He said he didn't want to leave and I didn't listen to him." She hadn't heard him at all. No, she was wrapped up in her own pity party.

Hope put her fingers against her lips and tried not to sob. "I'm supposed to take care of Anna's baby. I messed this up so bad."

Before she knew what was happening, Trevor had his arms around her. "It's okay, Hope," he soothed, his voice close to her ear. "We're all doing the best we can and you're doing better than most of us."

She pulled away from his warmth and looked into his eyes. "Where would he go, Trevor?"

"I don't know. Cole turned his phone into me on Sunday. I don't have a way to reach him. He could be anywhere." Trevor paused. "His favorite place on the ranch is the stables. He's not here. I would have seen him."

"The bookstore," Hope said. "It's the only other place I can think of. I'll drive into town."

"We'll go together. You go tell Gramps and Bess to keep an eye out for him. I'm going to have Jim take a ride around the ranch in the ute. I'll meet you at my truck."

"Okay. Okay. Yes." Hope raced out of the stables, her feet kicking gravel as she headed to the main house. She found Gramps in the kitchen making coffee and arguing with Bess.

"If that boy doesn't do something to stop her from leaving, I'm going to do it myself."

Hope cleared her throat as she entered the kitchen.

"I was just talking about you, Hope," Gus said.

"Cole is missing."

"What?" Bess dropped the towel in her hand. "Oh my. What can we do to help?"

"Have you checked the elementary school?" Gus asked.

"The elementary school?" Hope frowned. "What are you talking about?"

"While we were cleaning up after the event on Saturday, Cole asked questions about the elementary school. That got the boys telling stories about their days at that school. He seemed really interested. Said he wanted to go to school there. Trevor gently reminded him that he'd be in Oklahoma City for school."

"Oh, my," Hope murmured.

Sunday he'd commented on the banner on the school fence with details about enrolling. Had he really walked five miles into town to enroll himself in school?

His words came back to her. *Aunt Hope, I never get what I want.*

Cole wanted to stay in Homestead Pass. He was tired of adults who didn't hear him and had decided to take matters into his own hands. She didn't blame him one bit.

"You're right. I know you're right." Hope gave Gus a kiss on the cheek. "Thank you so much."

"We'll be praying," Bess called.

Trevor stood next to his truck when she rushed out of the house. "Gus thinks he's at the elementary school. I think he's right. My guess is that Cole is enrolling himself."

"Get in," Trevor said. "We'll find out."

The drive into town was silent. Hope imagined an eleven-year-old boy and his dog walking this stretch of road to get to Homestead Pass. Would he really walk five miles to town? In this heat?

"Maybe someone gave him a ride," she said aloud.

"Could be. Still, it's only five miles and he's a kid with a dog. I used to walk farther when I was his age."

"Cole's not used to walking five miles and it's so hot."

"You're underestimating him. He's worked all summer at the ranch in the sun. I taught him to hydrate. I think that boy is made of tougher stuff than you realize. He'll be fine."

Silence stretched between them once again.

"Were you going to leave without saying goodbye?" Trevor asked, his hands tightly gripping the steering wheel.

"I hadn't gotten that—that far," she stammered. "I have to return the keys to your house." She stared at his profile and then looked away, clasping her hands in her lap. Why was this so hard? Love wasn't in her long-term plans. Neither was an eleven-year-old boy, her heart whispered.

"Don't you think I deserve more than dropping off keys?" Trevor asked.

"Yes. You do. And, yes, I'm an incredible coward. I don't know what else to tell you."

"At least you're honest," he murmured.

Trevor guided the car down Main Street and made a left on Adams.

"Red shirt?"

"What?" Hope blinked and turned toward him confused.

"Is that Cole over there in the red shirt? There's a maple blocking the view. It's the playground of the elementary school."

Hope looked in the direction he pointed and

gasped. It was Cole. He sat on a swing in the playground with Patch at his side, looking sad and alone. Poor kid. She shuddered and caught her breath, offering a silent prayer of thanks.

"Do you want to go and talk to him?" Trevor asked.

"Maybe we could go together." Her heart pounded as she waited for his response.

Trevor's lips slowly moved into a smile. "Yeah. I'd like that."

She jumped out of the truck and waited on the sidewalk for Trevor. He caught up to her and took her hand.

"You're the smartest woman I know, Hope."

"Thank you." She paused. "Why are you telling me this?"

"I want you to do what your heart tells you to do, not what fear is whispering. That's what Cole needs from you."

Hope nodded. He knew her too well.

The gate of the playground creaked as Trevor opened it for Hope and then walked through behind her. Patch's ears perked and he looked up, delighted to see them. When he barked, Cole's head popped up. He got up from the swing.

"Aunt Hope." His gaze went from her to Trevor. "What are you doing here?"

"Cole, you forgot to tell me where you were going. I was worried about you."

"I'm sorry."

"What are you doing here, Cole?" Trevor asked.

The boy shrugged. "I wanted to find out about school here. You know. Just in case."

Hope's heart caught as she imagined this boy of hers bravely walking to town and going into the school, alone.

"What did you find out?" she asked.

"I can't enroll without a parent or guardian."

She nodded. "Good thing I'm here then."

Cole looked at her, hope in his eyes. "Really?"

"Yes." Hope pulled him to her and hugged his slim frame. He smelled like ranch and dog and maybe cookies too. She met Trevor's gaze over the top of Cole's head, and she offered a smile. To her surprise, he smiled back and nodded.

Then she released Cole, her hands still on his shoulders. "That's not to say that every time you want something you can walk into town without telling me, and I'll give it to you." She raised an eyebrow. "But it turns out I wasn't listening to you like I should have. This town is the best place for you to be right now and I'm sorry I didn't realize that."

She turned to Trevor. "We're going to go enroll in school. Do you want to join us?"

The cowboy grinned. "Wouldn't miss it for the world."

"Thanks, Trevor," she murmured as Cole and Patch bounded ahead of them toward the school.

"I didn't do anything."

"Yes, you did. You were my friend, and you didn't give up on me."

"I can receive that. What's next?"

"I don't know. Why don't you stop by the house tonight and we can talk."

Trevor nodded. "Okay," he said solemnly.

Okay. She could work with *okay*, and maybe between the two of them, they'd figure it all out.

TREVOR CONSIDERED THE late-afternoon storm to be a sign. Summer rains cooled the pavement and washed away the dust of life. He stepped over a puddle as he approached Hope's house.

When spits of rain started again, he picked up his pace and moved quickly up the porch steps.

"Come on in," Hope called. Someday he'd have to asked her how she did that. How she knew he was there before he even knocked.

For now, he'd focus on today. Today, she'd enrolled Cole in school in Homestead Pass. That left him breathless with hope that maybe there really was a way to a future together.

"Hi, Trevor," Cole said when he stepped into the house.

"Cole, remember what I told you," Hope called.

"Uh-huh, I remember. The grown-ups are going to talk, so read in my room." He rolled his eyes and giggled, which caused Trevor to laugh.

Hope walked into the room and looked at them. "What's going on?"

Trevor shrugged. "Not a thing." He looked at Cole, who snickered.

"Yeah, right." Hope blew a raspberry. "Come on outside. It's started to rain again and there's a breeze." She grabbed a sweater from the chair and led the way.

The rain fell in a gentle rhythm, its sounds soothing his nerves as he settled on a rocker, which he set in motion with his foot. He prayed his heart wasn't going to be broken tonight.

"Nice weather, isn't it?" Hope said. "Autumn will be here before we know it."

Trevor took a calming breath, inhaling the scent of the rain and the land. "You signed Cole up for school. That means you're staying in Homestead Pass, right?" He looked over at her, seated in the rocker with one leg tucked beneath her and the other on the floor, and sent up a silent prayer.

"I am. I don't understand it, but this is where I'm supposed to be. Of that, I am finally certain."

She rocked back and forth slowly for minutes and then stopped and looked at him. "You knew all along the results of the DNA test would be negative, didn't you? I mean, you kept hinting at it, but you knew."

He nodded. "I never had that sort of relationship with your stepsister."

"Why didn't you let us just get the tests and be done with it?"

"I told you. I wanted Cole to have time to heal. That was the truth." He raised a shoulder. "Besides, from the minute you stormed onto the scene, I knew there was something about you. If we had a quick test, you'd be gone, and I wouldn't get a chance to figure out why you were the woman who awakened my sleeping heart."

"What are you saying, love at first sight?" She cocked her head. "If anything, it was Cole who stole your heart."

"Nope. You did and I just didn't know it then. Nor did I know what to do about what I felt."

She nodded. "I get that... What I feel for you terrifies me as well."

He looked at her. Hope Burke, so in control, was terrified of her feelings for him. That was a revelation that gave him pause.

"I called Colin Reilly this afternoon. I have a job."

Trevor blinked at the words. She had a job and Cole was enrolled in school. Hope really was staying. He longed to let out a whoop, but he subdued himself, afraid he'd scare her off. "That's great."

"It is." She nodded. "Trevor, you and I know better than most people that every single day is a blessing. I've been cowardly. But I don't want to live life that way anymore."

"So what do we do about it?" he asked.

"The thing is, I'm looking for a forever home, just like Cole. This town, you, your ranch and your family, are more than I've ever wanted."

"I don't see the problem. Say the word and I'll get the ring."

She smiled. "Two and a half months, Trevor. We've known each other two and a half months. That's the problem."

"My parents knew each other thirty days and they were married twenty-five years, until they died."

"They aren't us." She sighed. "We come with our own baggage. Lots of it."

She was right. Recently, he lived in constant fear that this joy he'd found would be snatched away. "Okay," he said. "What do you propose? Pun intended."

"Cole and I are going to live in Homestead Pass. I'll find a place in town to rent. He can come out to the ranch on Saturdays." He nodded slowly.

"Ask me to marry you in a year. One year from the day we met. One year for you to learn to trust the Lord with your future, and put aside your past, and for me to learn to let go and let God." She looked at him tenderly. "One year to trust the Lord with all of our tomorrows."

His heart swelled as she spoke. He wanted to see her and Cole every day for the next year, until they could be a family. "You have yourself a deal. When do I get to let Cole know that I love his aunt and I'm going to be his father?"

She stood up. "Right now. He's going to be so happy." A smile touched her lips and the hazel eyes glowed with pleasure. "You really love me?"

"I haven't made that clear?" He got up as well. Taking her hands in his, he looked into her eyes. "Hope Burke, I'm in love with you. I'm fairly sure I have been since that day you arrived with your sassy attitude and your pink stethoscope."

She put her arms around his neck. "I fell for you at the same time. After all, how could I resist a man who growled at me?"

"Does that mean you love me back?" His heart thudded in his chest.

"I love you, Trevor. I wasn't looking for love, but it found me."

He touched his forehead to hers, inhaling the sweet scent of her hair. "You know that I'm a recovering alcoholic, Hope. I've made lots of mistakes on top of that."

"No, you're a sinner saved by grace. That's what you told me. Start believing it."

"I'm trying," he breathed. "I'm trying."

She pulled down his head and reached up to touch her lips to his. He returned the favor, kissing her with the intensity of all the love in his heart.

Then, he lifted his head, dazed with the wonder of knowing she loved him.

"Thank you for coming into my life."

"You're the one who called the home health agency. You brought me into your life."

"Gramps is right," he said. "I'm a lot smarter than I look."

Hope laughed and kissed him again. Then she took his hand. "Let's go tell Cole we're going to be a family."

Trevor smiled, knowing all the broken pieces of his heart had come together tonight. *Thank You, Lord. I am blessed.*

EPILOGUE

One year later…

HOPE STOOD AT the front of the church, with Gus Morgan at her side. One year ago, she'd gone looking for her nephew's father. Though she never found him, she found a forever family for her and Cole.

She touched the strand of pearls around her neck. Something borrowed from Liv. The single pearl drops at her ears were new. A gift from Gus. She'd cried when she opened the velvet-lined box.

Tucked inside her bouquet of pink and white roses was a small photo of her mother. Something old. Hope glanced down at her shoes. Baby blue.

Yes, she was more than ready.

Pastor McGuinness cleared his throat. "Dearly beloved, we are gathered together in the presence of God to join together this man and this woman in holy marriage.

"Let us bow our heads in prayer. Dear Lord, we ask You to bless this union between Hope Mary Burke and Trevor Augustus Morgan. Pour out Your abundant blessings in their comings and goings, in joy and in sorrow, and in life and death."

The simple but heartfelt prayer had Hope near tears, her heart bursting with joy.

The congregation that packed the Homestead Pass Church this Saturday morning in August chimed in, "Amen."

Hope blinked back her emotion and snuck a peek at Trevor. His eyes were glassy as they met hers.

Her gaze traveled to the groomsmen—Drew, Sam and Lucas—standing tall, dark and swoony, as Liv had described them a year ago. Directly to Hope's left was her beautiful bridal party. Bess, Liv and Sadie were dressed in soft pink dresses.

"Who gives this woman to be married to this man?"

Gus stepped forward. "I surely do. And it's about time."

A titter of laughter went through the congregation

"Thank you, Gus," Hope whispered.

"You can call me Gramps now," he said.

Hope kissed him gently on his cheek before he sat down. She handed her bouquet to Bess, her matron of honor, before stepping toward her groom.

Trevor took her hands in his, tender emotions shining from his blue eyes. In that moment, Hope knew that she would never love him more. He'd given her so much. A home, a family and his heart. His willingness to wait a year to get married broke down the last remnants of fear stubbornly guarding her own heart. In return, she had given him time to forgive himself and prepare for this new journey.

He claimed that waiting a year had only made his love grow more and more. She agreed. Her heart had expanded as she learned to trust that he'd never let her down.

Patch gave a short, excited bark and danced in a circle. "Sit, Patch," Cole said. Then he stepped back into his position next to Trevor as best man. The dog complied and sat at Cole's feet, the pink ribbon around his neck slightly askew. The obedience lessons with Jim had finally paid off.

Cole, so handsome in his tux, gave her a

thumbs-up. Anna would be so proud of her boy. "Thank You, Lord," Hope whispered.

"Please be seated."

It took a few minutes for the congregation to settle. Half of Homestead Pass was in attendance, and Hope wouldn't have it any other way. After the ceremony, they'd head to the Lazy M Ranch, where Liv's aunt had catered the outdoor reception.

As the church became quiet, the sweet babbling of Liv and Sam's twins echoed from the back where they sat with Liv's aunt.

Behind Hope, in the second row, she heard Eleanor Moretti whisper, "You know I got them together. I imagine they're going to name their first child after me."

The ensuing words of love and union were a blur of happiness to Hope's ears. Cole proudly produced the rings and moments later, Pastor McGuinness declared that they were man and wife.

Trevor held her tenderly and pressed a soft kiss to her lips.

"I love you, Hope. Always and forever."

"I love you too, my cranky cowboy."

Hope retrieved her bouquet, and they walked

down the aisle accompanied by the cheers of their family, friends and all of Homestead Pass.

As they sat in the limo, courtesy of Colin Reilly, Trevor leaned close and kissed her again. "When we get back from the honeymoon, I want to adopt Cole officially. I want us to be a family."

"Yes," she breathed against his lips.

From the front seat, the driver turned and smiled. "Ready to head to the reception, Mr. and Mrs. Morgan?"

"Yeah, we're ready," Trevor said.

"More than ready," Hope added.

★ ★ ★ ★ ★

WESTERN

Rugged men looking for love...

Available Next Month

The Maverick's Marriage Deal Kaylie Newell
The Rancher's Secret Crush Cari Lynn Webb

....

Expecting A Fortune Nina Crespo
The Doc's Instant Family Lisa Childs

....

 LOVE INSPIRED

Recapturing Her Heart Jennifer Slattery
The Cowboy's Return Danica Favorite

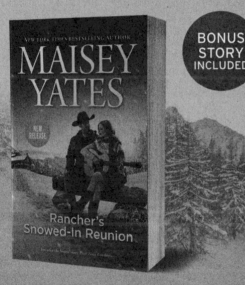